Mercy Street

ALSO BY JENNIFER HAIGH

Heat and Light

News from Heaven

Faith

The Condition

Baker Towers

Mrs. Kimble

Mercy Street

A Novel

Jennifer Haigh

HARPER LARGE PRINT

An Imprint of HarperCollins Publishers

FIRST HARPER LARGE PRINT EDITION

ISBN: 978-0-06-321107-0

Library of Congress Cataloging-in-Publication Data is available upon request.

22 23 24 25 26 LSC 10 9 8 7 6 5 4 3 2 1

To the one in four

I'm walking up and down Beacon Hill

searching for a street sign—

namely **MERCY STREET.**

Not there.

I try the Back Bay.

Not there.

Not there.

—ANNE SEXTON

WINTER

WINTER

1

It's hard to know, ever, where a story begins. We touch down in a world fully inhabited by others, a drama already in progress. By the time we make our entrance—incontinent and screaming, like dirty bombs detonating—the climax is a distant memory. Our arrival is not the beginning; it is a consequence.

The starting point is arbitrary. When Claudia looks back on that winter (as New Englanders can't help doing), the days fuse together in her memory: the weak light fading early, salt trucks clattering down the avenues, a bitter wind slicing through her coat. She had no sense, at the time, of forces aligning, a chain of events set into motion.

Like everyone else, she was distracted by the snow.

The season had arrived late, like a querulous old man

who refused to be rushed. The first weeks of January were arid and silent, bare pavement and short blue afternoons, a blinding glare off the harbor, seagulls diving in the slanted winter sun. Then a massive nor'easter roared up the coast, spinning and kicking like a kung fu fighter. A foot of snow fell overnight. Schools were closed, flights grounded, entire neighborhoods without power. The clinic's waiting room was empty, Mercy Street nearly impassable.

Three days later, the second storm hit.

Snow and more snow. With each passing week, the sidewalks narrowed. Pedestrians walked single file, stepping carefully. Parking spaces shrank and eventually disappeared, replaced by towering piles of snow.

On a frigid Wednesday morning in mid-February, a crowd gathered in front of the clinic, their backs to Mercy Street. Claudia stood at a second-floor window in the staff kitchen, counting heads.

"Thirty-six," she said.

Seen from above, the group looked organized. They stood in concentric circles like the growth rings of a tree. In the center were the professionals—Archdiocesan priests in slick nylon dress slacks, a few monks from the Franciscan monastery in New Bedford, the tails of their brown robes peeking out from beneath winter coats. In the outer rings were the regular people, holding rosary beads or carrying signs. They had come straight from church, their foreheads marked with dark soot. *Like gunshot victims*, Claudia thought. That morning, riding the MBTA train to work, she'd seen a lot of dirty foreheads. In Boston—still, despite recent events, the most Catholic city in America—Ash Wednesday could not be ignored.

Mary Fahey, the intake nurse, joined her at the window. "For Ash Wednesday, that's not so impressive. Last year we had twice that many."

Claudia said, "It must be the snow."

The staff kitchen was small and cluttered, a fresh pot of coffee brewing. The television was tuned to NECN, the New England Cable Network. Winter was the top story—the snowiest in 364 years, which was roughly how long people had been complaining about the weather here. Another storm was on the way, a low-pressure system forming in the Caribbean. *Batten down the hatches, folks. It's another monstah nor'eastah.* The weatherman, a shovel-faced man in an ill-fitting sports coat, couldn't hide his glee.

"Did you count those guys in back?" Mary asked. "Behind Puffy."

A few lurkers stood at the margins, staring at cell phones like bored strangers at a bus stop. Whether they were protestors or indifferent bystanders was impossible to say.

"No," said Claudia. "I wasn't sure about them."

Thirty-six, she felt, was a sizable number. In their bulky coats they might have been carrying anything. There were twelve staff working at the clinic—except for Luis the security guard, all female, all unarmed.

She studied the foreheads. The significance of the ritual was a little murky. The idea, apparently, was to remind the faithful of their mortality—as though anyone could possibly need that. How it all ended was a poorly kept secret. Spoilers were everywhere.

Thirty-six was a sizable number. And anyway, it only took one.

A monstah nor'eastah. It was that year's accepted usage, the agreed-upon nomenclature. In the winter of 2015, in Boston, a storm couldn't be called *severe* or *powerful* or even *wicked.* By Ash Wednesday, the season had been branded. Another Monster Nor'easter™ was on its way.

Mercy Street is barely a street. It spans a single block southeast of Boston Common, in a part of town once known as the Combat Zone. Long ago this was the city's red-light district, a dark, congested neighborhood of taverns and massage parlors, *peep shows* and *skin flicks*, twentieth-century perversions that now seem quaint as corsets. Prostitutes loitered in front of Good Time Charlie's, calling out to the men in uniform, sailors on shore leave from Charlestown Navy Yard.

They're all gone now—the girls, the sailors. Over the years, the neighborhood has gentrified. By all appearances, combat has ceased. After the Navy Yard closed, the dive bars were razed, the crumbling streets repaved. The porn theaters hung on a few more years, until the digital age finished them off completely. Now lonely men stay home to masturbate in front of computers, a win for technology. There's no longer any reason to leave the house.

Sex left the Combat Zone. Then the builders came. The new erections were office towers, parking garages, commercial space for shops and restaurants, easily accessible by the Chinatown and Downtown Crossing T stops. When they leased the building, the clinic's board of directors—a thousand miles away, in Chicago—had never heard of the Combat Zone. Completely by accident, they made a poetic choice.

The clinic is a member of Wellways LLC—a small but growing network of detox centers, drug-testing labs, and women's and mental health clinics, in eighteen states and the District of Columbia. Of these, the labs are the real moneymakers. Though technically a nonprofit, Wellways is a major player in the urine business.

Drug addiction and alcoholism, depression and anxiety, accidental pregnancy and sexually transmitted disease. These conditions are believed to share a common etiology, the failure of virtue. Whatever their diagnosis, all Wellways patients have this in common: their troubles are seen to be, in part or in full, their own goddamn fault.

Hanging above the clinic's front door is a wooden sign, painted blue and lemon yellow: WOMEN'S OPTIONS, a name no one uses. In Boston it is known, simply, as Mercy Street.

Down on the sidewalk, a priest led prayers into a handheld megaphone—at double speed, like a cattle auctioneer: *HAILMaryfullofgracetheLordiswithThee.*

The crowd answered in a low hum, like a swarm of bees.

"Hey, guess what?" Mary said with a certain satisfaction. "They're all men."

"Are you sure?" This was not typical. Claudia

blamed Ash Wednesday, the overrepresentation of religious professionals. "I could swear I saw a woman."

In hats and scarves and chunky winter coats, the protestors were ageless, shapeless, sexless. A few had set down their signs to pray the Rosary. A figure in a blue parka made its way along the middle ring, stooping to wipe the snow from each sign.

"There." Claudia pointed. "That's a woman. Coincidentally, she is cleaning."

"Coincidentally," Mary said.

The Ash Wednesday protest had been planned for weeks. Mary had heard about it in church. Her priest had made the announcement with great enthusiasm. On the first day of Lent, the faithful would hold a side-walk vigil on Mercy Street. They would ask the Blessed Virgin to inspire the young women, to save the unborn babies. They would pray for wisdom, for divine forgiveness, for grace.

HAILMaryfullofgracetheLordiswithThee. The words ran together like the disclaimer after a radio commercial, a glib announcer racing through the fine print.

"Those fuckers," Mary said, meaning the priests. "Anything to change the subject."

The subject, in her mind, was unchangeable: the child victims, the Archdiocesan cover-up, hundreds of lawsuits settled in secret. There was only one subject, and Mary would not be distracted. Her convictions were solid and unyielding. Each year on Ash Wednesday, she did patient intakes—height, weight, blood pressure—with a smudge of holy soot on her forehead. How or whether she explained this to the patients, Claudia had no idea. It was a lesson you learned over and over again, doing this work: people live with contradictions.

HAILMaryfullofgracetheLordiswithThee. Mary Fahey had heard these words from earliest childhood, her own name offered to the heavens in prayer.

Was that weird? Claudia asked her once.

I never thought about it, Mary said.

The protestors were a fact of life, a daily nuisance like traffic or bad weather. Some days there was only one, an old guy in a Sox cap. Claudia had given him a nickname, Puffy. He arrived each morning like a dutiful employee, in a down coat the color of trash bags. In May he'd swap it for a yellow windbreaker. To Claudia it was like the daffodils sprouting, the first rumor of spring.

In the beginning she tried talking with them. She had no experience with religious people and was surprised, actually surprised, at the way every conversation devolved into godtalk. It was like arguing a point of fact with a stubborn child who parrots a single refrain: *Because my dad said so!* To which a reasonable adult might respond:

He said that? What were his exact words? Are you sure you heard him right?

Or:

I've never seen your dad. Are you sure you have one?

Or:

Who asked him? Seriously, your dad needs to mind his own.

Her attempts at rational discourse went badly. On her very first day of work, a man approached her on the sidewalk—a stocky guy in Dockers and a fleece jacket, the most ordinary-looking person imaginable.

"Please, Mother," he said.

She can still recall his lilting voice, so gentle it seemed sinister. Also, it was the first time a grown stranger had called her *Mother*, which isn't something you forget.

"Please, Mother. Our Lord Jesus Christ is speaking to you. Please don't kill your baby."

He had been to Starbucks. She could smell it on his jacket.

"I work here," she said.

The change in his demeanor was immediate, like

an actor breaking character. He looked at her as though he'd stepped in shit.

"You are doing the devil's work," he said.

Claudia said, "So I've been told."

When he called her a cunt and damned her to eternal hell, the damnation didn't faze her; as a nonbeliever, she found it slightly comical. The name-calling was more disturbing. Not so much the word itself as the way he said it: triumphantly, as though winning an argument. For a certain type of man, *cunt* was a concealed weapon—discreet, portable, always at the ready. What did it mean to him, this angry stranger who didn't possess (and had possibly never seen) the body part it referred to? A body part he considered loathsome, the vilest thing a person could possibly be.

It was just a word; Claudia knew this. In Britain and Ireland, *cunt* was used casually, recreationally—a good-natured insult between mates who, go figure, were usually men. She had learned this years before, in the early days of online dating, from a Tufts professor of English literature. At a noisy pub a few blocks from campus, he explained that *cunt* was a synecdoche, a figure of speech in which a part stood in for the whole. ("Like *a head of cattle*," he added helpfully.) Then he delivered a discourse on synecdoche and metonymy, which weren't the same thing but were somehow related. Professing this took quite a while, and required him to use the word *cunt* several times. He seemed not to understand, or maybe he did, that to the female ear, *cunt* is brutal, exquisitely personal—half of humanity reduced to a body part, a single purpose: This is what you are. This is all you are.

The part stands in for the whole.

Claudia didn't explain this to the Tufts professor. She didn't want to say the word, and she particularly didn't want to hear him say it. He was just some guy she'd met on the internet. Her cunt was none of his business.

She filled her mug and went downstairs. The waiting room was bright and cheerful, painted a sunny yellow. There were comfortable chairs, tables stacked with cooking and decorating magazines, boxes of Kleenex strategically placed. One wall was covered with giant photographs, taken by the director's son while he was in the Peace Corps: smiling African women in colorful dresses, carrying bundles on their shoulders, backs, and heads. They carried water jugs, bushel baskets of bread or fruit or laundry. They carried all the things you'd expect them to carry, except babies.

That morning, half the chairs were occupied:

several pairs of women who might have been sisters or roommates or mothers with daughters; an Indian couple in professional dress, each staring at a cell phone. A boy and girl, college-aged, sat shoulder to shoulder holding hands. They wore look-alike hoodies and sweatpants, as though they'd just come from the gym.

She crossed the waiting room and continued down a long hallway to the call center. The door was open a crack. A woman was talking on the phone, a voice Claudia recognized. Naomi had worked on the hotline for as long as there'd been one, her most dedicated volunteer.

"What was the first day of your last menstrual period?" Naomi asked.

This was always the first question.

The call center was packed with cubicles. Each held a desktop computer and a standard-issue office telephone. At each workstation was posted a printed notice: SILENT CALL PROCEDURE.

In the corner cube Naomi consulted her chart, a cardboard wheel the size of a floppy disk, to calculate gestational age. The younger volunteers used the online version, but Naomi was old-school. She hunched over her wheel like a medieval soothsayer, reading tarot or tea leaves.

"You are eight weeks and five days pregnant," she said.

The volunteers came in two varieties. Half were gray-haired, old enough to remember illegal abortions, some from personal experience—Pam, Naomi, Janet, Karen. The rest were grad students in psychology or social work or public health—Meghan, Amanda, Lily, Marisol. They were called counselors, but it was a poor description of the work they did. Callers to the hotline needed many things: information, appointments, decent jobs, any sort of health insurance. Childcare, affordable housing, antibiotics, antidepressants. Counsel, honestly, was pretty far down the list.

This was especially true for AB calls. By the time a woman Googled "abortion Boston," she wasn't looking for advice from a stranger. Her decision was already made. The counselor told her what to expect on the day of the appointment: how long the procedure would take (ten to fifteen minutes), how long she'd spend at the clinic (two hours, including recovery), what to eat that morning (nothing), what to bring with her (socks and a sweater—the procedure room could get chilly).

"Are you diabetic?" Naomi asked. "Do you take methadone, Suboxone, or Subutex?"

Claudia slipped on a headset and settled in at her desk.

They explained the procedure and answered questions. Will I be awake? Does it hurt? Those were common questions, but not the most common.

The most common question was, how much does it cost?

"The first set of pills is mifepristone," said Naomi. "You'll take those here in our clinic. The second set is misoprostol. You take those later, at home."

More and more, women were choosing the medication AB over the in-clinic procedure. Either method, without insurance, cost $650—a drop in the ocean, compared to the cost of raising a child, but for many of the callers, it was an unimaginable sum. *Holy shit,* Claudia had been told more than once. *Looks like I'm gonna have a kid.*

Her first call was a Pill question. As the caller spoke, Claudia took the following notes: *Started pack three days late. Missed two white, took week two. Missed one pink. Only green left.*

She had long since mastered the Pill question, having heard every possible variation: started late, started early, vomited up a white one, took two pink ones by mistake. She could answer a Pill question in under a minute, in English, Spanish, or Haitian Creole.

"You'll need to use a backup method," she said. "Condoms for the rest of your cycle."

The caller was unhappy to hear this. No one was ever happy to hear this.

"It's those white pills I'm worried about. Unless you take them consistently the first week, you're not protected."

The moment she disconnected, the line rang again.

The second caller gave her name, Tara. In the background a television was playing. Claudia recognized the opening music of *Dr. Phil*, the Texas twang of the doctor himself, testifying like a revival-tent preacher: *This is going to be a changing day in your life.*

"What was the first day of your last menstrual period?" Claudia asked.

Tara was nine weeks pregnant, HIV positive, and sleeping on a stranger's couch. She took methadone, but not regularly, lithium, but not recently. She lit cigarettes one after the other—scratch, pause, inhale. At ten o'clock on a Wednesday morning, she was already high. As she spoke, Claudia thought of the word problems she'd solved in high school algebra, trains traveling at different speeds, in opposite directions. How long before their paths intersect? The problem, always, was knowing which variable to solve for. Tara's life was a burning building with a fire on each floor. Which fire did you put out first?

Tara had only one question.

"Six hundred fifty dollars," said Claudia.

You put out the pregnancy first.

What would become of Tara? Claudia would never know. The hotline was a portal into a stranger's life: ambient traffic and distant sirens, kids playing in English or Spanish or Portuguese or Hmong. Music playing, a dog barking, a child crying. A video game that must have been popular because she kept hearing it—the catchy electronic jingle, the cartoon gunfire with its plosive reports.

A dog crying, a child barking. Running water, dishwashing, ice cubes tinkling in a glass. Always there was a television. Even in the throes of a personal crisis, it didn't occur to the caller to turn off the TV.

Some counselors found the noise distracting. Claudia barely noticed it, having grown up in such a household. Her mother, Deb, had been a nurse's aide at the county retirement home. She came home from work exhausted and often in physical pain, and the first thing she did, always, was turn on the TV and light a cigarette, her reward for getting through the day.

That's what they called it—*the County Home*—which sounded nicer than what it really was: a place for indigent old people to grow older and eventually die, a process that sometimes took forever and sometimes only seemed to.

For most of Claudia's childhood, they lived in a single-wide trailer. Not a double-wide. If you know anything at all about mobile homes, you know that the difference is profound. A double-wide feels like a house because of the way it's constructed, in two separate halves that are bolted together on-site. A single is all one piece, like a shipping container, and like a shipping container it gets hot in summer and cold in winter. In a Maine winter it gets very cold, and a crying child produces a strange echo; it's impossible to forget, ever, that you're living in a can. On the plus side, a single is cheap and easy to get. Claudia's mother bought theirs at an RV lot—no mortgage, no credit check. She hauled it away herself, hitched to a truck her brother had "borrowed" from work.

When Claudia thinks of the trailer, she remembers the carpet—wall-to-wall acrylic shag, the pile so long and dense that it seemed to suck in whatever landed on it. Spilled milk, puzzle pieces, Smarties. Cat food, thumbtacks, melting Popsicles, Lego blocks.

The trailer was fifty feet long and eighteen across. Claudia has lived in smaller places, but never with so many people or such small windows. There was a kitchen and a living room. A bathroom and two tiny bedrooms opened off a narrow hallway. Later, to accommodate the fosters, her uncle Ricky built a flimsy addition, two-by-fours and fiberglass insulation and sloppy drywall, with a skin of Tyvek HomeWrap.

In point of fact, her childhood home was half house, half trailer. They were the sort of people who *built onto* their trailer.

She can still remember the first time she heard the term *white trash*. She was nine or ten years old, watching a stand-up comic on television, and she understood immediately that he was talking about people like her. Her family drank cola with dinner, store brand. They ate off paper plates as if each meal were a picnic. This was not a whimsical habit, but a practical one: her mother sometimes couldn't pay the water bill, and for a few weeks each year, there'd be nothing to wash dishes *in*. The paper plates came in cheap hundred-packs and were so flimsy they used two or three at a time, and as a result they produced vast amounts of garbage. Behind the trailer, under a carport of corrugated plastic, their trash barrels overflowed with it. In summer the smell was overpowering: soggy paper plates and food scraps rotting in the can. As a family they were both an environmental catastrophe and a sanitary one, as poor people often are.

When Claudia heard the words *white trash,* that is what she thought.

She never found out who that comedian was, or what compelled him to mock what was probably a large share of his audience. Poor people watch a lot of television. Claudia's family was sometimes without water, but they always had an expensive cable package, and her mother always managed to pay that bill on time.

If Deb was at home, the TV was playing. To fall asleep she watched something monotonous, golf or C-SPAN. Every day of her short life began in the chipper company of the network morning shows, with their simpering hosts and human-interest stories and celebrity guests preparing favorite dishes, as though movie stars actually cooked. She was out the door by seven thirty, leaving Claudia to dress and feed the fosters.

The minute her mother left for work, Claudia turned off the TV.

The fosters, Deb called them—as though it were their last name, as though they were brothers and sisters in a large, multicolored (for Maine), ever-expanding family. They had one at a time, then two, and finally three or four. Claudia was in middle school—old enough to babysit—when Deb hit on this way to make extra money. Each month, the state of Maine paid four hundred bucks per kid.

(Could that figure possibly be correct? After her mother's death, Claudia asked her aunt Darlene. "It sounds right," Darlene said, but she didn't sound sure.)

Importantly, each foster increased their monthly allotment of what were inexplicably called *food stamps*. These weren't actually stamps but paper bank notes, clearly labeled by the federal government: U.S. DEPARTMENT OF AGRICULTURE FOOD COUPON. The food stamps were blue or purple, to make absolutely certain no one would ever mistake them for actual money. It was important to make them look like what they were: government handouts for poor people. They were designed for maximum embarrassment. Times have since changed—single mothers on assistance are now issued debit cards—but back then, no one worried about shaming them. Shame was considered appropriate. Shame, it was felt, might teach them some restraint.

When Claudia was sent to the store for bread or milk, the cashier held the food stamps by their edges, as though they were not quite clean.

Claudia's mother grew up poor and having kids made her poorer and yet she continued having them, first her own and then other people's, long past the point where she had any patience for them. She didn't enjoy them in any discernible way, and yet she couldn't stop acquiring them. At a certain point Claudia began to see this as a sickness, her mother as obsessive-compulsive, a hoarder of children. Only later did she grasp what now seems obvious: Deb raised other people's kids because it was one of only a few things she could earn money doing. The world was full of discarded people, sickly old ones and damaged young ones, and she was a paid caretaker. It said something about the world that this was the worst-paying job around.

Raise wasn't the right word. The fosters were given food and shelter and more or less left to raise themselves. They were bathed twice a week—at Aunt Darlene's, if the water was out. They were fed adequately and were never hit, which put them miles ahead of where most had started out in life. Deb said, often, that she treated them like her own children, and Claudia can attest that this was true.

The fosters, her mother called them. There was no suggestion, ever, that they were Claudia's brothers and sisters. The fosters were their own category. At the time this didn't strike her as cruel.

After Tara, the lines went quiet. On Wednesdays the call volume waxed and waned for inscrutable reasons: twenty minutes of dead silence and then, suddenly, a half dozen calls were waiting in the queue. Tuesdays and Fridays were quieter, Thursdays busier. On Mondays the line rang nonstop—fallout from the weekend, its psychic detritus scattered like confetti after a parade. Women called from taxicabs, windy street corners, T stops, Dunkin' Donuts. Sometimes they called from work. Late period, broken condom, suspicious lesion, their narratives interrupted periodically to serve a customer. *You want fries with that?*

"Well, that was disheartening." Naomi peeled off her headset and took a tin of mints from her purse. In her real life she was an anthropologist at Harvard. For six weeks each summer, she did fieldwork in some developing country, where she seemed to buy all her clothes. That morning she wore a sack-like dress made of some rough fabric, like a medieval penitent, and a necklace that looked like a chicken bone hanging from a leather cord.

"That poor child is getting married next month. She's terrified she'll get her period on her honeymoon, because her fiancé would freak."

"She said that?"

"Her exact words. 'My fiancé would freak.'" Naomi gave her Edvard Munch look, mouth open in a parody of screaming. "And I'm thinking, Sweetie, you're sure you want to marry this guy? Every month, you're going to worry about him freaking?"

Claudia said, "It sounds like a long life."

Naomi rose, stretched, glanced out the window. "It's snowing," she reported.

"*Again?*" How was it even possible? Across the river in Somerville, Claudia's Subaru—its trunk packed with a shovel, blankets, and a bag of kitty litter to provide traction—was still encased in the snowbank where the plow had buried it. Digging it out would take a solid hour. It hardly seemed worth the effort.

"There's another system blowing in," said Naomi. "The Weather Channel is calling for a foot."

"Ugh. I was supposed to run up to Maine this weekend. To check on my mom's house." Claudia had long referred to the trailer this way—aware, always, that she was being deceptive. Her mother had used the same word, without hesitation; to her, *house* and *trailer* were interchangeable. Deb, when she said it, would have passed a polygraph. To her it wasn't a lie.

Naomi looked dumbfounded. "You're *driving?*"

If there was another way to get to Clayburn, Claudia didn't know about it. "I want to make sure the place is still standing. That last storm packed a wallop."

"That's crazy," said Naomi. "Can't you just call your tenant?"

"The tenant isn't reliable." *Tenant* was another approximation. Here, again, there was no right word. Nicolette had been the final foster, a sulky, unappealing girl who'd taken advantage of Claudia's mother and was now taking advantage of her. Nicolette had cornered her at Deb's funeral, asking if she could stay on in the trailer—rent-free—with her young daughter. A temporary arrangement, or so it had seemed at the time.

"The tenant is unreachable," Claudia said. "Her number isn't receiving calls."

Naomi said, "That doesn't sound good."

It didn't sound bad. To Claudia, it sounded normal: to the Birches of Clayburn, Maine, this sort of thing happened all the time. No one had a landline, or regular cell phone service; they relied on cheap, disposable Tracfones. When you made or received a call, you were charged by the minute. When your minutes ran out, the phone was unusable until you bought more of them at Walmart. Claudia didn't explain this to Naomi. To a Harvard anthropologist, aboriginal fertility rites would be less exotic.

The hotline rang again. As Claudia was reaching for her headset, Mary Fahey stuck her head in the doorway.

"Claudia, I need you. We've got an Access patient out front."

The patient was waiting in the counseling office—a cramped closet next to the waiting room, just big enough to hold a desk and three chairs. Vanessa M. was a cute round-faced girl with box braids and a wispy, timorous voice. According to her file she was seventeen years old, and ten weeks pregnant.

"Everything you tell me today will be kept confidential here at the clinic," Claudia began, "unless you tell me someone is hurting you or not taking care of you, or if you are going to hurt yourself or someone else. If you tell me any of those things, I have to tell someone outside the clinic so we can make sure you're safe." With minors, this was standard protocol. Every staffer at the clinic was a mandated reporter. Once or twice a year, sometimes more, Claudia placed a call to DCF to initiate a 51A report.

Vanessa answered her questions in monosyllables. Yes, she was aware of all her options. No, no one had pressured her to have an abortion. When asked about her plans for the future, she was more expansive. In September she would begin classes at UMass Boston, to study communications and later, speech pathology. Her sister was raising a deaf son. Someday, Vanessa would teach the boy to talk.

Vanessa M. The name abbreviated, AA-style, to protect the patient's privacy. This too was standard protocol.

"I definitely want kids someday," she said softly. "Most definitely. Just—you know—not now."

Claudia explained that with a medication AB, she could expect six to eight hours of heavy bleeding and strong cramping. "Like a bad period," she added. "Ibuprofen will help with the cramps."

Mary returned with Vanessa's legal guardian—a stout, pugnacious aunt who reminded Claudia of her own mother. The aunt had agreed to sign the consent form, but was palpably displeased.

She signed the form without speaking. Before leaving, she paused at the door. "It's Vanessa's decision, but I don't mind telling you, I'm not comfortable with this." She looked Claudia up and down. "You have kids?"

Of course, she'd been asked this before. The askers— often Black or Latina, and mothers themselves—were unsurprised by her answer. They eyed her with suspicion, a White woman who didn't love children. Claudia felt the sting of their judgment, but she couldn't argue with the verdict. She was White and she didn't love children—at least, not in the global, unconditional way women were supposed to. She loved them strictly on a case-by-case basis, having learned early on that some were intolerable. In the Maine foster care system, many were: unruly, needy, hemorrhaging rage and fear. That they had good reasons for being so didn't make them any easier to deal with.

"No," said Claudia.

"I didn't think so," the aunt said.

In truth, she had never decided *not* to have children. She had simply decided, *not now*—at twenty, at thirty, at forty. At every point in her life, there had been something else she'd rather do.

The aunt said, "I don't know how you can work here."

Claudia said nothing. People were always telling her this: old friends, distant cousins, strangers on airplanes. Her dentist. Her chiropractor. The woman who cut her hair. Her therapist had pointed out that a reply was unnecessary; it was a statement, not a question. The most obvious response was simple agreement. *No, you don't.*

"Vanessa will be fine." Claudia handed the aunt a card. "That's my direct number. If she needs anything, please call."

I don't know how you can work here.

Here's what Claudia didn't say, had never said: *I didn't always.* Long ago, in another life, she'd lived in

New York and worked at a magazine called *Damsel*. She got the job because she was young and cute and her boyfriend's mother knew someone. Claudia was hired as an assistant editor, the youngest on the masthead. It was her first lesson in how the world worked.

Damsel dispensed an unending stream of advice. They taught women how to be women. Service journalism, they called it.

Once a year, Claudia wrote without irony, *book a session with a professional bra fitter.*

It was a glamour job. The paycheck was small, but there were other compensations. *Damsel* paid for her gym membership, a monthly clothing allowance to cover dry cleaning. Enterprising salon owners offered free haircuts and massages and waxing and pedicures, hoping for a positive mention in the magazine.

When did bra fitting become a profession? Was there a licensing exam, an International Sisterhood of Bra Fitters, an annual convention to keep yes, abreast, of new developments in bra technology?

Color-treated hair demands TLC, Claudia wrote. *A violet shampoo will tone down brassiness.*

She wrote about breakthroughs in anti-aging skincare, fashion mistakes over forty. She was twenty-three years old.

A glamour job, highly coveted. The assistant editors skipped lunch to save money, and spent the hour smoking on the rooftop. In the evenings they went to *events*. An event was a cocktail party, a salon opening, a product launch: the spring line, a celebrity diet book. The assistant editors arrived en masse, crammed into taxis to protect their borrowed shoes. They sipped wine from plastic goblets. They made a meal of the free hors d'oeuvres.

Investment shoes, smuggled out of the photo department: stiletto heels worn only once, by a model for a cover shoot.

The fashion mistake, it seemed, was turning forty.

It was a time in her life when no one ever said, *I don't know how you can work here.*

The great unspoken irony of that job, which strikes her even today, was that a person raised in a trailer could be hired to do it. Not that she trumpeted this fact about herself, then or ever. At twenty-three, she was like a gangster in the Program. Discretion was the central imperative of her life.

She was good at the job, to the extent anyone could be. Her heds and deks were clever, her ledes witty. Her qualifications were the same as anyone's: she had been raised a girl. As a child she'd pinned diapers on a doll that wet itself. She dressed Barbie in bikinis and evening gowns, matched tiny plastic handbags to tiny plastic shoes.

The dolls taught you what you were supposed to want.

The dolls loomed large in her memory. As a child she'd preferred Barbie to the other type, the chubby baby doll, with its nifty faux-urination feature. Claudia's was a hand-me-down from an older cousin, and she never quite knew what to do with it. (You changed its diaper and then what? Carried it around with you?)

Deb considered toys a waste of money and took pleasure in saying so, but every year, for as long as Claudia can remember and somewhat against her mother's will, some unseen higher power sent a box of them a few days before Christmas. They weren't gift-wrapped and weren't meant to be surprises; Claudia had chosen them herself, after weeks of deliberation, from the pages of the Sears Christmas Wish Book. At her mother's insistence, she put her requests in writing—letters to Santa Claus and later, bulleted shopping lists, complete with item numbers and prices. When the package arrived, it would be the most momentous thing that happened all year.

The toys were shipped directly from Sears, and Claudia did not for many years understand that they were paid for by her father, that this was what he gave

Deb in lieu of child support, a few twenty-dollar toys at Christmas.

For Christmas 1980 she chose a popular board game called The Bride Game. It quickly became her favorite, outranking a game called What Shall I Wear? and another one licensed by the Miss America Pageant, in which two to four girls, aged eight to twelve, competed for the crown. Claudia knew about these games entirely thanks to Justine Webster, who lived up the hill and whom she believed to be wealthy because she owned all three.

The games taught you what you were supposed to want.

At *Damsel* she passed on her knowledge. Have a professional tooth bleaching, a salon blowout, a session on the Reformer. A low-carb diet prevented bloating, premenstrual breakouts, mood swings, existential anguish. A low-carb diet was your friend for life.

She edited a column called Ask *Damsel*, in which leading beauty experts answered readers' questions. Because readers stubbornly refused to ask questions that appealed to *Damsel*'s advertisers, Claudia invented the questions herself.

At the salon ask for highlights, ask for lowlights. Have a mani-pedi, a scalp massage, a Brazilian. How much money could be spent in the quest for perfection, the care and maintenance of a single female body? An upper limit has not been established.

You taught them what to want and so they wanted it.

Get a facial, a seaweed wrap, a few zaps with the pulse-dye laser. Do a five-day cleanse, a juice fast. Have your colon irrigated.

The upper limit was equal to the GDP of a small island nation.

The upper limit was an illusion. There was no upper limit. There was always more you could do. A woman could, theoretically, spend every waking moment making herself look better, as demonstrated by the one percent: the model/actresses, the pop stars, a small handful of elite prostitutes. The ornamental wives who could not, dared not, *let themselves go.*

Ask for highlights, ask for lowlights. Claudia knew the job was bullshit, but for a long time she didn't care. She had escaped her mother's trailer. She was performing a flattering version of her life.

She worked at *Damsel* longer than she should have. When she quit, she was replaced immediately. Twenty years later, the job was still being done. By whom exactly mattered not at all.

She moved to Boston—the place Mainers went when there was some compelling reason to be in a city, such as needing a kidney transplant. In Boston she waited tables at Legal Sea Foods. In her spare time she went to grad school. She was still a student when she started volunteering at the call center, where there was no need, ever, to invent the questions. The questions never stopped.

By the winter of 2015, she'd worked on Mercy Street for nine years. As Access coordinator, she did the same work she'd once done for free—answering calls on the hotline—but now she had a retirement plan and health benefits and what passed for a full-time salary in the nonprofit world. She spent most of her day in the call center, fielding phone calls, training and managing the volunteers. Several times a week, she counseled Access patients in person. These were ABs with special cir-cumstances: minors who needed parental consent; women with medical conditions that made terminating more complicated; latecomers who'd missed the legal cutoff, or were about to.

An AB. That's what they called it. Whenever pos-sible, they avoided saying the word.

Her predecessor in the job was a woman named Evelyn Dodd, who did it for twenty years before suf-fering a series of ministrokes and quitting for good. How she lasted that long was a mystery for the ages, because Access was stressful. Claudia liked the minors and didn't mind the medicals, but the latecomers cracked her open. In Massachusetts, AB was illegal after twenty-four weeks. When a patient terminated at the last minute, it was usually because she'd gotten ominous test results: a fetal brain tumor, a mass in the lung.

The latecomers were impossible to counsel, because they didn't want ABs. They wanted babies. They were pregnant by choice; some had gone to great lengths, and considerable expense, to get that way. Many were over forty, painfully aware that this was their last chance. By the time Claudia met them, they were mortally exhausted, like prisoners who'd been waterboarded. Some wept. Others were catatonic. A few were incandescently angry. None of these reactions surprised her. She was meeting them on the worst fucking day of their lives.

By week twenty-three, names had been chosen, cribs purchased, baby showers planned.

Minors were easier. First Claudia saw the girl alone. Then she met with the parent or legal guardian, who signed the consent form. To get an AB in Massachusetts before age eighteen, you needed a parent's permission, unless you happened to be married. In the eyes of the Commonwealth, having a husband made you an adult.

The consent form had to be signed in person. This made things difficult if the parent was missing or incarcerated or deployed overseas, unable to jet back from Afghanistan to sign a piece of paper. In other cases, parents were available, but—for one reason or another—the girl refused to tell them she was pregnant. For these patients, Massachusetts law provided an additional, equally shitty option: a judicial bypass, an order signed by a judge.

For one reason or another. For some girls, home was a dangerous place.

Getting a JB wasn't easy. Not every teenager had the *sangfroid* to stand before a judge—who was nearly always old, White, and male—and beg for permission to do as she wished with her one and only life. And yet, faced with the prospect of confiding in their own parents, a surprising number would rather tell it to a judge.

JBs were usually sixteen or seventeen. That isn't to say that younger girls didn't get pregnant, just that they were unlikely to pull themselves together to appear before a judge.

With some judges, the interview was a formality. Others asked probing questions: the girl's career and educational goals, her reasons for terminating, whether she'd been pregnant before, what form of birth control she planned to use in the future. Really, they could ask whatever they wanted, and *none of your fucking business* was never an acceptable answer.

Important note: younger girls did get pregnant. Depending on where and how and with whom she lived, a thirteen-year-old girl in America had, by Claudia's estimate, a medium to high chance of being messed with.

With the JBs she restrained herself. She resisted the urge to mother them, to scold and lecture: *Stay in school. Protect yourself. Choose the future over the present. Leave nothing to chance.* It was the only way—if you were born female, and especially if you were poor—to own your own life.

Claudia said none of these things. Instead she found them attorneys (at no cost to the patient—the lawyers were paid by the Commonwealth). Once a court date was set, she arranged transportation to the courthouse, a note from Dr. Gurvitch to explain the girl's absence from school. Then she prepped the patient for her interview with the judge.

Sometimes the patient resisted. A few years back, she'd prepped a JB whose career goal was to play in the WNBA. Claudia wasn't sure that would fly with the judge, so she suggested talking about other things—the patient's part-time job at Lady Foot Locker, the possibility of community college. But Ana F.—a gorgeous Dominican girl from Dorchester, lanky as a supermodel—wouldn't have it. She sat impassively in Claudia's office, her long arms folded across her chest.

No way, man. I'm gonna play ball.

I don't know how you can work here.

It was not, in Claudia's view, an extraordinary way to make a living. On the phone and in person, she took care of patients—as many women did, as her own mother had done. The patients—pregnant or not, in crisis or not—needed information. They needed pregnancy tests, birth control pills, STD panels. They needed Depo shots, IUDs, antibiotics, pelvic exams.

She took care of patients. The rest—the angry protestors, the threats and insults—didn't touch her. Each morning she rode the train to work. On Mercy Street she pushed her way through the crowd.

2

By the time she left work it was fully dark, the early dusk of deep winter. Traffic crept along the Methadone Mile, a grim stretch of Mass Ave studded with clinics. Panhandlers camped out at a busy intersection, holding handmade signs:

WOUNDED VETERAN
SOBER AND STRUGGLING
ANYTHING HELPS

Claudia picked her way along the icy sidewalk, into a stiff wind. When her phone rang in her pocket, she knew without looking that it was Stuart calling. She pictured him idling on the expressway in his silver Audi, part of the huffing bolus of German sedans creeping north to Andover.

"Distract me," he said.

Stuart was a collector of distractions. His phone was loaded with podcasts, videos, e-books, and sudoku. Claudia was simply another type of content he could access, her voice amplified by the excellent Bluetooth speaker on his steering wheel. When he wasn't consuming entertainment, he sculled the Charles and ran a biotech start-up and wrote numbingly detailed reviews of high-end audio equipment, which he posted to online forums read by other awkward men. In ten months of dating they had discovered no common interests beyond sex and dinner, a common condition among couples who'd met online.

Claudia told him about her day, the Ash Wednesday protestors. Stuart described a promising meeting with a venture capitalist. The unrelatedness of these topics made transitions impossible, so they simply took turns talking. It didn't matter. This was just a courtesy call, to confirm their intention to continue sleeping together. Glittering repartee wasn't the point.

The terms of their relationship were dictated by traffic. A weeknight date meant sitting in nerve-shattering gridlock, so their in-person contact was limited to alternating weekends, when Stuart's ex-wife had the kids. Twice a month they grilled steaks at his house in the suburbs and had sex several times, a two-week supply. Claudia excelled at this type of dating. Like a city gardener who grows tiny tomatoes in clay pots, she had realistic expectations. There was a natural limit on how big such plants could grow.

They weren't in love and never would be, but in one respect Stuart was the ideal man: late in his marriage, at his wife's insistence, he'd had a vasectomy. Nora had already decided to leave him, he told Claudia, and was looking out for the kids' interests: if he fathered more children with some other woman, their inheritance would be further divided at his death. His ex-wife had exhibited an adaptive behavior that favored the survival of her offspring, what mothers of every species were hardwired to do. Stuart explained this calmly, without rancor. His reaction struck Claudia as peculiar but generous, which made her like him. Combined with his inability to make her pregnant, it dramatically increased his appeal. After the STD test, they stopped using condoms. The careless sex was luxurious, like driving a car with heated seats or onboard navigation, some extravagant amenity she'd once considered unnecessary and now couldn't live without.

Garden tomatoes were always worth having, even if they were small.

"Traffic is moving up ahead. I'll call you tomorrow," Stuart said.

Claudia crossed the street to the T station and hurried down the stairs. Rumble and clatter, a squealing of brakes. A southbound train was near.

When she resurfaced, a light snow was falling. The sidewalks were crusted and slippery, rock salt crunching beneath her feet. Her destination was a side street off a busy avenue, a maze of crooked one-ways lined with parked cars.

The house on the corner looked like all the others, an unnumbered three-decker wrapped in grubby aluminum siding. If you've ever passed within five miles of the Charles, you've seen a thousand like it—cheap workers' housing, a hundred years old and built to last fifty. The inevitable synecdoche for the city of Boston; the part that stands in for the whole.

On the front porch, Timmy—she didn't know his last name—was smoking a cigarette, a big beefy guy with pale blue eyes and the terminally startled look of a person with blond eyebrows. He wore no coat, just the standard Boston street uniform: nylon track pants, wool watch cap, a short-sleeved T-shirt over a long-sleeved one. His most distinctive feature was a burly old-fashioned beard, the style favored by Ulysses S. Grant and the Smith Brothers, makers of cough drops. It hung halfway down his chest like a coarse woolen bib.

He waved her into a narrow entranceway—drafty, unheated, its tile floor encrusted with grime. The apartment door was ajar, three rooms connected shotgun-style, bedroom, sitting room, kitchen in the back. The floors were bare, stacked here and there with random clutter—sneakers, CDs, a sweatshirt—piled into plastic milk crates. The place was very warm and smelled intensely of marijuana. The windows were covered with a paisley tapestry the size of a bedsheet.

They sat in their usual spots—Claudia on the couch, Timmy in his magisterially large La-Z-Boy recliner. His massive television was tuned to TrafficCam. For someone who never seemed to leave his apartment, he was intensely interested in road conditions. A tray table held his daily necessities, arranged like surgical instruments: a cigar box, a remote control, a water pipe, and a small digital scale. Behind his chair, invisible from Claudia's vantage point, were several large glass jars with rubber seals, the kind used for storing sugar or flour.

He reached behind his chair and handed her a jar.

"This is Green Crack." He had a smoker's voice, deep and phlegmy. "It's high sativa. Trippy, a little heady."

Claudia opened the jar and sniffed, like a customer in a pretentious wine bar. The smell was fresh and verdant, like cut grass. From her spot on the couch she could see into Timmy's bedroom. The bed was unmade, the floor littered with dirty clothes, like the lair of some furtive, hibernating male creature. Under the bed, in a giant metal footlocker, was the rest of his inventory. She'd seen him dip into it to replenish the jars when they ran low. It says something about that time in her life that none of this seemed strange.

He passed her a second jar.

"This is Blue Widow. It's a hybrid, Blueberry crossed with White Widow. Your basic body stone." He always had a lot to say about the product, the relative merits of different strains. He preferred indica over sativa, pure strains over hybrids. Growing conditions mattered— the acidity of the soil, natural or artificial light. Men and their opinions: Stuart and his speakers, Timmy and his weed.

Blue Widow smelled darker, like freshly brewed coffee.

"Which one do you like?" Claudia asked.

"That depends." Timmy sat back in his chair, index fingers touching. With his insistent beard he might have been a wizard, an ancient seer, a warlord of the imperial era. "The question is, why are you smoking? What are you looking for?"

These questions were not easily answered.

She'd been coming to Timmy's for sixteen months exactly. One of the hotline volunteers had put them in touch. Claudia made her first buy in funeral clothes, having driven straight from Maine. In what would become their usual pattern, Timmy met her on the porch. Once inside, they smoked together and watched television. When money changed hands, both pretended not to notice. As though they were old friends just hanging out; as though there were any other imaginable circumstance in which they'd find themselves in the same room.

Was this normal weed-selling protocol? Claudia had no idea. She hadn't smoked in twenty years, and had never bought her own. In college she had no money for drugs, no money for anything. She smoked her first joint with a guy in her dorm, a rich boy from Concord, Mass, who was stoned for every minute of their freshman year. They had a rambling conversation about writers she hated (Jack Kerouac, Hunter S. Thompson) and music that bored her senseless (Pink Floyd, the Grateful Dead). While they talked, he lay on the floor and did sit-ups, his T-shirt riding up to show his ridged midsection. This interested her more than the conversation or the weed, which made her hungry and sleepy. His name was Scott McKotch, and he was never her boyfriend. He was just a guy in her dorm.

Smoking in middle age was a different business entirely. Hungry and sleepy were exactly what she wanted. In middle age, smoking a joint at bedtime made life possible. This was her thinking at the time.

Timmy was waiting for an answer.

"Work has been stressful lately," Claudia said.

Three days after Christmas, a suspicious package had been found in a patient restroom. The building was evacuated and swept for explosives. None were found, but the clinic closed for a full day of Threat Response Training, mandatory for all staff. For six hours, a former Green Beret led them through drills: active shooter drills, bomb drills. They were taught the Silent Call Procedure, in case the shooter was hiding in the building. (Press 1 for police, 2 for fire, 3 for ambulance.) Claudia hadn't slept through the night since.

Of course, she didn't explain this to Timmy.

"I mean, it's always stressful." She closed her eyes briefly. "I just need to *sleep.*"

"Ah." Timmy reached behind his chair and produced a third jar, smaller than the others. "This is Cocoon. A little pricey, but trust me." He fished out a bud, crushed it between his fingers, and packed it into the water pipe. Then he hoisted himself out of the recliner and sat beside her on the couch. He smelled, not unpleasantly, of marijuana and deodorant soap.

When he lit the pipe, she understood that she was to put her mouth on it, and she did—hesitantly, because the act seemed too intimate and the pipe was vaguely disgusting, the smoke warm and smelly and very moist.

She felt it immediately, a kind of unspooling, a slow dilation of the senses. "Wow," she said.

"Seriously?" Timmy looked impressed. "One hit, I don't even feel it. When you smoke as much as I do, it takes longer."

"How much is that?"

Timmy said, "All day, every day."

She took a second hit and handed back the pipe.

"I'll give you an eighth to start. See how you like it." Timmy ambled back to his recliner and placed the scale on the floor between his feet. Then he leaned forward in his chair, in the posture recommended to prevent fainting, and meted out her weed.

Their transaction completed, he packed a bowl and told her a story. Whether he did this with all his customers, she had no idea. It was her favorite part of the shopping experience, the prize inside the cereal box.

Last winter Timmy had taken a vacation. Never again would he do this, never a fuckin-gain. The trip was his buddy Kevin's idea. Kevin had a sister in Hawaii and could go visit anytime he felt like it, though in the ten years Timmy had known him, he had never once done this.

"I guess he never felt like it," Timmy said, passing her the pipe.

In Hawaii they'd have a free place to stay. Timmy agreed, grudgingly, to pay for their plane tickets. Because greed offended him, he avoided flying as a matter of principle. The fuckin airlines weren't getting his money, not when the CEO was paying himself ten million a year. For the Hawaii trip he'd made an exception, on one condition: when they landed in Honolulu, a bag of top-quality weed must be waiting for him. This point was nonnegotiable. Timmy would cover the cost of the weed, but someone else would have to make the buy. No problemo, said Kevin. His brother-in-law had a connect.

In this regard only, Kevin was as good as his word. The weed was excellent quality, worth every penny, the first and last part of the trip that went as planned.

Kevin's sister, it turned out, lived in a crappy one-bedroom condo. Kevin would sleep in the living room, on a child-sized love seat. For Timmy there was an air mattress on the kitchen floor. Each day, the sister and brother-in-law drove together to work, leaving Kevin and Timmy stranded in the apartment. To get to a beach, or anything else you'd actually want to see, they would have to rent a car.

At this point Timmy made a terrible discovery. Kevin had come to Hawaii with thirty dollars in his pocket. If they were going to rent a car or eat in a restaurant or do anything at all besides sit in the sister's apartment, Timmy would have to pay for it. This was no accident. Kevin had planned it that way.

Fine, Timmy thought, *I'll sit here*. I'll sit here all fuckin day and watch TV and smoke my weed. And for two weeks in Hawaii, that's exactly what he did.

One afternoon when he couldn't stand it any longer, he hiked along a busy highway to the one place within walking distance, an Outback Steakhouse. He sat at the bar nursing a beer and staring at the Weather Channel, the city of Boston buried in snow.

The one thing he'd wanted to do was see Pearl Harbor. To get there, they'd have to fly from the Big Island to Oahu, two more plane tickets he'd be on the hook for. A different type of person would have surrendered at this point, bought the tickets and rented the car and seen Pearl Harbor, but Timmy was not that type of person.

He sat in the sister's apartment and smoked his weed.

His story ended, Timmy reached for the remote. He flipped past music videos, the shopping channel, a cartoon dog speaking Spanish. NECN was rolling footage of a press conference at the State House. A crawl skated along the bottom of the screen: ATTORNEY GENERAL OPPOSES RECREATIONAL USE.

"You think that's going to pass?" Claudia asked.

This was the other thing they did together. They talked about what was on television.

"Nah. Never happen," Timmy said.

The couch embraced her like quicksand.

The crawl continued. IF THE REFERENDUM PASSES, MASSACHUSETTS WILL BECOME THE THIRD STATE TO LEGALIZE. COLORADO AND WASHINGTON APPROVED RECREATIONAL USE IN 2012.

"Colorado," Timmy said.

Those four syllables seemed to trip a switch in his head. As often happened, he told her something he'd told her before. Last summer, he'd gone to Denver for a buddy's wedding and was amazed to find a weed store on every corner, marked with a green neon cross. He chose one at random and went inside.

Long ago, when Claudia was briefly married, her in-laws took a trip to China. When they returned, they threw a party for themselves, featuring an hour-long slide presentation narrated by her mother-in-law, who had some sort of rapturous experience seeing the Great Wall and couldn't shut up about it.

The weed store in Denver was Timmy's Great Wall.

In a trance of stoned wonderment, he described its interior, the track lighting and exposed brick and blond wood floors. The product was displayed in glass jars, spotlit like sculptures in a gallery. He'd counted forty kinds of flower, from commercial-grade to fancy heirloom varieties, vials of cannabis oil, shelves of hookahs and ornate pipes, expensive LED inhalers kept under glass. The store stocked a full range of edibles, not just candy but tortilla chips, granola, frozen pizzas in slick packaging, all clearly labeled with grams of THC per serving. An entire convenience store worth of processed food, guaranteed to get you high.

"Capitalism run amok," he said, his final words on the subject. "The little guy can't compete."

He reached for the remote and began clicking through the channels. Finally he settled on a car show, which was what they usually watched. This one featured American cars of the 1960s: Falcons, Thunderbirds, the era of heroic winged creatures. It might have been ten minutes or an hour before the doorbell rang.

At Timmy's this happened all the time. There was a steady stream of random dudes in and out of the apartment. He stepped into the hallway and came back with a customer, a pale skinny guy with a receding hairline and—you couldn't miss it—a smudge of holy ash on his forehead.

"Claudia, Winky," said Timmy. "Winky, Claudia."

Winky sat at the other end of the couch. "Anthony," he said.

Timmy ignored the correction. "Winky, man. There's something on your face."

"It's Ash Wednesday," said Winky.

"Aren't you going to wash it off?"

Claudia was glad he'd asked. She'd been wondering about this for years, ever since she moved to Boston. How long was a Catholic expected to walk around with a dirty forehead? An hour, an entire day?

"You're not supposed to." Winky blinked rapidly, one eye at a time—left first, then right. Claudia felt that she'd seen him before, which made a certain kind of sense. If he smoked a joint a day, as she did, an eighth would last him four weeks. They had gotten on the same weed cycle, like roommates who menstruate in unison.

"I should get going," she said, clawing her way out of the couch.

Timmy followed her into the hallway. "Hold up, I want to show you something. It's just down the block."

Outside, the temperature had dropped. Claudia hugged her coat around her. Timmy, in his layered T-shirts, seemed impervious to the cold. Walking beside him, she was aware of his hugeness—a foot taller than she was, easily twice her weight. Usually she forgot this. Sitting in front of his television, they were roughly the same size.

When they turned the corner, she saw the car parked across the street: a Plymouth Barracuda from the early 1970s, dark green, lovingly restored.

"Whoa." She crossed the street to study it. "It's, what, a seventy-one?"

"Seventy-two," Timmy said.

"Oh, right, the headlamps. They went back to the singles, for whatever reason." She peered through the passenger window. The leather seats looked smooth and glossy. The dashboard was a marvel of midcentury futurism, the dials and gauges ringed in chrome.

"I just got it back from the body shop," said Timmy. "That's fresh paint. I need to drive it over to my buddy's garage, but I wanted you to see it first."

"It's *yours*?"

"For now," said Timmy. "I picked it up last summer for cheap. I figured I'd put a few grand into it and double my money."

She wanted to ask why anyone would sell such a car; how, if such a miraculous object came into your possession, you could ever part with it. The question seemed too personal. He was just her weed dealer.

Such a car could take a person anywhere, to an entirely different life.

3

When Claudia was growing up, her uncle Ricky worked at a body shop in town, and for a while she spent a lot of time there. In later years she'd be busy after school, minding two or three fosters, but at the time they had only one. Erica was easy, a quiet, shell-shocked girl who was always hungry. As long as she was eating, she was happy, even if it was only grape jelly and soda crackers. Claudia's mother complained that the child was eating them out of house and home, but crackers, even Zesta or Krispy, weren't expensive. The ones Deb bought, in plain white cartons labeled SALTINES, were practically free.

Each day after school, Claudia put Erica in front of the TV with a box of crackers. Then she rode her bike across town to Street Rodz, where the guys would be

jacking up a rear end or ripping out an original bench
seat to replace it with buckets, atrocities that should be
covered under the Geneva Convention. Besides these
"customizations," Street Rodz also offered detailing. Claudia was a skinny kid, small enough to wedge
herself into tight spaces, and for two dollars an hour
she attacked seats and floor mats with a shop vac. It
was criminal what people did to their cars. She vac-
uumed out pounds and pounds of dog hair, cigarette
butts, shredded Kleenex. Under the seats she found
candy wrappers, costume jewelry, roach clips, used
condoms—and often, a few dollars in coins. She was
allowed to keep whatever she found.

It was the first time in her life she had money of
her own, which would have been incentive enough, but
she also liked the cars. Most were junk, but a few were
authentically beautiful: a Plymouth Belvedere, midsix-
ties vintage; a '63 Ford Falcon in mint condition—kept
for years in a widow's garage, her dead husband's pride
and joy.

In the 1980s these models weren't as rare as they are
now. Sometimes you even saw them on the road, the
sort of rusted-out wreck a teenager could pick up for a
hundred bucks and spend his entire adolescence lying
under, trying to get the thing to run. Later, in high
school, Claudia would date one of those boys, a mute

gearhead with black fingernails. At Clayburn High almost nobody had a car, but if you did, that was who you were.

She loved the body shop, with its smell of tires and Turtle Wax. She even liked the guys. Growing up in a female household, she was unnerved by deep voices and especially, male laughter. But the body shop guys—Ricky, Roy, Tip, and Gary—laughed all the time, so she got used to it. The body shop guys found themselves hilarious. They cursed and crowed, they waged meaningless arguments: the best sandwich, bass guitarist, kung fu movie. The most lethal poisonous snake. The best goalie of all time. Each guy had a role to play—Ricky the wiseass, Roy the mimic, Tip the straight man. Gary, the quiet one, spoke only in riddles: Polish jokes, blonde jokes. His jokes were never funny, which made them funny.

The body shop guys ignored her completely, which was all she wanted. She zoned out and listened to the radio, Led Zep or Iron Maiden or sometimes, the oldies station. This happened mainly on Fridays, when the owner, an old greaser with a graying pompadour, stopped by. The owner was a throwback in every way: his hair slick with Brylcreem, the novelty bowling shirts he wore to hide his high belly, which began at the sternum. He had a surprisingly beautiful tenor voice, and when he sang along with the Beach Boys or Del Shannon, Claudia fell a little in love with him.

She also fell in love with the Falcon. Due to its age and pristine condition, it was kept in an indoor bay, and once, when the guys were busy at the front of the shop, she tried the door and found it unlocked. Its interior smelled of lube and gasoline and some kind of male grooming product, deodorant or aftershave.

She didn't sit in the driver's seat. She sat in the back like a daughter on television. A cherished daughter being driven somewhere, her mother in the passenger seat, her father at the wheel.

It was an acknowledged fact in the Birch family that Claudia was *born out of wedlock*, an expression used without irony in their part of Maine. Even her mother used it. Claudia can remember her talking on the phone to Aunt Darlene, about a wedding announcement in the Clayburn *Star*. Deb knew for a fact that the bride had a kid already, *born out of wedlock*.

Wedlock. The word sounded ominous, punitive, faintly medieval. Also, *wedlock* rhymed with *headlock*, a word Claudia knew from WWF wrestling—a perennial favorite with the fosters, boys and girls alike.

The phone was a central feature of Claudia's

childhood, a princess model bolted to the kitchen wall, its receiver connected by a long spiraling cord. Stretched to its full length, the cord reached to every corner of the trailer so that Deb could spend every waking minute on it, as a princess would presumably do. While making dinner or changing diapers or washing dishes or sitting on the toilet, she squabbled with her mother or gossiped with Darlene, their conversations punctuated with cawing laughter. She was happier on the phone than off it, and who could blame her? Trapped in a trailer with a pile of hyperactive kids, many people would do worse.

Claudia knew little about the circumstances of her conception, because her mother was a prude and a secretive person generally. Deb had given birth at seventeen, which meant dropping out of high school; her parents—stern Yankees who believed in paying the piper—weren't about to clean up a daughter's mistake. The man who got her pregnant was older and married and did not in the end divorce his wife, as Deb wanted him to do.

The man who got her pregnant. That's how Claudia thought of him. That is what he was.

Her mother was secretive, so she sought answers elsewhere. According to Uncle Ricky, the man had worked as a linesman for the electric company. Deb met him when he came to the house to restore power after a storm. Whether the man had a wife or children, Ricky didn't mention. It wasn't the sort of thing he paid attention to. He'd had several of each, and had barely noticed his own.

Her aunt Darlene told a different story. Deb had earned pocket money by babysitting for a family in town. At the end of the night, the man of the house— who may or may not have worked for the electric company—would drive her home.

Don't you want to find him? Claudia had been asked this more than once—usually on a second or third date, by men who were themselves fathers. The question said more about the person asking than it did about her.

She was conceived in May of 1971, when her mother was a junior in high school. The age of consent in Maine was sixteen. As far as the state was concerned, there was nothing wrong with a grown man impregnating a teenager, a girl who still collected stuffed animals and dotted her *I*s with tiny hearts: Debbie Birch.

(*No*, Claudia told her date. *I don't want to find him.*)

In the spring of 1971, abortion was still illegal in Maine. If Claudia had been conceived a year later, would she even be here? She had never asked her mother that question. The answer was none of her business, and anyway, she didn't want to know.

The man, whoever he was, eventually moved away, with his wife and other children, to North or South Carolina. Probably he did it to get away from Deb, who didn't take betrayal lightly and, Claudia strongly suspected, had made a nuisance of herself.

(*Why would I want to find him?*)

The annual package from Sears. Claudia has tried to work out exactly how it happened. Did her mother call the man on the phone? Did she say, "This is what Claudia wants for Christmas"? Did her father even know her name?

There was no point in asking. On this subject and others, Deb was a vault. Claudia consulted various sources, reliable and unreliable, and made reasonable assumptions. She pieced together a story that seems plausible and may in fact be true.

Clayburn, Maine, was a town of four thousand. There was a Congregational church, a gas station, a Dairy Queen, and a Hannaford supermarket. The nearest town of any note was Farmington, which had a U of M campus and was the birthplace of the guy who'd invented earmuffs. Growing up there, Claudia and her friend Justine Webster affected a snotty disdain for the place, as though they were just passing through on their way to somewhere more exciting. Claudia believed this about both of them, but especially about Justine. Never mind that Websters and Birches had served life sentences in that poor woodchuck county for many generations, the girls' forebears so lazy or unimaginative that not one, ever, had found his way out.

How exactly you'd do that wasn't clear. Forty percent of Claudia's high school class went on to *further education*, a deliberately vague category that included shady for-profit colleges and low-end trade schools that advertised on matchbooks. Girls went to the Downeast Academy of Cosmetology or got mall jobs or got pregnant. Boys drove trucks or joined the army or worked on road crews or went to jail. Between the two of them, Justine and her husband had done most of those things, shuffling through the same sad options like a losing hand of cards.

Her best friend, her entire childhood. When they were eight and ten, Claudia saw Justine twirling a baton in her backyard, and from that moment she had to have one. That's how it always was between them, Justine out front and Claudia two steps behind, doing as Justine did and wanting what she had. There should be a special word for it, the adoring love of a little girl for a slightly older one. Claudia has never loved anyone else in precisely this way.

Justine could toss a baton high above her head, whirl around twice, and catch it. She could spin it around her wrist in a way that defied gravity, a trick Claudia practiced for many, many hours and never managed to perfect.

Hundreds and hundreds of hours.

At college she'd meet people who knew how to do things she couldn't imagine doing. Their childhoods had been curated by concerned adults: piano lessons, ballet class. In summer they were sent to camps, where paid instructors taught them to play tennis and ride and sail and row. And if how you spend your time is what you eventually become, baton twirling was a significant feature of her childhood, and Justine's: the uncountable hours spent honing an entirely useless skill.

Their childhood was uncurated. On rainy summer days they made earrings out of dandelion stems. You peeled the stem into thin strips and dropped them into a puddle. Instantly, magically, they curled up in a snail-shell spiral. Later they stole real earrings from a kiosk at the mall, cheap metal hoops that turned their skin green. They stole constantly: candy bars from Hannaford's, perfume and lipstick from Justine's mother, who sold Avon cosmetics and kept a sample case under the bed. They swiped old shirts and sweaters from the Websters' closets. At the time, L.L.Bean offered a lifetime guarantee on all merchandise. Anything with a Bean label, no matter how ancient, could be returned for a full refund, no questions asked.

They stole nips of bourbon from the bottles Mr. Webster hid in the basement, the toilet tank, a toolbox in the garage. Claudia can remember rolling down the hill behind Justine's house at age ten, outrageously drunk and delighted by the motion. She remembers Justine holding her hair as she retched; their hysterical laughter as Justine's dog Daffy, the sweetest and dumbest beagle Claudia has ever encountered, lapped up the puddle of sick.

They did what they wanted, when they wanted, and if no laws were broken and no one was injured, it was largely a matter of luck. Justine's mother had four other kids to nag, and Claudia's was always working. Every so often she came home—cranky and exhausted, her knees and back aching, to sprawl on the couch and watch television and complain and cough and smoke.

But that is a later version of Deb. If Claudia reaches way back, she can conjure up an earlier iteration: young Deb in denim cutoffs and a halter top, long hair in a ponytail, washing her Chevelle with a garden hose. Deb vacuuming the trailer with the radio blasting, burning strawberry incense; painting Claudia's toenails, and Justine's, in rainbow colors to match her own. After the funeral, sorting through a box of junk from the trailer—pay stubs, expired coupons, dead scratch-off tickets—Claudia found that girl in a photo: her mother young and impossibly slender, lying on a foil blanket in a purple bikini, her skin slick with baby oil and lobster pink from the sun.

The photo was shocking. That it had been taken at all (by whom?), that it had been kept. Most astonishing of all was the expression on Deb's face. For as far back as Claudia could remember, her mother had despised being photographed. The few surviving family photos show her glaring at the camera, jaw clenched: *Get that thing away from me!* The bikini photo was different. Young Deb wore a mischievous smile, amused, playful. Incredibly, she was having fun.

On the back of the photo, in her mother's familiar round cursive, was a date that explained everything: July 4, 1984. That was the summer of Deb's thirtieth birthday, the summer she fell in love with Gary Cain.

There were other boyfriends, but Gary is the one Claudia remembers—silent Gary from the body shop, who spoke only in jokes; a tall, gawky man with orangutan arms and bushy sideburns that stretched nearly to his jaw. When and how he and Deb got together, Claudia has no idea. She simply woke one night with an urge to pee and found Gary standing in their bathroom in boxer shorts—dick out, pissing with tremendous force.

"Jesus Christ," he said. "Don't you people knock?"

It's my house, Claudia thought—but didn't say, because she was twelve and dumbstruck, physically unable to speak to a grown man with his dick in his hand.

Everyone says that kids are adaptable. If that's true, it's because they have no choice. Claudia was already used to fosters coming and going—most recently Erica, who'd been picked up by the caseworker one Saturday morning and was never heard from again. Gary's arrival was no different. She came home from school one day to find a hose running from the bathroom to Deb's bedroom, Gary filling his waterbed. This was how she learned he'd moved into the trailer. Like a new foster, he was just suddenly *there*.

There is an extreme intimacy to living in a trailer. Claudia fell asleep each night to the sloshing of the waterbed, low voices behind her mother's bedroom door. Gary was a big man, so tall he had to duck to clear the doorjamb. His work boots were the size of cinder blocks, and nearly as heavy; at least once a day Claudia tripped over them on her way out the door.

Even after he'd left for work, he filled the trailer with his presence: blond stubble in the sink, fine as sugar; a cigarette butt floating in the toilet, urine dribbled at the rim.

That winter was endless, the three of them shut up in the trailer like the rabbits her grandfather kept. Actually, the rabbits had it better: to prevent endless litters of babies, they were at least separated by sex. The skinny jumpy male got his own private cage, with a mesh floor so that his droppings fell to the ground and nobody had to clean up after him.

But even in Maine, the snow melts eventually. In the spring, Gary built a carport behind the trailer and spent most of his time there, working on his motorcycles. He owned two, a Kawasaki he actually rode and a beautiful old Vespa that wouldn't start. He spent months trying to get it to run—a complicated proposition in rural Maine, where parts were impossible to get.

Every once in a while, he took Claudia for a ride.

When she thinks of that summer, this is what she remembers: sitting on the back of the Kawasaki wearing Gary's helmet, her arms around his waist. She took to it instantly. Unlike her mother, who'd nearly toppled them over the one time Gary took her riding, she knew instinctively how to shift her weight when they turned a corner.

Claudia, you're a natural.

She can still remember where they were standing when he said this—behind the carport, Gary squinting into the noonday sun. The words were thrilling. She had no experience receiving compliments of any kind.

When Claudia told Justine about the motorcycle, she squealed in disgust. "You *touched* him?"

The question was confusing. Did you touch a chair when you sat on it? To Claudia, Gary's body was just furniture. The ride was the point.

"He's such a loser," Justine said, perplexingly. (Who, in Clayburn, could be called a winner?) Her dislike of Gary seemed excessive, which was probably Claudia's fault. She'd been complaining about him for months, beginning with his first appearance at the trailer, standing at the toilet with his dick out. Seen in this light, Justine's antipathy was understandable. It affected the way you thought of a person, if you were told immediately about his dick.

Claudia shut up about the motorcycle. She was sorry she'd mentioned it at all, because now when she climbed onto the seat she was aware of Gary's long back, his rib cage expanding, blond hairs curling at the nape of his neck. He wore an old flannel shirt, washed in the same detergent her mother used, but there was a different smell underneath, Old Spice and alcohol and something like potting soil, a rainy earth smell Claudia couldn't identify.

She'd gotten used to having him around. Once you got past his physical presence, he was easy to ignore. In the evenings they watched TV together, Gary and Deb cuddled up on the couch—orange-and-brown plaid, a sagging hand-me-down from Claudia's grandparents. Claudia sat in a beanbag chair that leaked tiny Styrofoam pellets onto the floor. From her low vantage point, she experienced a strange parallax: with Gary's long arm draped over her shoulder, Deb seemed to disappear entirely. Only her head was visible. Until then, Claudia had never thought of her mother as small.

Another thing that happened that summer: in July or August, during a rare heat wave, Gary brought home a secondhand air conditioner. The project seemed doomed from the outset. Trailer windows are tiny, and Deb had never managed to find a unit that fit. This one didn't either, but in Gary's eyes it wasn't a problem. Mother and daughter watched, dumbstruck, as he sawed a neat hole in the living room wall.

Most people have their qualities, and even after what happened later, installing the air conditioner was a testament to Gary's. It was a magnificent gesture. If you've ever spent a summer in a single-wide trailer, you understand that it was like giving sight to the blind.

Gary was there, and then he wasn't. One Monday afternoon in late September, Claudia came out of school at the final bell and saw the Falcon idling in the parking lot. The windows were down, the radio blasting. She recognized the long orangutan arm hanging out the window, the green mermaid at the biceps.

"Get in," he called over the radio—red-faced, as though he'd spent the day on his motorcycle. He seemed in high spirits, ready to celebrate. He'd borrowed the Falcon from Street Rodz, he told Claudia. As a birthday present, he was going to teach her to drive.

There were obvious logical problems with this statement—her birthday wasn't for another week, and anyway, she was only thirteen. Explaining this seemed too complicated, so she got into the car.

They set out driving. North of town, in the parking lot behind the Amway store, they switched places. Gary showed her how to slide the driver's seat forward, to adjust the mirrors. They didn't bother about seat belts; it's possible there weren't any.

She started the car.

It's hard to say how long she drove. It might have been minutes or hours; even at the time she wasn't sure.

The feeling was dreamlike, trees and barns and houses slipping past. Indian summer, the clear light tinged with sadness. The leaves had begun to turn. The black vinyl seat stuck to her bare legs, superheated from the sun.

The driving lesson finished where it had begun, in the Amway parking lot. Claudia pulled around to the back of the building and engaged the brake, and Gary reached across her lap to cut the engine. The silence was a little shocking. Birdsong in the distance, the quiet tick of the motor cooling down.

"Happy birthday," he said, and kissed her on the mouth.

He had been drinking, which was normal. She wouldn't have said that he was drunk. Gary was a big man with a high tolerance, and the beer he liked was cheap and watery. He could demolish half a case with no apparent ill effects. In a person who rarely spoke, drunkenness was hard to discern.

She didn't want to kiss him, and she certainly didn't want his cold muscular tongue in her mouth, but Gary seemed not to notice.

He said, "I've been wanting to do that for a long time."

Many years later, Claudia would tell her therapist about that kiss, but at the time she kept quiet. She didn't even tell Justine. Their conversation about the motorcycle (*You* touched *him?*) still haunted her. She feared Justine would think it was her fault, that she'd given Gary the wrong idea, and that this was possibly true.

Of course, she didn't tell her mother. She didn't have to. When she came home from school the next day, Gary's motorcycles were gone.

"I kicked him out," Deb said flatly. It was a Tuesday, her day off, and she was lying on the couch with a heating pad under her back, watching *Wheel of Fortune.* "I had enough."

Enough of what? Claudia didn't ask. Her cheeks burned as though she'd been caught in a lie.

There was a long silence.

"He came to my school," she said finally. It was hard to get the words out. "We went for a drive."

She didn't have to say it. She could tell by her mother's face that Deb already knew.

Another silence in which they both stared at the TV screen. Pat Sajak had cut to a commercial, a chorus of exuberant kids singing about vitamins. The commercial seemed endless. Even as a child, Claudia hated the sound of children singing.

Deb said, "He shouldn't have done that."

Claudia waited for her to say more, but there was no

more. Her mother reached for the remote and clicked through the channels.

"He's gone now," Deb said. "He won't bother you again."

Here's one final fact about Gary Cain. This is something Claudia doesn't like to think about. As he kissed her in the Amway parking lot, he pressed her left hand to his groin.

It was a confusing moment. Her knowledge of male anatomy had come from diapering fosters, and this had in no way prepared her for what felt like a clenched fist beneath Gary's button fly. In those two or three seconds she thought of Justine's dog Daffy, who had a fast-growing tumor between her shoulder blades that would eventually kill her. Claudia loved Daffy and continued to pet her, even though her tumor was disgusting. When Gary pinned her hand to his lap, she felt a similar mix of revulsion, pity, and alarm.

Poor sweet dog.

To his credit, he understood immediately that he'd done something wrong.

"Fuck!" He flung her hand away as though it had burned him. "I shouldn't have done that. You're just a kid."

Gary leaned back in his seat and covered his eyes with his hand. He had to go, he said. Living with Claudia had become impossible. He said other things too, but years later, those were the words she'd remember: *Living with you has become impossible.* He didn't say, and she didn't ask, what exactly she had done.

When he threw away her hand, she didn't know what to do with it. *Keep it,* she wanted to tell him. *I don't want it anymore.*

Gary talked and talked, more words than she'd ever heard him speak, as though he'd been saving them up for months. He would miss her, but she had to understand that it was only temporary. In three years, when she turned sixteen, he would come back for her. Claudia didn't ask what he would do with her then. Adopt her? Marry her?

In the end they swapped seats; Gary drove back to the trailer in silence, having used up all his words. Claudia stared out the window, her left hand in her pocket. It felt different from the other one, as though she'd been sitting on it for a while and starved it of blood.

Really, it was nothing. What occurred in the front seat of the Falcon was so minor that there wasn't even a word for it. Claudia wasn't raped or assaulted; she was only messed with. Worse had been done to young girls all over the world, on every day of every year for as long as people had kept track of days or years.

It was nothing at all.

She never saw Gary Cain again. He quit his job at the body shop and—she found out later—set off on a cross-country motorcycle trip, and when she turned sixteen he didn't come back for her. She didn't want him to, and yet some part of her was sure he'd remember. By then she was desperate to be elsewhere, but she understood that no rescue was forthcoming. If she wanted to get out of Clayburn, she would have to do it herself.

With Gary gone, the trailer seemed spacious. The junk he'd left behind—fetid sneakers, random motorcycle parts, a few sweaty ball caps—Deb hauled to the dump. She agonized over the waterbed, but in the end decided to keep it. (She'd injured her back at work, and for the rest of her life would struggle with chronic pain.) These chores completed, she called the caseworker.

The new fosters, Dylan and Daryl, were identical twins. Taking two at once set a dangerous precedent, though at the time this wasn't apparent; the boys were so alike that they seemed to count as only one. Each morning, after Deb left for work, Claudia fed them and coaxed them into school clothes. In the afternoon she did the same things in reverse.

The twins lived in the trailer for just over a year, until their mother got out of jail. By then Deb had gotten used to the chaos (also, probably, the extra money), so they got Troy and Danielle.

Childcare is exhausting, even for a child. With two or sometimes three fosters to keep track of, Claudia's life changed dramatically. She'd already stopped going to the body shop. Now Justine found a new best friend, a girl in her own grade. After school, while Justine and Lori smoked cigarettes at the reservoir or returned merchandise to L.L.Bean, Claudia was stuck in the trailer, waiting for the fosters to return. In that time and place, no one thought twice about letting kids walk home alone from the bus stop. That no child was ever abducted was probably a question of supply and demand. In Clayburn, unsupervised kids were everywhere. You couldn't give them away.

The fosters came home ravenous. They all qualified for free school lunches (ground beef in a variety of disgusting configurations—sloppy Joes, meat loaf, shit on a shingle), but by three p.m. were hungry again.

Claudia's first task, always, was to feed them. Their favorite treat was a delicacy of her own creation, known as Cheesy Ramen.

Many years later, married to a man who reviewed restaurants for a living, she learned that there was a term for this type of cooking, the recipes printed on cereal boxes and soup can labels, featuring name-brand ingredients ("1/4 c. Durkee French Fried Onion Rings"). These creations—processed foods in fanciful combinations—were referred to, snottily, as *vernacular cuisine.* But Cheesy Ramen didn't come from a recipe; it was Claudia's own invention. Cheesy Ramen hatched from her brain like Pallas Athena, the baby daughter of Zeus. This happened early in the Reagan era, when Maine foster families received, as part of their food-stamp benefits, a monthly allocation of government-surplus cheese. The free cheese came in giant blocks and tasted vaguely like cheddar. Its color was bright orange, its texture smoothly plasticated. Mixed with milk and shiny yellow margarine, it melted almost instantly into a thick sauce for ramen noodles, which cost ten cents per brick and could be boiled up four at a time in a spaghetti pot.

None of this is important. The only important thing about Cheesy Ramen is how much the fosters loved it. Nothing else Claudia has done in her entire life has brought another human being such pleasure. This is objectively true.

The fosters kept coming. Jackson, Levi, Kylie, Brianna. Cody, Nevaeh, a second Danielle. Those are the names she remembers, though there were others, tiny refugees who stayed for a day or a week while relatives were located, responsible adults of any description willing to take them off the state's hands.

The fosters were usually White, but not always. In Maine—at the time, and maybe still, the Whitest state in America—this attracted a certain type of attention. When Deb took the kids shopping for school clothes, there were looks and whispers, pointed comments from salesclerks. ("Is that your boy? I guess he looks like his daddy.") Even as a kid Claudia grasped the subtext: a White woman who'd let herself be impregnated by a Black man was an outlaw. In the spirit of a citizen's arrest, the salesclerks were putting her mother on notice. *I see you. I see what you've done.*

Claudia hated shopping and still does, and this is possibly why.

But the Maine summers were exquisite, the state parks free and plentiful and gloriously empty a hundred miles from the coast. Her mother's idea of heaven was to broil herself beside a man-made lake while Claudia towed the fosters around in circles on an inflatable raft. She has vivid memories of those afternoons, but no photos. Deb's unease around cameras had by then evolved into out-and-out horror, in the years when she was getting big.

She had always been a yo-yo dieter, sugary binges followed by days of atonement (black coffee, cottage cheese, SlimFast, Special K). As a child Claudia adapted cheerfully to this regimen. Dieting was a kind of shared project, a thing mother and daughter did together. Each morning, they weighed themselves. They recorded their numbers on a sheet of paper held by magnets to the refrigerator door.

130 LBS.
52 LBS.

After Gary Cain, there were no more diets. Grocery shopping became a weekly celebration, a festive ritual like trick-or-treating. Deb and her children subsisted on family-sized sacks of Fritos and Chips Ahoy!, tubs of Cool Whip straight from the freezer. They ate the way every kid would eat, if no adults existed in the world.

Claudia's mother got bigger, and finally big, and the therapist in her can't help making certain connections.

After Deb got big, there were no more boyfriends lurking around the trailer. After Deb got big, they were both safe.

At the time Claudia didn't see this. Like most teenagers, she saw only herself. At fourteen, fifteen, she lived in a constant state of embarrassment, a self-consciousness so intense it was nearly paralyzing, and having a suddenly fat mother (this does not speak well of her) only made it worse. Her mother's weight gain had coincided with her own puberty, which was traumatic in all the usual ways. (Claudia was a *late bloomer*—a phrase that should be outlawed—and the blooming process did not fill her with joy.) As she watched her mother expand, her own budding breasts seemed ominous, a harbinger of things to come.

At sixteen she stopped eating. At first it was unconscious: she was so busy shoveling food into the fosters that feeding herself was an afterthought. Later she was more intentional. She discovered that she liked being hungry—the peculiar energy it gave her, the feeling of clarity and control. She could eat what she wanted, when she wanted. Unlike anything else in her life, it was entirely up to her.

She ate what she wanted, when she wanted, which was almost nothing and almost never. When her breasts disappeared and her periods stopped, it felt like victory. She had proved, definitively, that she was not her mother.

She wasn't, would never be, anything like Deb.

At college she met people who summered in Maine, in vacation houses on the coast, but she never met anyone who lived there year-round, and certainly not inland. When the freshman directory—the original facebook, printed on glossy paper and known on campus as "the Pig Book"—listed her hometown, she had no reason to be ashamed. To her classmates at Stirling College, Clayburn had no shabby connotations, no associations of any kind. Raised in East Coast cities and their tony suburbs, they had never been to such a place.

They were from good families. A significant percentage had flunked out of elite prep schools. Stirling was their *safety school*, an expression Claudia had never heard before she arrived on campus. She'd applied nowhere else and wouldn't have applied there, if not for a saintly teacher at Clayburn High—a proud Stirling alumna who (bless her all of her days) urged her to try.

When the acceptance letter came, Deb wouldn't let her see it. As they shouted over the television, she held Claudia's future in her hand.

A private college was expensive. This was both

true and obvious, but it wasn't the reason her mother wouldn't let her go. By then Deb had a second job with a home nursing agency, visiting patients in the evening. With Claudia away at college, who would look after the fosters? Without her round-the-clock unpaid labor, life as they knew it would crumble.

Her mother didn't say, *Don't leave me.*

She did say, *You're no better than anyone else.*

If Claudia wanted more school (Deb may have added *for whatever reason*), there was the community college in Bangor. With a nursing certificate, a job at the County Home was virtually guaranteed.

It was a persuasive argument, though not in the way she intended. At that moment, Claudia would have crawled across broken glass to go to college.

Even during a conversation of this import, they didn't turn off the TV.

4

At six a.m., Timmy opened for business. He was an early riser, though not by choice. It was what he had to show for two hitches in the Marine Corps: a lifetime of early mornings and one bad tattoo.

He smoked a bowl and waited for the text message, the phone call, the knock at the door.

The apartment was freezing. He cranked up the heat and turned on the TV, a reality show about cops in Miami: body cams, traffic stops, search and seizure, cops giving chase. In Miami the suspects were shirtless, the sun blazing. In Timmy's apartment the radiator clanked rhythmically, as if someone were whacking it with a hammer. A roar in the distance, a snowplow barreling down Washington Street. The western sky looked gray and heavy, Boston winter bearing down.

He was about to pack a second bowl when his phone lit up: **hey its Brent (Ian's friend) U around this am?**

The name Ian was vaguely familiar, so he responded immediately: **yep, any time.**

In Miami the sirens were screaming. Timmy was selling drugs while watching a TV show about drug crime. He was aware of the absurdity of this.

Which Ian exactly, he couldn't remember and had no way of finding out. Text messages from customers were deleted immediately, his standard operating procedure. Timmy was cautious in such matters—*risk-averse*, a term he'd learned watching Bloomberg. If he ever got busted, the cops would have to earn their money. He wasn't about do their job for them, hand them a complete case when they cracked into his phone.

When Brent arrived, Timmy would be waiting on the porch. He liked to see what the customer was driving, how he presented himself to the world. Remember the douchebag who double-parked his Hummer directly in front of the house? The guy put on his flashers like he was delivering a pizza—engine idling, subwoofers thumping. He didn't even turn off the radio. Timmy sent him away empty-handed: *Sorry, man. This ain't the drive-thru.*

On the front porch he waited. Potheads were unreliable people. They arrived hours or days late—bleary, unwashed, haphazardly dressed. Timmy kept, in a kitchen drawer, a growing collection of their misplaced keys and sunglasses, earbud headphones, cigarette lighters, guitar picks. Not one of these items had ever been claimed.

The street was quiet except for an unfamiliar green Nissan parked two doors down, its engine idling. Timmy lit a cigarette and monitored the situation. He watched the idling car.

In Boston, winter was endless. He could barely remember how it felt to open the windows, walk unarmored out in the open, sunshine on his skin. His aversion to winter was a recent development, middle age creeping in. Growing up on the South Shore, he'd been impervious to the cold, made it to Christmas with nothing but a jean jacket. Florida had ruined him, lost years in Tampa Bay. At that time in his life, he had trouble making decisions. Civilian life was a shock to his system. He was like water spilled everywhere. He no longer had a container for his life.

In Florida he didn't need one. There was a landscaping job, year-round, for anyone who wanted one, a tropical peninsula covered in Bermuda grass and soaked in ChemLawn, fifty thousand square miles of ornamental plantings and dwarf date palms. Timmy— young then, and still in Marine shape—worked like a slave in the hundred-degree heat. At night he slept hard, blackout sleep, then woke at dawn to do it all again. It didn't sound so bad from where he was standing at that moment: hip-deep in the frigid Boston winter, obsessing over a parked car across the street.

He'd been selling weed for twelve years. He hadn't planned on a career in the retail space (or, let's be honest, in any space at all). Like everything else in his life, it had happened by accident. In Florida he'd sold a joint here and there, a favor for a friend. When his wife kicked him out, he came back to Boston and got a job driving a Coors truck. Then his uncle, who had thirty years in the Stagehands, got him a union card.

Remember the Stagehands? It was, no question, the best job of his life. Anytime a show loaded in or out of FleetCenter, ten or twenty Stagehands would get the call. Timmy had loaded in Springsteen shows, Bowie, Prince, U2. If you wanted to play Boston, you had to use the Stagehands. Always and forever, Boston was a union town.

He worked for the Stagehands, but not enough. There were too many nephews and cousins on the list, too many guys like him. *I'm dead wood*, he told a guy named Paul Pruitt, as they broke down an Aerosmith show. And just like that, Pruitt offered him a job picking up packages at the UPS Store.

Packages of what? Timmy asked.

Pruitt said, *You don't want to know.*

To limit his exposure, Timmy took precautions. He opened a UPS account in a fake name, Brock Savage, and invented a cover story to tell the clerk. Brock had his own business building custom skateboards. He had business associates all over the country, customers and suppliers who, once or twice a week, sent him small, lightweight packages shrink-wrapped in clear plastic.

When a package was due, Timmy ran the tracking number through the UPS website. Then he waited in the parking lot for the truck to roll in, keeping an eye out for police. If everything looked legit, Brock Savage would flash his fake ID and claim his package. Pruitt paid him a hundred bucks a box.

This went on for nearly a year, until Paul Pruitt accused him of stealing: Timmy had brought him an empty box that should have contained three pounds of medical-grade kush. Timmy saw right away that Pruitt was forcing him out, so he invented a new story for the UPS clerk. Brock was in a dispute with his business partner. If a stranger tried to claim one of his packages, the clerk should give him a call.

A day later, the call came. *I didn't give it to him*, the clerk said proudly. *I'll call the cops if I have to.*

Don't do that, Timmy said.

The parcel, when he opened it, was a dense brick of midgrade commercial bud, wrapped up like a welcome package.

Welcome to selling weed.

He sent Brent away with an eighth of Lemon Haze. Then he stepped out to pay the cable bill. Comcast would take cash if you paid in person. On his way home he ran into his upstairs neighbor, Mrs. Rivera, crossing Washington Street. As always, she carried several shopping bags.

"You got another visitor," she said. "He been standing there for half an hour."

Mrs. Rivera had lived in the upstairs apartment basically forever. Timmy knew nothing about her except that her mailbox overflowed with catalogs—for shoes and luggage and home decor, rugs and kitchenware and discount pet food. The catalogs came addressed to Maria Elena Dominguez Rivera; was she all of them? Had there ever been a Mr. Rivera? (Or Dominguez?) Timmy had no clue. Every so often, a Rivera child or grandchild sent her a massive fruit basket wrapped in yellow cellophane, so heavy she could barely lift it. Timmy carried the basket up the stairs and placed it at her door.

Back at the house, he found Winky Blanchard waiting on the porch.

"Winky, man, how long you been standing here?" Timmy glanced up and down the block, at the cars parked on either side of the road. Ten, maybe fifteen, had a clear view of the porch.

Winky Blanchard was a fucking moron.

"You could've texted me," said Timmy.

"I did," Winky said.

Timmy reached for his phone and sure enough, there was Winky's text: **This is Anthony. Are you home?**

Inside, Winky settled into the couch. Timmy clicked on the television. Then he reached behind his chair and fished two fat buds out of the jar. "I'm out of Bay One. This is Bay Two."

Winky did his signature blink: left eye first, then the right, like a breeze blowing across his face. He said, "I like the One."

Timmy was tired of hearing this. All his customers liked the One, which should have been good news but wasn't. His inventory was unreliable—and in the retail space, supply chain was everything. In the retail space, you lived and died by its whims.

Bay Two was a dense bud, slightly seedy so it weighed heavy. Timmy placed two fat buds on the scale between his feet. The digital display read .125—an eighth ounce precisely, Winky's usual order. Week after week he rode the commuter boat up from Grantham, forty minutes each way, to buy his tiny bag of weed.

Winky Blanchard was a fucking moron, but this was possibly not his fault. There was a story Timmy vaguely remembered—an accident, a lawsuit. Somewhere along the way, Winky had gotten his eggs scrambled. Whether he was any sharper before the accident was impossible to say.

As he double-bagged the weed, Timmy found himself telling the story—he wasn't sure why—about the douchebag in the SUV. *This ain't the drive-thru.*

"I can't play it like that," he told Winky. "I have a kid."

Winky's eyes darted around the room—nervously, as if he expected Timmy's kid to jump out of a closet. "You have a kid?"

"In Florida. He's fourteen." Was it possible he'd never mentioned his son? He lost track of what he said to people. He'd known Winky his whole life, in the same vague way he knew everyone who grew up in the neighborhood. Winky still lived in Grantham with his mother, two blocks away from Timmy's parents.

"He's not getting along with his mother. Which, believe me." Timmy reached for the clicker and turned up the volume. "I tell her, send him up here if you can't handle him."

They stared at the TV screen. The NECN news anchor was a woman who didn't belong on television. On every other network, the female reporters looked like porn stars. This one was sturdy and plain-faced, like an intrepid mail carrier who spent her days out in the cold.

Winky took a pipe from his pocket and packed a substantial bowl. Say what you want about Winky, he always shared his weed.

In the afternoon Timmy set out driving. He made the trip once a month—oftener than he'd like, oftener than he should have to, but Marcel was stubborn about how much weight he'd sell.

Timmy didn't mind the drive north. Driving was his favorite activity, his one talent, the thing he did best in life. The return trip was the problem, untold hours idling on Route 128 with several pounds of Class D controlled substance stashed in his trunk.

He weaved along surface roads, through dense

neighborhoods. The snow piles were stupendous. The narrow side streets were lined with decrepit cars—wounded veterans of the traffic wars, the city's disintegrating roads and bridges; cars in such beshitted condition nobody would believe they were still operable and yet you saw them everywhere, locked bumper-to-bumper on Storrow Drive, muscling into packed rotaries, crowding onto the Tobin Bridge.

His favorite activity, despite the dangers. The simple fact of owning a car exposed him to risk. It was how the government tracked you, monitored your movements: title, insurance, licensing, inspections; an E-Z Pass transponder stuck to the windshield. He'd drive ten miles out of his way to avoid a toll booth, the Commonwealth's cameras pointed at his license plate. Speed limits, moving violations, parking tickets, traffic court. If you drove for any length of time in the state of Massachusetts, sooner or later you'd have to deal with cops.

Here Timmy thought of Dennis Link, the childhood friend he'd smoked his first joint with: a teenage burnout who, for inexplicable reasons, went on to become a Massachusetts statie—a grown man who spent his days hiding under highway overpasses with his radar gun, waiting for speeders to blaze past. It was, Timmy felt, an undignified way to make a living.

He merged onto the interstate.

His favorite activity, and yet it made him lonely. A passenger only made it worse. Conversation of any kind blunted his enjoyment. What he wanted, truly wanted, was someone to drive *with* him, to participate wordlessly in the unending series of decisions: when to signal, to change lanes, to overtake or yield.

His ex-wife had viewed long car rides as opportunities for conversation. She particularly enjoyed starting arguments when he was trapped behind the wheel.

On the open road he looked for drivers like himself, fast but cautious, who sped down the middle lane and used the left lane only for passing, as the God he'd like to believe in intended it to be used. When he spotted one, an exchange was sometimes possible. Timmy passed courteously, then retreated to the middle lane, an invitation for the other guy (it was always a guy) to pass him. In this way, a rhythm was established. They shared possession of the passing lane, swooping in and out at intervals like cyclists in a peloton. It was the best conversation he'd ever had.

Marcel was Canadian but called himself French. He lived on a farm in far-north Vermont, twenty miles from the Canadian border. What unlikely circumstances had landed him in that remote place, Timmy had no idea. As a kid, on a school trip to the whaling museum in New Bedford, he had marveled at a piece of scrimshaw—a fragment of whalebone no bigger than a nickel—carved, in letters so small you'd need a magnifying glass to read them, with a single Bible verse. That was how much he knew about Marcel: one scrimshaw's worth. Marcel's entire biography would fit on a Bazooka comic, a scrap of paper so small you could swallow it whole.

The house sat at the end of a gravel lane, wooded on both sides. From somewhere in the distance came a breathy whistle, like someone blowing across a bottle. An owl, maybe? Timmy peered into the forest looking for movement, a rustle of wings.

The place looked deserted, which was intentional. He waited, idling, until Marcel appeared on the porch and waved him around to the barn behind the house. He was dressed in his usual attire—jeans, leather vest, some kind of weird paisley blouse. He had a distinctive style, like a journeyman folk musician: flowing silver hair, beard neatly trimmed. Nicotine-stained teeth, the color of buckwheat honey, gave him a rakish air.

The barn doors were open. Timmy pulled in and parked, twisting a little to unkink his back. Marcel pulled the doors closed.

"I heard something out in the woods," said Timmy. "An owl, maybe."

"A drone," said Marcel, as though this were an established fact. He climbed a ladder to the hayloft and returned with a green trash bag. "The drones, they are everywhere. I had a dream last night. The subconscience is always working, even when I sleep."

"Subconscious," Timmy said.

"The subconscience is very intelligent. A change in the atmosphere, the subconscience will tell me." Marcel knelt on the floor and opened the bag. Inside were several smaller bags, black plastic, labeled with masking tape: Blue Widow. Green Crack. Bay Two.

"No Bay One?" Timmy said, without hope. The supply chain was merciless. Asking Marcel for anything was like praying for rain.

Marcel barely shrugged, a microscopic movement of head and shoulder. "Sorry, man."

Timmy lifted the bags one at a time, testing their weight. He trusted Marcel, but it never hurt to check. He could guess a bag's weight to the ounce.

"What about edibles?" he asked. "You got any more of those gummy bears?"

"I have lollipops," Marcel said.

The lollipops were pineapple-flavored and achingly sweet, with an aftertaste of yard clippings. Timmy had invested in several cartons and couldn't get rid of them. Nobody had ever bought them twice.

"Nah, I'm good on those," Timmy said.

He counted off tens and twenties, grubby pothead money from the roll in his pocket, bulging there like a giant hard-on. Then he packed the bags into his trunk, around and inside the spare tire. The overflow he stuffed into an Igloo cooler, beneath a case of Sam Adams he'd bought years ago for this purpose. The beer froze solid each winter and nearly boiled in summer and was probably, by now, undrinkable.

Unusually, Marcel took a joint from his pocket. "I have some news." He inhaled deeply. "Florence and me, we are going to sell the farm."

"*What?*" said Timmy, taking the joint. "For Christ's sake, why?"

"We are going back to Canada. At the end of the summer, I think. After that, I am a pensioner." Marcel took another drag. "You know that I am selling weed now for forty year? I think it's enough."

Stoned, he was expansive, professorial—the kind of pothead who lives to explain the world to other potheads. The weed business had changed, he said. Top-quality bud was no longer enough. Younger customers wanted wax, cannabis oil. They wanted edibles. The weed business was officially going to shit.

"And when it is legalize, forget it," he said. "It's finish."

"*If*," said Timmy. "*If*."

"You're dreaming, man. It's going to happen." Marcel inhaled heroically. "For me it's okay. I am old. But you're still a young man. What you are going to do then?"

Can you hear the clock ticking? Timmy could. He'd been hearing it for a long time.

Naturally he'd thought about it: renting his own storefront, selling weed out in the open like candy or breath mints. The start-up costs were intimidating. The weed store in Denver had stocked, in Timmy's estimation, a hundred grand worth of product. That didn't include rent and utilities, the shelving and track lighting and refrigerator cases, none of which came cheap.

And the problem was bigger than money. Even if he could scrape together a down payment on a storefront, he had no way to explain where the money had come from. He hadn't filed a tax return in ten years. There was licensing to think about, insurance, a background check. Later there would be sales tax to collect, a blinding shitstorm of paperwork to complete. His ineptitude in these matters was half the reason he started selling drugs in the first place.

The truth was inescapable: when weed was legalized, Timmy would become a displaced worker, like his dad when Raytheon closed the plant in Northboro. The legal weed business would be run by lawyers and bankers, the same douchebags who ran everything else in the world.

"You want my advice? Win your money now. In a couple year, it's going to be impossible. Im-poss-*sible*." Marcel grinned, showing caramel-colored teeth. "If I were you, I would make a plan."

"If they legalize it, I'm out," Timmy told Winky Blanchard.

Weeks had passed since his conversation with Marcel. In that time, he'd come to certain conclusions.

"If they legalize it, I am officially retiring from weed."

He handed Winky the pipe. It was a Tuesday afternoon, the light already waning, the TV tuned to a golf match they weren't watching. Timmy didn't understand golf but found it soothing: the rolling green lawns, the announcers speaking in hushed voices as though a baby were sleeping.

Winky looked dumbstruck. "What will you do then? I mean, I guess you could get a . . . *job*." He pronounced the word hesitantly, like he couldn't imagine Timmy doing such a thing.

Timmy couldn't imagine it either. The sort of job he could actually get wouldn't cover his child support. It wouldn't cover his adult support, though his needs were simple. He didn't travel or go to restaurants or buy things. All he did was smoke weed.

Winky closed one eye, as though trying to remember. "Weren't you going to open a tattoo parlor?"

It wasn't a bad idea. But Timmy, disconcertingly, had no memory of saying such a thing to Winky. He wondered, not for the first time, if he was smoking too much weed.

"Nah," he said, as though he'd considered the idea and rejected it, which he probably had. "Too much red tape." A tattoo parlor meant licensing, inspection certificates, the Board of Health sticking its nose in. Military life had left him with an aversion to regulations, official dealings of any kind. He'd been told he had a problem with authority. He didn't like hearing it, which proved it was entirely true.

Anyway, he had a better idea. He would open a Laundromat. A cash business—no license required, no employees to deal with. Just Timmy and his machines.

The more he talked, the better it sounded. The plan seemed somehow virtuous—cleanliness, godliness. He would be providing a necessary service. He'd still have to figure out the tax questions, but he'd rather deal with the IRS than the DEA.

The first step was to raise some cash. Timmy had done a little research. A brand-new commercial washer went for a thousand bucks. Dryers were a little cheaper. Then there were the monthly costs: rent, water, electricity. He'd need a hundred grand to get up and running.

"Holy crap! That's a lot of cake." Winky blinked: left eye, then right. "Can you get a business loan?"

Timmy was speechless. Never in a million years would he qualify for such a loan—a fact he understood on a cellular level, which was why the thought hadn't occurred to him and never would. His own calculus was simpler: To open a Laundromat, he needed a pile of money. To make a pile of money, he had to sell a pile of weed.

If the referendum passed—he explained this to Winky—nothing would change overnight. The state would need a year or two to get its act together. Timmy would use the time to his advantage, to make some serious bank.

His plan was to cut out the middleman. His old buddy Wolfman had been growing for years, on a hidden corner of his family's strawberry farm in Pasco

County, Florida. The Wolfman had washed out of basic training, washed out of life in general, but in this one respect he was an overachiever—endlessly experimenting with new strains, gleefully cross-pollinating, a mad scientist of weed. Crucially, the Wolfman was no salesman. At the moment he was sitting on a bumper crop, more product than he knew what to do with.

"The main problem," Timmy said, "will be moving the weed."

Pasco County to Boston was fourteen hundred miles, through thirteen states. Timmy would drive the stash back himself—on weekends to avoid the traffic, the soul-killing rush hours in DC, Baltimore, Philadelphia, New York, and Boston.

Winky blinked. "What about cops?"

Timmy was way ahead of him. Over the years—countless trips back and forth to see his son and fork out child support—he'd made a study of this. Up and down the I-95 corridor, speed traps were everywhere, the Dennis Links of the world plying their trade. The stopped vehicles were usually SUVs, always with Yankee plates. He would need the right car—discreet, reliable, a car that would attract no attention.

This was his thinking last week, when he bought a three-year-old Honda Civic, in cash, from a stranger on Craigslist.

To make the trip worth his while, he'd need to move some quantity. He'd heard about a Russian kid in Quincy who did customizations. For five grand he could retrofit a car with hidden compartments—invisible, virtually undetectable—ideal for stashing product.

"Real James Bond shit," Timmy said.

He took a final, hopeful drag, but the bowl was kicked. He dipped into his own stash to refill it.

Marcel was right. There was power in having a plan.

5

The storms kept coming. There was a feeling of meteorological unease. The pigeons of Copley Square whuffed their displeasure. At the corner of Mass and Cass—the epicenter of the Methadone Mile— volunteers handed out blankets. Commuters waited for buses that never came.

Schools closed for a day, a week, for two weeks, prompting a citywide childcare crisis. In the Savin Hill section of Dorchester, streets were taken over by boys on sleds.

Boston descended on Star Market girded for battle. Toilet paper, bottled water, frozen pizzas. It was impossible to keep these items in stock. Checkout lines were staggering. Shoppers read the same headlines over and over, the aging starlet who was married again or pregnant again or fat again. They studied the contents of each other's carts, a stranger's secret comforts: cartons of cigarettes and extra-sensitive condoms, tubs of ice cream and cases of IPA.

In the neighborhoods, shoveling took on a feverish intensity. Parking spaces were saved with wheelbarrows, with lawn chairs, with recycling bins.

The boys attacked Savin Hill with whatever was handy: cafeteria trays, trash can lids. They raced down the slopes with war whoops, shrieks of terror and delight, because childhood always finds a way.

Years ago, when Claudia was just starting out on the hotline, the callers' questions amazed her. For a startling number of people, the basic facts of human reproduction were shrouded in mystery. She answered calls from women who douched after sex, or had sex only while menstruating, and were stunned to find themselves pregnant. More than one truly believed she'd contracted herpes from a toilet seat. And these weren't teenagers; they were grown women. Teenagers would have known better.

Considering what passed for sex education thirty years ago, in the public schools of Clayburn, Maine, this made a certain kind of sense.

It happened in a single afternoon that fell, in 1983, on

the first warm day of spring. In Maine, it is a holiday of sorts: the hats and gloves packed away, the Bean parkas moved to the back of the closet. These are the rituals of a primitive people blessing the return of the sun. At Clayburn Middle School, the sixth-grade boys whooped it up during an extended recess. The girls, meanwhile, were trapped indoors, sequestered in the cafeteria for a Very Special Presentation by a sales rep for the Modess corporation, an ebullient young woman whose entire job was to drive back and forth across New England showing schoolgirls a filmstrip about menstruation. After the movie, she handed out sample packs of Modess sanitary napkins. At age eleven, the girls had no possible use for these items; in 1983, synthetic hormones had not yet reached alarming concentrations in the American food supply, and puberty was still a ways away. Still, most were poor enough that getting something—anything— for free was worth crowing about.

The sales rep showed them how to wrap a used napkin in toilet paper and dispose of it properly. Through the open window they heard the crack of ball against bat, boys cheering and shouting. Someone had scored a run.

Along with the napkins they were given a booklet printed on heavy paper, with a title in curlicue script: *Growing Up and Liking It*. It looked like a child's storybook, and in a way it was. The main character was a girl named Patty, whose family had moved to a new city and who kept in touch with her old friends, Beth and Ginny, by writing letters (a quaint notion, even in 1983). The girls swapped news about school and boys, but mostly about getting their periods and using Modess products. They discussed the mysterious requirements of "heavy flow days" and "light flow days," and whether you could wash your hair or shower during your period.

Who would even ask such a question? Why would anyone think you couldn't? Even Claudia knew better, and she knew almost nothing. Her information about sex came mainly from Justine, who knew as little as she did, but with greater certainty. From the moment Justine got her period, Claudia wanted one desperately. This was Justine's superpower. She could make anything—even bleeding from the crack—seem glamorous.

Of course, none of that had anything to do with sex. For that, Claudia turned to television. Vague references to the act—what Bob Eubanks, the toothy host of *The Newlywed Game*, called *making whoopee*—were everywhere, but actual information was rare. At least once per episode of *The Love Boat*, a make-out scene would cut to a close-up of the DO NOT DISTURB sign being placed on the cabin door.

What happened after the door was closed? Answers

were elusive. Her mother, naturally, was no help. If forced to speak of certain body parts—for instance, when toilet-training a foster—Deb resorted to euphemism. A girl's private area was called her *princess*. This caused a comical confusion in the summer of 1981, when Deb, who loved weddings, woke the whole family at dawn to watch the British royals get married. When Prince Charles made Lady Diana Spencer his *princess*, the fosters couldn't control themselves. Their giggling could not be contained.

Her mother loved weddings.

Given the quality of her education, Claudia has done reasonably well in life. Given the quality of her education, she should have ten unwanted children and be riddled with syphilis.

Her afternoon with the Modess rep did nothing to enlighten her, and yet, for some reason, she'd needed a parent's permission to attend the session. Deb had signed the form without comment. They'd never had a conversation about sex and never would. The following year, when Claudia started bleeding, she saw no reason to mention it. She simply swiped a maxi pad from the box under the sink.

Naomi and Claudia were working the hotline.

The caller gave her name, Brittany, and asked how

Claudia's day was going. Never underestimate the politeness of mannerly young women! Even those who'd been date-raped or infected with chlamydia were happy to observe the conventions, reflexively eager to please.

Brittany sounded anxious. Four days earlier, she'd had unprotected sex. She was scared to death she might be pregnant.

"It just happened," she said—apologetically, as though she had wronged Claudia personally. "It was all my fault."

Over the years, Claudia had heard the same words from teenagers and middle-aged women; from nurses and teachers, cops and soldiers; sex workers and rape victims and survivors of incest. It was a lesson they'd been taught from birth, swallowed and digested: at all times, in all circumstances, the woman was to blame. Claudia resisted the urge to correct them. *If you're pregnant, you had help.*

Brittany said, "What can I do?"

It was a simple question with a confusing answer. Most pharmacies in Massachusetts dispensed emergency contraception without a prescription. The morning-after pill could be taken within five days of unprotected sex, but its effectiveness diminished with each passing day. To complicate matters, it was less effective in overweight women. Explaining this to a caller was delicate.

"This is a little personal," Claudia said, "but how much do you weigh?"

Silence on the line. Of all the prying questions she asked the callers (*Does it burn when you urinate? Is the lesion red, or crusted over? Is your husband circumcised?*), this one incited the most outrage. She'd been called a nosy bitch, a body Nazi. Occasionally a caller hung up in disgust, but no one ever said *I don't know.* Claudia had yet to encounter a woman who didn't know her own body weight. (Her mother—a woman who could polish off a can of buttercream frosting in a single sitting—had known her weight to the ounce.)

Grudgingly, Brittany named a number.

Claudia explained that for a woman her size, the safest bet was an IUD, which prevented implantation. The insertion took just a few minutes. Dr. Gurvitch had an opening in her schedule and could see Brittany that afternoon.

But there was a complication: Brittany lived in rural western Massachusetts, far from public transportation, and didn't own a car.

There was always a complication.

In Brittany's case, the answer was clear. She lived half a mile from a CVS drugstore, which dispensed the morning-after pill without a prescription. After four days it would be less effective than an IUD, but far more effective than doing nothing at all.

"I'll go tonight," Brittany promised.

Claudia said, "Go now."

When she hung up, Naomi stripped off her headset. "Was that another EC? That's the third one today."

"It's the snow," said Claudia. "Storm babies. It accounts for half the population of New England."

"These girls," Naomi said, shaking her head.

She spoke of the callers as if they were her own daughters: *What are these girls thinking?* Exasperation in her voice; affection, amusement, a grudging admiration. She seemed to be rooting for them. Naomi was the mother Claudia wished she'd had.

She often had this feeling about acquaintances and even strangers, as though parents were parts of a life that could be swapped out like an alternator or a fan belt. The truth, she knew, was more complicated. If Naomi had been her mother, she would be someone else entirely, unrecognizable to her current self.

Unlike Claudia's mother, and unlike Claudia herself, Naomi was patient. Answering the same questions— month after month, year after year—Claudia sometimes wanted to throttle the callers. Their crises seemed unnecessary. Truly, it was not that difficult to avoid getting pregnant.

"How was Maine?" Naomi asked.

"I didn't go. I came to my senses."

"Did you have a talk with your tenant?"

"Not yet," Claudia said. Nicolette's phone still wasn't answering, which might mean anything or nothing. "I'll run up there next week, maybe. It isn't urgent," she added, which may or may not have been true.

At noon, predictably, the line fell silent. Friday afternoons were always dead; young women were otherwise occupied, furiously calling and texting, making plans for the weekend. In a few hours they'd be off doing the things they'd be calling the hotline about on Monday morning. Claudia was about to step out for lunch when the phone rang again.

She slipped on her headset.

"Hello?" The caller was male—unusual, but only a little. About a third of the STD patients were men. This one had a deep voice, a hard Boston accent. "What is this numbah?"

"We're a medical facility," said Claudia. "This is the counseling line."

"A facility," he repeated. "Like, a hospital?"

"How can I help you?" Claudia said.

"My wife has been calling this numbah." Traffic noise in the background, a motorcycle roaring past. "Her name is Alicia Marzo. *M-A-R-Z-O.* Is she a patient there?"

"That information is confidential," Claudia said.

"Oh, for fuck's sake! It's a simple question. Is she or isn't she?"

"I can't tell you that," said Claudia. "It's against the law."

A car horn in the distance, the Dopplered wail of an ambulance passing. The caller was driving somewhere.

"Are you shitting me? This is *my wife* we're talking about."

"It's called the Health Information Privacy Act," she said evenly. "You can Google it."

Another car horn. The caller, clearly, was a lousy driver. *Hang up the phone, buddy,* she thought. *Keep your eyes on the road.*

"This is bullshit," the caller fumed. "Let me talk to your supervisor."

"I *am* the supervisor."

"I'll come over there if I have to," he said, louder than necessary. "Someone will have to talk to me."

"I wouldn't advise that," said Claudia, but the line had gone silent. He'd already hung up the phone.

There was a procedure for handling such calls. Verbal threats were to be documented using the Suspicious Caller Report.

Date and time of call: _____

Duration: _____

Did the caller make a specific threat?
Check all that apply:

Shooting___ Explosive device___ Fire___
Sexual assault___ Other threat (please
specify): _____

How did the caller sound? Check all
that apply:

Male___ Female___ Indeterminate gender___

Young___ Elderly___

White___ Black___ Hispanic___

Angry___ Weeping___ Laughing___
Agitated___ Calm___

Slow talker___ Fast talker___ Stutter___
Lisp___

Other speech impediment (please
specify): _____

Foreign or regional accent (please
specify): _____

The Suspicious Caller Report was unpopular with the staff. When the former Green Beret introduced it during Threat Response Training, he was severely interrogated by one of the volunteers, Marisol Leon.

Sir, I have a question. Do I sound Black or Hispanic?

He smiled uneasily. *Ma'am, that's not for me to say.*

Well, this form is asking us to make a judgment. "How did the caller sound?" I'm merely asking you that same question. Do I sound Black or Hispanic?

The Green Beret blushed a shade not found in nature. The Suspicious Caller Report was designed, he explained, to give law enforcement as much actionable intel as possible. There was no other agenda.

Marisol repeated her question.

Ma'am, he said, *I'm not going to engage with you on this.*

The deli was packed at midday, hungry people lurking in the vestibule. The overflow crowd spilled onto the sidewalk: elderly couples, women pushing strollers, loud-talking men in suits. All day long the place smelled of breakfast, bacon and coffee and fried potatoes. Every few months, Phil dragged Claudia there for lunch. As far as she could recall, he was the only person who'd ever cared what she ate. When they were married, it drove her crazy. After their divorce, it was the thing she missed the most. He'd been her college boyfriend, first lover, starter husband. His mother got her the job at *Damsel.* They married the summer after graduation and lasted two years.

She was a divorced person. It was her natural state— preferable, she felt, to either alternative. Marriage didn't appeal to her in any way, and yet she was glad to have tried it. If she were forty-three and never married, she might attach undue importance to the fact. Her never- marriedness would seem the root of all sorrow, the cause of every small dissatisfaction in her fortunate and mostly happy life.

"Sorry I'm late," she said as they waited for a table. "The phone rang just as I was leaving. It got com- plicated." She explained about the Suspicious Caller Report, the angry husband. *My wife has been calling this numbah.*

"I don't like the sound of this," Phil said. "Be careful."

"What would careful look like?"

It was an honest question. At the clinic they took every precaution imaginable. She felt incapable of greater care.

"I'm serious, Claudia. What are you going to do if he shows up there?"

"He won't. People say things on the phone that they'd never say to your face. Honestly, it was nothing."

"You said that last time."

"Last time was also nothing."

"If I were you," Phil said, "I'd get myself a gun."

"Seriously?" Claudia was gobsmacked. "Can you seriously imagine me pulling a gun on someone?"

"You'd do what you had to do," said Phil.

"I would lose my shit." They'd known each other twenty-five years; how could he not know this? It suggested that he hadn't been paying attention, that he had no idea who she really was.

They slid into a booth and glanced at the menu, which Phil knew by heart but studied for pleasure. Early in his career he'd reviewed restaurants for the *Globe* and had single-handedly put several out of business—fake, overpriced dim sum; a gastropub in Somerville that served an appetizer of flavored steam. But the deli never disappointed. The dumplings and brisket and homely kugels were, to him, the pinnacle of human culinary achievement. Claudia could remember when these foods seemed exotic to her. In rural Maine, pre-internet, even bagels were unheard of. It wasn't like that anymore; no place was. It was hard to believe, now, how little they'd known of the world, how isolated they'd been.

"I drove past the clinic the other day," said Phil. "There must have been fifty people out there."

"Thirty-six," she said. "It's Lent. They'll be out there until Easter." She reached for her phone to show him a photo. "See? No more buffer zone. Now they come right up to the door."

For years, protestors had to stay fifty feet away from the clinic's entrance—a Massachusetts law recently overturned by the courts. Now they could crowd around the door, praying and singing to their hearts' content, cursing and screaming and speaking in tongues. Their insults and obscenities were protected under the First Amendment. Unless they laid hands on a patient, or threatened to, or physically barred her from entering, the law was on their side. It was up to the patient—whatever her physical or emotional condition—to muscle her way through.

When Claudia explained this to Phil, he looked incredulous.

"You're kidding. That's *legal*?" The son and grandson of attorneys, he believed—reflexively, unconsciously—in the overarching wisdom of the law. That the law could be shortsighted or capricious, or simply wrong, was an impossible thought.

"It is now," said Claudia. "Do I like whitefish?"

"That's outrageous. Someone's going to get killed."

He had an eye for calamity, an actuarial sense of all that could go wrong in life: identity theft, radon leak, Bell's palsy. Tsunami, heatstroke, spinal meningitis. It seemed like a complicated way to live.

"Enough on that subject," she said. "Joy is good? The girls are good?"

Joy was Phil's second wife, a woman she had never met. Claudia wasn't invited to their wedding, a lavish affair at a golf club in suburban Ohio, with a six-piece swing band for dancing after the surf and turf. Her own long-ago wedding to Phil, at city hall, took ten minutes.

"Isabelle has a boyfriend. *Logan*," Phil said with wry distaste. "I am unprepared."

"How is that possible? You've been worrying about this since she was in diapers." Back then he'd played it for laughs: his reflexive mistrust of male children, an entire generation of infants with designs on his daughter's virtue. Joking, but not really. It was a quirk of male psychology Claudia would never understand, a weird oedipal protectiveness she found slightly creepy. But what did she know? She'd never had a father.

"He's two years older," Phil said. "I find that ominous."

"You don't like Logan?"

"Haven't met him. No one has. Logan is a mythical whatever. A Sasquatch."

"Loch Ness monster," said Claudia. "Jersey devil."

"Funny you should say. He does go to Princeton."

"That doesn't sound ominous."

"That's what Joy says. I'm lucky: the girls tell her everything. I'm happier that way. The less I know." He took a pair of reading glasses from his pocket.

"Oh ho! When did this happen?"

"It's been happening. Joy has been reading menus to me for two years." Phil pondered the special, a brisket plate. "Talk about yourself. Wasn't there a boyfriend? His name escapes me."

"That's understandable," she said. *Boyfriend* was an overstatement. Stuart was an e-boyfriend. They were two moderately attractive divorced people of comparable age and educational level, living in a twenty-mile radius, because those were the boxes they'd checked. The internet provided a limitless supply of such men, pleasant strangers Claudia could plausibly date for six to twelve months.

"Stuart," she said, "but never mind. I've been thinking lately that I'm done."

"Done as in done?"

"Done as in, they can retire my number. I'm forty-three years old. At a certain point, dating becomes preposterous."

"I can't believe what I'm hearing."

"Believe it. Now it's all repeats. Every guy reminds me of someone I've already dated."

"But not me."

"You are singular," she agreed. "There will never be another."

It was true: they'd been young together. Back then Phil had a full beard and a nimbus of curly hair—packing material, she thought, to protect his outsized brain. Now he had life insurance and acid reflux and a spreading bald spot, yarmulke-sized, on top of his head. Claudia knew, in a factual way, that they'd once shared a bed, that they'd seen each other naked, but she had no memory of it. Mainly she remembered dinners. After their divorce she'd reverted to old habits, lazy meals of toast or cheese and crackers, but occasionally she still ate with Phil, in dreams.

"How does Stuart feel about this?"

"Stuart has not been consulted."

Phil studied her. He had a way of scrutinizing a person. When they first met, in college, she'd found it unnerving. It seemed, then, that he was the first person who'd ever really looked at her.

"Claudia, are you sleeping?"

"Right now?"

"In general."

"I sleep enough." This was a blatant lie. But talking

about her insomnia made her anxious—which, in the end, made it harder to sleep.

"You need to get away," Phil said. "When's the last time you took a vacation?"

"I'm going up to Maine next weekend. To check on my mom's place."

"Not exactly what I had in mind." He signaled the waitress. "You can't keep this up, you know. That job is killing you. I don't know how you can work there."

It was tiring to have these conversations.

"Look," Phil said. "I'm on your side. You know I have no problem with abortion, assuming there's a good reason."

"There's always a reason," she said. "Define *good*."

The reasons were many and varied. Occasionally a patient would volunteer hers, as though trying to convince herself.

My son is autistic and day care won't take him. I can't handle another kid.

I got fired. Evicted. I got into law school.

I'm afraid to go off my meds.

I just need to finish (high school, chemo, probation. My PhD. My tour of duty.)

My mother would never forgive me.

I want a different kind of life.

"Last summer we had a call on the hotline," she

said. "A 603 number, so New Hampshire. She said that if her ex found out she was pregnant, he'd come to her house and shoot her kids."

Phil looked up from the menu.

To the list of reasons, add another: *I must escape this monster, raise the drawbridge, bar the door. If I bear his child I will never be free of him; he will take up residence in my life.*

"It's possible she was delusional, or a compulsive liar. Honestly, I have no idea. All I know is what she told me." Out of the corner of her eye Claudia saw, at last, a waitress approaching their table. "The point is, what's a good reason? Who gets to decide?"

Phil ordered the brisket.

It was hard to believe they'd ever been married. Claudia's recollections of that time were like blurred photocopies, memories of memories of memories.

She hadn't disliked it, exactly. Married life was like walking around in shoes that almost fit. She wore them every day for two years, and still they gave her blisters. Like most shoes designed for women, they were not foot-shaped.

She saw, in retrospect, that she'd been a poor candidate for marriage. She had never seen a happy one up close. Her Yankee grandparents were so taciturn that it was impossible to tell if they were happy or not, but their children, who were less well behaved, lived in raucous misery. Aunt Darlene and her husband bickered constantly. Uncle Ricky drove his first wife to drink and his third to Jesus. Claudia wasn't sure what happened with the second one, but none of them hung around for long.

She didn't know how to be married, but she wanted to learn. It was part of her master plan to live like people on television. Phil was raised in Westchester County, New York, in a handsome Tudor house filled with books. His father and grandfather were law partners. His mother owned a high-end catering business and was a personal friend of Martha Stewart. The Landaus were people of quality. By marrying Phil she hoped to become more like them, and less like herself.

She took his name happily, gratefully. As Claudia Landau she could be someone else entirely, which was all she wanted. To be relieved of her Birchness seemed like a gift.

Her in-laws, Joel and Nadine, were educational parents. They were always telling Phil how to do things better: save money on car insurance, prevent jet lag with melatonin, allocate contributions to his 401(k). This, she later learned, was called *parenting*. (Nadine was the first person she'd ever heard use *parent* as a verb.) It had been going on for Phil's entire life and explained why he was good at everything, competent in ways Claudia would never be.

A landau is an elegant horse-drawn carriage. A birch, in Maine, is the commonest sort of tree.

Next to Phil she felt like an orphan, unparented. It wasn't a question of being poor—or not only. Like many poor people, she'd been raised by a teenager. Years later, working on Mercy Street, she would meet her mother every day—pregnant girls *in extremis*, half-educated, without resources. Adolescents charged with the monumental task of raising a human being and utterly unqualified for the job.

That Claudia had been inadequately parented must have been obvious. Phil's mother, in particular, seemed alarmed by her ill-preparedness for life, so she took Claudia shopping. Claudia learned to write thank-you notes, to make hollandaise sauce, to iron sheets with a few drops of rosewater perfume. In Nadine's world, these were basic life skills.

At first this attention was thrilling. Later it became oppressive. Phil had been raised in a greenhouse, fed and watered and protected from the elements. Such relentless care and tending was stifling if, like Claudia, you were nothing but a weed.

In those years she rarely spoke to her own mother.

When she did, Deb's stories never changed: a cranky resident at the County Home, senseless beefs with co-workers, a foster who had nightmares or played with matches or started fights or wet the bed. Deb, notably, asked no questions. Her daughter's life in New York—the glamorous job, the handsome husband, the exemplary new parents—didn't interest her at all.

Phil hated to be alone, so they arranged their lives accordingly. They shared a small apartment in a congested neighborhood of a vast teeming city. There were weekly brunches with his parents, drinks and dinners and movie nights with their lively circle of friends.

For their first anniversary he gave her a cell phone. It seemed an extravagant gift. At the time they were expensive and not everyone had one, but Phil felt it was necessary, in case he needed to reach her. To Claudia this made no sense—there was a telephone in their apartment, and another in her office at *Damsel*—but she didn't say that to Phil.

She took the phone with her to work, to the gym, to yoga class—feeling, always, that she'd been assigned a tracking device, like Uncle Ricky after his DUI. At least once a week, she'd leave it behind in one of those places, and there would be a mad scramble in which she tried to remember when she'd last had it and where.

Later it would seem obvious that she lost the phone

on purpose, for reasons she couldn't have explained at the time. She wanted simply to be alone, to wander aimlessly through the vast teeming city, unnoticed and unaccounted for. To prove to Phil, but mostly to herself, that she was not incarcerated. That unlike Uncle Ricky, she had a choice.

They might have gone on that way forever—Claudia losing her phone, Phil losing patience—if chance hadn't intervened. A few months into her cell phone contract, she fell pregnant—an expression she'd learned at *Damsel*, from a South African photo editor who worked there until she too fell.

Claudia's pregnancy was unintended. The Pill gave her blinding migraines, so she'd quit taking it. She and Phil used condoms most of the time, which was only slightly better than not using them at all.

When she fell pregnant, that was exactly how it felt: a plummeting sensation, the plane losing altitude. She didn't want a baby but was, apparently, going to have one. She didn't consider doing otherwise. At that age, she had a horror of making decisions. She'd been raised in a sea of lost potential, people trapped by their own bad choices. Her own judgment seemed equally suspect. A choice of this magnitude—of *any* magnitude—was paralyzing. Every possible outcome seemed like a mistake.

When she miscarried at eight weeks, it seemed like a miracle. Her relief was unspeakable, so she didn't speak it, and her silence passed for grief. Eventually Phil's mother took her to see a therapist. She had married into a family where this was a normal thing to do.

Therapy embarrassed her. It was hard to talk about herself for fifty minutes straight. She was young and there wasn't much material—at least, none she was willing to share. Her background, her entire history, was unmentionable, so she complained about her in-laws. Phil's family was half the reason she'd married him, and yet she'd come to resent their generosity and concern and relentless advice, which she badly needed but couldn't bear to receive. She had misrepresented herself to them and they had believed her, which made them seem stupid. The Claudia they loved was a fiction, the person she pretended to be.

Their sorrow at her miscarriage seemed disproportionate. She'd never told them about the fosters—of course she hadn't—but she blamed them for not knowing. Children, actual children, were dying every day—of abuse, neglect, wholly avoidable causes—while these kind silly rich people cried over a fetus the size of a gumball.

It wasn't a baby; it was a menstrual period. That's what she wanted to say.

She went to therapy for four months, twice as long as she'd spent being pregnant. In the end, she and Phil divided their CD collection. At their age, it was what divorce looked like.

She has no idea what became of the South African photo editor, whose fall was cushioned by a breathtakingly extravagant baby shower. She married a Wall Street trader and moved to Connecticut and was never heard from again.

Boston didn't, after New York, feel like much of a city. Restaurant kitchens closed at nine p.m. The slow, creaking underground trains went nowhere she wanted to go. In December Boston came into focus, a city with a certain idea of itself. On Beacon Hill, snow danced under the streetlamps. Men wore long wool coats and Burberry mufflers. Historic cobblestones were carefully preserved. Diplomas were the local industry, like steel or textiles, so she earned a master's in social work. She'd been skeptical of therapy, which seemed like an expensive crutch for whining rich people, but it had helped her. It might have helped her mother or Uncle Ricky or any one of the fosters. Social work was therapy for people without money, for people like her.

Back at the clinic, the crowd had thinned. Puffy had put down his sign to eat his usual lunch, French fries and Chicken McNuggets. He nodded in Claudia's direction, a friendly guy in his real life. She gave him a half wave.

She was two paces from the door when she noticed the protestor leaning against the side of the building, a beardo in a red jacket, a ski lift ticket hanging from the zipper. He didn't accost her, didn't even see her. It was his sign that caught her attention—hand-painted, a bespoke creation. ABORTION CAUSES BREAST CANCER. Beneath this caption was a cartoon drawing of a naked woman, rendered in pornographic detail: melon breasts, nipples like small fingers. Over one grotesquely large breast was a red bull's-eye.

It is said that certain animals—ornery males, bulls and roosters—are inflamed by the color red. Claudia imagines they have no idea why the color provokes them and no memory of their aggressive behavior unless, like her, they see a video posted later on the internet.

In the video she starts out calmly, conversationally, explaining that the sign is factually inaccurate. *Just so you know, there is no connection at all between abortion and breast cancer.* Her smile is tense, wincing. *I mean, just so you know.*

She can remember feeling a human presence behind her—a slowing of sidewalk traffic, pedestrians stopping to listen—but she had no idea that someone was filming her with a cell phone.

By the end of the video she looks and sounds like a shrieking madwoman. (*Abortion is not a risk factor! Having breasts is a risk factor!*) It was the man's smugness that inflamed her, his undeserved power. The power to threaten strangers—female strangers—with the illness women fear most.

The video is sixty-eight seconds long. It ends with heavy footsteps, a male voice off camera. Luis, the security guard, had been watching on closed circuit.

Sir, please step out of the way.

The video doesn't show what happened next: Luis dragging Claudia into the building, grasping her arm, hissing into her ear: "For God's sake, have you lost your fucking mind?"

When they were safely inside, he let her go. "Claudia," he said, more gently. "Are you all right?"

It was a hard question to answer. Was anybody all right? At best, she was mostly right. Objectively speaking, *all right* was an impossibly high bar.

6

Anthony went to the morning Mass, not every day but most days, often enough that he was seen and recognized. At St. Dymphna's, early Mass was poorly attended, the crowd made up entirely of old people. He would remember it as the defining ritual of his time on Disability: the sonorous language of the liturgy, old people croaking out the hymns, the familiar prayers welcome as rain. Not to mention he needed to get out of the house.

The advanced age of the congregants didn't trouble him. At Sunday Mass the mean age was younger, but this came with its own complications. For instance: some of the younger people had been known, during the recitation of the Lord's Prayer, to raise their hands to heaven like Pentecostal snake handlers calling forth spirits, a practice that struck him as distinctly Protestant. The old priest, Father Cronin, wouldn't have tolerated this. His replacement, Father Quentin Roche, seemed not to have noticed. He was twenty years younger, a brisk, busy man who zipped through a full Sunday Mass in thirty minutes, endearing himself to the congregation and earning a genial nickname, Quentin the Quick.

The Mass ended, Anthony lingered in the vestibule. It was a slow-moving crowd, what with the canes and walkers and Mrs. Paone's wheelchair creating a bottleneck in the aisle. As he watched their halting progress, Mrs. Morrison touched his shoulder.

"How are you feeling, dear?"

Mrs. Morrison looked a hundred years old, but possibly wasn't. Possibly she was his mother's age, which was sixty or seventy. At a certain point the exact age no longer mattered. Mrs. Morrison had passed that point long ago.

He had a theory about old people, their greater devotion. Like everything in life it came down to timing, the historical moment, large impersonal forces at work in the world. Mrs. Morrison's generation had hit it lucky. They were products of a better time.

Mrs. Morrison talked about a new medication she

was taking, her daughter in Arizona with the fertility treatments and the one in Methuen who'd been diagnosed with lupus.

A better time, a better church. Anthony wanted the church of his grandmother's day, the Kyrie and the Gloria, the Latin Mass in all its lugubrious perfume. In those days people dressed accordingly, understanding that it was the most important hour of the week. Hats and gloves for the ladies, ties and jackets for the men. Modern Catholics (he included himself in this) dressed like they were stepping out to Tedeschi's for a pack of smokes.

He had never been to Methuen, a town that sounded like a sneeze.

He wanted fasting and indulgences, Baltimore catechism and fish on Fridays. Anthony missed these things as though he'd experienced them personally, when in fact it was all over by the time he came along. His generation got Reconciliation instead of confession. They got altar girls and folk Mass and guitar-playing nuns in blue jeans.

He took Mrs. Morrison's arm and guided her down the church steps. "I saw your father in the post office the other day," she said. "He was limping."

Anthony didn't know how to respond to this. His old man had walked out when Anthony was a teenager, though he didn't walk far. For nearly thirty years he'd lived just across town, in the apartment above Grandma Blanchard's garage. His departure was barely noticed. Anthony's day-to-day life was unaffected. His dad was never home anyway. He'd simply found somewhere else to sleep.

"I asked him why and he said, *I'm not limping*. But I'm telling you, he *was*."

It was Grandma Blanchard who'd kept the old traditions alive. For his First Communion she gave him a scapular, which was two pictures, one of the Sacred Heart, the other of the Virgin Mary, each the size of a postage stamp and laminated in plastic. The pictures were connected by a length of brown ribbon and were to be worn under his shirt, one against his chest, the other against his back. The wearing of the scapular conferred a plenary indulgence when combined with certain prayers, recited in a particular sequence.

He followed Mrs. Morrison into the parish hall, where volunteers were setting out donuts and coffee. He took a frosted donut and a cup of coffee that was mostly Cremora.

A plenary indulgence wiped out all your accrued purgatory time, for all the unabsolved sins committed in your entire life. A plenary indulgence reset the counter to zero.

The laminated pictures stuck to his skin.

The saints were prayed to for specific purposes: seasonable weather, relief of headaches, the protection of firefighters. Each saint was in charge of his own department, like middle managers in a corporation. The system was comprehensive. His own patron saint, Anthony, handled the finding of lost objects. There was a saint to help actors remember their lines, to prevent mines from collapsing, to liberate fish bones caught in the throat.

The Latin, the fish on Fridays. He'd seen photos from fifty years ago, Sunday Mass in Boston packed elbow to elbow. Now the churches were nearly empty. In ten years they'd be completely empty, the old faithful Catholics—Anthony's entire social circle—gone to their eternal reward. There were no young people to replace them, due to the thing with the priests.

The scapular was to be worn day and night. Grandma Blanchard had been insistent on this point. In her final years she lived strategically, to collect the maximum number of indulgences. Spring was her busy season, the forty days of Lent like a January white sale, an annual event during which the best bargains could be had. Certain prayers doubled or tripled in value if said on a Friday, in the presence of the Blessed Sacrament. Lent brought opportunities for extra credit, like managers' specials: Stations of the Cross, the Friday fast. Mary Frances Blanchard took full advantage. In her heart she was a packrat—a thorough, organized, highly efficient hoarder of grace.

Under the Grandma administration, the Blanchard family had enjoyed peace and order. They had a blueprint for living, a clear and unconfusing path. In hindsight, which was always twenty-twenty, Anthony understood her power. After she died, his dad stopped going to church beyond the two inescapable holidays, Christmas and Easter. He walked across town and never walked back.

Hindsight was always twenty-twenty, which was the only thing anybody ever said about it.

Anthony wore the scapular until the cord frayed and the whole thing fell apart. For a long time after he missed the feeling, a square of plastic stuck to his back.

From across the room Mrs. Morrison waved him over to a table. She was still talking about the barren daughter in Arizona, but now four people were listening: Mrs. Paone and Mrs. Giuliucci, Mrs. McGann and her senile husband, who wasn't paying attention but was always pleasant, which was how you could tell something was wrong with him.

The thing with the priests was bad, very bad. Innocent children had been approached sexually. Anthony didn't doubt this, and yet he couldn't help feeling that the average person was better off not knowing. For his grandparents, being Catholic was something to be proud of. Now it was a dirty joke, an easy laugh for the late-night comics. For the average Catholic, knowing had been a net loss.

Mrs. Morrison admitted that the daughter in Methuen had always been a problem. First there'd been a divorce. The lupus was probably a coincidence.

"She takes sixteen pills a day," she reported.

There was a murmur of sympathy or dismay.

He didn't doubt it, exactly. And yet he'd spent a good part of his childhood in the company of priests and was not approached sexually.

"That's why I won't go to the doctor. They're turning us all into drug addicts." Mrs. McGann nodded firmly, as though the question were settled. "I saw it on the news."

St. Dymphna was the patroness of incest survivors, children raped by fathers. Her subspecialties were neurological disorders, depression, and anxiety. The modern saint was expected to multitask.

At morning Mass he studied the old people, the embers of his Church, and pondered its disintegration. The Church was like an old car driven past its limit, to the stage when everything broke down at once: brakes, transmission, the decrepit engine running hot. The Church was basically flying to pieces.

It was possible that he simply wasn't a type of person who was approached sexually. History, certainly, had borne this out.

He'd like to meet someone his own age, a young mother, Hispanic maybe. If he could have one made to order, he'd choose a beautiful Spanish-type girl with two kids, a boy and a girl.

A little-known fact was he'd like to have a family. Not his own kids, necessarily: he wouldn't mind taking over ones that some other guy had started. In a way, he'd prefer it. For some guys it was all ego, passing along their genes and whatnot. Anthony figured his genes were something the world could go on without.

They were better off when they didn't know.

In the afternoon he took the commuter boat into Boston, a ritual he performed weekly. The boat was uncrowded, the commuters having already commuted. The only other passengers were an old couple pushing suitcases on wheels.

A thrill in his stomach as the boat pulled away from Grantham Pier. On a clear day, which this wasn't, you could count the islands: Sheep Island, Nut Island,

Georges Island. Anthony had never been to any of these islands, but even through the fog he sensed their presence. He knew exactly where he was.

To prevent dizziness, he kept his eyes on the horizon. At one time, not long ago, this journey would have been impossible. The motion of the boat would have tripped a switch in his head.

The boat stopped briefly at the airport ferry dock. The old couple pushed their suitcases ashore, and for a full ten minutes Anthony had the boat to himself. At Long Wharf he debarked like a visiting dignitary, delivered to the City of Boston by his own private fleet.

From the pier he set out walking. The clinic sat on a busy corner. That had surprised him at first, how it was all out in the open, like a regular doctor's office. Around the front door a small crowd had gathered. A few of them were carrying signs. He spotted only one familiar face, the old guy in the Sox cap. The rest were fair-weather protestors, which Anthony had no use for. For a few weeks a year, during Lent, they cared about the unborn. The rest of the year, the unborn could go screw themselves.

He visited the clinic once a week, one of his regularly scheduled activities in the City of Boston. A schedule, he'd learned, was a critical component of right living, one of the necessary conditions for healing to occur.

The priest at the megaphone was one he'd seen before, a big-bellied man with a booming voice. At first Anthony had liked this priest—his broad smiling face, the authority conferred by his portliness—but over time his affection had dimmed. Each time they met, the fat priest introduced himself. It was one thing to make no impression, another to be reminded of it continually. Still, he preferred the fat priest to the Franciscans, in their sandals and brown dresses, smug in their humility. The Franciscans had never given him the time of day.

In the beginning he'd been unsure where to stand, and hovered at the outer edge of the crowd. Now he took his place up front. He wanted to be close enough to see their faces, the women who'd come to kill their babies. He wanted to look them in the eye.

He found these interactions strangely exhilarating. As a boy, on a family trip to Cape Cod, he'd sat for hours in a traffic jam caused by a jumper on the Saga-more Bridge. Anthony would remember it for the rest of his life, the terrible proximity of death. Anytime he crossed a bridge, he felt a morbid thrill. Watching the pregnant women make their way into the clinic, he had a similar feeling. He was witnessing the final moments of someone's life.

His phone was charged and ready. He kept his eyes on the door.

From the clinic he went to Tim Flynn's, four stops away on the T. As per Tim's instructions, he sent a text message from the T station: **This is Anthony. I'm on my way.** He made a point of using his given name, hoping Tim would take the hint, which never happened. Tim had never called him anything but Winky, for a childhood facial tic that acted up when he was nervous. Anthony hated the nickname, but from Tim he accepted it, understanding that being insulted was a part of friendship. After he bought his weed they'd smoke and have a conversation. Tim Flynn was his best friend. Buying weed was the highlight of his week.

Anthony followed him into the apartment. The massive TV was tuned to the Guide channel, an endless scrolling chart listing all the shows they weren't watching because they were watching a list of their names.

They sat in silence, staring at the list. Finally Timmy chose a show about cops in Miami. It gave Anthony an idea of something to say.

"My ma is going to Florida. Didn't you use to live there?"

Timmy grunted what could be a yes or a no. He reached behind his chair for a jar of weed.

"Jupiter, Florida. Is that a place?"

"I have no fuckin idea," Timmy said.

"Her sister lives there. She's going to stay for a month, until the snow melts."

Timmy said, "I've seen this one before."

The Miami cops were conducting a traffic stop. The driver, a scrawny dark-skinned guy with Rasta dreads, was asked to step out of the car.

Timmy said, "Dude is gonna run."

Anthony had never been to Florida, or anywhere else.

"There he goes!" Timmy shouted, pointing at the TV screen, where the Rastafarian was running full tilt across eight lanes of traffic. "Did I tell you?"

"You told me," Anthony said, reaching for his wallet.

When the excitement died down, Timmy double-bagged the weed and handed it over. Anthony took his pipe from his pocket and packed a substantial bowl. "How's your sister?"

Timmy looked surprised. "How do you know Maureen?"

"From school," Anthony said.

Timmy felt around for the remote and found it behind him. "She's all right. Mick got a job in Nashua. Her husband."

The word *husband* soured Anthony's mood somewhat. "I thought they were separated."

"They were. Now they're back together. Don't ask."

When Timmy began clicking through the channels, Anthony closed his eyes. The rapidly changing picture gave him vertigo. The TV screen was the size of a child's swimming pool, far too large for the room.

On the boat back to Grantham, he thought about Tim's sister, whom he had not known in school. He'd lied because the truth was humiliating: Maureen Flynn had been his babysitter. Anthony was, at the time, twelve years old—by Grantham standards, old enough to stay home alone while his mother played Monday night bingo. He had done this many times without incident, until the night of the toaster fire, which he extinguished by the accepted method of throwing a carpet over it. His mother was mad about the carpet, so she paid Maureen Flynn to stay with him, unaware of the shame it caused him. Maureen was only four years older, a junior in high school and the great love of his life, a title for which there'd been, to date, no serious competition.

His experience with women had been lackluster.

With Maureen he blamed the circumstances, which were not auspicious. Looking back he wondered: *What the hell was wrong with her? Why was she messing around with some little kid?* Which probably should have occurred to him at the time, but didn't.

When it was over she said, *It's supposed to take longer.*

He said, *I'll do better next time.*

But there was no next time. When he heard some years later that she'd gotten married, the news affected him powerfully. It was as though he'd missed the bus that was supposed to take him to the rest of his life.

The rest of his life was a country he had yet to visit. Nothing, nothing had turned out as planned.

He'd made a promising start, two semesters at Curry College. When he ran out of money, he worked as a helper at Mancini Construction. Each morning, with his dad, he rode to the job site at dawn, not talking but listening to the same radio. It was the most time he'd ever spent in his father's company. This lasted five weeks, until he was loaned out to another crew driving piles on the Big Dig, the biggest mistake of his life.

When he disembarked at Grantham pier, he felt that he'd been gone a long time, though of course the town was exactly as he'd left it. This would be true if he'd been gone ten minutes or twenty years. A beer-drinking teenager loitered at the waterfront, pursuing his delinquency. Fifty years ago, he might have been Anthony's father. Thirty years ago, he might have been Tim Flynn. In the sad B movie that was life in Grantham, actors were recast periodically, replaced with younger models, but the script itself never changed. It was that kind of town.

He found the house empty, his mother at the beauty parlor for her weekly wash and set. There was nothing interesting in the refrigerator, so he filled a bowl with Lucky Charms and took it downstairs to his headquarters. As a teenager, for privacy, he'd relocated his bedroom to the basement. Over the years he'd made key improvements: a stereo system, cable TV, and wireless internet. Plugged into headphones, he could ignore the creaking overhead, his mother going about her business in the kitchen, where she spent ninety-eight percent of her waking life.

His headquarters was comfortable, if a little dark. The only daylight came from a couple of high windows set at ground level. They looked out on window wells made of corrugated tin.

The darkness had come in handy in the year of holding his head.

He ate his cereal in front of the computer, scrolling through the site. For two years, he'd been the webmaster for Catholic Heritage of New England, an organization that existed for one reason only: to convince priests to say the Latin Mass.

The webmaster gig paid nothing; then again, it was almost no work. Once in a while he made an addition to the calendar of events: a Rosary rally, Stations of the Cross, a bus trip to a community theater in New Jersey for the annual performance of *Veronica's Veil*. After a while he requested, and was given, the title webmaster, which Father Renaldo was happy to do as it was cheaper than paying him. Immediately Anthony printed up business cards with his name in raised gold letters: ANTHONY BLANCHARD, WEBMASTER.

He noticed a backward parenthesis on the Calendar of Events. As he made the correction, he heard footsteps overhead.

His mother called from the top of the steps: "Anthony, are you home?"

She clomped down the stairs. Her gray hair was teased into its usual configuration, bubble-shaped and hard as a helmet, lacquered with hairspray to last the week.

He met her at the foot of the stairs. "Ma, what did I tell you about knocking?"

"Sorry, sorry. You want me to go back and knock?"

"I'm a grown man. I have a right to privacy. I could have a girl down here." He didn't add that he could be jerking off, which was far more likely, or that he could be smoking a bowl, which was likelier still.

His mother sniffed dramatically. "It smells down here."

"I don't smell anything."

She said, "Where have you been?"

"Where have I ever been? I went to Mass."

"Don't get snippy. I'm just asking."

"After that I went into town," he said, "to see a friend."

His mother brightened. "You have a friend?"

"I have lots of friends."

"In Boston?"

Anthony sighed, exasperated. "It was Tim Flynn, if you must know. Maureen's brother."

"Who?"

"You remember Maureen. My girlfriend."

"When did you have a girlfriend?"

Anthony did not dignify this with a reply. Lately he got the sense that his mother thought he was gay, an impression he didn't bother to correct because the truth was even less flattering.

"Well, at least you got out of the house. Maybe you should look for a job," his mother said, as though this had just occurred to her. As though it hadn't been their *number one subject of conversation for his entire life.* "They're hiring down at Stop & Shop."

"A grocery checker," he said.

"You could work your way up, like Sal with the frozen foods."

This was her second-favorite subject of conversation. Anthony's cousin Sal, on the Fusco side, was the frozen foods manager at a Star Market in Lynn or Saugus or wherever the fuck he lived.

Anthony said, "I have no interest in frozen foods."

"It's not about interested. It's about you have a job."

"I have a job," he said for the thousandth time. "On the internet."

His mother, who had only a vague idea what the internet was, had no answer for this.

"I've explained this," he said with infinite patience. "I get some crap job at Stop & Shop, I lose my Disability."

He'd been collecting for fourteen years: longer than he spent in school, longer than he'd done anything in his entire life. In the deadbeat Olympics, he had won the gold medal: permanent and total incapacity. All because of a single moment on a Tuesday afternoon, in a South Boston tunnel pit.

His monthly check was modest—sixty-six percent of what he'd earned at Mancini Construction, plus an annual cost-of-living adjustment—but it beat Stop & Shop money, frozen foods money. Broken down to an hourly wage, it was even more impressive. He spent zero hours earning his monthly nut. He got paid just for staying alive.

The particulars of the accident weren't real to him, they lived in the realm of rumor and conjecture. According to witnesses, an unsecured beam had made contact with Anthony's hard hat. The force was great enough to knock him out cold. On the Glasgow Coma Scale, he was rated a nine. (Loss of consciousness for less than thirty minutes, cognitive impairments that may or may not resolve.)

At a certain point the hospital discharged him. Anthony was hazy on the details. The state was involved, workers' comp, the union maybe. Claims were processed. He was assigned a caseworker whose name he forgot immediately.

He sat in a dark room holding his head.

In that year, 2002, he lived nowhere. He lived only in his body, a troubled neighborhood rapidly going to seed. Ringing in his ears, a sickening vertigo. He sat very still and listened to his interior weather, his organs slipping and sliding against one another like a bag of dying fish.

The body in all its exigencies, its variegated symptoms, its colorful complaints.

His mother hired an attorney who advertised on

TV, in between reruns of *Law & Order*. A caseworker whose name he couldn't remember gave him advice he couldn't remember.

"Total permanent. I can't imagine they'd refuse you," she said, looking him up and down, and in spite of himself he was offended because she didn't look that great herself.

His head was examined by every means possible. He lay in a metal tube that made otherworldly noises. After an hour or a month, who could tell, he was excreted through the tube. His vitals were taken—blood pressure, resting pulse. The numbers were a kind of code, elegant, inscrutable. Anthony added them together to discern their meaning, the unreported stories of the body contained therein.

He was given a PET scan and a CAT scan but curiously, no dog scan.

By every means possible, short of cutting his skull in half.

He sat in a dark room holding his head. Upstairs his mother watched *Law & Order*. In between scenes came the chinking noise he could hear through the floorboards, like the door of a prison cell being closed.

His brain didn't work the way it once had. Reading made his head ache. He had trouble matching names and faces. An Indian doctor with a musical accent

peppered him with questions. Were these new defi-
ciencies? Was his memory better before the accident?

"I don't remember," Anthony said.

His traumatic brain injury was classified as moder-
ate. There had been some impairment of his executive
functions. To Anthony, who wasn't aware of possessing
any to begin with, it was confusing news.

He listened for the chinking noise.

Each doctor referred him to another doctor. The
acupuncturist, the inner-ear specialist. He swallowed
capsules and was palpated. A psychologist asked questions about his childhood. He lay on a table listening to
soothing music while a Chinese woman stuck needles
into his neck.

When he was advised to resume his normal activities, it was like being told to burst into flames.

Head injuries were unpredictable. On this point
only, the doctors agreed. A mild concussion could cause
symptoms for years afterward. A massive, bell-ringing
concussion basically doomed you for life—according
to the Traumatic Brain Injury message board, which
Anthony checked daily. The posts were like dispatches
from another planet—a bleak, ruined planet inhabited
by dizzy, nauseated, clinically depressed people who'd
lost all interest in living.

On the message board they shared useless informa-

tion. Melatonin, B vitamins, a drink containing elec-
trolytes. Plastic bands around the wrists to prevent
seasickness.

Days got longer, shorter, longer. Warmer, colder,
warmer. In this way, years passed.

Unpredictable was the sole point of agreement. The
doctors were happy to take his money. Several times
a week he rode the Care Van, a free shuttle that made
regular stops in Grantham—to ferry decrepit elders
to their medical appointments, multiple stops on their
journeys to the grave.

On one of these trips, the driver—a friendly old
hippie whose name he couldn't remember—gave him a
hand-rolled cigarette.

His brain didn't work the way it once had. He felt,
always, that he was moving at half speed. Smoking
weed didn't make him any quicker, but it quelled his
seasickness, the gyroscope spinning inside his head.

He smoked the joint at bedtime and slept deeply.
The next morning he went for a walk.

On the bus driver's advice, he called Tim Flynn.

Each day he walked a little farther. One morning he
made it as far as St. Dymphna's. The church was warm
and smelled of candle wax, birthday candles, the best
moments of childhood. Gradually the pews filled; the
morning Mass happened around him.

He sat in a back pew holding his head.

At Mass he was the kid in the room, the object of geriatric cooing. At Christmas Mrs. Paone knitted him a muffler. Mrs. Morrison baked him a pie. It may not have been accurate to say that faith saved him. If he'd gone through the motions of daily Mass without actually believing, it might have worked just as well.

Each morning he set out walking. He took off his hat so the salt breeze could aerate his brain.

When he returned to his computer, an alert was flashing on his screen, an instant message from Excelsior11—after Tim Flynn, his second-best friend.

Excelsior11: How was turnout?

Not bad, Anthony wrote. **Maybe 30, give or take.**

Excelsior11: Pix?

Anthony wrote, **Uploading them now.**

They had known each other for six months, in the peculiar way strangers know each other online: screen name, alleged age and gender and whatever else the other chose to reveal or embellish or outright fabricate about himself. Excelsior11 lived in a log cabin in Nowhere, Pennsylvania. A Vietnam vet and former long-haul trucker, he now devoted himself, full-time, to the defense of the unborn. These facts were, of course, unverifiable, but Anthony accepted them at face value. It wasn't the sort of biography anyone would bother to invent.

Excelsior11 was not Catholic. His insistence on this point was, at first, disquieting.

Excelsior11: I reject the worship of saints and angels. But I can see that you are a righteous man and I have no quarrel with your beliefs.

Anthony found these words reassuring. He had never been called *righteous* before. That his second-best friend was a Protestant made him feel worldly, cosmopolitan. He began to see Excelsior11 as a kind of mentor—like the old Japanese coot in *The Karate Kid*, the all-time favorite film of his youth.

Excelsior: *ever upward.* Though not Catholic, he had chosen a Latin screen name.

His method was Socratic. Each day, he sent Anthony a question to ponder.

Excelsior11: How would you defend the Right to Life if you found yourself in discussion with a Nonbeliever?

Excelsior11: What is the appropriate legal punishment for a woman who chooses to kill her child?

These questions lit up his brain. In thirty-nine years of attending Catholic Mass, he'd sat through so many sermons about abortion that the word itself had a soporific effect, like the "midnight sedation" he'd been given when his wisdom teeth were removed. To Anthony, who had never impregnated anyone and had little hope of doing so, abortion was a distant, abstract problem—a thing you were supposed to care about, like the national debt.

Then, a few months back, Excelsior11 had approached him with a proposition—a mission, he called it. There was an abortion mill operating in plain sight, just off Boston Common. Anthony's mission was to document its activities, the daily holocaust of the unborn.

7

The patient had a diamond chip in her face. A Monroe, she called it.

It took Claudia a moment to grasp the reference. The diamond sat an inch above the girl's top lip and slightly off center, the exact placement of Marilyn's famous mole. Under the fluorescent lights her skin looked pale and waxy, like the petals of a lily. She was dressed in stretch pants, a thermal undershirt pulled tight across her belly, a man's plaid shirt hanging open in front, sleeves rolled down to hide her arms. Claudia had seen her before, underdressed for the weather, panhandling on the pedestrian mall at Downtown Crossing. Or maybe she hadn't; it was hard to say for certain. That winter in Boston, there were plenty of girls who looked like Shannon F.

The diamond chip flashed, it twinkled, it caught the light like an errant tear. Claudia asked the usual questions, but Shannon didn't want to talk about her pregnancy. She wanted to talk about her Monroe—a gift, she said, from her new boyfriend, Kyle.

"Is he the man involved with this pregnancy?" This was how Claudia had been trained to phrase it: no assumptions, no judgment.

"None of your fuckin business," said Shannon F.

Women in crisis were not always charming.

Did Shannon have a phone number? Did she feel safe where she was living? Had she received any prenatal care?

No, yes, no.

Claudia asked, "How often are you using?"

Shannon crossed her legs, twig-like in the black stretch pants. It was hard to believe she was pregnant. Her suede boots—battered Uggs, probably fake—seemed too large for her feet.

She said, "Whenever I can."

Her habit, like most, had started with a prescription. At fifteen she was thrown from the back of a motorcycle and broke her shoulder. When the Vicodin ran out, heroin was stronger and cheaper. In Boston—in all of New England—it was easily found.

She found heroin and lost weight, perspective, memory, inhibitions. She lost her keys and her phone, lost minutes and hours. Her period came a few times a year, or didn't.

She lost her keys and her phone, but what did it matter? She had no car and no apartment and no one left to call.

A janitor found her unconscious in a gas station restroom, a scenario familiar to them both: it was the janitor's second such discovery, Shannon's third overdose. The emergency room doctor ordered an ultrasound. Her pregnancy was dated at twenty-three weeks.

"We have until Saturday," Claudia told her. "In Massachusetts the cutoff is twenty-four weeks. After that, *we can't help you.*"

Shannon's eyelids looked heavy.

"Shannon, do you understand?"

No response.

"Shannon?"

Her eyes clicked wide open like a doll's. "*Jesus.* Yes, I understand."

"Okay, just checking." Claudia kept her voice even. The patients could be as rude as they wanted; they could tell her to go fuck herself, as long as they stayed awake. If they nodded off before the procedure was explained, they couldn't give informed consent.

"Oh, for Christ's sake! I know all this," Shannon said. "They explained it all last time."

She'd been pregnant twice before. The first time she gave birth to a son, now six years old and in DCF custody, her parental rights terminated. The second time, she came to Mercy Street. She explained this to Claudia matter-of-factly, without embellishment. Her narrative had a succinct, executive quality, as though she were in a hurry. As though, on the pedestrian mall at Downtown Crossing, urgent matters demanded her attention: questions of global economic collapse, impending crises of state.

Claudia explained that at twenty-three weeks, the procedure was more complicated. Shannon would need to see the doctor twice, on two consecutive days.

Shannon rolled her eyes heavenward.

The boots were definitely fake.

Informed consent, that was the standard. A lawyer might argue that it wasn't possible at all, if the patient was high. By that measure, Shannon's consent was unattainable. Claudia would have had to travel back in time several years—long before there was a pregnancy to terminate—to find a day when Shannon didn't use.

For such patients—Claudia knew this—consent

was a fairy tale. Shannon's entire sexual life had happened without it. She'd lost her virginity at fourteen, an age when legal consent was impossible. By the time she reached the age of consent, she was high every day. This AB, or the last one; the haphazard intoxicated couplings that landed her, periodically, at the door of the clinic: Had she consented, legally, to any of it? Her childhood and her addiction had overlapped seamlessly. At no point, ever, had she been a sober adult.

Claudia explained that on the first day, Dr. Gurvitch would insert laminaria, sterilized seaweed sticks that expanded gradually to open the cervix. "It doesn't hurt," she added, though Shannon hadn't asked.

She thought of Shannon's son, the little boy who was now, in all likelihood, someone's foster. Would he ever see his mother again? Did he even remember who she was?

Shannon's eyelids fluttered.

"Shannon, are you with me?"

"Yeah, yeah," Shannon said.

The following day the doctor would remove the laminaria. Then plastic tubing would be inserted through the cervix. The tube would be attached to a gentle suction machine.

"That's it?" Shannon seemed wholly unimpressed.

In the context of her life, this didn't qualify as a disaster.

"Dr. Gurvitch can insert the laminaria first thing Monday morning. We open at eight."

"In the *morning*?" Shannon looked aghast. "I mean, can't we just do it now?"

Women in crisis were sometimes unbearable. Sometimes, honestly, you wanted to break them in half.

"I explained this," Claudia said. "You'll need two appointments, Monday morning and again on Tuesday. Remember?"

She explained the procedure again.

This time Shannon was outraged. "This is bullshit," she fumed. "I mean, why did I even come here today?"

Claudia said, "To have this conversation with me."

"What a fuckin waste of time! First some asshole takes my picture. Now you tell me—"

"Wait, *what*?" Claudia frowned. "Someone took your picture?"

"One of those assholes outside. I see him again, I'm gonna kick his ass." Shannon sat up very straight—wide-awake now, blinking rapidly, her pupils dilated. She seemed alert but disoriented. She seemed—in

Claudia's professional opinion—out of her fucking mind.

"Shannon, I'm confused. Can you tell me exactly what happened?"

"Fuck this." Shannon rose awkwardly from the chair, hand over her belly. "I'm outta here."

"Wait," Claudia said, but it was no use. Shannon was already out the door.

Claudia thought, *No way in hell will she show up for that appointment.*

It took a certain kind of person to do this work, and she was that kind of person. She believed this most of the time.

Some years back—it must have been the spring of 2008—Claudia was riding the T to work when a story in the *Globe* caught her eye. A jogger on Deer Island had discovered a pile of debris washed up on the beach—a black plastic trash bag, the thick, sturdy type used by building contractors. Protruding from the bag was a tiny hand.

The bag held the drowned body of a child—a little girl, perhaps two years old. Her face was bloated beyond recognition. Her waterlogged body, wrapped in a Hello Kitty blanket, weighed twenty-four pounds.

Her eyes were blue, her ears pierced though she wore no earrings. She wore a disposable diaper and pink cotton leggings printed with tiny hearts.

Who was she, and where had she come from? For the next several months, these questions would dominate the metro pages of the *Globe* and the *Herald*. The little girl had no fingerprints; the tides had damaged the skin of her hands. To readers of both papers—to the entire city of Boston—she became known as Baby Doe.

The child was found barefoot. Her shoes, if she'd been wearing any, had been stolen by the tides. Her toenails were painted cherry pink, and this was a detail the press would seize upon, a detail almost too painful to bear. Imagine someone, her mother presumably, taking the plump little foot in hand and dabbing the brush over each tiny toenail, the child squealing with delight.

Someone had loved her. The pink leggings proved it—the sort of garment a young mother might spot in a store and coo over, a miniature version of ones she herself might have worn not so long ago.

Baby Doe's mouth was studied. Her first molars had come in, but not her second. Her teeth had been brushed regularly and were in good condition. There were no marks on her body, no signs of abuse or trauma.

She appeared well nourished and well cared for, yet no one had reported her missing.

The pink cotton leggings were a brand sold only at Target, toddler size three. The word *toddler* made it all too real. Too painful to read and too painful to write. Imagine this child in life, wearing her pink cotton leggings, barefoot, her toes tipped in pink. Now imagine her toddling.

Well nourished and well cared for. Baby Doe appeared to be in perfect health, except for the fact that she was dead.

No one had reported her missing. How was it even possible? In a walk-in cooler on Albany Street, the little girl waited. She had been assigned a bar code and zipped into a plastic bag.

An investigation was mounted. Tides were analyzed. The beach at Deer Island faced eastward. The Coast Guard calculated reverse drifts. In salt water, at high tide, how far would a twenty-four-pound bag be carried? The terrible power of mathematics: there was, apparently, a formula for this.

The autopsy showed no drugs in her system, no pathogens, toxins, or diseases. A cause of death could not be determined. Suffocation seemed likely, but impossible to prove.

DNA was extracted. The child's hair and clothing

and blanket were combed for pollen. Incredibly, though she'd spent God knows how long in the icy Atlantic, specimens were found.

The pollen samples were sent to a lab in Houston.

The girl's DNA was compared with databases of missing children. Incredibly, this was someone's job. The missing children numbered in the thousands. No match was ever found.

The pollen analysis showed local pine and oak pollen mingled with soot. Baby Doe was a Boston girl.

A forensic artist made a composite image, using Adobe Photoshop: chubby cheeks and blue eyes, red-gold hair the texture of cotton candy. The hair made her distinctive even in Boston, a city with more than its share of redheads. Someone, surely, would recognize that hair.

The composite image appeared on television, in newspapers, on billboards. At city hall, a press conference was held. Police appealed to the public for assistance. A tip line was established, a toll-free number. *Text GIRL to 61717.*

The tip line was inundated. Calls from concerned neighbors, from day care workers, from frantic grandparents. The most agonizing ones came from parents whose kids had been taken by DCF. Their children were safe in state custody, they were told again and again. No one actually believed this. The state, the world entire, could not be trusted. Your child was safe only in your arms.

The composite image was seen by sixty million people.

On the beach at Deer Island, an impromptu shrine was erected. Strangers left flowers and stuffed animals, a dozen Hello Kitties. A candlelight vigil was held.

The tips kept coming, more hay for the haystack. A funeral home in Worcester offered to bury the child free of charge—"To save her," the *Globe* reported, "from a pauper's grave."

The mystery was solved in the most banal way imaginable. A drunk at a bar overheard a conversation, a young couple arguing. The woman and her boyfriend were questioned by police.

The man, Mark Keohane, was indicted for second-degree murder. The child's mother, Lisa James, was charged as an accessory after the fact. Security video showed Keohane tossing a black contractor's bag from the Tobin Bridge while his pickup truck idled nearby. Sitting at the wheel was Lisa James.

The security video went viral. Mark Keohane had confessed to the murder, but it was Lisa James who was called a monster—the woman who'd helped him dispose of the body, who had failed to protect her own child.

Her dismal history became, briefly, a subject of local fascination: the arrests for possession and prostitution, the evictions, one known overdose. According to the *Globe*, DCF had investigated her as far back as 2003, when another child was removed from her care.

To Claudia, the particulars of the story were eerily familiar. She combed through her predecessor's notes. Mercy Street's medical records had long ago been digitized, but Evelyn Dodd—seventy years old and resistant to technology—had been granted an exception. Each Access patient—minor, medical, or latecomer—was the subject of a detailed entry in a spiral-bound notebook, in Evelyn's careful hand.

Claudia pored over the notebooks. The entries painted a vivid picture of the daily workings of the clinic—and, over time, of Evelyn's physical and cognitive decline. Her notes, increasingly brief, became hard to decipher, full of underlines and cryptic abbreviations.

In the spring of 2006, a latecomer was seen in clinic, a nineteen-year-old woman named L. Jones (or, possibly, L. James—after her initial stroke, Evelyn's handwriting had deteriorated). The patient was twenty-five weeks pregnant, just past the legal cutoff. Her baby would have been born that November—a child the Commonwealth forced her to bear, a child with no safe place to land.

Was this patient—a latecomer turned away at twenty-five weeks—Baby Doe's mother? Claudia would never know.

Anything was possible. It was even possible (not likely, but *possible*) that Evelyn's patient had found a happy ending. That L. Jones or L. James—poor, addicted, nineteen years old and unhappily pregnant—had risen to the challenge of sudden motherhood, that she'd detoxed, found housing, devised a way to support herself. In the final weeks of her pregnancy, she might somehow (somehow) have acquired the wherewithal to defend herself, to protect herself and her child from a man like Mark Keohane.

A man with a criminal record, a raging drug habit. A big man who could snap a child's neck with one hand.

Nothing was certain, except this: Baby Doe had died violently. The little girl had disappeared from the world without explanation, for months on end, and nobody, nobody had noticed. If the tides had shifted that day in March 2008—if one additional nor'easter had battered the Massachusetts coast that winter—the contractor's bag would have been swept out to sea. The child's body would never have been found.

These were Claudia's thoughts as she watched Shannon zoom down the hallway toward the reception desk, her fake Ugg boots sparking the carpet. On Monday morning, she would be a no-show. Her baby would be born addicted, to an addicted mother—a child with no soft place to land.

Claudia thought of the protestors gathered on Mercy Street: the churchgoing faithful, the celibate priests and monks. Would they have any interest in Shannon F.—a homeless addict who haunted the brick sidewalks of Downtown Crossing, harassing tourists for spare change—if she weren't pregnant? Preventing her abortion was all they cared about. The bleak struggle of her life—the stark daily realities that made motherhood impossible—didn't trouble them at all.

What made a person a person? Her mind and her memories, all that she had done and felt and known and created, thought and wondered and seen and understood. A fetus had no thoughts or memories; it had made nothing, understood nothing. And yet, this mute, unthinking knot of tissue—alive, yes, but unformed, unconscious, incapable of tenderness or reasoning or even laughter—was the life that mattered. The woman carrying it, the complex creature formed by twenty or thirty years of living in the world, was simply the means of production. Her feelings about the matter, her particular ideas and needs and desires, didn't matter at all.

A fetus was living tissue, no question. But it was not a person.

A fetus, at most, was raw material. The woman carrying it could, if she wished, make it into a person. But what was the point of making yet another person, when the woman herself—a person who already existed—counted for so little?

Baby Doe had been a person, a little girl who felt love and joy, who delighted in her pink leggings and giggled when her toenails were painted and who, in the end, felt shock and fear and betrayal and pain. As a fetus she'd been protected by Massachusetts law, the twenty-four-week cutoff. As a person she was utterly dependent on a woman who couldn't raise her and didn't want to. Once she became an actual person, Baby Doe was on her own.

The bar was a neighborhood place, a stale-smelling dive known for cheap beer and—in summer—extravagant air-conditioning, delivered by massive units anchored high on the wall. In February the place was the same temperature. As they did most Friday nights, the clinic staff staked out a corner table. Bolted to the gantry were dueling televisions: at one end, the NECN weatherman making dire predictions, another monster nor'easter; at the other, the Bruins pummeling Detroit.

"The Bride Game," said Claudia. "Does anyone remember this?"

"The what?" said Heather Chen, the nurse practitioner. She was roughly Claudia's age, old enough to recall the cozy pastimes of an analog childhood: board games, jigsaw puzzles. "I'm drawing a blank here."

"Don't look at me," said Florine, the executive director. "This is not a Black thing."

"Mary will remember." Claudia waved to Mary Fahey, who'd just returned from smoking a cigarette. "The Bride Game. Go."

"Oh, Jesus." Mary sat heavily, cold air and tobacco smoke radiating from her coat. "My sister had it. They never let me play. Mostly I just watched. Remember the cakes?"

"Cakes," Florine repeated. "I'm losing the thread here." She was the clinic's public face—telegenically charming, a former Miss Tennessee who'd grown up on the pageant circuit. She was also a lethal debater, a frequent guest on the cable news channels. Claudia had seen her take apart a right-wing congressman with effortless grace, like an expert chef disarticulating a chicken.

Another arctic blast as the door opened, Luis coming to join them. Claudia slid over to make room.

"The point of the game," she said, "the *object* of the game, was to plan your wedding. You needed a dress and a ring and a wedding cake and I'm forgetting something."

"Flowers," said Mary. "Also the groom."

"Groom, yes. And you rolled the dice and moved around the board and when you landed on a Ring space you got to choose which ring and then the cake, et cetera."

"An actual ring?" said Florine.

"Well, no. There were no actual rings. No actual cakes. You picked a card with a drawing of a ring or a cake. It was a simpler time." Claudia sipped at her beer, which tasted flowery. This happened whenever she sat next to Florine, who took her name seriously. That day she wore silver earrings shaped like peonies and her trademark jasmine perfume.

"The winner was the one who put a whole wedding together first. But there was a hierarchy: the best flowers, the best cake. The wedding dress, I remember, was hotly contested. There was a particular one everyone wanted. You wanted to land on a Dress space right away, to get first pick."

"What about the groom?" said Heather.

Luis raised his palms to the sky. "I was going to say."

Mary said, "The groom was a secondary concern."

"The *cake* was secondary," said Claudia. "The groom was tertiary. The primary concern was the dress."

"And you were *how* old?" said Mitch—Carolyn Mitchell, Heather's wife, who was younger than the rest and had a moral severity Claudia found endearing. Mitch volunteered as a clinic escort, leading patients through the gauntlet of shouting protestors in her fluorescent blue vest, like a school crossing guard for adults.

"Eight, nine."

"That's disturbing," Mitch said.

"I don't know about *disturbing*," said Luis. "*Disturbing* is a strong word."

"We didn't have the game," Florine said, refilling her glass, "but, you know, we did it anyway. I had my whole wedding planned by the time I was twelve."

"That's mental," Luis said.

Mary cackled, a husky smoker's laugh. "You're telling us boys don't do this. There was no Groom Game."

"You're kidding me, right?"

A cheer rose up in the bar. The Bruins had scored a goal.

Mitch took the empty pitcher to the bar for a refill.

Florine and Mary stepped outside for a smoke. Claudia turned to Luis—remembering, suddenly, what she'd been meaning to tell him.

He listened, frowning.

"Someone took her *picture*?" he said. "Claudia, are you sure?"

"Well, no." She drained her glass of beer, which now tasted like beer. "That came straight from the patient. And like I said, she's not the most reliable witness."

"Why would someone do that?" Luis looked mystified. "I mean, what the hell for?"

8

The world is full of signs.

    Excelsior11 drove at night, south and east into the Maryland panhandle, holding a bag of frozen peas to the left side of his face. Wedged behind his seat were a shovel and mallet and posthole digger. In the bed of his pickup, beneath a clean blue tarp, was a stack of freshly painted signs.

    He rolled through Hagerstown just before dawn. The streets were deserted. His target was a tract of state land outside Cumberland. When possible, he preferred to work in darkness.

    The installation went smoothly. In Maryland the snow had melted. A few crusts hung on at the margins, but the ground was soft and moist.

    He finished just as the sun was rising. There was another tract he had his eye on, along State Road 36. According to the public records database, the land was privately owned, a delicate matter. He believed, ardently, in the sanctity of ownership. He would not knowingly violate a citizen's property rights, even in the service of good.

The site was in a field gone fallow. It had not been plowed in many years. The owner lived across the street, in a sturdy brick house with a deep front porch, set far back from the road.

He parked in the driveway and rang the doorbell. The wide grassy yard was studded with lawn ornaments—garden gnomes, oversized plastic mushrooms, a miniature wishing well cast in cement. An old lady in a housecoat opened the door.

"Good morning, ma'am. Are you a Christian?" His speech was a little mushy. He was trying not to move his mouth.

"I am." She hugged her robe around her, studying him—a barrel-chested man in what he thought of as his sign-planting uniform: blue jeans, denim shirt, orange hunting vest. "Why do you ask?"

"My name is Victor Prine, and I believe in the sacredness of all life. With your permission, I'd like to put one of my signs on your property."

The old lady looked confused. "What kind of a sign?"

"Let me show you. I have a couple in my truck."

She followed him outside. In the driveway he lowered his tailgate and peeled back the tarp. On top of the stack was one of his favorites, a dark silhouette of a pregnant woman. Only her womb and its contents were rendered in color—a chubby pink infant, blond-haired and blue-eyed. The lettering was bright pink, all caps. IT'S A CHILD NOT A CHOICE.

"Oh my," she said. In the clear morning light she looked very old, one eye milky with cataract. "The baby is darling. Is he waving?"

"That's right," he said.

She seemed at a loss for words.

"I have other ones," he said, moving it aside. The three remaining signs were identical. He had a dozen more at home, stacked in the hayloft of his stepbrother's barn. The caption read AMERICAN CARNAGE.

"Good heavens," she said. "What on earth am I looking at?"

"I took that photo myself. It's a dumpster behind an abortion mill in San Antonio." He had said this so many times that it had become true; he could nearly remember taking the photo, despite having cribbed it from a pro-life website he viewed as a competitor. The deception didn't trouble him. He *could* have taken the photo. No one could prove he hadn't.

"Get off my property," the old lady said.

He'd been planting signs for half his life. In his thirty years as a long-haul trucker, he'd placed them in national parks, on grazing lands, and once, in the oil fields of Williston, North Dakota. SAVE GOD'S PRE-BORN CHILDREN. He'd posted a photo of that one on his website—a pump jack bobbing behind it, dipping its head to sip the earth like some exotic waterfowl.

In the West, the land was anyone's. There were literally millions of acres of land with no owner to speak of. The degenerate federal government had no authority, legal or moral, to own anything, in Victor's firm view. He'd explained his position at length to a county sheriff outside Laramie, who'd threatened to cite him for trespassing and defacing public property.

All he'd done was plant a sign.

That was how he thought of it: each sign was like planting a seed in the ground. It pleased him to think of all the people who'd seen them, year after year, the young mothers moved to spare their babies. It was humbling to think how, in a split second, a life could be saved.

Later he saw the flaw in his reasoning. How many pregnant females were driving across the empty western states, the great thunderous trucking routes of North America? In the average two-week hitch, he saw no women at all, never mind pregnant ones.

The sheriff in Wyoming did not cite him. He stood and watched while Victor took down the sign.

In those years he lived everywhere, he lived nowhere. Every couple weeks he'd stop off at his stepbrother's in Pennsylvania, where he slept and did laundry and saw no one. Except for hunting and occasional trips to the lumberyard, his waking hours were spent in Randy's barn, lifting weights and painting more signs.

He crisscrossed the country and listened to talk radio—a show out of Kalispell, Montana, hosted by a man named Doug Straight. Listening, he began to understand the world. The voice on the radio was the voice of adulthood, the bearer of hard truths. Doug Straight didn't pretend that the world was fair or generous. The America he spoke of was a place Victor recognized, the tough neighborhood where he himself was raised.

There was something in the air in those years. The news was full of cryptic signals, random happenings that seemed to be building toward something. The European states lining up in a shadowy alliance, a New World Order emerging. Race riots in Los Angeles; in Idaho, a Christian family gunned down on their own sovereign land. In Texas, a faith community of women and children, executed in cold blood—immolated by the federal government, at taxpayer expense.

There was a hatchet-faced boy with a soldier's hair-cut, a face he had seen before.

Something in the air. Victor blamed the glad-handing cracker president, a type he recognized: the glib salesman, the apple-polishing smart boy. He hated Bill Clinton's toothy smile, his undeserved ease in the world, as though he'd forgotten where he came from. Watching him on television, Victor thought: *You're no better than I am. You are hill trash just like me.*

He left Maryland feeling defeated. The remaining signs clattered in the truck bed. In a gas station men's room he studied his face in the mirror—his father's face, the same bristled white eyebrows and fleshy earlobes and handlebar mustache. The resemblance was startling. Turning into his father wasn't something he'd planned on.

It was a thing no one talked about, what age did to a man's earlobes.

The swelling of his jaw was now visible, as though he'd been socked in the mouth.

His bag of peas had turned squishy and tepid, so he bought a pint of ice cream and got back into his pickup. The cab had a distinct human odor, as though someone had been breathing and farting and perspiring inside it for hours on end, as was in fact the case.

He got back on the road and set out driving, holding the pint of ice cream to his face. The offending tooth, a rear molar, had spread its poison widely, a kind of guerrilla warfare. The ache stretched from his jaw to his sinuses, in solidarity, as though the entire maxillofacial neighborhood had joined in the fight.

He had not been blessed with good teeth, but through obsessive brushing and absolute avoidance of sugar, had made it to his sixties with most of his dentition intact.

The paternal resemblance was not accidental. Nature—this had been proved time and again—always had a reason. Faced with the female's swollen belly, the male of the species naturally had questions. The paternal resemblance existed for one reason only: to prove that the female was not a whore.

Victor Prine had never seen dental floss, nor known of its existence, until he saw it for sale at the PX at Fort Benning.

He drove and drove.

As a boy he'd had a headful of rotten baby teeth, a casualty of lax dental hygiene and the wanton consumption of Kool-Aid, red or orange or mouthwash-green, which his mother mixed in a mayonnaise jar and which they all drank like water. Milk teeth were temporary anyway, the thinking went, not worth the inconvenience of toothbrushing or even the small expense. His father, careless of his own teeth—he wore false ones, top and bottom, by age thirty—had a hillbilly skepticism of dentists, who after all were paid by the cavity. Who could say that the dentist hadn't put them there himself, with his nerve-squealing drill?

His father was not a trusting man.

His father was a coal miner. Lovell Prine went underground at sixteen and any vestige of the boy he had been went down there with him, never to resurface. For the rest of his life he did not hunt, did not fish. He would not watch a ball game or play cards or throw horseshoes or read a newspaper. He did not even whittle. As far as his son could recall, mining and drinking were the two things he did.

Not a trusting man. Once, while working underground, Lovell had opened his dinner bucket and found his water jug empty. Someone on the crew was stealing his water. Thereafter, when he filled the jug each morning, he dropped his bottom denture into it. No one ever drank his water again.

Victor crossed the state line, glad, as always, to leave Maryland, with its speed traps and degenerate radio stations, the snazzy rhymes of angry Black people. In Pennsylvania the voices quieted. The radio emitted a gentle static. The road was pleasingly empty, laid in segments; every twenty feet his tires crossed a seam in the pavement. This produced a gentle cadence, like the clop of a horse's hooves.

He exited the highway and drove back into winter—frozen fields, a vast emptiness. A radio preacher urged repentance: the End of Days was coming. Dead animals littered the highway, as if to prove the point.

The road jogged and jumped, winding around the hills. Here and there, in the valleys, were clusters of ramshackle houses, as though a great flood had washed through the mountains and left this detritus behind.

He scanned the dial until he heard, through the static, the voice of Doug Straight, now in national syndication. In the satellite era, you were always in Straight Nation. Doug was never far away.

Today Doug was talking about the Founding Fathers, a favorite topic. In drafting the Second Amendment, they had shown remarkable prescience. The Founding Fathers had seen hundreds of years into the future, when private citizens would need enough firepower to protect themselves from the government the Fathers had just created.

That was the whole idea, libtards: every free man locked and loaded, ready to defend life and liberty when the need arose.

Victor didn't disagree; how could you? And yet it was the Founding Fathers who'd made the original mistake.

Doug cut to a caller, Roger in Boise. Victor recognized the voice, a high-pitched drawl with a western twang. Roger in Boise had called the show before.

The mistake was indisputable, a matter of historical record. The Founding Fathers hadn't invented slavery, but they had embraced it. Exhibiting a striking *lack* of foresight, they'd seen no downside to importing boatloads of captured people from the other side of the world, with no possible way of sending them back.

If the Founding Fathers really *were* visionaries, they might have asked themselves certain questions.

What happens when the boatloads of people get sick of being whipped and beaten and worked like pack mules, when they decide they'd just as soon *not* plow your fields and pick your cotton and build your new country for you, for free, for as many centuries and generations as it's going to take in the absence of irrigation and gas motors and simple shit like insecticides and power tools? Hey, Founding Fathers: What happens then?

Victor didn't blame the Blacks, who hadn't chosen to come here. They'd been brought by force and now, like it or not, America was stuck with them.

He didn't blame the Blacks, necessarily. Which wasn't to say the country needed so goddamn many of them.

The radio station came in and out, bright bursts of static. Roger in Boise was creaming himself over the Second Amendment. Roger in Boise, honestly, sounded a little nuts.

The truck climbed Saxon Mountain, its old engine chugging. At the top of the ridge was the landmark sign. SAXON COUNTY WELCOMES YOU. In recent years the letters had faded. At highway speed they were impossible to read. The sign was like everything else in Saxon County, a place that no longer looked like anything. You couldn't see it clearly unless you knew what it used to be.

The letters had faded, or maybe they hadn't. Victor couldn't say for sure. A doctor at the VA had told him his eyes were going. "Horseshit," he told the doctor, but in his heart he wasn't surprised. Life, at his age, was an escalating series of physical humiliations.

At least he'd hung on to his teeth.

The world is full of signs.

The town, Bakerton, was quiet at that hour. Even at rush hour, there was nowhere to go. When Victor was a boy, the place had come alive at the shift change, traffic backed up in both directions along Number Twelve Road. Now the shift change was a distant memory. The mines had closed a generation ago. The old train station was now the volunteer fire department. Unlike most buildings in town, it was at least being used for something. On the hill behind it was another faded sign: BAKERTON COAL LIGHTS THE WORLD. In the old days it had been repainted annually. Riding the train into town, it was the first thing you'd see.

He passed the bank, Saxon Savings—flanked, now, by empty storefronts. Across the street was the old Fridman's Furniture, a cursed location that had housed a long series of failed businesses: a fruit market, a storefront church, a bridal shop. Recently a new tenant had moved in—COAL COUNTRY TAXIDERMY, according to its homemade sign.

At the center of town, two stores, Dollar General and Dollar Bargain, squared off at an intersection. The sidewalks were empty. A flashing yellow light directed traffic that wasn't there.

He drove past the Pennzoil station, closed now. The pumps had been removed long ago, leaving craters in the ground. On the side of the building was a hand-painted mural, silhouettes of men in hard hats. TOUGH TIMES NEVER LAST, a caption insisted, in defiance of all evidence. TOUGH PEOPLE DO.

He gunned the engine up a steep hill. Number Twelve Road was high and winding, the pavement crumbling. He turned down the new access road, built by the gas company so the drill rigs could come through. At the end of the road were six wells—drilled at the peak of the gas boom, and still producing. Every month the company sent his stepbrother a royalty check.

He peeled off down a narrow lane. The truck bounced along, scattering gravel. Deep in the forest, dogs were barking. The road ended at a checkpoint, a sturdy gate with cement pillars on either end, each mounted with a camera. The gate was hung with signs he'd painted himself:

YOU HAVE INVADED THE PRIVATE PROPERTY
OF A SOVEREIGN CITIZEN

TRESPASSERS WILL BE SHOT ON SIGHT
SURVIVORS WILL BE SHOT AGAIN

SMILE FOR THE CAMERA!
YOU ARE BEING WATCHED

He parked on the gravel pad next to the house. Behind it sat the old wooden barn, painted fifty years ago, the letters now faded: CHEW MAIL POUCH TOBACCO. From the glove box he took the .45, his everyday carry

(EDC). He unlocked his tailgate and carried the left-over signs to the barn.

The barn was dark inside, with an odor of paint and mineral spirits. He'd tidied up before he left: neat stacks of plywood, paint cans arranged on rough wood shelves. Leaning against the walls were a dozen new signs, the paint still drying.

ALL LIFE IS SACRED
END THE SLAUGHTER OF THE INNOCENTS
ABORTION STOPS A BEATING HEART

He set down the leftovers he'd brought back from Maryland: three copies of AMERICAN CARNAGE, plus the happy baby waving from the womb.

He had always been a visual thinker. Seeing his work spread out in front of him, Victor understood what should have been obvious from the beginning: AMERICAN CARNAGE was confusing. The babies recovered from the dumpster didn't look human. They looked like hamburger. The image was powerful, but only if you understood what you were looking at. Barreling along at highway speed, how could you possibly tell?

The realization was disheartening.

The realization fed into his larger frustration, his disillusionment with the entire sign-making operation, which more and more seemed like a vanity project—an archaic pastime like candle-dipping, the useless hobby of an eccentric old man.

The log house was freshness-sealed, tight as Tupperware. Victor had built it with his own two hands. When you closed the front door, the world went silent. When you opened it, you heard a kissing sound. Daylight came from small windows, each the size of a shoebox, set high in the walls. Bedroom, living room, kitchen, a small back room he used as an office. Crucially, the house had a full basement, accessible by a fireproof steel door. A trapdoor in the floor led to the subbasement, where he kept his guns.

The basement resembled a crowded warehouse. Along three walls he'd installed floor-to-ceiling shelves—loaded, now, with jars and cans. Stacked against the fourth wall were cardboard cartons, some labeled: MINUTE RICE. QUAKER INSTANT OATMEAL. COWBOY BAKED BEANS. CHARMIN ULTRA 40 ROLLS.

He stocked six months' worth of provisions at all times. Six months was the bare minimum, according to Doug Straight, though this advice was possibly outdated. Conditions had shifted since 1999—the year Victor began paying attention, the year the threat became clear. That was the year he acquired his first computer, a Macintosh Plus he'd picked up at a yard sale. With his dial-up modem he'd ventured onto the information superhighway, not understanding that his life was about to change.

In the Usenet groups he was no longer Victor Prine, a backwoods trucker hauling loads across the continent. He became Excelsior11, a renegade soldier for good.

Usenet, in those days, was alive with chatter. Excelsior11 had joined the conversation at a panicky time. The programming of computers had been short-sighted, the dates encoded in two-digit format: 97, 98, 99. As the century wound down, it seemed that the world was heading toward a precipice, beyond which no future could exist.

Doug Straight laid it out clearly: At the turn of the millennium, the world would stop working. Banks would fail, telecommunications, the electrical grid. Citizens would be forced to shelter in place. The End Times were coming, but there would be no conflagration, no sea of fire. Mankind would be undone by simple mechanical failure, the machines he'd trusted to make the world work.

In the spirit of new beginnings, certain preparations were made.

In the final days of 1999, Victor withdrew the entire

balance of his savings account. He tested and retested his emergency generator, bought extra batteries for his night-vision goggles. He stocked up on ammo and cleaned his guns.

When possible, he observed the Rule of Three. To every imaginable problem, he planned three possible solutions. Water jugs, filtration tabs, charcoal filters. Rifle, pistol, semiautomatic.

At ten minutes to midnight, on the final night of the millennium, he filled the bathtubs. When the lights went out, Victor Prine would be ready. He wore a halogen headlamp, an updated version of the light his father had worn underground. His night-vision goggles waited next to the door.

But at the stroke of midnight, the lights stayed on. The TV didn't even flicker. Victor stepped outside and saw, in the distance, his stepbrother's porch light. The night sky was clear and cold.

The initial disappointment was crushing. Later he saw the experience for what it was, the world's most elaborate dress rehearsal. The real collapse was coming. It was only a matter of time until Shit Hit The Fan (SHTF).

America had been built on self-sufficiency, but modern man had forgotten those lessons. To the average flabby, pampered American, water came from plastic bottles. Food came from the drive-thru window. Take away his cell phone and internet and he'd be helpless as a child. After three days he'd strangle his own mother to get a piece of bread.

Mankind had been given fair warning. For those who chose not to hear it, Victor had no sympathy. There were people in town who'd made serious money on their mineral rights, and blew it on foolishness. A local jagoff named Wally Fetterson had quit his mail-carrying job, bought a new truck and a motorboat. In his backyard he'd dug a goddamn swimming pool. When SHTF, he'd run crying to the government begging for a handout. And this was a White man! The country was so far gone that even the White people had that freeloader mentality, like the government owed them something.

When SHTF, Wally Fetterson would be banging on Victor's door.

The collapse was coming. Forget Y2K and natural disasters and nuclear Armageddon. In the end it would come down to numbers: the White race at the mercy of all others, the immense and cresting brown wave.

Organized society was nine meals away from anarchy.

When SHTF, Victor would be just fine.

He lingered a moment, looking around him with satisfaction. It always soothed him to visit his preps. He shut off the light and climbed the stairs.

It all came down to numbers.

This was the organizing principle of democracy, a truth baked into the system: The majority owned the minority. In a well-functioning democracy, the minority was the majority's bitch.

The Blacks understood this better than anyone, having spent hundreds of years on the wrong side of the equation. And Black people were no fools. For centuries, now, they'd been growing their numbers, industriously fucking and birthing, and their efforts had paid off. Already they dominated professional sports; they'd taken over colleges and universities, and infiltrated the military. They had elected their very own president.

You had to hand it to them.

Blaming the Blacks was too easy. The fault—Victor knew this—lay with his own race, which had squandered its advantage. The White heroes who'd tamed the vast wilderness of North America, who'd built the greatest civilization in human history, were an endangered species—slated for extinction, their numbers dwindling. The White race had surrendered its majority with no thought to the consequences, no appreciation of what would be lost.

If you looked at historical birth rates, as Victor had done, the roots of the problem were clear.

A Black female born in 1950—the same year as Victor Prine—produced, on average, four viable offspring. A White female born that year produced only two. Since then, the situation had only worsened. Today's underachieving White female produced only one precious Caucasian child.

The numbers were abysmal.

The numbers came directly from Doug Straight, his only trusted source.

A change was coming. White people, if they knew this, bore the knowledge lightly. They stumbled through life like oversized children, spending and consuming and giggling at sitcoms, a tribe of obese dimwits in NFL-licensed sportswear. As far as Victor could tell, White people didn't have a clue.

One viable offspring. This was the White female's pathetic output—even after the so-called sexual revolution of the 1970s, which Victor did not experience personally. In the 1970s people were going at it like rabbits, sex in groups, among strangers, sex in every wild permutation. And yet, despite all that fucking, birth rates had dropped precipitously—*but only among White women.*

Victor did not experience it personally, having spent most of that decade in the joint, but he was aware of it happening. He read about it in the magazines of the day.

One viable offspring. He chalked it up to laziness. A pregnancy took only nine months, and females were living longer and longer. A healthy one could squeeze out an entire baseball team with decades to spare. But the White female, for whatever reason, refused to see this. Nature had entrusted her with an awesome power she was incompetent to manage. The White female lacked the focus and discipline, the practical intelligence, to understand what her life was *for.*

At suppertime he wandered over to Randy's, lured by the smell of fried meat. His stepbrother lived in a tin-roof shack at the bottom of the hill, a square box with half its shingles missing. He lived exactly as he always had, though he was sitting on a pile of frack money big enough to tear down all of Bakerton and rebuild it from scratch.

They were as close as brothers, though they were not blood-related. Childhood had sealed them together, their two parents careening into each other like drunken motorists, skid marks and squealing tires, the sky raining broken glass. The two boys grew up in the wreckage, or maybe they *were* the wreckage. And here they were sixty years on, two odd, lonely men growing older and now old.

Victor was blood-related to no living person he knew.

Randy was sitting in the kitchen, at an old card table draped with a vinyl cloth. At his elbow was his dinner, a gristly pork chop spread with ketchup. As always, he was staring at his laptop.

"You hungry?" he asked. "I can make you a chop."

"I can't eat," Victor grumbled. "My fucking tooth."

Randy's laptop was old and monstrously large, so heavy that it caused the card table to bow in the middle. He could afford a new computer, he could afford it many hundred thousand times over, but he was not the sort of person to replace a thing that still worked. The computer was slow, but fast enough for his purposes, buying junk on Craigslist and jerking off to internet porn.

"Luther is selling his generator. I seen it on Craigslist," said Randy. "Same model as our one. You might could take a look."

It was Randy who'd given him the idea. Last fall, Victor had returned from a marathon week of sign-planting to find Randy at his laptop, scrolling through

USA Today. Now that it could be read for free online, it was his sole source of information. His favorite section was "News From Around Our 50 States," brief items culled from local papers across the country.

They raided a hoorhouse in some little piss-ant town in Alabama, he told Victor. *Look at this poor bastard. They caught him with a girl and put his pitcher in the paper.*

Sorrow in his voice, genuine empathy. After he got his first frack money, Randy had been a prodigious consumer of prostitutes. An online pharmacy kept him supplied with Canadian Viagra, and once a month he'd disappear for a weekend and come back with tiny soaps and shampoos from Pittsburgh motels. It took a drunk-driving arrest to break his habit. The fine was eight hundred dollars. After that he stuck close to home, his needs satisfied by anonymous women with webcams. Such women existed all over the world, apparently. Randy's monthly subscriptions cost less than a single night in a motel.

That could of been me, he told Victor. *Makes you stop and think.*

And Victor did just that. He stopped and thought. Shame, he knew, was a powerful motivator. You could shame a person into just about anything.

He built the site himself, over several weeks. Technically, it was nothing special; he knew this. Still, he was proud of what he had accomplished. He had a fifty-year-old diploma from a backwoods public high school. Nobody would have called him an educated man. And yet—with the help of *Web Design for Dummies*—he had brought the Hall of Shame into being. Everything he knew, he had taught himself.

The idea was elegant in its simplicity. On any given day, thousands of pregnant White females walked into abortion clinics; thousands of precious White children were executed in secret. The Hall of Shame would shine a light on these crimes.

The abortionist plies his trade behind closed doors, Victor wrote. *Those who commission these murders count on his discretion.*

The writing came easy to him. He had always been good with words.

They present themselves to the world as responsible employees, neighbors, wives, and even mothers. Do you recognize these faces?

Getting the photos was easy. Every major American city had an abortion clinic, or several; every pro-life American had a cell phone in his pocket. Victor put out a call on 8chan. Within hours, he had an army of volunteers. The response was heartening. American heroism was alive and well, the country full of right-thinking men, eager to be of service. Their can-do spirit touched and inspired him—total strangers volunteering their time and talents to make a Whiter world.

San Diego, Boston, Minneapolis. Orlando, Phoenix, Colorado Springs. Once or twice a week, a new collection of photos appeared in his inbox. Victor picked through them carefully, long nights at the computer in his dime-store reading glasses, which never seemed strong enough. Every few months, he bought a new, more powerful pair.

9

The Russian kid worked out of a garage in North Quincy. Timmy pulled his new Honda Civic into the parking lot just as the shop was closing. As instructed, he parked behind the shop and texted: **I'm here.** And then, as an afterthought: **This is Tim.**

He got out of the car, twisting to stretch his back. He missed the legroom of his Ford Escape, the roomy seat that reclined to the perfect angle. After a week of driving the Civic, he'd developed a chronic twitch in his sacrum. In nearly every way, the Civic was a disappointment. Mechanically, aesthetically, it was a piece of crap. Its only virtue was its banality. The Civic was the sort of anonymous tin can a law-abiding citizen would drive.

His naked face tingled in the cold.

That morning, after a long shower, he'd studied his face in the mirror. It was not the face of a law-abiding citizen. The beard was the problem. The beard would have to go.

He had planned ahead, bought shaving cream and a razor—an item he hadn't owned in years and that now, apparently, cost twenty dollars. First he went at the beard with a pair of scissors. Hair mounded in the sink like some exotic plankton.

What am I doing? he thought as he took the first swipe.

His face didn't look the way he remembered it. The last time he saw it, the face was twenty-nine, the face of a new husband and father. His face had missed its thirties. Under all that hair it had sagged and softened into the face of a middle-aged man.

The garage door opened. A teenager with a patchy goatee waved him inside.

The Russian kid came highly recommended. There was a story Timmy had heard many times, now legendary among the weed sellers of Greater Boston. One of the kid's customers, a Portaguee from Fall River, had been traveling west on I-84 when he was pulled over by a Connecticut statie, his SUV searched with a sniffer dog. The dog alerted at a spot behind the rear seat, the exact location where the Russian had installed a trap. The cop searched by hand, but found no loose wires or extra rivets or signs of jerry-rigging. The Portaguee drove back to Fall River a free man, with twenty pounds of product in his truck.

In the shop's back office, they smoked a joint to get acquainted. Alex Voinovich was a skinny kid, possibly still growing at age nineteen. Since childhood he'd enjoyed ripping shit apart. A vacuum cleaner, a stereo, the thermostat in the snug apartment where he lived with his mother and sister. He was no more destructive than the average boy. He dismantled these machines not to destroy them, but to see how they worked.

He explained this emphatically, as though Timmy had argued otherwise. He seemed to enjoy explaining himself. In the daytime he installed car stereos at Def Jam Sound Design, a job he found unsatisfying. He did the same two or three generic installs over and over again, for punks with no sense of style; they cared only about the size of the speaker and the whomping bass line it could put out.

"Punks," he repeated. He had a faint accent that didn't sound Russian. He could have come from Chicago or Philly or Detroit or New Jersey. To Timmy he sounded American, nothing more.

The punks had no interest in the kind of sick in-stallation Alex had done in his own car, a rebuilt Golf hatchback: custom subwoofer mounts in fantastical shapes, wood frames he'd cut himself and covered in fiberglass. And so it was boredom, ultimately, that had brought him to this body shop in North Quincy, owned by a distant cousin. The cousin let him use it nights and weekends, on the DL, to do his real work.

His real work, his money work, was building traps.

He led Timmy to a newish Toyota Camry, parked at the rear of the shop. "This is just an example," he said. "Your job will be a little different. Every customization is unique. No two vehicles have same code."

A Camry was the one car Timmy could think of that was even lamer than a Civic.

He thought, *I should've bought a Camry.*

"Basically there's four steps," said Alex. "You got to do them in the exact order or it won't work. First all the doors got to be closed. If you have that driver door open, it's not going to work. So like if you get pulled over, that cop, he's not going to search your car with all the doors closed. Meaning he ain't going to find shit."

"Doors closed," said Timmy. "Got it."

"Then you sit in the driver's seat," said Alex. "There's a pressure sensor in the seat so it knows if someone is there."

They got into the car, Alex behind the wheel, Timmy beside him in the passenger seat. "Next you turn on the rear defroster," said Alex, switching it on. "But here's the key thing: at the same time, you got to push these two." He indicated the switches for the front and rear passenger-side windows.

Timmy pressed one switch, then the other.

"No, at the same t-time." The kid was jazzed, nearly trembling with some weird manic excitement.

"Like this?" Timmy said, holding down both switches.

"Yeah, but you messed up the order, so you got start again from the beginning. Watch."

Alex demonstrated again, flicking on the defroster while holding down the two window switches.

"That's it?" said Timmy.

"No. Now you got to swipe the card." He took a white plastic card from his chest pocket and swiped it across the center air-conditioning vent.

On the passenger side of the dashboard, a compartment opened soundlessly, in the spot where an airbag would go.

"Holy shit." Timmy peered into the compartment. It wasn't big, but big enough. "What's that inside it? Wood?"

"Cork," said Alex. "It soaks up the smell."

"Goddamn. That is some James Bond shit."

The kid fidgeted. Timmy saw in that moment how young he was, proud of what he'd built but mistrustful of praise.

"How much is all this going to set me back?"

"The base cost is eight grand. That's for two compartments. If you need more than two, that's extra."

"*Eight?*" said Timmy. "Andy told me five."

"It was five last year. Now it's eight."

There was no point in haggling. Timmy saw that he had no leverage in this negotiation. He said, "I only brought five."

Alex frowned, deliberating.

"I could take half up front," he said grudgingly—as though he were going out on a limb, as though he wouldn't have an entire fucking car as collateral.

Timmy took the envelope from inside his jacket. "You do a lot of these?"

"I don't know about a lot. I do some."

Timmy did that math. If the kid did one installation a week, he'd clear thirty thousand in a single month. Probably he had a girlfriend spending it for him. Timmy had been the same way at his age, every dollar he earned spent—directly or indirectly—on getting laid.

"Enjoy," he said, counting out the cash. For four thousand dollars, the kid should get plenty of tail.

Older than cave painting," said Connor. "It's the earliest form of writing. I shit you not."

Timmy was sitting in Connor's chair, naked to the waist.

"Thirty-two hundred B.C. That's the oldest known example." Connor was famous for making asinine pronouncements about tattooing, its importance as an art form. He had personally done all Timmy's ink but the first one, an eagle on his right biceps. He'd had the eagle since boot camp at Parris Island, which made it older than Connor.

"They found this dude in a bog in Denmark, the oldest known human. The skin was perfectly preserved. Sixty-one tats."

Connor was not a critical thinker. His information came from old tattoo magazines he bought on eBay. There was so much ludicrousness packed into his stories that Timmy didn't even bother.

A warm lick of blood trailed down his back.

"You need a break?" said Connor.

"Nah. I'm good," Timmy said.

The current piece was an elaborate back tattoo, an

ongoing project. Every few weeks Connor outlined a new section, or filled in what he'd outlined last time. It had begun with a massive Celtic cross centered over Timmy's spine, its crossbar extending from shoulder to shoulder. Timmy had drawn the cross himself, on grid paper to get the scale right. He had a large back, and it took Connor three hours just to get the outline on his skin. Filling it in took longer. Timmy chose three colors: black, red, and green. He'd lost track of how much money he'd spent, the countless hours in Connor's chair.

The cross, in the end, was not what he expected.

What's the problem? said Connor. He had an artistic temperament, sensitive to criticism.

It looks kind of—Christian.

It's a cross, Connor said.

The cross had been a problem from the beginning. First it looked too Christian. Then it looked too Celtic. Timmy feared turning into his father, whose flabby sentimentality about Ireland embarrassed him. If it was so fucking great over there, why did everyone leave?

After some discussion, he and Connor decided on a solution. The solution was more ink. Connor added a border around the cross, meant to resemble chain mail, then a leafy vine winding through the chain. Birds were added, thorny roses, a slithering snake. Timmy's back looked better and better. Now Connor was filling in what was theoretically the final piece, a sliver of moon above the left shoulder blade.

The needle was very hot, digging into his flesh. His phone rang in his pocket.

Connor said, "You need to take that?"

With any other customer, he would have pitched a fit—more evidence, to Timmy, of his artistic temperament. Connor was so touchy about being interrupted that he'd hung a sign above the mirror: NO CELL PHONES PLEASE. He made an exception for Timmy, whose phone calls typically lasted less than a minute.

Timmy answered without looking, which was always a mistake.

"It's February," said his ex-wife. No *hello*, no *how are you?* They'd dispensed with the pleasantries long ago.

Connor gave him a quizzical look. Timmy held up a finger.

"Yeah, I know," he said. "I can't get down there right now." Every few months he brought her a wad of cash, hand-delivered. Tess knew, had always known, what he did for a living. And yet she refused to understand that he couldn't simply drop a check in the mail.

Connor reached for his vape and stepped out the back door for a smoke.

"Well, what am I supposed to do?" said Tess. "Put it on your tab?"

"Look, you know I'm good for it. I've got it right here." It was nearly true; at least, it had been true a week ago—before he bought a Honda Civic from a stranger on Craigslist, before he handed a Russian teenager four thousand dollars in cash. "Don't I always pay you eventually?"

"My car payment is due tomorrow. Not *eventually.*"

"Fuck your car payment," he said, filled with righteous indignation. "This is *child support.* Food and clothes and whatever."

"I already bought his food and clothes. That's why I can't make my car payment. Do you get that?" Tess spoke very slowly, as though he were hard of hearing. "We need a better system. Or any system. We could set up direct deposit like Paige and Bill." Paige, her best friend, had ditched her husband last year. To Tess she was like a patron saint of divorce.

"Direct deposit? Are you crazy?" To set up direct deposit, Timmy would have to open a bank account. He might as well send a handwritten note to the feds: *I made this money selling drugs.*

"I can send you a money order," he said.

"Do money orders still exist?"

"How the fuck do I know? Tess, what do you want from me?"

Marriage, he'd learned, was a negotiation. In the beginning, Tess's goodwill could be purchased with sex, money, or weed. By the time his son was born, two of those currencies had ceased to matter. Tess had quit smoking dope, and screwing was by then a distant memory, but they continued to fight about money. Ten years divorced, they still did.

"I want you to act like a father," she said. "Did he tell you he got suspended?"

"That little shit," said Timmy. "What did he do?"

She'd answer the question eventually. First he'd have to sit through an angry monologue on the inconvenience of her life, his global failure as a father, the monumental difficulty of raising a kid alone. He waited for her to finish. Then he said, "If you can't handle him, send him up here."

"You always say that." Tess sounded disgusted. "You say it because you know I'll never do it. No way in hell would I let you raise my son."

At one time he would've flown off the handle. *Your* son? *You got knocked up all by yourself?* Hard years of marriage had taught him there was no fucking point.

"There are laws about this," said Tess. "I can have your wages garnished."

"What wages?" Timmy said.

When she hung up there was simply nothing. Timmy missed the old days, when they argued on a landline, the crude satisfaction of a dial tone when one of them slammed down the phone.

Remember the rooftop? A summer party in St. Pete. They smoked a joint and danced a little—something Timmy never did, but somehow Tess compelled him. She danced with him. It was his first glimpse of her willfulness, the sheer force of her personality, though at the time he didn't see it. That night she seemed sweet and dazed and dreamy, a barefoot hippie girl in a long cotton skirt. She shaved her legs but not her armpits, which shocked him at first but later seemed kind of hot.

Remember Tess's apartment? Pillows everywhere, perfumed candles, the curtains drawn. It reminded him of the bottle where *I Dream of Jeannie* lived, the old TV show in constant reruns throughout his childhood. Jeannie's bottle had one room—round, of course, with a pink upholstered couch shaped like a Lifesaver. You wanted to stick your dick in that bottle.

He'd known her just a month when she got pregnant. Remember Tess pregnant? When she slept in his arms he was holding his entire family, his future, the rest of his life. He wouldn't have believed that a girl with a huge belly could be sexy. But it was different, everything was different, when it belonged to you.

Getting married was his idea. That they barely knew each other didn't seem important. Marriage would fix that. It had worked for his parents (or maybe it hadn't). Anyway, it seemed like the right thing to do.

His son was born in July, a seething Florida summer. Timmy was present for the birth, a moist and surprisingly violent spectacle that would have traumatized him if he hadn't been stoned out of his mind. Afterward he stepped out to meet a customer. When he got back to the hospital, the birth certificate was already filled in with the name Tess had chosen, Dakota Blue.

You're fuckin kidding me, Timmy said.

Dakota was bad enough. Dakota was some faggot on a soap opera. Dakota Blue was worse, a stripper or a hooker. A transvestite hooker. That's what she'd named his son.

Dakota Blue Flynn, he said aloud, but what he heard was *bluefin*. And from that day on, he called his kid the Tuna.

Those first months were like a dream to him, the

exhilaration and the exhaustion feeding each other so that weed was superfluous. Without smoking anything, he woke up stoned. He watched the Tuna while Tess went rollerblading to regain her figure, which took no time at all. *You look great,* he told her, but secretly he missed the big tits and belly, the sexy fat chick carrying his son.

The crazy part, the completely inexplicable part? All these years later, he still missed her. Not the shrieking bitch who blew up his phone every month, but Tess as she once was, the dazed, horny hippie girl. Remember how her hair smelled? Smoky sweet, like sandalwood incense. It gave him an instant hard-on. No other woman had ever affected him that way.

Timmy smoked a bowl to fortify himself. Then he muted the TV and called his son's cell phone.

"Tuna, my man. What's going on?"

"Nothing," he said in his new deep voice.

There was an unusual silence. Normally their calls had a soundtrack, an unending loop of electronic noises.

"Pretty quiet there. No Xbox?"

"Nope." The *P* landed with an aggressive pop, a tidal wave of adolescent anger packed into a single consonant. "Mom took it away."

"Why'd she do that?"

Another silence. Timmy eyed the water pipe on the coffee table, contemplating another hit.

"I know she told you," said the Tuna. "Why ask me, if you already know?"

"I want to hear it from you."

"I got suspended." The voice was a little shocking. Just a few weeks ago, he'd sounded like a little kid.

"What for?" Timmy said.

The Tuna didn't answer, which wasn't surprising. He was a brick wall when confronted. At fourteen, Timmy had been the same way.

"Mom said you cut class."

The kid inhaled loudly, a moist snotty sound. "It wasn't a class. It was a fucking pep rally. Did she tell you that?"

"No," said Timmy. Fucking Tess! It was a lesson he'd learned a hundred times: her version of events, any events, was not to be trusted.

"I mean, why do I have to sit there and clap for some asswipe with a basketball?"

"That is some bullshit," Timmy agreed.

Another silence.

Timmy said, "Well, at least you get a couple days off school."

"And sit here all day with Rudy? No thanks. I'd rather go to school."

Rudy was Tess's Cuban boyfriend, a Lexus-driving douchebag.

"Doesn't he have his own place?" Timmy knew, had been repeatedly told, that the answer was none of his business. He felt it was entirely his business if some random guy was living under the same roof as his kid.

"Supposedly," said the Tuna. "But he's always here."

Another silence. There was plenty Timmy could say, should say. Parental shit like *Your mother's a pain in the ass, but she's still your mother. High school isn't forever; in a few years you'll graduate and do whatever the fuck you want.*

When he opened his mouth, he said none of those things.

"You could come up to Boston," he said. "Not to visit. To live." He hadn't planned to say it, not yet. The words had simply fallen out of his mouth.

"Not right away," he added hurriedly. "But soon. Next year, maybe." In a year his Laundromat would be up and running. The Tuna could help out nights and weekends, valuable work experience for a kid. It would get him started on the right path in life, a path that had eluded Timmy for forty years.

"I'll see you next month," he promised. "I have some business down there."

A month seemed reasonable: ten days to install the

traps in the Civic, another week or two to scrape together some dough. He was three months behind on
child support. Unless he showed up with a fistful of
cash, there was no way Tess would let him see his son.

In the evening Sean Barry washed up on his doorstep—
Timmy's uncle, his mother's brother. In the family he
was referred to, always, by both names—this to dis-
tinguish him from Sean Flynn, Timmy's uncle on his
dad's side.

There was a recognizable Barry look, snub-nosed
and round-cheeked. As a young man Sean Barry had
camouflaged it with hippie hair to his shoulders, a
goatee to cover the leprechaun chin. In his sixties he
was clean-shaven, his face grown soft and womanish.
His hair, what was left of it, was slicked back from his
forehead with some brittle-looking adhesive.

"Christ on a cracker," he said. "What happened to
your face?"

Timmy's hand went to his chin. "I figured it was
time. What are you doing here?"

"What do you think?"

They went inside, Sean Barry stepping elaborately
around the pile of shoes, the snow shovel, the pail of
rock salt. "I love what you've done with the place."

"Fuck you." Timmy wasn't in the mood for company.

But Sean Barry, being both his uncle and his landlord, couldn't be turned away.

How this arrangement came to be was Barry family legend. After Timmy's grandmother died, the house was left to her two children, and Timmy's mother sold her share to Sean Barry. No one could have predicted, then, how the neighborhood would change, the shabby houses gutted and carved up into apartments. Twenty years later, the street was still noisy and trash-strewn and pocked with potholes, but somehow the rents had tripled. Timmy's mother lived in a constant state of outrage. Her brother had taken advantage of her youth and greed, her ignorance about real estate and business and, let's be honest, everything else in life. (*I paid her fair market value*, Sean Barry insisted to anyone who'd listen.) To shut her up, he rented the ground-floor apartment to her drug-dealer son at a special family rate.

He took a seat on the couch and Timmy brought two beers from the kitchen. From the cigar box he handed over an envelope of cash.

"Feels a little light." Sean Barry picked through it skeptically. "That's it?"

"How much did you smoke last month? You should be paying *me*."

For years they'd operated on the barter system,

Timmy's monthly rent weighed against Sean Barry's epic consumption of what he still called *reefer*. At this point Timmy effectively paid his rent in weed.

"How's your mother?" Sean Barry asked.

"The same, I guess. I'll tell her you said hi."

"That's all you'll tell her," Sean Barry said with a raised eyebrow, as if the entire family didn't already know he was a smokehound. Except for Timmy's parents— who instead drank like fish—all the Flynns and Barrys smoked, but there were unspoken rules about who knew what and who would smoke with whom. Timmy's sister, Maureen, would smoke with him, but not with their older brother. Sean Barry would smoke with his niece and nephews, but not with his own kids. Sean Barry's kids would smoke with their Flynn cousins, but not with the other Barrys. Timmy would smoke with anyone, anytime, anywhere.

"You got any more of that Bay One?" said Sean Barry.

"Sold out."

"You were sold out last time. You have a supply problem."

"I'm aware," Timmy said.

Sean Barry took rolling papers from his pocket. "How about some of those gummy bears?"

"You're kidding me. You ate them all?"

"I got half of one left. I already bit the fucker's head off."

"All right. Hang on." Timmy hoisted himself out of the chair and stepped into the bedroom. His inventory was stored in a fireproof, coffin-sized strongbox beneath the bed.

When he came back, Sean Barry was trying to roll a joint. "I can't see a fuckin thing. Turn on a light, will you? It's like a cave in here."

Timmy did.

"Seasonal affective disorder," said Sean Barry. "It's a problem in the northern latitudes, which we are a part of. It affects your serotonin, your melatonin. All the tonins are affected." He ticked off the symptoms: low energy, oversleeping, overeating. "Not to mention," he added.

"What?" said Timmy

"When's the last time you got laid?"

"None of your fuckin business," Timmy said.

Sean Barry seemed pleased with this answer.

"This is my point. Low libido is a notorious symptom. Get yourself a light box. Full spectrum, to get the longer wavelengths." He took a drag off the joint, which was burning too fast on one side. He evened it out with a wet fingertip and passed it to Timmy, who eyed it with distaste.

Since Tess there'd been no one important, and almost no one unimportant. A year ago he made a mistake with a customer. She arrived on a bicycle—a skinny little thing, wide-eyed like a girl in a Japanese cartoon, a ripped T-shirt over black spandex, a metal stud in her nostril that made him wonder where else she was pierced. They started on the couch and finished in his bed. When he woke several hours later, the girl was gone. She hadn't paid him for the weed. He figured he'd never see her again, but a few weeks later she knocked at his door.

I can't give you any more free product, he said. *I don't work that way.*

The bike girl said, *It wasn't free.*

For months afterward, Timmy was haunted by this vision of himself: a clueless participant in prostitution, dumbly taking what was offered, believing, foolishly, that her motives were the same as his: simple desire, aching need. He'd failed to understand the terms of the transaction, the girl paying for her purchase with something of equivalent value. He was disgusted by her but mostly by himself, a middle-aged guy with a receding hairline, going soft around the middle.

Of course she didn't want him. She only wanted his weed.

So no customers. He needed another way to meet

women. He made himself a profile on a dating site, with a ten-year-old photo and a career he invented on the spot—driver's ed teacher, something he'd always thought he'd be good at. He went on one date with a woman named Sharynn and heard the stupid spelling every time he said her name. She asked him about teaching driver's ed, and Timmy made up answers he would never remember. They made a second date he later canceled. It was all too much fucking effort.

He needed a woman who understood what he did for a living, the one advantage of dating a customer. He didn't have the energy to pretend to be something he wasn't. The problem was that he'd never be able to break up with her. A pissed-off ex-girlfriend could call the law on him.

Before he'd even met her he was planning their breakup. That was how his mind worked.

He could date a customer only if she had no vindictive impulses whatsoever. Timmy had never met such a woman.

He took a long drag on the joint. "How's it going with the Stagehands?"

"Slow. It'll pick up in the spring."

Timmy said, "I need to get back on the list." He didn't say, *I'm a forty-year-old man without a bank account. I do not exist in the world.*

"The list," Sean Barry repeated. "What for?"

"You don't need to know what for."

"This is how you ask a favor." Sean Barry reached for the joint.

"My kid is coming. Not to visit. He's coming to live with me." Timmy said it just to say it, to hear it in his own voice.

Sean Barry looked flabbergasted. "Does Tess know?"

"Of course she knows." In that moment it seemed entirely true. "She doesn't know, it's an Amber Alert."

Again the eyebrow. "And she's happy about this?"

Well, no. Tess wasn't happy. It wasn't, in general, a word you'd associate with Tess.

"She's fine with it," said Timmy. "She's fine, I'm fine, everybody's fine. I am fuckin thrilled, you want to know the truth. He lives with me, and I'm done giving her money every month. I never have to deal with her again."

"There's that." Sean Barry nodded gravely. He had two ex-wives of his own. "You can't put a price tag on that."

They drank in silence.

"So what about this?" said Sean Barry, gesturing with the joint. "What do you do about this, with a child in the house?"

"He's fourteen," said Timmy.

"Meaning what?"

"Meaning I don't know what it means." It was a question he had never confronted. The Tuna had visited Boston only once, nine years ago. Back then he was too young to notice the skunk smell of Timmy's apartment, the all-day parade of visitors coming and going. Now that he was older, their visits took place in Florida. Twice a year, Timmy got a motel room in Pensacola. They spent a week playing video games, fishing and body-surfing and lying on the beach.

They passed the joint in silence. Timmy inhaled deeply, an alternate vision of his life coalescing in his head. The kid would come to live with him, finish high school in Boston. Together they would run the Laundromat, a family business the Tuna would eventually inherit. In this way, Timmy would give his son a decent start in life. His own parents hadn't given him squat.

"Forget the list. The list is a nonstarter. The list, I will tell you now, is not going to happen." Sean Barry squashed out the joint in the ashtray. "You need cash? Here's my advice. Sell the Cuda."

The car was a sore subject. Timmy had spent more on it than he'd intended: the rebuilt engine, bodywork, a new paint job. He garaged it, also on the barter system, at his buddy Andy Stasko's—for free, but not really. It was depressing to think what the Cuda had cost him in time, money, and weed.

He said, "I'm not going to sell the Cuda."

Sean Barry looked disgusted. "Jesus Christ and his mother! Was that not the whole goddamn point? An investment, you said."

"It was," Timmy admitted. "Now, I don't know." There was more he could have said. In thirteen months, when the Tuna got his license, the Cuda would be the coolest birthday present in history. It would make up for a lifetime's worth of fuckups, the best gift any father ever gave his son.

10

Jesus Christ, not another storm.

Five nor'easters in five weeks. It was like living in wartime. Weather alerts were updated twice an hour. Public utilities sent stern warnings via text message: **Storm preparedness is a civic responsibility.** The homeless were urged to seek shelter indoors.

In the neighborhoods, parking wars intensified. Spaces were saved with lawn chairs, with recycling bins. Sofas and armchairs were dragged into the street. Workers called in sick to avoid driving. It was worth burning up a vacation day to hang on to a parking space.

The text messages arrived like digital precipitation, what the Weather Channel called *wintry mix*. **The homeowner is responsible for clearing sidewalks.**

Ice dams were a serious problem. This was a thing people talked about.

Five nor'easters in five weeks. It's fair to say that Boston took it personally. Boston blamed El Niño or La Niña, global warming and fossil fuels, corruption in the State House, the city's cursed geography. Boston blamed the New York Yankees, just because.

Long underwear, wool sweater, down parka, balaclava. Boston packed into train cars, awash in sweat and indignation. Boston—not the jolliest city on its best day—was feeling cantankerous. Resentment hung in the air like a toxic gas. **Clear your dryer vents! Blocked vents lead to carbon monoxide poisoning.** The resentment was visceral, a physiologic response to known phenomena—dew point, bulb point, barometric pressure—and to others not yet identified.

Meanwhile the rest of life was still happening. Claudia worked too much and slept too little. She made appointments (haircut, dentist, mammogram); she showered and laundered. She shoveled the sidewalk and dusted it with rock salt, read the newspaper and ate toast. On alternating weekends she drove to Stuart's house in Andover, to eat steaks and fuck. (Occasionally they watched a movie.) Once or twice a week, her car was buried by the snowplow. Once or twice a week, she dug it out. All this took time.

At work, the hotline kept ringing. Condoms broke, eggs were fertilized, periods came or didn't. Symptoms flared, worsened, required attention. The body, indifferent to weather, made its demands.

Each morning on Mercy Street, protestors gathered. Puffy fingered his rosary beads—a kind man, well-meaning. He wore a wedding ring. Claudia imagined him long married—widowed, maybe—and lonely in retirement, eager to do good in the world. He spoke gently to the young women he met at the clinic, not understanding that most of them were not actually pregnant.

A female body is a lot of work. Puffy, not having one himself, was possibly unaware of this fact. Women go to the doctor all the time, just to keep things running smoothly. On any given day the clinic was full of them, women of all ages and colors sitting in stirrups for the annual tribulation—an experience they'd all happily forgo, if they had any say in the matter.

Bring in your pelvis for its twelve-month checkup. Failure to perform scheduled maintenance may void the warranty.

These drab medical realities didn't interest the protestors gathered on the sidewalk. Only abortion mattered, a stranger's crisis. The rest was too mundane, too visceral: the messy business of secretions and hormones and cyclical seepages, the routine (expensive, embarrassing, occasionally lifesaving) interventions a female body required.

There was no way to explain this to the crowd on the sidewalk. Claudia didn't even try.

Hannah R. was seventeen, a tall, slender girl with silky hair and a flawless complexion, a senior at Pilgrims Country Day School. According to her file, she was six weeks pregnant.

Hannah. The name had become inexplicably popular. To bookish girls of Claudia's generation, Hannah had been the family housekeeper in the Nancy Drew mysteries. Now, suddenly, Hannahs were everywhere.

"Have a seat," said Claudia. "First we're going to talk privately. When we're finished, Mary will bring in your parent or legal guardian to sign the consent form.

"Everything you tell me today will be kept confidential here at the clinic, unless you tell me someone is hurting you or not taking care of you, or if you are going to hurt yourself or someone else. If you tell me any of those things, I have to tell someone outside the clinic so we can make sure you're safe."

She verified that the abortion was Hannah's own

choice, that no one had pressured her to have it. She explained the procedure step by step. Hannah might have some bleeding afterward. Her periods were likely to be irregular for the next couple of months.

Hannah absorbed this silently. She seemed preternaturally calm.

"Any questions?" Claudia asked.

"Not really?" Hannah replied.

Was this a statement or a question? With teenage girls, it was hard to know. They seemed at every juncture to be looking for agreement, consensus, affirmation. To be reassured that they weren't wrong.

Hannah stared at the box of tissues on Claudia's desk. "Am I supposed to be crying? Like I'm doing this terrible thing and I should at least be upset about it? But you know what? *I'm not.*"

"That's not unusual," said Claudia. "Every person responds differently." A year ago she'd have said, *Every woman responds differently.* The new gender-neutral language still felt awkward in her mouth, but she'd get used to it. It didn't happen every day, but every once in a while, a transgender patient did fall pregnant. "If I think back on everyone I've counseled, the most common reaction is relief."

"*Exactly,*" said Hannah. "I mean, it's just the worst time *ever.* I'm applying to college?"

Yale and Dartmouth, she said when Claudia asked.

"And Stirling?" Hannah added. "It's kind of my safety school?"

I went to Stirling, Claudia could have said but didn't. It was the first rule of counseling: it's never about you.

"I don't know how this happened. I mean, I *know*, but . . ." Hannah hesitated. "I'm like, under a ton of stress? I know that's no excuse, but . . ." Her voice trailed off.

Claudia waited for her to say more.

"I feel *so stupid*. It just kind of—happened? I mean, it was *totally my fault*." This time Hannah sounded certain. There was no question in her voice.

Claudia asked about the man involved with the pregnancy.

"We don't see each other that often. He's at Georgetown?" Hannah said. "Anyway, he's been really cool about everything? He even offered to pay for it, which . . ." Her eyes welled.

Claudia slid the tissue box across the desk. "Which isn't really the point."

"*Exactly.*" Hannah swiped at her eyes—impatiently, as if annoyed to find tears there. "This whole experience, I don't know. I just think maybe he's not the right person? I mean, are we even going to be together a year from now? Is that even what I want? *Anyway*," she

said, "I can't think about that right now? I just want
to, you know, get it over with and get on with my life?"

"Fair enough." Claudia picked up the phone and
dialed Mary Fahey's extension. "We're ready to sign."

"My mom's been *so great*," said Hannah. "I thought
for sure she was going to freak out? But the second
I told her she was like, whatever you want to do. No
drama, you know? My dad is another story."

"Have you talked to him about it?"

"No!" Hannah looked aghast. "He's, like, an anxious personality? I feel like he'd totally overreact, and
then I'd feel bad, and it would be all about making him
feel better? My dad's awesome," she added. "But he's,
like, a lot of *work*."

The door opened. Hannah's mother was a tall, lean
woman in a thin leather jacket—older than Claudia,
though at first glance this was not apparent. She seemed
energetic and radiantly healthy, like a woman advertis-
ing vitamins or yogurt.

"Julia Ramsey. Nice to see you," she added smoothly,
as though they'd crossed paths at a cocktail party and
she couldn't quite recall whether they'd met before.

She signed the form briskly, without comment.
"Thank you *so much*." Her eyes went from Claudia to
Mary. "Really. All of you. Hannah and I are so grateful
for the work you do."

Claudia watched as Mary led them down the hall. In an hour the procedure would be over, and Hannah's visit to the clinic would become part of her past. When she thought about it at all, she'd remember a youthful mistake, quickly corrected. In the spring she would graduate from Pilgrims Country Day. Whatever happened next—Yale or Dartmouth, the future unfolding—would stem directly from the choice made on Mercy Street. For Hannah R., every door remained open. Her life was entirely her own.

At noon Claudia stepped out for a sandwich. Outside, the sky had darkened, storm clouds gathering. At twelve thirty in the afternoon, the streetlamps were bright.

When she returned to Mercy Street, the wind had kicked up. A woman stood in the shelter of the building, trying to light a cigarette. She looked very cold, underdressed in her chic leather jacket. It took Claudia a moment to recognize Julia Ramsey, Hannah's mother. The cigarette confused her. It seemed at odds with the vitamins-and-yogurt thing.

"Here." Claudia approached and stood with her back to the wind. "Let me block you."

Julia tried again: scratch, pause, inhale. "Got it. Thank you. God, that's good." She studied the cigarette in her hand, as if unsure how it had gotten there. "I never smoke. Honestly, I haven't had one in twenty years."

"No worries," said Claudia—an expression she loathed. What exactly did it mean? Nothing, which was why people said it, an innocuous filler for an awkward pause. "Are you okay?"

"I've been better. This day has been—unbelievable." Julia closed her eyes as if the subject pained her. "I just want it to be over."

"Hannah said the same thing." Claudia studied her. "She's a lovely girl. I enjoyed meeting her, despite the circumstances."

"She's a good kid." Julia smiled wanly. "Kind, thoughtful, straight As at school. She's never been in trouble. Honestly, I never saw this coming."

A garbage truck roared past, dieseling loudly.

Julia took a long final drag. "Three puffs. That's all I need." She dropped the cigarette and squashed it beneath her heel. "I had one."

It took Claudia one second to grasp her meaning. In her line of work, such confessions were common. One in four American women would, at some point, terminate a pregnancy. Most, it seemed, carried the secret for the rest of their lives.

"A hundred years ago, when I was in college." Julia

blinked rapidly, her eyes tearing. "I didn't tell my mother. I didn't tell anyone."

"Have you told Hannah?"

"No." She seemed startled by the question. "I mean, would you?"

Claudia considered this.

"Yes," she said finally. "Yes, I think I would."

11

11

His earliest memory was of his mother. Victor must have been very small. They were in the kitchen of the old house and she was giving him a bath in the sink. A flicker of memory, fleeting, strobelike: the warm water running over him like a blessing, the porcelain cold against his back.

His mother was a whore named Audrey, a name his father would not speak.

After she left, father and son lived in three rooms above a pool hall. When his father worked Hoot Owl, the boy was alone all night in the apartment. He lay awake thinking of the loaded shotgun in the kitchen closet, and waited for an intruder to come.

His mother was a whore because what other kind of woman would leave her child?

Her blonde hair dark at the ends where it dipped into the sink.

His father switched to day shift and in the evenings went out prowling. Victor witnessed adult behavior, drunkenness and fornication. Later he understood that this had warped him, shaped his character in ruinous ways.

He was nine when his father married Junie Thibodeaux. She was not a virtuous woman, which was to be expected. What virtuous woman would have anything to do with his father?

Junie was not virtuous, but she was kind. She approached little Victor cautiously, like a feral cat she meant to tame. Naturally he resisted. In the rooms above the pool hall he'd bathed when he felt like it, which was never. If he got hungry he boiled up a hot dog from the fridge. At Junie's house—a tin-roof shack out in the sticks—the food wasn't much different, but they ate it together at a table. There was mustard and ketchup and a slice of Wonder bread to wrap around the hot dog.

Junie had a son his own age, a shy, undersized kid who stuttered when nervous, a choke chain of consonants jammed in his mouth. Randy was born small and had stayed small—not the worst thing that could happen to a child, but in the mid-1960s, in the public schools of northern Appalachia, it opened the door to the worst things. Randy Thibodeaux—technically Victor's stepbrother—was a runt, it was true. But holding his head in the toilet bowl—the accepted and time-honored punishment for runthood—seemed excessive. As the biggest boy in his class, Victor felt a certain responsibility for maintaining order, like a junior county sheriff. When his stepbrother's head was held in the toilet bowl, he did not let it stand.

After the incident in the boys' washroom, Randy didn't say *thank you*. He thanked Victor silently, wordlessly, for the rest of his life.

Junie was not virtuous, but Victor was fond of her and sorry when she died. Her days had begun, always, with five minutes of convulsive hacking that woke the household. The cough was a part of her, like her choking laugh and sandpaper voice and the beaded vinyl case that held her Virginia Slims, the brand advertised on the back of *Cosmopolitan* magazine. Junie kept a stack of back issues in the family's one bathroom—a convenient arrangement for young Victor, who for one fevered youthful summer masturbated over them twice a day. He was just a boy; he knew nothing of sex. Without the young whores leering out from the pages of *Cosmopolitan*, he might never have found his own cock.

The magazines taught you what you were supposed to want.

The young whores had accompanied him to basic training, to Vietnam, to highway rest stops across the country. The actual women in the photographs would be grandmothers now, a fact he didn't like to think about. Fifty years later, their young faces and bodies were still burned into his memory, a mental repository of images he could flip through when the need arose.

Now, when he reached for his cock at night, a new set of pictures flooded his mind.

When the Hall of Shame was up and running, he built a private version just for himself. He chose the best photos and arranged them in a slide show, with a slow dissolve in between.

Occasionally a particular girl caught his attention. In San Diego there was a freckle-faced blonde. Victor gave her a name, a complete biography. Bonnie was twenty-three years old, a kindergarten teacher. She had been raped by a (White) stranger when her car broke down by the highway. The attack was not her fault; Victor knew this for a fact, having visualized it in great detail. He imagined comforting her, holding her close, explaining, gently but firmly, her duty to the White race, Bonnie agreeing through tears that he was right.

Thanks entirely to Victor, her precious White child would be spared.

Bonnie, it must be said, was not typical. For the most part, the Hall of Shame was full of whores.

Sometimes you could tell by looking: the hair dyed unnatural colors, the tattoos and slutty makeup. Some were fat or brutishly ugly. One wore an actual ring in her nose. What sort of man would want to fuck such a creature, Victor could not imagine. Though, in point of fact, he would have fucked most of them.

He set the slide show to music.

Fallen women were everywhere, fucking indiscriminately with no thought to the consequences. The precious life that resulted was merely an inconvenience, a problem to be dealt with. In a lifetime of whoring, a female could kill a staggering number of children—up to six a year, by Victor's arithmetic. Of course, she'd have to do a tremendous amount of fucking to get pregnant six times a year. By the looks of them, many did.

They killed their babies so they could go on fucking.

He sat back and watched the parade of whores.

He ran the slide show on a continuous loop. Occasionally he drifted off to sleep. The late-afternoon nap was a pleasure he'd rediscovered in his sixties. Like a reversion to earliest childhood, this slow toddle into drooling old age.

His dreams were unnaturally vivid. Victor blamed the pills. The VA doc had prescribed them for his prostate, which still did whatever a prostate was supposed to but was so swollen that pissing took ten minutes.

He dreamed he saw his mother outside the clinic. He called her name—*Audrey!*—but she didn't hear him. She walked purposefully toward the clinic like a runway model, her long hair lifted by the breeze. In the dream he ran after her, his heart pounding. If Audrey went inside the clinic, he himself would be aborted. He was running for his life.

The day, like all days, began strategically. He rose at first light and drank his coffee at the computer, sorting through a new batch of photos. In Boston the snow was still flying. Anthony had sent three dozen photos of women in winter coats.

The coats depressed him. It had been shortsighted to launch the Hall of Shame in winter. The women's bodies, if they had bodies, were impossible to discern. Victor thought of women in Arab countries, swathed head to toe in fabric. Say what you want about Muslims; they were realistic about human nature in a way regular people weren't. Male urges—Victor knew this from long experience—were not to be trifled with. If you didn't want your wife or daughter to become stroke material for some horny male stranger, measures had to be taken. An extreme but highly effective precaution was to swaddle her in cloth.

Say what you want about Muslims, they knew how to manage their women.

He respected the Muslim discipline. And yet, if Muslims ran the world, there would be nothing to look at. Single men like Victor would die alone, of unrequited horniness, without ever seeing another ass or breast or thigh.

He respected the discipline, no question. But he wouldn't want to live in such a world.

A knock at the door. "I'm going to Costco," said Randy. "Where's my list?" He was dressed for town, in what Victor thought of as his Daniel Boone outfit: a fringed buckskin jacket that had cost him six hundred dollars—for a cheapskate like Randy, a stupefying sum. He was still a runt—five-three on tiptoe—but over the years had made peace with his stature. On his whoring trips to Pittsburgh he'd dressed flamboyantly, in a long trench coat and leather ranchero hat. He was a crackerjack mechanic, a competent electrician, a better carpenter than Victor, skills acquired through a lifetime of overcompensating. Randy was so good at so many things that it was easy to forget he was short.

"On the fridge," said Victor.

His computer pinged loudly.

Randy leered. "Is that one of your lady friends?" Impressed by the number of hours Victor spent at the computer, Randy was convinced he had a wild sex life, with dozens of virtual floozies on the hook. That a computer had other uses besides the viewing of pornography was a rumor he didn't quite believe.

Victor ignored the question. "I'm going to the show later. Leave your license on the kitchen table."

"Roger that. Put some ice on your face, will you?" said Randy. "It's swole up like a basketball."

Victor returned his attention to the screen. One girl had real potential—long curly hair, soulful brown eyes—but the effect was ruined by the puffy down jacket she wore, a ridiculous garment for women. For Victor, a pretty face wasn't enough. He needed at the least the suggestion of a body.

He reviewed the photos in reverse order, trying to imagine these same women in sundresses, in bikinis, in virginal white underwear, and found it impossible to do.

He should have waited until summer.

For women anyway, the puffy jacket should be outlawed.

All things considered, the Boston photos were a

disappointment. Half were completely useless. Despite clear instructions, Anthony had sent a motley collection of Blacks and Orientals and Spanish, females in every conceivable shade of yellow, beige, and brown.

Anthony was not the brightest bulb.

Anthony, poor bastard, had missed the point entirely. There was *no reason whatsoever* to shame these women. Privately, Victor had no problem at all with them having abortions, though he knew better than to say so. His lieutenants, all Christians, were delicate flowers—fragile creatures raised on fairy tales, the addictive fantasy of prayer.

Victor was not, himself, a Christian. His only god was nature, the blind force that ran the universe. Nature was reliably impartial, indifferent to outcomes. It had no special loyalty to Black or White, it did not take a rooting interest. With nature, prayer was useless. There was no appeals process. The White race would simply have to fend for itself.

The crisis was a concrete matter, a mathematical problem with a clear solution. Disaster could be averted, if immediate action were taken. If the White female rose to the challenge, and did her part.

To date, he'd seen no evidence of this happening. The blithe unconcern of White females was infuriating. Victor encountered them every day on the internet, chatting and LOL-ing and posting selfies, squandering their precious reproductive years on nonsense.

For decades, now, the White female had defied nature, fighting her destiny with every weapon possible: swallowing pills, injecting herself with hormones, shoving tiny pieces of copper up inside her to keep a baby from implanting. (Implanting! That was the word used. Victor had read about it on the internet.)

The depravity was breathtaking. The depravity, truly, was hard to fathom.

And there were other consequences. Just think of the urine! All over the world, untold millions of females were jacked up on estrogen. Each time one took a piss, a dose was released into the water supply. By now, every drop of water on earth had cycled through some female's bladder, a thought that haunted Victor each time he turned on the tap. How much estrogen had he himself ingested in his lifetime? All over America, testicles were shriveling. Teenage boys were growing tits. Maleness itself was under attack.

The White female was drunk with power. She was holding an entire race hostage. In the interests of humanity, an intervention was necessary. It was a matter of survival. The female body was a natural resource, like coal or iron. It belonged to the entire world.

An instant message appeared on his screen.

LostObjects1977: how do you like the pix??

Victor tapped out a reply, two-fingered. He had never learned to type properly.

Excelsior11: Too many black girls

Anthony fired back immediately. His instant messages were entirely too instant. They came at lightning speed.

LostObjects1977: did you watch the vid?? that one was white

Oh, for Pete's sake, Victor thought. Like the rest of his generation, Anthony was overly impressed by technology, so dazzled by the bells and whistles that the mission itself went out the window.

Excelsior11: Video?
LostObjects1977: sent it to you yesterday

Victor scrolled halfheartedly through his inbox.

Excelsior11: I don't see it. Are you sure you sent it?
LostObjects1977: resending now

It occurred to Victor—not for the first time—that he had a personnel problem. He needed a better quality of lieutenant.

The expo hall opened at ten in the morning. Victor was first in line when they unlocked the doors. He'd been standing there for forty minutes, determined to beat the crowd.

The show got bigger every year: hundreds of tables, thousands of firearms. In recent years the organizers had branched out. There were night-vision goggles, antique swords, a vast selection of helmets and body armor. There were blowguns and stun guns, Gadsden flags and kukri knives, an enticing display of high-end surveillance cams. Victor took his time wandering the aisles. It was, in point of fact, the only type of shopping he enjoyed. Back in his driving days, he'd visited gun shows in thirty states. He was, by then, some years sober, and there wasn't much for a solitary man to do along America's interstate highways that didn't involve a shot glass.

He made a slow tour of the perimeter, scoping out

the merchandise. Certain vendors, he knew by sight: the Civil War reenactor with his muttonchop sideburns, the enormously fat man who sold nunchucks and ninja stars at suspiciously low prices, the young skinhead with his vast inventory of knives.

He stopped to look at some night-vision goggles and heard a noise behind him, a low electrical humming. He turned to see Luther Cross rolling up in his chair.

"Jesus God, Victor! What happened to your face?"

"I got a tooth that's giving me trouble."

Luther grinned broadly. "I can pull it for you, if you want. Wouldn't take me a minute."

"Don't get any ideas," Victor said.

They had known each other since high school. Luther, a few years older, had gone to Vietnam ahead of Victor and left his legs there. Since then he'd rolled around town in a motorized wheelchair, his hair tied up in a ponytail, his lap covered with a blanket to hide what was missing.

Luther looked him up and down. "How you been, man? Still driving?"

"Naw. I retired last fall." Victor chose his words carefully. Luther Cross was a talker. Telling him anything was like writing it in the sky.

"*Retired?*" Luther looked astonished. "What the hell happened?"

"Nothing happened," Victor said irritably. "Time to hang it up, is all." On some level it was probably true, though failing the eye test had helped him along. His old boss might've let it slide, but the new manager was an uptight kid who played by the rules. *You get pulled over with an expired license, and I'm in deep shit.* Victor surrendered his rig and left quietly. He retreated to the log cabin in the valley and waited for the world to burn.

He said, "I hear you've got a generator to sell."

"Yessir," Luther said.

"My backup one crapped out. I might be interested."

"All right, then. Come over to the house and take a look."

Victor continued on his rounds. He wasn't in the market for anything in particular. Already the sub-basement contained more firepower than he needed, more ammo than he'd use in a lifetime in the pre-collapse world. Strictly speaking, he didn't need a goddamn thing, which—in his experience—was when lightning struck. He found the exact right piece when he wasn't even looking. He'd acquired most of his arsenal this way, a series of happy accidents.

Buying a weapon was like falling in love.

He passed a table of ladies' guns, pistols and revolvers in shades of lavender and pink. A young lad with acne and a sad attempt at a mustache stood studying the merchandise, as though he were on intimate terms with a woman who'd appreciate this type of gift. Victor had been looking for such a woman his entire life, and had long ago concluded that they didn't exist. If they did, it seemed unlikely that this kid would have acquired one.

He stopped to study a display of crossbows.

As always, the shoppers were ninety-nine percent men. The vendors too, unless you counted the handful of peroxide blondes who'd been hired to stand at certain booths, in a blatant attempt to drive horny male foot traffic. This tactic was effective. Victor himself had fallen for it, but only once. When he tried to make conversation about the merchandise, he was sorely disappointed. The girl knew nothing about guns.

He stopped at the table of a guy he knew, a dealer named Wayne Holtz.

"Victor, man. How you been?"

Victor let the question sit. He had never been good at small talk.

"You in the market for anything special?"

"Just looking," he said. In fact, one piece in particular had caught his eye, a used Ruger Mini-14 in perfect condition. Well, why not? In the spirit of preparedness he wore, beneath his shirt, a ripstop nylon security pouch he'd ordered off the internet—filled, at that moment, with hundred-dollar bills.

"How much is this here?" he asked.

"Four fifty," said Wayne. "But I can give it to you for four."

Wayne Holtz was a cretin. New, the piece would go for a thousand. Victor didn't need another semiautomatic; already he had a half dozen in his arsenal. But he was constitutionally unable to pass up a bargain.

"Sold," he said.

Wayne reached under the table and handed him a form. "For the background check." He offered Victor the pencil from behind his ear.

Victor reached for his wallet and placed a Pennsylvania driver's license on the table. Wayne understood the particularities of his situation. They had done business before.

Wayne studied the license. "How do you say that, anyway? Thibadoo?"

Victor said, "Tib, bow, doe."

Squinting, he filled in Randy's address and birth date and Social Security number, information he'd long ago committed to memory. The form was hard to read: the type was large enough, but the letters looked wavy. As he wrote he felt a presence behind him. He turned to see an armed Black man.

Ringing in his ears, a flash of alarm.

The guy was a Pennsylvania statie. His uniform shirt was neatly pressed, his head shaved shiny bald. Immediately, instinctively, Victor made a series of calculations. He did this routinely whenever a cop came into range. This one—L. WASHINGTON, according to his nameplate—was taller than Victor, thirty years younger, and built like a brick shithouse. His service revolver was holstered at his hip.

"Hey, man," Wayne said, shaking the cop's hand. "You on duty?"

The friendly tone took Victor by surprise. He wouldn't have thought Wayne was the type to buddy up with cops, never mind Black ones.

"Not for another hour." The cop leaned on the table. "Right now I'm just shopping."

Victor kept his head down and continued writing. A lick of sweat trailed down his back. Randy's license sat in plain sight on the table, six inches from the cop's hand.

"I see you made a sale," the cop said to Wayne. He took the Ruger from the table and raised it briefly to his shoulder. "That's a good-looking weapon."

Victor's back was now slick with sweat.

The cop handed the Ruger back to Wayne. Then he noticed Randy's license on the table. "What's this?"

Wayne looked suddenly alert. "I ran a background check on that guy a while ago. Poor bastard left his license behind."

In spite of himself, Victor was impressed. He had discounted Wayne as a slow-witted blowhard. Who would have guessed he could think on his feet?

The cop slipped the license into his pocket. "There's a lost and found at the front office. I'll turn it in for you."

"Thanks," Wayne said.

When the cop moved away from the table, Wayne met Victor's eyes. "Jesus, Victor. That was a close call."

"Yeah. Sorry about that." Victor was a little rattled. He looked longingly at the Ruger. "He's gone now. Can you run that background check real quick? I wrote down all the numbers."

Wayne looked panicked.

"Victor, man. I get caught doing this, I could lose my license."

"Oh, for Pete's sake," Victor said.

At that moment the PA system crackled, an announcement coming on: *Will Randy Thibadoo please come to the office to claim a lost item? Randy Thibadoo.*

Victor's face—he could feel it—flushed scarlet. *It isn't worth it,* he thought. The last thing he needed was to get slapped with a gun charge.

He really wanted that Ruger.

He said, "I should hit the road."

He drove home in a foul mood, thinking of the Ruger and of L. Washington—an armed Black man, vested with the full authority of an immoral government. He thought about what he'd say to Randy when he wanted his license back.

He tried to look on the bright side. The trip was not entirely wasted. To cheer himself up, he'd made an impulse buy. In the parking lot, a kid had sold him a rifle on cash and a handshake, a Mosin-Nagant in mint condition. In Pennsylvania, only licensed dealers were required to do background checks.

The law was hopelessly misguided. No question, it had complicated Victor's life. He hunted at odd hours to avoid the game warden. He steered clear of gun shops and shopped only at shows. When he struck a bargain on a piece, it was always Randy's license he handed over, Randy's Social Security number the vendor entered into the FBI database. That his stepbrother didn't know one end of a gun from the other was, to the law, an insignificant detail. Randy could buy anything he wanted—except for a six-year-old DUI, his record was clean. To Victor—a lifelong hunter, former army sniper and gun safety expert—

the injustice was galling. He himself was the second-best shot he'd ever known, after a Kentuckian he'd met in the service—a boy who'd grown up with a rifle in his hand, in a place where men who couldn't hunt had long ago gone extinct.

The injustice was intolerable. Like all his dealings with government, it reduced him to a state of blind rage.

Fucked by the bureaucracy, the petty rules of a corrupt and illegitimate federal government.

Fucked, again and still, by Barb Vance.

They met in summer, a few years after he came back from Vietnam. She was a bartender at the Commercial Hotel, old enough to serve drinks, but just barely; a fox-faced redhead with full-body freckles and schoolgirl tits that disappeared when she lay down. A scrappy, mouthy girl, a ballbuster. Cursing came as naturally to her as breathing. In the beginning Victor found this exciting. Her foul language inflamed him, made him want, urgently, to teach her a lesson.

One night she called the law on him for no goddamn reason, or so it seemed at the time. It was a Friday night in late May, the beginning of the Memorial Day weekend. He and Barb had gone out drinking, then stumbled back to her place to fuck. Immediately afterward they began fighting, their usual pattern. If they were not fucking or fighting, they had just fucked and were about to fight, or had just fought and were about to fuck.

That night, like most nights, the fight/fuck cycle began anew.

Their argument was heated, but they'd had a dozen worse ones. When Victor put his hands on her it wasn't to hurt her, he explained to the town cop. Barb was a hellcat. He was only protecting himself.

The cop refused to see his logic. Victor was led away in handcuffs. Due to the holiday, district court would be closed until Tuesday morning. He spent four nights in the county lockup for no goddamn reason, or so it seemed at the time. While he was locked up, Barb went to see a doctor in Pittsburgh. He hadn't even known she was pregnant on the day she killed his child.

He wouldn't know it to this day if not for her sister, who'd driven her to the appointment. When the sister told him this, Victor knew immediately that it was true. The timing convinced him: when Barb called the cops on him, she'd already made the appointment in Pittsburgh. She'd deliberately goaded him into an argument, then had him locked up to get him out of the way.

When Barb came out of the Commercial that night, he was waiting for her in the parking lot. *How could you do it? What did that baby ever do to you?*

To his astonishment she did not cry, did not apologize.

Oh, Victor. She sounded weary and amused, as though he were a child talking nonsense. *What else was I going to do?*

It wasn't the reaction he expected. There was no sorrow in her, no shame at what she had done.

(If she had come to him, if she had touched him. *I'm sorry, Victor. Forgive me, Victor.* If she had shed a single tear.)

I would have married you, he said.

She said, *Who'd marry a crazy motherfucker like you?*

It was very late, the parking lot deserted. It would have been laughably easy, it would have been the most natural thing in the world, to kill her with his bare hands. For all her fire, she was a skinny little thing. It would have taken him two minutes, his hands around her throat.

What he did instead was harder and more calculated. He waited. No one will ever understand the effort it cost him, the superhuman restraint.

They sent him to prison—the Great Lakes Correctional Institution in Erie County, ten miles west of nowhere. The judge gave him seven years. Because the apartment was occupied, he was charged with first-degree arson. It didn't matter that Barb wasn't home when it burned, having hiked across town to watch the fireworks with the new guy she was now fucking. Purely by accident, Victor had torched the building on yet another patriotic holiday. The timing was unconscious, or maybe it wasn't. The coincidence seemed significant. For years afterward he would ponder what it meant.

In prison, the Lord found him. It's the one part of the story he is slightly ashamed of: his own suggestibility, his weak-minded surrender to fantasy. The prison chaplain had caught him at a vulnerable moment. Later Victor would come to his senses, but at the time it had felt real to him. He had wanted so badly to believe.

At first he resisted. He and the Lord had no prior relationship. They ran in different circles and had no acquaintances in common, and Victor did not, as a rule, open the door to strangers. Out in the world he would have run from grace, he would have died running. In prison there was nowhere to run.

Why would the Lord want him? Why would anyone? He subsisted like livestock in a pen ten feet square. Each morning he shat in a concrete toilet, two feet from where he'd laid his head. There wasn't a single one of God's commandments he hadn't violated. In Saigon he'd paid a girl who gave him the clap. He had fornicated with Barb Vance while she was pregnant with his child.

His brief, hysterical conversion had no ill effects, and one positive one: encouraged by the chaplain, he began painting. At the time he had only one subject—the child Barb Vance had taken from him, his baby son (he is certain it was a son) slaughtered in the womb.

He served his full seven. The parole board refused to see his side of things. *The prisoner shows no remorse.*

To Victor it was the crowning insult. Barb Vance had killed his baby so she could go on fucking. It was *Barb Vance* who had shown no remorse.

The injustice was intolerable. It was, truly, more than he could bear.

Victor regretted the lost time—seven years of his youth, gone forever—but he did not regret what he had done. He came out of prison a stronger man, larger in all ways. They had not broken him. They had only increased his resolve.

He was thirty-three years old, the age of the mythical Jesus. Long-haul trucking paid well, and for the first time in his adult life there was no lieutenant barking orders, no shift boss hanging over his shoulder, no CO busting his balls. He'd been truthful on his application, but the manager didn't care that he was a felon. As long as a load arrived on time, no one cared how it had gotten there.

Driving, he thought of Barb Vance. For a while he

tried to find her, but this proved impossible to do. After the fire she'd moved south, to Maryland or Virginia, where she married, divorced, married, and divorced. Over the years she'd had different names, become different people. To Victor it was the ultimate injustice. Barb had been given multiple lives, while he could only ever be himself.

Being Victor Prine was a life sentence.

What exactly he'd have done if he'd found her, he wasn't entirely sure.

The injustice, in the end, was bearable. He had borne it, but only just. *It will get easier with time*, the prison chaplain had told him, but this proved to be untrue. When Victor died, five or ten years from now, it would be as though he'd never existed. No part of him would be left in the world.

Single-handedly, Barb Vance had erased him. In a few short years he would be expunged from human history, his line extinguished. Victor Prine would be gone without a trace.

Day and night, he dreamed of women.

On an endless loop he watched the parade of whores. The killing of an unborn child wasn't just a murder; it was also a theft. Always there was a second, invisible victim, a man robbed of his progeny. It was a perversion of the natural order, the female trying to run the table. For a brief, frightening time, she had absolute control of a man's legacy. She could hold his line hostage out of stupidity, whorishness, laziness, or spite. The female had been put on earth for one reason only, a single exalted purpose. Stubbornly, perversely, the Barb Vances of the world refused to play their part.

For such females he felt the same contempt he'd felt for hippies, the whiny longhairs who'd burned their draft cards while he'd offered up his life. Women who refused to be women were no better—they were far worse—than men who refused to be men.

The female who slaughtered her offspring was an abomination. She had committed an atrocity, a high crime against nature. At best she was irredeemably sick, deformed by some extreme mental illness. If you saw a dog eat its own pups, you'd be disgusted. You'd do anything to prevent its sickness from spreading.

In the interests of herd health, you would put that bitch down.

12

Ladan B. was twenty-six, from South Sudan by way of Ethiopia. Her name, she told Claudia, meant *healthy*. Her mother had died in childbirth shortly after giving her this name.

"We're too late." Mary Fahey handed Claudia the ultrasound report. "Twenty-four weeks and three days. She's just over the line."

"Four days!" The patient had a notable voice, deep and resonant, too big for the tiny room. "I come four days ago, it would have been no problem. Is this true?"

Her eyes were red from crying. Claudia slid a box of tissues across the desk.

"Massachusetts law is very specific," she said. "To get an abortion, you have to do it before twenty-four weeks."

"Okay, but four *days*?" Ladan sank into the puffy yellow jacket they'd given her at the church, a type of garment she'd never had a use for, never known existed, until she came to Boston. "What difference does it make, four days?"

It was a reasonable question. Morally, the law made no sense. On Monday an AB would have been acceptable. On Thursday it was a crime.

"I'm sorry, but we have no choice in the matter. That's the law." Claudia had said these words before, and would say them again. It was the one part of her job she hated, the moment she dreaded most.

Ladan made a sound low in her throat, a moan ending in a sob. "So what am I going to do now?"

"We can talk about that," Claudia said, feeling her heart. "But first I want to understand why you waited so long. Did you have second thoughts about having an abortion? Are you sure this is what you want?"

"No second thoughts," Ladan said firmly. "No baby. I know from the beginning it's not possible."

She explained that she had a child already, six years old, born over there when she still had a husband. The boy was her heart and her life and yet he made everything harder. When you were just yourself you could live anywhere, sleep anywhere. You could work the worst kind of job cleaning floors at South Station; you could work all day and all night because what else did you have to do?

"One child already makes it harder," she told Claudia. "Two is not possible."

When Claudia asked about the man involved with the pregnancy, Ladan waved a hand dismissively. "Dee is his name. He's just a kid."

In fact he was her age exactly; he only seemed younger. "Born in America makes you younger," Ladan said.

That morning, when the security guard asked him to empty his pockets, Dee had said, *What for?*

Dee was good with her boy, but that didn't mean she was going to have a baby with him. Where did he work? Where did his money come from? He wasn't putting on a uniform to go work at Burger King. Dee would end up in jail or dead like her husband, and then what would she have?

"You sound very sure," Claudia said. "About the abortion. So why did you wait so long?"

"*I didn't wait!*" Ladan cried, loud enough to be heard in the waiting room. "Three months ago I call for an appointment. They put my name on the list. They say they'll call me back so I wait and wait, but they never call. I call again and they say okay, but I have to have counseling first. Then, for the abortion, I need to make another appointment."

"Wait, *what?*" Claudia could make no sense of what she was hearing. "Who told you that?"

"The counselor. Katie was her name. The girl who answered the phone." Ladan looked perplexed. "Did she make a mistake?"

No, Claudia thought. *Please, not again.*

Some years back, a new clinic had opened in the Fenway, two miles west of Mercy Street. Claudia learned, later, that *clinic* was the wrong word, since no actual medicine was practiced there. Women's Health Network was a crisis pregnancy center, run by an Oklahoma nonprofit called the Whole Family Initiative. It existed for one reason only: to trick women out of getting abortions. The place was a fraud.

The con was simple. When a woman called to make an appointment for an AB, she was connected to a friendly young "counselor," recruited from a Christian college in the Midwest. An appointment was made, an ultrasound performed—the image enhanced to make the fetus look like a full-term infant, a plump and adorable Kewpie doll. After the ultrasound came a lengthy counseling session, an aggressive sales pitch by a Christian adoption agency. If the patient still wanted an AB, she was offered a second appointment, which would be canceled and rescheduled several times. By the time she figured out what was happening, it was usually too late to terminate. This was no accident. It had been the goal all along.

When the bogus clinic first opened, Claudia and Mary made a recon trip to check it out. Walking through the front door was a surreal experience. The Whole Family Initiative had gone to great lengths, and considerable expense, to replicate the peculiar atmosphere of their workplace: the same potted plants and comfy chairs, well-thumbed magazines on the same innocuous subjects: cooking, travel, decorating. (Everybody eats. Everybody likes sunsets. Everybody has a couch.) The sign out front was painted in the same colors, blue and sunny yellow. Even the typeface—a rounded sans serif—was identical.

To the untrained eye, the overall effect was convincing. To the trained eye, it was all wrong. The place had no metal detector, no cameras, not even a security guard. At a real clinic, such measures would be automatic. At a real clinic, the staff would be afraid.

The other difference was the toys. The reception area resembled a day-care center, or the waiting room of a pediatrician's office. In one corner was a Fisher-

Price workbench and a racetrack for tiny cars; in the opposite corner, a miniature kitchen with toy stove and sink. Toys for boys and toys for girls.

The ruse was breathtakingly elaborate—and from what Claudia could tell, it sometimes worked. The victims were usually poor, usually young. Some, like Ladan, were recent immigrants. The Hannah Ramseys of the world—rich White girls torn between Yale and Dartmouth—rarely fell for the con.

The fake clinic stayed open for nearly a year, until the Whole Family Initiative quietly folded; its founder, caught in a sexting scandal, had resigned in disgrace. The building in the Fenway sat empty for months, until it reopened as an Aveda hair salon. Claudia hadn't thought about the fake clinic in years. Now, apparently, another crisis pregnancy center had opened its doors.

Ladan was skeptical.

"But that's *crazy!*" she said when Claudia had finished explaining. "Why do they want to trick people like that?"

"Religion, mostly. They think God is on their side."

Ladan said that she was familiar with that argument. Everything she'd ever been forced to do was because God said so.

Claudia was impressed by her equanimity. Considering that she was pregnant and hadn't eaten in twelve hours and had been conned into having a baby she didn't want, her composure was remarkable. *If she slapped me,* Claudia thought, *I would understand.*

Ladan leaned forward and laid her head on Claudia's desk. "I'm so *hungry*," she moaned. Her hair was twisted into tiny braids, each thinner than a pencil and glistening with hair oil that smelled like oranges.

Claudia reached into the desk drawer and handed her a granola bar.

"I feel so stupid," Ladan said, chewing. "I should have known it was taking too long."

"You're not stupid. None of this is your fault." Claudia handed her a second granola bar. She'd demolished the first one in three bites.

"The counselor was so nice," Ladan said. "Katie was her name. She even gave me her cell phone number. She said I could call her anytime."

"Do you still have that number?"

Ladan took a phone from her pocket, poked and swiped at the screen. As she read off the digits, Claudia wrote them on her desk calendar, an annual gift from their sales rep at Quincy Adams Medical Supply.

"So what am I going to do now?" Ladan asked.

It was the only question that mattered.

Claudia explained that in some states, the law was different. In Virginia, abortion was legal up to twenty-five weeks.

"Okay, then. I'm going to Virginia." Ladan got to her feet, gingerly stretching her lower back, as though preparing to lift something heavy.

"Where is Virginia?" she said.

Claudia spent her lunch hour on the phone. It took some doing, a few heated exchanges with receptionists, but she managed to secure a last-minute appointment at the Wellwoman Clinic in Alexandria, Virginia. The AB would cost two thousand dollars, more than three times what Mercy Street charged. Ladan would pay half. A Massachusetts charity, the Reproductive Choice Action Network, would cover the difference, plus a round-trip bus ticket to Alexandria.

These arrangements in place, Claudia made two more phone calls. The first was to Ladan. The second was to the number she'd written on the desk calendar. She had no clear idea what she was going to say to the fake counselor at the fake clinic. Mainly she needed information. At the very least, she needed a name.

The line rang twice before voice mail picked up. A young female voice, full of sunshine: *Hi there! You have reached Katie at Women's Choice Boston. I can't take*

*your call right now, but leave me a message! I'll call you
back the first chance I get. Have an awesome day!*

Claudia was tempted to leave a message. The urge
was nearly overpowering. *Katie, this is Ladan. Guess
what? I'm still pregnant. Please advise.*

In the end she hung up without speaking, having
gotten what she needed. She had a name.

"Women's Choice," a name intended to confuse.
The clinic on Mercy Street was called Women's Options. A few miles to the west, in Brookline, was the
Choice Center for Women's Health. Across the river,
in Cambridge, was the Women's Center for Reproductive Choice.

Claudia booted up the hulking desktop computer,
rarely used. A Google search for "Women's Choice
Boston" took her to a slickly designed website:

WOMEN'S CHOICE
Free pregnancy testing
State-of-the-art ultrasound
Options counseling
A caring, patient-centered approach

She clicked around the site. There wasn't much else
to it, just that landing page, photos of smiling young

women pretending to be patients. Predictably, it had been made to look exactly like Mercy Street's website. Anyone would have been fooled.

Claudia felt a pulsing behind her left eye, the beginnings of a headache—premenstrual, or possibly not. Her cycles were unpredictable. Thirty years after her teenage flirtation with malnutrition, she still bled grudgingly, on her own mysterious schedule—two periods in a single month, or sometimes none at all. It was a basic, incontrovertible truth of female life: everything that ever happened to you unfolded against this backdrop, the unending play of shifting hormones. Month after month, year after godblessed year, there were logistics to be managed, symptoms to be treated, effluvia to be absorbed.

Mary knocked briefly at the door frame. "How'd it go with Ladan?"

"It went," Claudia said. "Women's Wellness was booked solid, but Wellwoman can see her tomorrow."

"Thank God for Wellwoman! Can she get herself down there?"

"The bus leaves at midnight. I got RCAN to spring for the ticket."

"RCAN still exists?"

"Apparently." Claudia felt suddenly exhausted. "Of course, it's an eight-hour bus ride, and she has a six-year-old at home, and two jobs and no sick days and no family and no childcare. So, you know, what could go wrong?"

"Jesus," said Mary. "Why'd she wait so long?"

"She didn't. She's been trying to get an appointment for months." Claudia swiveled the monitor around to show her the screen. "She called *them*."

Mary frowned. It took her exactly ten seconds.

"Oh God," she said. "Not again."

"This one's on Shawmut Ave. I can't tell how long they've been open."

"How did she find them?" Mary perched on the edge of the desk. "I mean, why didn't she come to us first?"

"How does anybody find anything?" At the keyboard Claudia typed "abortion boston." As Ladan had surely done; as any unhappily pregnant woman in the city would naturally do.

The search took two seconds. The first result was the Mercy Street website. Second was the site Claudia had just visited—the homepage of the dummy clinic, Women's Choice. The scammers, clearly, were tech savvy. At least, they knew enough about search engine optimization to make their site easy to find.

The other search results were just what she'd expected—links to hospitals, legit private clinics, a slew of reputable gynecology practices in Cambridge, Brookline, Arlington, and Newton. She was about to close the browser when she noticed a link at the bottom of a page:

Abortion: An Insider's Guide.

She clicked on the link.

The page took a long time to load. When it did, it had a distinctly homemade look. At the center of the screen was an ornate picture frame—clumsy clip art from the 1990s, the awkward early days of web design. At the top of the page was a caption in curlicue script:

Hall of Shame

Click to begin slide show.

Again she clicked.

Slowly, one pixel at a time, a female face appeared in the frame. The girl was young and blond, her hair in a ponytail. She wore a pink ball cap and headphones and looked away from the camera.

"Mary," said Claudia. "You've got to see this."

They watched, fascinated, as the image fragmented and was replaced. Another photo of a woman—older, a redhead. She too looked away from the camera, seemingly unaware that she was being photographed.

"What the fuck?" said Mary.

They watched speechlessly as one image dissolved into another. Candid shots, slightly out of focus. They'd been taken outdoors, in a variety of locations: a busy urban street, a strip mall parking lot. Some were close shots, tightly focused on the woman's face. In others, background was visible: parked cars, a palm tree, the golden arches of a distant McDonald's.

Mary said, "What the hell am I looking at?"

"Clinics," said Claudia. "All these women are patients."

On the screen, another blonde dissolved into a brunette wearing sunglasses. Over her shoulder, in the distance, was a green street sign, the letters so tiny they were barely legible: MERCY.

"Mary," said Claudia. "That's us."

When Claudia left work it was already dark, a fine snow falling. Behind her left eye, the pulsing continued. She and Mary had spent the afternoon studying the demented website, trying to determine which of the women were Mercy Street patients. It wasn't easy to do. In an average week, Mary did hundreds of intakes—ABs, Pap smears, IUD insertions, STD tests. In the end they identified nine patients. All had been seen within the last five months.

Claudia paused in front of the clinic, noting the position of the security cameras. One was aimed at Mercy Street, the patch of sidewalk where protestors typically gathered. A second camera pointed squarely at the front door. A patient arriving for her appointment would walk past both of them. With any luck, whoever had taken the photos had been captured on video.

She crossed the street, looking over her shoulder. At the corner, two pedestrians waited for the light to change. A guy in tights sat astride his bicycle, one foot on the curb. In front of the dim sum place, a man in an apron smoked a cigarette. Each was staring at a cell phone.

At any given moment, the entire city of Boston had a camera in its pocket.

It could have been anyone.

That night sleep was impossible. When Claudia closed her eyes, she saw the crowd on Mercy Street, patients arriving for their appointments, protesters carrying signs. A faceless man lurking near the entrance, waiting with his cell phone. The man was everywhere, he was nowhere. It was possible—likely, even—that she'd seen him herself.

At midnight she got up and turned on the television. She clicked past reality shows, comedies, the Home Shopping Network, and settled on a rerun of *Dateline*.

There was literally nothing in the world she'd rather watch than a rerun of *Dateline*, except maybe a brand-new *Dateline*. Supply was the problem. The show was produced at the glacial pace of one episode per week. There was simply not enough *Dateline* in the world to satisfy the appetite of a fan like Claudia, if that is what she was.

She was not uncritical.

That the victim was nearly always a woman wasn't, strictly speaking, *Dateline*'s fault. The *Dateline* producers didn't kill these people. Statistically, men were murdered more often than women, but apparently in a less entertaining way.

Claudia was aware that the show had shaped her worldview. She would never even consider buying life insurance. She carried her driver's license at all times—to aid police in identifying her body, should the need arise. The first forty-eight hours of an investigation were crucial. A little advance planning on the victim side could save precious days or weeks.

Because the killer was nearly always the victim's boyfriend or husband or ex-husband, celibacy was another commonsense precaution she was seriously considering.

Boyfriend, husband, ex-husband. Because every viewer knew this, the *Dateline* producers had to work hard to maintain suspense. Alternative suspects were identified, investigative blunders explored. Time was spent developing the character of the victim. The heartbroken parents were interviewed, the bereaved siblings, the teary best friend.

Like most serial killers, *Dateline* was drawn to a particular type. Its ideal victim was relatable and sympathetic, a devoted wife and mother. She need not be wealthy; it was enough to be attractive, young, and White. When prompted, her survivors would agree that her children were the center of her world. Such a devoted mother, surely, didn't deserve to be shot or bludgeoned or shoved off a cliff.

Once in a while, a childless woman would have the temerity to turn up murdered. This was not ideal, but the *Dateline* reporters found workarounds. If the victim was young enough, a case could be made that she was desperate to start a family. Ideally, she had discussed this ambition since childhood. Ideally, she'd already picked out the babies' names.

When there was no way to work children into the narrative, it was entertaining to watch the reporter scramble. The victim's hobbies were mentioned, her devotion to nieces and nephews. Occasionally there was a dog. In such cases, the reporter's questions smacked of desperation: *What did your sister do for fun?* It was a bit like watching an awkward blind date, the leading questions, the anxious search for common ground.

From her ongoing study of *Dateline*, Claudia had extracted several lessons. In the world of service journalism, these would be bullet points.

- Before shooting or strangling or bludgeoning your wife, **get rid of your cell phone**. Your text messages will be retrieved, your calls triangulated between cell towers.
- **Google search terms to avoid:** "antifreeze poisoning," "fatal gunshot," "how to overdose." Police will seize your computer, so do *not* create a Google map of the burial site. The internet is not your friend.
- **Don't smoke.** Cigarette butts retain your DNA.
- **Cameras are everywhere.** Avoid ATM machines. Do not stop at a gas station. If you must buy gloves or bleach or tarps to wrap the body in, don't do it at Walmart.
- **Let someone else find the body.** If you must find it yourself, remember: your 911 call will be recorded. Try to sound upset.

When the episode ended, Claudia was still wide awake. Her alarm was set, as usual, for seven a.m. In six short hours, she'd have to get up for work.

She set out driving.

Timmy's porch light was on, a yellow mosquito bulb left over from summer. When he came to the door, his face shocked her. The Rasputin beard was gone. Without it he looked younger, cleaner, unexpectedly handsome. If she'd met him on the street, she wouldn't have recognized him. His skin had the moist, rubbery look of an infant's after a bath.

"This is your face?"

She had never given a second's thought to what his bare face would look like, so why did it look wrong?

Timmy touched his chin gingerly, as if to make sure it was still there. "I have a business trip coming up," he said. "I figured it was time."

"How does it feel?"

"Like half my head is missing," he said.

She followed him inside. The TV was playing, a nature show about piranhas. From his TV tray he took the water pipe and offered her a hit.

The weed was more aromatic than the stuff he sold her, and stronger. "What is this?" she asked in a choked voice.

"Train Wreck. My private stash."

"It's kind of—intense."

When she handed back the pipe, Timmy waved it away. "Hang on to that awhile. You need to catch up."

Then he muted the volume and told her a story. Claudia understood that this was exactly why she'd come: to stare at his immense soundless television, to sink wordlessly into the embrace of his couch.

The story was about his uncle Frank—his dad's brother, a Brockton firefighter. In his youth Frank had been a Golden Gloves champion, a handsome guy, a guy women loved. After he blew out his knee and could no longer fight fires, he retired to Delray Beach, Florida, where there was nothing to do all day but drink and go to strip clubs and get obsessed with one of the girls, a paid professional who danced around a pole.

"So Frank watches her every day," said Timmy. "Spends all his money on her. Eventually he blows his whole retirement to set her up in an apartment. She's twenty-six and Frank is a hard seventy, but in his mind he's still a good-looking guy. He has no problem believing this girl is in love with him."

"I have a bad feeling about this," Claudia said.

"Well, yeah. Uncle Frank is in for a rude awakening, because guess what? The stripper has a boyfriend, a Florida statie. And one night Frank gets pulled over on the highway and the cop—for no apparent reason—starts whacking his Eldorado with a tire iron."

"Shit," said Claudia, filled with genuine anguish.

The scene was entirely too vivid: headlights racing along the interstate, palm trees swaying in the wind.

"Frank being Frank, he gets out of the car and takes a swing, but the cop is forty years younger," said Timmy. "Also, he has a tire iron."

Claudia handed back the pipe.

"So Frank spends two months in the hospital." Timmy took a long drag. "The doctors say he's going to spend the rest of his life in a wheelchair. By the time he gets out of the hospital, his wife is long gone, and he spent all his life savings on the stripper, so he has to live off his daughter. Who, go figure, still idolizes him."

He handed Claudia the pipe.

"The daughter—my cousin Bridget—married some rich douchebag and lives in a fancy housing development, a bunch of McMansions around a man-made lake. And of course Uncle Frank hates it there. So one night he's had enough, he's at his fuckin limit, and he drives his chair straight into the lake."

"No!" said Claudia.

"He waits until the middle of the night, when the daughter and her husband are sleeping, so they won't hear him if he changes his mind and starts screaming for help. Which he does." A long pause. "Finally one of the neighbors hears him and goes in after him, but it's too late."

They sat in silence. Claudia studied the piranhas darting across the screen.

"Jesus," she said finally. "That's a depressing story."

"Wait, there's more. They find the chair a week later," said Timmy. "They have to drag the lake."

Why tell her this story? Was there even a reason? It didn't occur to her to ask. She inhaled deeply, his words washing over her like water—a warm rinse of received experience, not to be questioned. Train Wreck had done its work.

Timmy went to the window and peered out from behind the tapestry at the silent street. "Where is everybody? It's like a bomb went off out there."

This was briefly confusing, until Claudia remembered that she'd left her house after midnight.

"It's late," she said. "I should go."

"Not yet." Timmy jangled his keys in his pocket. "Let's go for a ride."

In retrospect—Claudia knows this—her behavior raises certain questions. What was she thinking, getting into a car in the middle of the night with a known drug criminal? Was she aware that she was engaging in high-risk behavior?

She was aware.

And yet, in her gelatinous state, it didn't feel risky.

She felt safer than she had in weeks or months or possibly ever; safer, certainly, than she felt showing up for work each morning. Timmy's hugeness was comforting, a powerful visual deterrent to any *Dateline*-type predator. Walking down a dark alley with Timmy, she would not be messed with.

With Timmy she would be perfectly safe, unless he decided to kill her himself.

Washington Street was deserted, the traffic lights flashing. As they crossed the street, Claudia noticed the lightness in her pocket.

"Shit. I left my phone in your apartment."

She could picture exactly where she'd left it, beside her on Timmy's couch.

"Get it later. You won't need it," Timmy said.

More high-risk behavior: without her cell phone, her GPS coordinates could not be traced. A stern male voice—the voice of *Dateline*—whispered this in her ear.

They walked several blocks to somebody's garage. Inside it, the Barracuda was draped with a canvas cover, like a giant toaster. Timmy rolled back the cover and unlocked the passenger door. "Madam," he said, opening it with a flourish.

She got into the car. They were both beaming like idiots, flush with excellent weed, the magnificence of the car, the sheer unlikeliness of the moment.

"It's beautiful," Claudia said.

It wasn't the right word. It wasn't the wrong word either. The dashboard was set with round dials that looked vaguely nautical. The bucket seats, dark green leather, felt smooth and cold. The sleek cockpit was a psychic time capsule, a sacred artifact of a lost tribe. Encoded in the design were all its secrets: the collective unconscious of an extinct people, its unspoken, unspeakable beliefs.

The interior was spanking clean. The chrome ashtray shone like a mirror. Claudia found herself babbling about Street Rodz, her early career cleaning cars for Uncle Ricky.

"I always do my own detailing," said Timmy. "There's no one else I can trust." He glanced at her sideways. "You, maybe. Because you were a professional. I could maybe trust you."

They sat in silence, their breath fogging the windshield.

"I can't believe you're selling it," she said.

"It's already sold. Sight unseen. The guy is coming tomorrow." Timmy stroked the steering wheel with unabashed tenderness, as though petting a cat. "This is the final ride."

"But *why*?" Claudia was filled with an inexplicable anguish. "I don't get it."

"I need the cash. I have obligations; it's a long story. Anyway," he said, "I bought another car."

Claudia could make no sense of this explanation.

"There is *no other car*," she said, with emphasis. "What could you possibly?"

Timmy grinned broadly. "A Honda Civic."

It was the funniest thing anyone had ever said. Claudia and Timmy laughed until suffocation was a real danger. They laughed to the point of physical pain.

Timmy turned the key in the ignition. A thrill in her stomach as the engine roared to life. Claudia felt the vibration all through her, as if she'd been dancing near the speakers at a loud concert, her body a blind antenna picking frequencies from space.

The heater came on with a huff.

"Where to?" said Timmy.

"Anywhere," Claudia said.

They rolled east, in the vague direction of the expressway. Dorchester slipped past like a film they weren't watching. The streets were strangely deserted. Claudia remembered that it was two in the morning.

They stopped at a red light just to watch it blink.

The car's heater smelled like a lawn mower, it smelled of petroleum and burning dust, it smelled like it might cause mesothelioma. They skated along the empty streets, the blinking red lights like leftover

Christmas. Timmy drove with great concentration, in some enraptured state. Claudia turned a little to watch him, his hands large and square and strangely young looking, the hands of an overgrown boy.

As they pulled into the garage, a light snow was falling. Deliberately, almost reverently, Timmy engaged the parking brake, closed the door and locked it. They stood a long moment looking at the car.

On the sidewalk in front of Timmy's they said good night. Snow dusted their shoulders, their hair and eyelashes. The snow was an afterthought, light and powdery, a snow of no consequence. It would be gone in the morning, leaving no trace.

Timmy said, "What about your phone?"

Claudia followed him inside. The radiators were hissing. Her head was swimming from the joint, the sheer exhilaration of riding. The overheated air burned her cheeks.

Her phone wasn't on the couch where she'd left it. Her phone was nowhere to be seen.

"Don't worry, we'll find it. Happens all the time. Jesus Christ, it's like a sauna in here." Timmy peeled off his wool sweater and tossed it onto a chair.

He dropped to his knees and dug around in the recesses of the couch. Claudia knelt beside him to help.

"Hang on, I feel something." He reached in elbow-deep, like a fearless midwife, and pulled out Claudia's iPhone, still in its orange plastic case.

The relief was intoxicating. To a veteran phone-loser like Claudia, the feeling was familiar. The upside of losing things was the joy of finding them eventually—which may have been (she reflected) the entire reason she lost them in the first place. In her fractured state she saw a perverse logic to this, like wearing uncomfortable shoes for the sheer pleasure of taking them off.

They got to their feet. She noticed, then, a dime-sized spot on the back of Timmy's T-shirt—one in a larger constellation of rust-colored stains, as though someone had shaken a wet paintbrush in his direction.

"You're bleeding," she said.

Timmy turned his head to look. "Eh, that's nothing. The new ones always bleed a little." Then, as though it were the most natural thing in the world, he peeled off his shirt.

"Whoa," said Claudia. "That's a lot of ink."

What had been done to his back was extraordinary. You couldn't look at it quickly. There was simply too much to take in: a giant cross, a complicated tapestry of roses and chain mail, an actual wolf howling at the moon. The style was psychedelic, like album cover art from the sixties, Santana or Steppenwolf or King Crimson. In that moment it seemed perfectly reasonable to stand in Timmy's living room, studying his large naked back—his secret hieroglyphics, an obscure language of his own invention, evidence of some deeply strange inner life.

She would wonder, later, how long they stood there. Time had gotten slippery, expanding and contracting like an accordion.

His skin was warm as bathwater.

"Your hands are freezing," he said, which was how she knew she'd touched him. Her intentions were scientific. She expected the red roses to feel warmer than the silvery moon, but the temperature was exactly the same.

The bedroom was very cold, as though a window had been left open. It's possible he carried her there. A streetlamp cast shadows through the paisley curtains. In the half-light his body seemed decorated for battle, streaked with paint or clay.

Sometime later she woke in the dark, her throat aching. She crept into the living room to gather her clothes, dressed silently, and went out into the cold.

13

When Timmy woke she was already gone, the room filled with sunlight. The light was disorienting. He felt that he'd been asleep for days, weeks possibly. He hadn't slept so deeply in years.

Naked, he wandered into the living room, which looked normal—the usual disaster, ashtrays overflowing. The living room looked exactly the way it always looked, except that one couch cushion was slightly askew. There was no other suggestion that anything extraordinary had happened. He felt a stupid affection for the misplaced cushion. If not for the misplaced cushion, he'd have thought he'd made the whole thing up.

He would have liked to wake up with her, to see her in daylight. He imagined them drinking coffee, eating breakfast, doing the ordinary things people did. He tried to see the apartment through her eyes: the chin-up bar he'd hung in the doorway, the unused weight bench. The plastic milk crates overflowing with clutter: a pair of busted headphones, power cords and remote controls to electronics he no longer owned.

He had never seen her in daylight.

The apartment wasn't set up for visitors. He had a coffee maker somewhere, an old Mr. Coffee that had once belonged to his parents. His refrigerator contained batteries, a case of beer, and a crusted assortment of aging condiments.

The apartment wasn't set up for anything but what it was actually used for: the smoking and selling of weed.

Timmy replaced the couch cushion and saw that she had, in fact, left something behind: the bag of product she'd bought and paid for, an eighth of Cocoon. *I should call her*, he thought, but of course it was impossible. Every text message they'd ever exchanged had been deleted immediately, his standard operating procedure. He had never saved her number to his phone.

He met the buyer in a grocery store parking lot. They had exchanged a half dozen messages: the condition of the engine, the asking price, when and where to meet for a test drive. The guy, Ross Weaver, was clearly new to Craigslist. Timmy had used the site for years, to buy and sell car parts, vinyl records, Bruins memorabilia, electronics. Never once had he given anyone his last name.

Weaver rolled up in a taxi, a tall, skinny guy underdressed for the weather, in faded red chinos and a floppy trench coat.

"Sorry I'm late," he said. "Intense traffic coming from Newton." Over Timmy's shoulder he studied the car. "Wow. Wow. She's in beautiful shape."

Timmy flinched. There was, he felt, a special section of hell reserved for people who referred to cars as "she."

Weaver ran his finger along the trim. "Is this original?"

The question offended him slightly. "Yep," Timmy said, popping open the hood. "Like I said, the transmission is completely rebuilt. New alternator and fan belt. The battery is a year old. You should get another five years out of it."

"Awesome," Weaver said, barely looking. "Can we take her for a spin?"

They got into the car. Timmy sat in the passenger seat, where Claudia had sat the night before. He slouched down low and studied the dashboard. He wanted to see everything from her perspective, the Cuda exactly as she had experienced it, the world through the windshield of this magnificent car.

Weaver backed out of the parking space. Timmy was aware of holding his breath. Years ago, working a show for the Stagehands, he spotted in the crowd a girl he'd banged in high school and had all but forgotten, now making out with some dirtbag who never let go of her ass. When Ross Weaver turned the key in the ignition, he had a similar feeling: that he'd been robbed of a thing he'd thrown away with both hands.

Timmy noticed, then, the guy's bare ankles.

"Dude," he said gravely. "Where'd you come from?" There was still a foot of snow on the ground. No local guy—not even a douchebag from Newton—would walk around without socks.

"The Bay Area. San Francisco," Weaver said.

They pulled out into traffic. Timmy saw immediately Weaver was a terrible driver, anxious and aggressive. He braked too hard, signaled too early. He shifted clumsily, grinding the gears.

Timmy imagined telling the story to Claudia. *So the fuckwad stops at a yellow light.* Claudia, he felt, would share his outrage.

"I haven't driven a stick in a while," he said, confirming a truth Timmy had always known. Only a twat drove an automatic.

"You'll get used to it," Timmy said. "Drive this car for a week and you'll never want to drive anything else."

"The car isn't for me, actually. It's for my son."

"No shit." A sour feeling in Timmy's stomach. "How old is he?"

"Sixteen. He just passed his driver's test."

"I have a kid that age," said Timmy. "Well, almost. He'll be fifteen next month."

Weaver grinned. "Good luck, my friend. Fifteen is the worst. Luke put us through hell. Three schools, rehab, you name it. But he's come out the other end. The car is his reward."

Timmy thought, *You get a reward for that?*

"I've been looking for one of these for a while," Weaver said. "Plenty of scammers out there. *Everyone* says mint condition. Then you find rust in the undercarriage."

"Not this one," said Timmy. "Have a look if you don't believe me."

"No need. I can see she's in great shape. You made a great investment," Weaver said. "It's a hell of a business model. You buy a car that's forty or fifty years old, the cars we wanted when we were kids. The nostalgia market. It's how you get guys our age, at their peak earning power. That's the sweet spot. The old guys don't care anymore, and younger guys don't have the dough."

They rolled back into the parking lot. Weaver pulled into a space and engaged the brake. He reached into his coat and handed Timmy a sealed envelope, looking over his shoulder. "This feels a little sketchy. I mean, I never carry cash."

Timmy, who always carried cash, slid his finger beneath the flap.

Weaver looked alarmed. "You're going to *count* it?"

"No offense." Timmy thought, *Why the fuck would I not count it? I've never seen you before in my life.*

"None taken. Just . . ." Weaver glanced around nervously. "This isn't the best neighborhood."

Timmy blinked. He'd chosen the meeting place carefully, a high-end grocery store in gentrified Jamaica Plain, where a small apartment went for a half million—still a rough neighborhood, apparently, to a man in pink pants.

He counted quickly. After twelve years in a cash business, he could have done it in his sleep. "Looks like we're good," he said.

"It's been a pleasure doing business with you." Weaver offered his hand. "Sorry, I never got your last name."

For a second, from long habit, Timmy hesitated—

stupidly, because the guy would see his full name the minute he handed over the title.

"Flynn," he said. "Tim Flynn."

He watched the car drive away. Even at twenty miles per hour, Ross Weaver rode the brake. Handing him the title, Timmy had felt a wave of sadness and guilt. Selling the Cuda to this douchebag was unfair to the Cuda.

Timmy thought how he and Claudia had driven it together, almost without speaking. Her eyes had never left the road.

As the car disappeared around the corner, he raised his hand in a salute.

With Weaver's cash in his pocket, he set out walking. The snow had melted and refrozen, melted and refrozen. The surface was crusted over with grime.

When he arrived at the tattoo shop, Connor was sitting at the front flipping through a magazine. Timmy saw him through the plateglass window: his skinny arms and Cub Scout chest, the knobby bones of his shoulders poking through his T-shirt. He looked not much older than Timmy's son, and yet he possessed an awesome talent. The last twenty-four hours of Timmy's life, remarkable as they were, were due entirely to Connor. Connor's ink had gotten him laid. How exactly this had happened was, to Timmy, a mystery. Taking off his shirt had seemed natural, inevitable even. He hadn't even remembered to suck in his gut.

The hours spent in Connor's chair, the hundreds of dollars he'd spent, the countless bags of weed. Timmy understood, now, the point of it all. He'd done it so somebody would read him, the entire story of him written on his skin.

He studied his back in the mirror.

"I had an idea," Timmy said. "Is there room for a person?"

Jumping the gun, probably, but he couldn't help himself. Later, if things worked out, they could add her name.

14

"This is pointless," Luis said.

They sat shoulder to shoulder in the front office, looking at security footage on his computer screen. Claudia wished that she'd gone home to shower. From Timmy's she had driven straight to work, in yesterday's clothes—reeking, probably, of sex and weed.

The front office was tiny. One wall was mounted with video screens, six different views of the clinic: the waiting room and reception desk, the long corridor that led to the exam rooms, the front and back doors, the sidewalk out front. On the desk beside Luis's computer sat Claudia's laptop, the browser pointed to the *Hall of Shame*.

"My eyes are starting to cross," Luis said. "I need a break."

"Ten more minutes," Claudia said.

The security footage was grainy, indistinct. To save time they watched it on quadruple speed. Even compressed, it was short on action. The protestors were unbelievably boring to watch. Claudia thought of Puffy, who showed up at the clinic each morning to do absolutely nothing. How could he stand it? What, exactly, kept him coming back?

Luis leaned forward in his chair and fiddled with the laptop. *Click to begin slide show.* They watched in silence as one woman after another flashed across the screen.

"You know what's weird about this?" he said.

"Everything?"

"Well, yeah. But also . . ." He paused. "They're all White."

Claudia blinked. In truth, she hadn't noticed. It was, for her, an illuminating moment: the limits of her vision, her own dumb parallax. What else had she failed to see?

Luis stared intently at the screen. "Whoa, what's he doing?"

"Who?"

"That guy in the back." He paused the playback and rewound by a few seconds. On the screen, a slight female figure moved jerkily toward the front door.

"Okay, watch this guy." Luis pointed to the bottom left corner of the screen. A male figure hovered at the edge of the crowd. He stood awkwardly with his elbows out, hands at chest height. He seemed to be holding something.

"He's taking a photo," Luis said.

They rewound the playback and watched again, on the slowest speed. One frame at a time, the female figure—dressed in black tights and clunky boots—made its way to the door.

"Wait. I know her," Claudia said, squinting. "Maybe. I think she's one of my Access patients." As soon as she said it, she wasn't sure. The video was grainy, the resolution muddy. "Can you zoom in on her face?"

Luis did. The resolution got even fuzzier, but Claudia could discern the point of flickering light, the diamond stud above the girl's top lip.

"That's Shannon," she said, her heart racing. "The patient I told you about that night at the pub. She said some guy took her picture, but I didn't believe her."

They paused the playback, rewound and played it again. Frame by jerky frame, Shannon approached the door. From the bottom left corner of the screen, the guy in the Sox cap moved toward her—a White guy in a down jacket and Red Sox cap, holding a cell phone.

"Can't you get any closer?" Claudia asked.

"Nah, that's the best we can do."

She squinted. The man was younger than Puffy, a little taller, but identically dressed. He raised the phone to chest height for just a second. Then he glanced briefly over his shoulder, his hand to his face, and stepped out of the frame.

"Did you see that?" she said, pointing. "He hid his face!"

She felt vindicated, weirdly elated. The guy had avoided the security cameras on purpose. To Claudia it was an admission of guilt.

Her feeling of triumph was short-lived. What had they learned, exactly? The photographer was a non-descript White guy in a Sox cap. There was no more common phenotype in the city of Boston. She saw this guy fifty times a day.

"Now we know who to look for," said Luis. "The next time he shows up, I'll be waiting for him."

For the first time in many months, Claudia left work early. She felt grimy, overcaffeinated, desperate for a shower. She retrieved her car from the garage under the Common and joined the scrum of traffic—remembering, again, why she always took the T.

Rush hour huffed and honked around her, the daily

disaster. A motorized wheelchair stalled in a crosswalk. An irritable driver leaned on his horn. Driving in Boston was like being inside a video game, a closed system with its own interior logic. The streets were booby-trapped with hidden dangers: broken glass in the road, raised manhole covers, kamikaze pedestrians. On a traffic island a man was weeping. It seemed like a reasonable response.

When her phone rang she nearly didn't answer. The caller was an unfamiliar number with a 617 area code.

"Oh, *Stuart!*" she said when she heard his voice. "I didn't recognize the number." They had spoken only yesterday. It felt like a long time ago.

"I'm at the lab," he said, sounding rushed. "Listen, Nora just called. I know it's last-minute, but is there any chance you're free Saturday? She wants to switch weekends."

Such conversations had become routine between them: the complexities of Stuart's custody arrangement, the ongoing negotiations with his ex-wife. His life was complicated. If he and Claudia wanted to get laid regularly, they had to be organized.

"I can't," she said quickly. "I have to run up to Maine. To check on my mom's place." Already she'd postponed the trip twice, due to two *monster nor'easters.* Now she was grateful for the excuse. Twelve hours earlier, she'd climbed out of another man's bed. She needed to collect herself.

At home she showered at great length. The spray landed like needles on her skin. She thought of Timmy's bare face, the face of a stranger. When he'd answered the door he'd already seemed naked.

The first part of the evening, she recalled vividly. The magnificent car, traffic lights flashing. The dull thump of windshield wipers, regular as a heartbeat; a thousand snowflakes melting on the glass. What happened later, in the half-light of Timmy's bedroom, was less clear, but the sting of the shower offered certain clues.

His face was not as smooth as it looked. She had experienced this before: the treachery of blond stubble. Her breasts were scraped raw, her thighs and belly.

Her skin remembered everything.

That night she lay awake a long time, thinking of the bag of weed she'd bought from Timmy—still sitting, probably, on the couch where she'd left it. All she had to do was text him: **Hey, are you awake?** In half an hour she could be smoking a bowl and watching his giant television. In thirty-five minutes she could be back in his bed.

Finally she gave up on sleep and turned on the television. Once again, *Dateline* was in full swing.

This episode did not disappoint. It satisfied in all the usual ways. The victim was a mother of four, a beloved Sunday-school teacher, a loyal wife, sister, neighbor, and friend. And yet her virtue did not save her. Her husband had snuffed out her life using a pillow from the marital bed. He was, it developed, a man of unsavory habits, a compulsive gambler with a much younger, distinctly nonmaternal piece on the side.

"The victim lived a low-risk lifestyle," the homicide detective said.

The victim did not venture out after dark without male supervision. She did not drink or take drugs or associate with people who did. She did not, *even once*—in an impaired state, at the end of a long winter, in a *grand mal* seizure of loneliness and anxiety and paralyzing grief—fuck her weed dealer.

Not even once.

When Claudia went driving with Timmy, she left her phone behind. She wanted to disappear with him. She wanted never to be found.

If someone strangled her tomorrow, *Dateline* would have no interest. Of this she was absolutely sure.

15

Luther lived in a prefab house in the north end of Bakerton—a single-story cracker box held together with cheap plastic siding, textured to look like wood. To Victor the place looked flimsy as a Popsicle stand. Its only notable feature was the sturdy wooden ramp that led to the front door.

He parked his truck and stepped down, thinking how it took balls to live in such a house, which announced to the world that a disabled person lived there—a man unable to navigate the world on his own two legs, whose survival depended on a battery-operated chair. In the post-collapse world, the ramp would be a liability. Knowing this, Luther had taken appropriate precautions. Long ago he'd given Victor a tour of his arsenal: enough firepower to equip a small army.

Luther, no question, had balls of steel.

The front door was open a crack, the screen door latched. Victor could hear the whir of the chair as Luther rolled to the door. He was already deep in conversation, which was classic Luther. You simply tuned him in, like a radio station. It was clear he'd be having the same conversation anyway, whether or not you were in the room.

Today he was talking about the Ebola virus, which had been created in a lab in New Mexico by Purdue Pharmaceuticals. He paused briefly to acknowledge Victor's presence.

"You been following this horseshit?" he asked rhetorically, pushing open the screen door.

Victor stepped inside. It was best to let him talk awhile. Luther's house was very dark, the shades pulled to the windowsills, the few pieces of furniture spaced far apart to make a path for the chair. The perimeter of the room was lined with cardboard boxes, stacked three deep. A regular customer at the VA, Luther had made friends with a nurse there. For years he'd been stockpiling medicines and syringes, surgical masks and latex gloves.

"First they cook up the virus. Then—believe it!— they try and sell you a cure."

Luther was obsessed with infections, communicable

diseases of all kinds. In prepper circles he was considered odd, but not extraordinary. The community was full of lunatics—Rapture lunatics, climate change lunatics, Gold Standard lunatics. Luther was a virus lunatic. He could talk about viruses for hours on end. Victor found him tedious, but for strategic reasons maintained friendly relations. Luther would be a valuable ally when SHTF. It was the great lesson of prepping: everyone had their pluses and minuses. Luther couldn't outrun an assailant, but he was a trained medic. He could set a bone, dress a wound, excise a bullet. In the post-collapse world, these would be valuable skills.

"You believe this shit?" Luther demanded.

Victor waited for him to continue. When he didn't, a response seemed necessary.

"Fuckin' A," Victor said.

He followed Luther outside to the patio, where the generator was waiting. It looked to be in decent shape, the same model Victor had at home.

"Crank her up, if you want," said Luther. "I tested her out this morning, but I guess you want to see for yourself."

Victor did. The motor turned over with a satisfying roar.

"Looks good to me," he said. "I got one already. This is just for backup. What do you want for it?"

Luther said, "Got any meat?"

Victor felt his face heat. This time of year, the chest freezer in his basement should have been full of wild game.

"Nah," he mumbled. "I got nothin'."

"Huh. I thought for sure you'd have something. Don't get your back up," he added hastily, reading Victor's glowering face. "What else have you got?

For the first time in forty years of hunting, Victor had failed to get his deer.

It wasn't for lack of trying. In retirement he had nothing but time. He could hunt every day if he wanted to, and for most of the fall and winter, this was exactly what he did. The results were disappointing, a succession of inexplicable near misses. He blamed the Commonwealth of Pennsylvania. Early in the season, after a close call with a game warden, he'd switched to bow hunting. (In Pennsylvania, even a convicted felon was permitted to own a bow.) This should have posed no problem, and in other years it hadn't. But in the winter of 2015, for reasons Victor couldn't fathom, he did not get his deer.

The third week in January, on the final day of archery season, he'd set out in darkness. A fresh snow had fallen, ideal for tracking. The moon was bright and full. High on the ridge north of Garman Lake, he settled in. An ideal spot, patchy forest with good sightlines. Time and again, it had proved lucky. A dozen deer had met their ends here. His shooting spot was so extremely lucky that Victor had kept it secret for twenty years. He'd have revealed its location only on his deathbed and only to his son, if he had one. Being sonless, he would carry the secret to his grave.

But this time, luck failed him. He waited two full hours and spotted nothing. This late in the season, the population had thinned. He was about to give up when he glimpsed, in the periphery, a flicker of movement. A sleek little doe nosed at the ground beneath a stand of bushes. Too small and too far, Victor decided, and did not take the shot.

The doe wandered off and then came back, closer this time. She paused a moment, broadside, as though daring him to take the shot.

He took the shot.

He would regret it later, but at the time he couldn't help himself. The doe was taunting him. She was at most—at most!—fifteen yards away.

The doe sprang up high, then crashed into the bushes. Victor scrambled to his feet.

Fifteen yards away, the bushes were still moving,

but the doe was gone—immediately and completely, as though she had never existed. On the snow was a round blood spot the size of a ripe plum. Victor bent and touched a finger to it.

Deep dark blood. Good hit.

He plowed his way into the bushes, stiff and ungainly, a slow, lumbering creature on two feet.

The sun was rising now, the doe's tracks clearly visible. Her hooves had barely nicked the snow. At regular intervals the ground was spotted with blood, brighter now. The effect was festive and strangely beautiful, like rose petals in the snow.

North of the ridge, without warning, the trail disappeared. How was it even possible? No blood, no hoofprints. It was as if the doe had been whisked into a helicopter.

Victor retraced his steps.

How had he missed her in the first place? A stationary creature, standing broadside, barely fifteen feet away.

He tracked the doe for a solid hour and never found her, a fact that shamed him. Somewhere north of Garman Lake, his doe was bleeding out.

In the end he slunk back to the house empty-handed. *No luck?* said Randy.

Victor said, *I didn't see a goddamn thing.*

He drove away from Luther's feeling satisfied. His truck felt heavy, sated, its rear end anchored to the road by the generator's weight. He'd brought along a couple of two-by-fours to fashion a ramp; with the help of Luther's neighbor, he'd pushed the generator up the ramp into the truck. He would come back later with a cord of firewood from Randy's back forty, a massive dead tree they'd cut in the fall.

When he arrived back at the cabin, the front door was unlocked. Unlocked! Immediately his adrenaline kicked in, the fight-or-flight response. He doubled back to the truck and took his EDC from the glove box. He crossed the living room on tiptoe and crept down the hall.

In the office he found Randy sitting at the computer. "Jesus Christ, Victor! Don't shoot!"

Victor lowered his weapon. "Randy, man. What are you doing in here?"

"Just looking. I wanted to see your girls." Randy frowned, clearly mystified by Victor's taste in pornography. Splashed across the screen was a digital contact sheet, twenty or thirty thumbnail images of fully clothed women.

Victor said, "It's not what you think."

He explained, then, about the Hall of Shame. "Every

one of those girls is a cold-blooded killer. I want the world to know what they're up to."

Randy closed one eye, as though pondering this. He seemed genuinely perplexed. "What for?"

"What do you mean, what for?" Victor felt his face heating, his patience draining away. "What if that was *your* child she's carrying?"

Randy's eyes widened. "It *ain't!*" Outrage in his voice, the righteous indignation of the falsely accused. "I'm dead serious, Victor. I never touched a single one of them girls."

"I never said you did. I said *what if. What if* that was your child?"

Randy looked dumbfounded. "How could it be?"

"Never mind that. That isn't the point." Victor set his weapon carefully on the desk. "The point is, innocent lives are at stake. These whores are about to kill their precious babies."

"They're hoors?"

Randy studied the screen with renewed interest.

"*To kill their precious babies,*" Victor repeated for emphasis. "I guess that's all right with you."

"It ain't my business." Randy hoisted himself out of the chair. "I'm going to go start supper."

Victor sat in the chair, now unpleasantly warm from another man's ass. He took his time opening his email, prolonging the anticipation. Checking email had become the source of all pleasure, the most exciting moment of the day. More and more, the rest of his life seemed like filler, a feeling familiar from his drinking days. He waited for new photos the way he'd once waited for eight o'clock, when he'd park for the night, stretch out in the cab with a bottle of Jack Daniel's, and drink himself happy.

He glanced at the clock. It was nearly four in the afternoon, a promising hour: his West Coast lieutenants finally awake, his East Coast lieutenants winding down their day. At four p.m., he might have photos from San Diego or Kansas City or Atlanta. He might have photos from absolutely anywhere.

But not today.

His inbox was full of garbage, mail-order pharmacies selling steroids and painkillers and Mexican Viagra, lonely Danish virgins seeking companionship online. His inbox contained nothing of note except a message from Anthony. **THE VIDEO!! See attached.**

Victor clicked irritably—not understanding, yet, that everything was about to change.

In the video, snow was falling fast. Traffic noise, a car horn in the distance. The camera seemed unsure where to focus. The first few seconds were a jumble of back and legs. Finally it homed in on a small dark-haired figure in—surprise!—a puffy jacket.

For Pete's sake, Victor thought.

As promised, this one was White, but as far he could tell had nothing else going for her. Her hair was chopped short. A name, **Columbia**, was embroidered on her jacket, in the spot where a breast would be. To Victor she looked neither male nor female, a small stubborn asexual person in a stocking cap.

The video was poor quality. Anthony's breathing was audible, snotty and adenoidal. The female—definitely a female; the chirping voice was unmistakable—was talking to someone off camera. A man's left arm and shoulder were visible, holding a colorful sign. ABORTION CAUSES BREAST CANCER.

Well, goddamn.

Victor had to admit, the sign was good. Better than good: the sign was terrific. The sign was so mind-blowingly good that he wished he'd made it himself.

Your sign is factually inaccurate, the female shrieked. *There is no connection at all between abortion and breast cancer.*

Her face came in and out of focus. Anthony, clearly, lacked a steady hand.

The snowflakes flashed and flickered. They glowed like volcanic ash.

The female talked and talked. Victor's mind began to wander. Her voice annoyed him. Also, Anthony's breathing was getting on his nerves.

Abortion is not a risk factor! Having breasts is a risk factor!

And in that split second, everything shifted. Victor saw exactly why Anthony had recorded this moment.

He went back to the beginning and watched again, analyzing his own reaction. The female wasn't particularly attractive, not at all his type. She had a sharp little face and very dark eyebrows, which made her look angry. For the first minute exactly, he hated her: the nagging voice, the butch haircut, the certainty. The inescapable, infuriating, should-be-melted-in-an-oven puffy jacket.

Then, at sixty seconds, the earth shifted. He heard the quaver in her voice. There was no question in his mind that tears were coming. There was no question in his groin.

The snowflakes flashed and flickered. He wished that he could zoom in closer. He wished that Anthony would stop breathing.

At sixty-two seconds her eyes began to fill.

Victor paused the video to study her face.

Columbia.

He had a thing about women crying. A woman crying cracked him open with love.

The video ended abruptly. Heavy footsteps, a male voice somewhere off camera. *Sir, please step out of the way.*

Victor watched the video at half speed, at double speed. He watched it again and again.

He had so many questions.

Who was she, and how had she gotten herself into this situation? Was she a prostitute? Why did she hate children? Or was it men she hated, the man she'd been fucking? Most importantly: *Who was that man?*

Watching, he memorized every detail. A car alarm shrieking, traffic noise, a bicycle whizzing past. In the middle distance, just above her left shoulder, a street sign was visible. mercy.

Columbia, he thought. It wasn't really her name— Victor knew this—but he needed something to call her. She cried efficiently, with heroic force. At fifty-nine seconds her face was impassive, still as granite. At sixty-one seconds, her eyes closed briefly.

At sixty-three seconds she cried two tears exactly. A single fat tear shot down each cheek.

Every small, blessed detail. Her earlobes were

pierced with tiny silver hoops. Victor imagined her getting dressed that morning, choosing the outfit she'd wear for her abortion. That she had worn jewelry bothered him deeply. It seemed inhuman. This was more or less what he'd expect from a woman about to kill her baby, except that Columbia was not inhuman. Her distress was palpable. It couldn't have been clearer to Victor: *she didn't want to do this.* She seemed ready to collapse from grief.

mercy. The name seemed significant.

Every detail seemed like a gift.

The deep male voice at the end of the recording. *Sir, please step out of the way.* Was it his imagination, or did the guy have an accent? Was this the man Columbia had been fucking, whose baby she was about to kill?

When he thought of it that way, he almost felt sorry for the guy. Almost, but not quite.

He watched the video again. He was starting to hate the protestor a little. It was more than sign envy: the guy, whoever he was, was standing too close to her. It was a pet peeve of Victor's, an uncontrollable impulse. He had a similar reaction while watching porn. A solitary female, that was his preference: a beautiful female undressing, preparing herself for him. Seeing another man touch her ruined his pleasure. It distracted him from the business at hand.

If another man touched her, Victor lost all interest in fucking. He wanted to beat the crap out of the guy and keep the female for himself.

At sixty seconds he hit pause. He studied her frozen face, the frowning dark eyebrows, and suddenly it hit him.

He had seen her before.

16

Anthony stood at the curb waving. From a distance he might have been a father putting his child on the school bus, except that the bus was an airport shuttle and the person waving back was sixty or seventy years old. His mother looked ready for battle, her hair helmet freshly lacquered, frozen in place. Beneath her gray wool coat, she wore a new pink tracksuit, suitable for walking the beaches of Jupiter, Florida, with his aunt Doris.

He watched the bus disappear down the street. Then he went back inside the house, where clocks were ticking. This was not a new situation. It had been true his entire life, but he had only just noticed.

Tick, tick.

The kitchen clock had a jerky second hand, like an old man with a tremor. The digital display on the microwave oven had been flashing 12:00 for twenty years. In the living room was a grandfather clock that had belonged to Grandma Blanchard. Every half hour it bonged long and low like a foghorn. If Anthony stood sideways in front of it with both arms outstretched, his other hand would be touching an anniversary clock, which chimed on the quarter hour but ran two minutes fast.

Why did his mother, or any human being, need so many freaking clocks?

From somewhere in the house his phone rang.

He scrambled downstairs to his headquarters and found it on the desk, ringing and vibrating, jumping like a cricket. Its excitement was understandable. The phone was not accustomed to ringing.

"Who is she?" a male voice barked.

"Who is who?"

"Who do you think? The girl in the video."

The grandfather clock bonged portentously.

"How should I know?" said Anthony. "I never saw her before in my life."

"I beg to differ." Excelsior seemed out of breath. "You seen her a bunch of times. She was in that first batch of photos you sent me, way back in October. And again in November. And again on January fifth."

This was news to Anthony.

"Are you sure?" he said.

"Hell yes, I'm sure."

"Hang on, let me look." Anthony sat at the computer and located the folder for October, the first set of photos he'd taken last fall.

"Okay, I have October open. What number?"

"Zero one one," Excelsior said.

Upstairs the cuckoo clock started up, a half second behind the grandfather clock. *BONG cheep cheep. BONG cheep cheep.*

Image 011 showed a small, slender woman—a type he saw often in Boston, youngish but not young, in narrow jeans and a strange, choppy haircut. The overall effect was confusing, like a person going out of her way to be unattractive. Her eyebrows were very dark, which made her look angry. The haircut looked self-inflicted, the work of a mental patient or an untalented child. Such women did not appear on television, where everyone was attractive, or in Grantham, where no one was.

"Are you sure that's the same one?"

"Are you blind?" Excelsior seemed ready to choke. "Now look at November seventh. Number zero zero four."

BONG cheep cheep. BONG cheep cheep.

Image 004 showed a woman in a blue rain slicker. She had eyes, a nose, a mouth. Only the eyebrows were similar. If not for the eyebrows, she might have been anyone.

"I'm not great with faces," Anthony admitted. "But yeah, I guess there's a resemblance."

"Now look at January fifth. Image thirty-one."

Anthony did. In January she'd worn a puffy jacket, a stocking cap pulled down low. He couldn't see her eyebrows.

"That's HER!" Excelsior barked. "The one from the video. What's she doing at an abortion clinic in October *and* November *and* January? How many abortions can one female possibly have?"

BONG cheep cheep. BONG cheep cheep.

Anthony studied the images side by side.

"She's there all the time," he said, suddenly certain. "I think she works there."

Silence on the line.

"She *works* there," Excelsior repeated. "Which means—what? She's there every day?"

"How should I know?" Anthony was getting aggravated. He'd sent Excelsior hundreds of photos, and had never received a thank-you. Every once in a while he hinted—*How did you like the pix?*—and rarely got a response. He hated himself for asking. Asking for praise was like reminding someone it was your birthday. He shouldn't have to ask.

"I need more pics," Excelsior said. "Of her specifically. Can you do that?"

BONG cheep cheep. BONG cheep cheep.

Anthony said, "I can go tomorrow."

Excelsior said, "Go today."

The commuter boat was crowded. The ride was choppy, a brisk wind blowing, the first hint of a nor'easter rolling in. Anthony stared intently at the horizon. Though he badly wanted to, he knew better than to close his eyes.

In the City of Boston, snow was flying. The sidewalks had all but vanished. Grainy piles marked the intersections, studded with the usual inclusions—cigarette butts and gray chewing gum, frozen dog turds like artworks on display. People stepped carefully around the piles, trudged through snowbanks. Some gave up and simply walked in the road.

On Mercy Street a small crowd had gathered. The fat priest mumbled a half-assed Rosary. Anthony recognized the old guy in the Sox cap, who had a kindly face. Inspired by his example, Anthony had begun wearing his own Sox cap to the clinic. He wasn't a fan, exactly, but he wasn't *not* a fan. In baseball season, which it now wasn't, the cap would be a conversation starter. He and the old guy could talk about how the Sox were doing, as men did.

He took his place at the edge of the crowd. As per

usual, no one acknowledged his presence. As per usual, he was the invisible man.

He chose his position carefully, mindful of the security cameras. A few women came and went. He took a discreet photo—realizing, too late, that the girl in the photo was Chinese. *Well, too bad,* he thought. Taking photos in a nor'easter was a precarious exercise. Already his feet were numb, his hands freezing; he'd had no choice but to take off his gloves. Whoever showed up was who he photographed. If he managed to get the girl's face in the frame without dropping his phone, it counted as a win.

Anthony waited and waited, feeling irritated. He had missed the morning Mass, the coffee and donuts. His entire day was off-kilter. He was about to hang it up when a woman approached, sipping from a Starbucks cup—a small woman in a puffy jacket, her dark eyebrows knitted in a frown.

He was reaching for his phone when a man came out of the building.

"Sir," he called in Anthony's direction. "Sir, what are you doing?"

Anthony froze.

"One of our patients told me that someone was out here taking pictures. You know anything about that?"

Anthony blinked furiously. Excelsior had warned

him that this might happen. In this instance, Anthony was to assert his First Amendment rights. He was to stand tall, and stand his ground.

He looked around helplessly. For the first time ever, the priest and the Sox fan watched him with interest.

"I'm talking to you, sir. Are you the one who was taking pictures?"

Anthony opened his mouth to answer, but nothing came out.

He took off running.

He ran past the parking garage, the T stop, block after block of Chinese restaurants, fluorescent-lit like bus stations. Finally he glanced over his shoulder, but no one was following.

He felt that he had traveled a great distance. According to Google Maps, he had covered three blocks. Sick to his stomach, his head pounding, he looked around and spotted a cash machine. He withdrew a hundred bucks and texted Tim Flynn.

It's Anthony. I'm on my way.

On Tim's porch he knocked and waited. Strictly speaking, the visit was unnecessary; he still had half a bag of weed at home. But it was winter in New England, the TV weathermen full of dire warnings. *Storm preparedness*, they called it. For Anthony, that meant laying in a supply of weed. Moreover: it wasn't possible to show up at Tim Flynn's without buying something. Such were the terms of friendship.

He knocked again, thinking about Tim's face. Beardless, he looked younger, cleaner. He could literally be anyone—a Little League coach or a plumber or a bus driver, some sort of regular person who didn't sell drugs. He looked more or less the way he'd looked in high school, the smooth cheeks and clefted chin. Anthony had forgotten about the chin, which he found troubling. It was a bully's chin, the chin of a guy who might beat the crap out of you, just because.

He waited and waited, but no one came to the door.

17

The roads in Maine were clearer than Claudia had expected. At midday the sun was blinding, the power lines dripping. Wet clumps of snow fell heavily from the trees. Clayburn, Maine, seemed half-asleep. Commercial Street was quiet, the brick storefronts oddly sepulchral, like some designated historical site—a public memorial to the way people shopped in the great long-ago, before Walmart came.

She drove past the body shop, Clayburn Junior High, the Amway store—the exact route Gary Cain had taken that September afternoon in 1985, the day he taught her to drive.

North of town the roads were slippery, untraveled. On either side of Oak Hill Road, the snow looked clean enough to eat. At the bottom of the hill stood the eponymous oak, an important Birch family landmark: on a drunken Christmas Eve some years back, her uncle had wrapped a snowmobile around it. Paralyzed from the neck down, Ricky spent his final ten years in a wheelchair at the County Home, where his sister Deb still worked—conveniently located just a half mile down the road. Just beyond it lay Ricky's current address, the Congregational cemetery, as though on that snowy Christmas Eve—O Holy Night!—he had simply traveled in a straight line.

The trailer sat on a full acre just past the cemetery. Claudia's grandfather had bought the land back in the 1950s, believing it would one day be worth something. He hadn't expected his youngest daughter to park a trailer there and stay for thirty-eight years.

Of course, Deb hadn't expected that either. A trailer always seemed like a temporary solution, but Claudia knew this was an illusion. People died in them all the time. For an entire cross section of humanity, a trailer was the end point. Untold thousands of American lives ended in aluminum cans.

Her mother was fifty years old when she found the lump, younger than seemed fair or even possible. She had no family history of breast cancer, no discernible risk factors.

On a completely unrelated note, she'd never had an abortion.

A female body comes equipped with parts—breasts, ovaries, uterus—not necessary to its own survival. It was a lesson Claudia would learn over and over again, working on Mercy Street: each of these parts had the potential to kill you and might do so at any time, for reasons you would never know.

The lumpectomy left a dimple in her mother's left breast, a divot the size of a fingertip. Deb had worse scars on her knees, her elbows. Didn't everyone?

During her treatment she'd been told, again and again, how lucky she was. Her cancer had been caught early. Her prognosis was excellent. *You know what's really lucky?* Claudia thought. *Not getting breast cancer.*

If the scar were on her knee or elbow, it would not have been disfiguring, because a woman is not her knees or elbows.

Claudia could remember a student nurse—she looked to be fifteen years old—studying Deb's scar with palpable dismay. She exuded certainty, a healthy person's smug confidence: she herself would never be so unfortunate, the luckless one in nine.

Tag, you're It.

Objectively speaking, the student nurse was right: the odds were in her favor. The odds, technically, were in everyone's favor. And yet, inevitably, someone was going to be the one in nine.

In any industry Claudia could think of, this failure rate would be unacceptable. If breasts were a consumer product, the manufacturer would be forced to issue a recall.

As countless medical professionals had pointed out, her mother was lucky. Her left breast was gouged with a scalpel, blasted with radiation. Lucky, lucky! A week after the surgery, Deb was back at work, eager for life to return to normal. For her, *normal* meant taking care of kids, so she got Nicolette.

Their physical resemblance was striking. Of all the kids Deb had raised—Claudia included—Nicolette was the one who most *looked* like her daughter: sturdy and round-cheeked, a miniature Deb. Ten years old when she arrived, a chubby dark-eyed girl Deb called "part Indian," though whether she meant Native American or from the Indian subcontinent was never clear. Maybe she didn't know, or it simply didn't matter, because in her eyes Nicolette was hers entirely. She'd been raising fosters for twenty years, but this time was different. Deb herself was different.

Cancer had changed her, in ways Claudia didn't yet understand.

From the very beginning, Nicolette was a trial. She was not a lovable child. Most fosters started out wary and tongue-tied, but Nicolette's shyness evaporated quickly. By the time she entered high school, she had confidence to spare. In Claudia's opinion—and to her utter astonishment—Deb spoiled her. Not materially— she didn't have the means—but she tolerated more eye-rolling and teenage sarcasm than most people could bear. Her attempts at discipline were halfhearted. Nicolette was always in trouble: suspended from school for smoking cigarettes, arrested twice for shoplifting, busted for underage drinking when the town cop raided a kegger in the woods.

When Nicolette flunked ninth grade, Deb blamed the teachers at Clayburn High.

Claudia had shoplifted too, but she had never been caught.

In those years, Claudia learned of family news via Facebook—a rich source of local gossip, the modern equivalent of the Clayburn *Star*. Nicolette, a power user, posted a dozen times a day, so often that it was hard to imagine her doing anything else. At a certain point she'd sent a friend request that Claudia thoughtlessly accepted. Moments later she received a notification: *Nicolette Fleming has identified you as her sister. Click to Confirm.*

She didn't click. Nicolette was her mother's project, a problem she had no desire to inherit.

She thought, *You are not my sister.*

Halfway through her junior year in high school, Nicolette fell pregnant. Claudia marveled at the timing: at eighteen she would have aged out of the system, but now there was no question of her moving out of the trailer. After the baby was born, they would need a place to stay.

As Deb explained this—late one night, by phone—Claudia thought immediately of her grandparents. When Deb fell pregnant, they'd done nothing to help. Her predicament, in their eyes, was a problem of her own making—a reasonable and customary punishment for female misbehavior, no more than she deserved. With Nicolette, Deb had the opposite reaction: protective, jubilant, generous.

Her joy at the girl's pregnancy was, to Claudia, bewildering. Nicolette was a walking catastrophe. It was hard to imagine a person less equipped to raise a child.

"I know you don't want to hear this," Claudia said, "but are you sure this is a good idea?"

She pointed out the obvious: Nicolette had no high

school diploma, no job, and, with several misdemeanors on her record, little hope of finding one. Motherhood would put an end to her education, circumscribe her future. Her adult life would be a series of dead ends, over before it began.

As Claudia ticked off these items one by one, Deb said nothing. She listened in silence as Claudia lectured her on the difficulties of young single motherhood.

"She's seventeen years old," said Claudia. "She has another twenty-five years to have kids, if that's even something she wants to do. There's more to life than having babies."

She believed it then and believes it still, but she wishes she hadn't said it. For years they'd tiptoed around the subject of her work. Now, suddenly, there was nowhere to hide.

Deb said, "I don't know how you can work there."

(Here's how: never respond to this provocation. The person who says it—even if she is your mother—is trying to start a conversation you don't want to have.)

"She doesn't have to do this. Just let me talk to her. Mom," said Claudia, "this is what I *do.*"

"*No,*" Deb said sharply. "Claudia Marie, *don't you dare.*"

They were her final words on the subject. A moment later she hung up the phone.

They didn't speak again for many months. Claudia left a few messages on Deb's answering machine, but her mother didn't call back. Clearly she had nothing more to say.

At least, not to Claudia. On Facebook she posted constantly: umpteen photos of Nicolette's pregnant belly, a sonogram image bordered, literally, with hearts and flowers. Her captions were full of exclamation marks. (*My grandbaby!!!!*) Her online persona was, to Claudia, confounding: breathless, effusive, nothing at all like the stolid, taciturn woman she was in real life.

From what seemed a great distance, Claudia followed the saga of Nicolette's pregnancy. The prenatal checkups, the gestational diabetes—for Deb and Nicolette, yet another experience to be shared. For years Deb had kept a container in the bathroom to dispose of her own syringes, a plastic sharps bin she'd swiped from work. When Claudia was growing up, this had seemed normal. In Clayburn, everyone was diabetic; shooting insulin was a badge of adulthood, like getting a driver's license. She learned later that this wasn't unique to Clayburn; it was true wherever people were poor. At work she encountered diabetes all the time, in shockingly young patients from Dorchester or Chelsea—urban food deserts where moldering produce

334 • JENNIFER HAIGH

was shrink-wrapped and sold at a premium and shitty fast food was practically free.

Nicolette's food cravings, her backaches and heartburn. Claudia read the posts grudgingly, sourly, filled with childish aggrievement. Later she saw the feeling for what it was, a kind of sibling rivalry. By getting knocked up in high school, Nicolette had accomplished something Claudia had never managed. She had made their mother proud.

Their mother. Nicolette wasn't her sister, but she was—Claudia saw it clearly—Deb's daughter. She had followed in Deb's footsteps, made the exact same choices, while Claudia had done the opposite. For as long as she could remember, her mother's example had informed her every decision. For Deb, getting pregnant at seventeen had been determinative. For Claudia, dealing with unplanned pregnancies—prevention, remediation—was more than a career. It was her mission, her life's work.

Nicolette's pregnancy was, for Claudia, a surreal reversal. She felt wounded by her mother's joy. At the time it felt like a personal rebuke, a resounding judgment on the life she'd made for herself, Deb flipping the bird at all she'd done and all that she was.

As (a reasonable person might argue) Claudia had always done to her.

Nicolette's baby was born on May first, Deb's birthday. It was—Deb wrote on Facebook—the best birthday present of her life. That was . . . four years ago? Five? Claudia couldn't say exactly. It was the defining feature of a life without children: the ability to ignore the passage of time.

The trailer faced westward, a magnet for snowdrifts. The place looked deserted. Under the carport were fresh tire tracks, but no car. In the front yard was a large plastic nativity scene, with figures the size of first graders: Mary and Joseph, baby in the manger, shepherd and camels in supporting roles. The rickety porch was laden with junk—a child's bike with training wheels, a hibachi, an electric bug zapper, remnants of a long-ago summer now encrusted in snow.

Claudia parked on the road and picked her way through the snow. The curtains were closed, the front-facing windows covered in plastic sheeting— "winterized," her uncle Ricky used to say. When she was a kid they'd done this every year, in October or November, to cut down on drafts. Claudia's job was to hold the plastic tight against the window frame as Ricky duct-taped it into place. Seen through plastic, the outdoors had appeared remote and indistinct. For half the year, the universe narrowed to the dimensions of the trailer. In May the plastic would be peeled away, and the world would come back into focus.

The porch steps were unshoveled, the railing strung with tiny lights. Illuminated on a snowy night they may have been beautiful, but in the bright sunshine they looked like what they were: cheap plastic destined for the landfill.

The door was hung with a pine wreath, decorated with a printed ribbon: JOY TO THE WORLD! THE LORD IS COME. When Claudia knocked, a shower of dry needles fell to the floor.

"Nicolette?" she called. "It's Claudia. Are you home?"

A curtain moved in the kitchen window, or maybe it didn't. Her mother's wind chimes, rusted now, tinkled in the breeze.

She knocked again, listening for movement.

"Nicolette, I'm coming in."

Her key slid into the lock but wouldn't turn. She saw, then, that the door handle had been replaced.

Nicolette had changed the locks.

Well, now what? She'd driven three hundred miles on winter roads to be locked out of an empty trailer. She dialed Nicolette's number, but still no one was answering. She had no idea where Nicolette was, how long she'd been gone or when she would return.

She got back into the car and started the engine, cranked the heater to warm her hands. She was about to head back to Boston when the porch light came on. A moment later, Nicolette opened the door.

"Claudia?" she called. "What are you doing here?" She looked sleepy, disheveled, older and heavier than Claudia remembered. It seemed inconceivable that Nicolette was half her age.

"I was just about to leave," she said, stepping out of the car. "I knocked, but you didn't answer."

"I was sleeping."

Claudia thought, *It's one in the afternoon.*

"I came to check on the place," she said, climbing the icy porch stairs. "I guess you made it through the storm okay."

Inside, nothing had changed. Deb had been a lackadaisical housekeeper, and Nicolette was no better: dirty dishes in the sink, the carpet dusted with potato chip crumbs like some persistent dandruff. The place smelled the way it always had, like cigarettes and air freshener. Nicolette plugged them into every spare electrical outlet, filling the trailer with the unlikely scent of potpourri.

"The power went out." Nicolette ran a hand through her lank hair—bleached blonde, but not recently. The dark roots extended nearly to her ears. "I had a bunch of meat in the freezer. I had to throw it all away."

"That's too bad," Claudia said.

"Twenty bucks' worth. I just went to the store that morning."

As always, Claudia had the distinct impression that the girl was trying to shake her down for money. A few months after Deb's funeral, Nicolette had called Claudia to complain that the lights wouldn't work. When asked if she'd paid the electric bill, Nicolette seemed taken aback, as though she were owed free utilities in addition to free rent.

Nicolette sat heavily at the kitchen table. The other chair was piled with magazines and junk mail, so Claudia remained standing.

"How've you been?" she asked.

"All right, I guess."

What was going on in her life, Claudia had no idea. On Facebook she posted jokes and prayer chains, images of sunsets with inspirational slogans: *A smile can change the world. Hope is the heartbeat of the soul.* Mostly, though, she posted photos of her daughter—a plump, serious-looking child with a bowl haircut—dressed in elaborate outfits: mermaid, Disney princess, a miniature Scarlett O'Hara with ruffled petticoats and an actual parasol. The costumes were weirdly revealing, in ways unflattering to a chubby child, her plump thighs squeezed like bratwurst into lacy stockings. The little girl seemed to know this. She wore an expression of profound dismay.

From the next room Claudia heard a child coughing, a deep, guttural hacking. "Yikes, that doesn't sound good. Has she seen a doctor?"

"It's just a cold," Nicolette said, lighting a Virginia Slim.

You shouldn't smoke indoors, Claudia thought. But she wasn't Nicolette's mother or sister or even, technically, her landlord. How Nicolette raised her child was none of her business.

"You changed the locks," she said.

Nicolette's eyes flickered. "There was a break-in up at Roy Bishop's. I was just being careful."

Claudia said, "You should have talked to me first."

Nicolette said, "I ran out of minutes."

You should've kept the landline, Claudia thought. A few weeks after Deb's funeral, the phone service was terminated, Nicolette-style: she neglected to pay the bill. Claudia would never forget calling the trailer— her childhood phone number, the first one she'd ever known by heart—and hearing an automated voice.

This number is no longer in service. Her mother's lifeline, her portal to the world. The princess phone with its endless spiraling cord.

No longer in service.

Nicolette said, "The fucker charged me a hundred sixty bucks."

It took Claudia a moment to understand that she was talking about the locksmith. First Nicolette had changed the locks without permission. Now she expected Claudia to pay for it.

She wasn't going to pay for it.

"I need a copy of the key," she said.

"I just have the one."

"No problem. I'll go to Walmart and make one." Claudia held out her hand.

"Fine." Nicolette took her key chain from its hook by the door and removed a shiny new key.

Claudia tried it in the lock to make sure it worked. She wasn't taking any chances. She thought, *I don't trust you at all.*

18

Victor waited and waited. Several times an hour he checked his inbox.

The video obsessed him. He had watched it so many times that it played constantly in his head. Even his sleep was affected. He lay awake thinking of Columbia.

I think she works there.

It was galling to know that she was at the clinic every day, unphotographed. Victor zoomed in to read the street sign in the video—MERCY—and located the address. He studied the building on Google Earth. He knew exactly where she was, and yet he couldn't get to her. It was a feeling he remembered vividly from his years inside, Barb Vance running loose in the world, forever beyond his reach.

I think she works there.

His mind glossed over this fact. What exactly Columbia did at the clinic was impossible to imagine. Was she a nurse—assisting, in some unfathomable and horrifying way, a doctor who butchered babies? Morally speaking, it was the worst news imaginable, yet in a way Victor was relieved. Better a nurse than a patient. He would rather think of her killing babies than wantonly fucking, impregnated by some guy who wasn't him.

He checked his inbox until certain conclusions were inescapable. Anthony had gone dark.

The nurses at the VA dressed in pastel scrubs, mint green or powder blue. In the video Columbia wore boots and blue jeans. She was not dressed for nursing, or any other job he could imagine a female doing.

He watched the video again, which was probably a mistake. The video was like a piece of gum rapidly losing its flavor. He knew that he was using it up, yet he couldn't stop chewing.

He needed more gum.

19

The messages were incessant. The messages, honestly, were a little much.

Excelsior11: Where are my PIX???

Thinking to buy himself some time, Anthony wrote:

LostObjects1977: You're right, she definitely works there.

Excelsior responded immediately.

Excelsior11: PIX! I need PIX!!

It was, Anthony felt, an untenable situation. He had promised more than he could realistically deliver. On the one hand, his second-best friend in the world was counting on him. On the other hand, he couldn't imagine going back to the clinic, now or ever.

(The Latino security guard, big and burly, shoulders straining his shirt.)

To get away from his computer, he put on his coat and set out walking. Mass wouldn't start for an hour, but he didn't mind being early. The choir would be practicing, Mrs. Morrison praying her Rosary, Mrs. McGann and her senile husband lighting a candle. The place would be lively as a discotheque compared to his mother's empty house.

But when he arrived at the church, the windows were dark. The stairs to the front door were covered in snow.

For Christ's sake, Anthony thought. *They couldn't shovel the freaking steps?*

For the Mrs. Morrisons of the world, the church steps were hazardous in the middle of summer. Now, encrusted with ice, they were a danger to every hip in the congregation.

He looked around for a shovel. Finding none, he walked around to the back of the church. The sidewalk was nearly impassable. He tried the door of the parish hall and found it locked. The priest's black PT Cruiser was parked in the driveway, nearly buried in snow.

"Anthony."

He turned. Quentin the Quick stood in the rectory doorway. Over his black clericals he wore a down jacket.

"Morning, Father," he called. "I was just looking for a snow shovel. Those steps are pretty icy."

"No need. Morning Mass is canceled. I asked the janitor to put a sign on the door." The priest hugged his jacket around him. "We lost power around midnight. Half the town did, apparently. Everyone east of Lisbon Avenue."

"I'm on the west side," said Anthony. "No problems over there."

The priest zipped his jacket all the way to the chin. "I'm glad you're here, actually. Won't you come inside for a moment?"

Anthony followed him into the rectory, stamping the snow from his boots. He'd been inside it only once— twenty years ago, with his father, to see the priest about Grandma Blanchard's funeral. He'd been struck, then, by the somberness of the place, the dark heavy furniture, the purple-tinged daylight through stained-glass windows. The place hadn't changed in any way he could identify. The room was so cold he could see his breath.

The priest led him into a rear office—more dark furniture, more stained glass. "Have a seat. I was going to make the announcement today, but Grantham Electric had other ideas. I'm relieved, actually. It's hard to be the bearer of bad news." The priest folded his hands on his desk. "The archbishop has informed me that St. Dymphna's is slated for closure."

The word landed with a thump.

"Closure," Anthony repeated stupidly.

"It was a fiscal decision. St. Dymphna's is an aging congregation. The parish gets smaller every year. And keeping the church open costs money. Utilities, maintenance, a custodian to shovel the snow. The Archdiocese can't afford to maintain so many small parishes. Not to mention finding a priest." Father Quentin smiled apologetically. "There's a reason we're always praying for vocations. We've had a shortage for many years, and it's only getting worse. Most of us are already covering two parishes. I spend half my life racing back and forth between Grantham and Framingham. It's an untenable situation."

There was a silence.

"So what happens now?" Anthony said.

"St. Dymphna's will be absorbed into another parish. Sacred Heart, in Dunster."

"*Dunster?*" A single two-lane road connected the

towns. On weekday mornings it was clogged with rush-hour traffic, commuters fighting their way to the interstate. Anthony thought of Mrs. Morrison and the McGanns, Mrs. Paone in her wheelchair. No way would they make that trek. He himself wouldn't make it. He tried to imagine his life without the walk to St. Dymphna's, the daily ritual that had healed his head.

"I'll make the announcement tomorrow, assuming the weather cooperates. I imagine it will be upsetting news. You seem to have quite a rapport with the older parishioners. It would be very helpful to have you on hand." The priest got to his feet. "I'm sorry, Anthony. Please understand, I have no say in the matter. I'm very fond of St. Dymphna's and I'm sad to see it go."

"Me too." Anthony had been baptized at St. Dymphna's. Grandma Blanchard had been married there, fresh off the boat from Ireland. Quentin the Quick had been there seven months.

"The Church has weathered storms before," said Father Quentin. "It is, I'm afraid, a season of storms."

Outside, the snow kept falling. Anthony spotted his own footsteps heading in the opposite direction, barely visible now, dusted over with fresh snow.

Grantham was silent, the streets muffled. Father Quentin was right: to the east of Lisbon Avenue, all the houses were dark. Dunkin' Donuts looked dead, its electric sign extinguished. Only Rite Aid appeared to be open. Anthony thought of the empty house waiting for him, its many clocks ticking. Like a refugee, he trudged toward the neon sign.

For a weekday morning, the place was hopping. At the pharmacy counter he took his place in line. His doctor had called in a new prescription—another drug that would not help him, but if Medicaid was paying he might as well pick it up. As he explained this to the clerk, he noticed a stooped, balding man studying a display of knee braces.

"Dad," he said.

His father looked startled to see him. "Antny," he said gruffly. "What are you doing here?"

They stood a moment staring at each other. His dad looked gaunt, elderly. He wore a battered Carhartt jacket, a relic from his days at Mancini Construction that now seemed too big for him. A smell clung to it, an old-person odor of mothballs and flatulence and Halls Mentho-Lyptus.

"Getting my prescription," Anthony said.

"How's things?"

"Okay, I guess."

"You working?"

"I'm on Disability."

His dad frowned as though he had some vague memory of this. "What's the matter with you?"

"My head," Anthony said.

There was a silence. Somewhere a radio was playing. A woman whose name Anthony couldn't remember sang, *I haven't got time for the pain.* He wondered if the song was part of a special pharmacy playlist, each song chosen for its special relevance to the Rite Aid customer.

The old man jammed an index finger into one ear and twiddled violently, as though he had an itch in his brain. "How's your mother?"

"She's all right. She's in Florida with Aunt Doris."

"Good for her." He turned his head and Anthony saw, then, the reason for the twiddling: a hearing aid, flesh-colored plastic, the size of a lima bean. It looked like a wad of chewing gum jammed in his ear.

No, I haven't got time for the pain.

"There's a storm coming," Anthony said.

"There's always a storm coming."

Another silence.

There was more, much more, to say: about St. Dymphna's and Quentin the Quick, the inexplicable betrayals of the Boston Archdiocese. Anthony couldn't imagine saying any of it—or anything else, really—to his father.

"Anthony Blanchard!" the pharmacy clerk called from behind the desk.

"That's me," Anthony said to the man who had, in fact, given him this name.

They stood there staring at each other. In roughly two minutes, they'd run through all their material. After two minutes, there was nothing left to say.

"They're closing St. Dymphna's," Anthony blurted.

"The church?"

"Effective immediately. They want us all to go to Sacred Heart. In Dunster."

"It happens," his father said.

Anthony was dumbstruck. His father had been baptized at St. Dymphna's, made his First Communion there. He seemed not to remember or care.

"What do you mean, 'it happens'?"

The old man looked disgusted, or maybe he didn't. Maybe that was just his face.

"Jesus, Antny. I mean it happens for a reason. They're selling off the churches to settle the lawsuits. The kids who were abused."

There was nowhere left to put the snow.

Five nor'easters in five weeks. Boston was up to here with this shit.

Life had ground to a halt and would stay ground.

Until further notice, everything was suspended: deliveries, trash pickup, mail service, bus service. Animation, judgment, disbelief.

Six feet in thirty days. The volume was unimaginable. At undisclosed locations around the City of Boston, snow farms were established. Fourteen hundred truckloads were dumped at a vacant lot in Southie. The snow was compacted dense as cement, twenty-five thousand cubic yards of snow. At city hall a plan was floated: load it into dump trucks, to be emptied into the Boston Harbor. Environmental activists cried foul. It was rumored that the snow was flammable. Spontaneous combustion was considered a danger. A hazmat team was dispatched.

Freak accidents were reported, the season's morbid fascinations. The elderly frozen in their beds, the children speared by icicles. The doomed family sedan, crushed by a falling tree.

Anthony read of these developments on his computer screen, courtesy of a satellite signal that came all the way from space. It was easier than putting on his boots and parka and trudging out to investigate; quicker, in point of fact, than stepping out onto the porch.

Because what was out there, really? Where did people actually go?

They're selling off the churches to settle the lawsuits. The kids who were abused.

A week passed, then two. One morning, for no good reason he could think of, he made his old morning trek to St. Dymphna's. The parking lot was empty, the windows dark. For a moment he contemplated driving to Dunster, the morning Mass at Sacred Heart. He was technically still licensed to drive by the state of Massachusetts. His mother's car waited in the garage, an Oldsmobile sedan from the last millennium. All he had to do was dig it out.

The garage door was blocked by a knee-high wall of drifted snow. When he took a shovel to it, it would not give; it had melted and refrozen so many times that a carapace had formed, an icy shell hard as glass.

He went back into the house and sheltered in place.

More days passed. How many days was impossible to determine and frankly, not worth the effort. Periodically he shuffled upstairs for a bowl of Lucky Charms. When the milk turned, he ate the cereal dry from the box.

He ran out of weed.

Excelsior11: Where are my PIX???

Without weed, his sleep was shallow. Tim Flynn was only a boat ride away, but the thought of getting on a boat made his stomach lurch.

He dreamed fitfully, distractedly, brief snippets of

dreams that seemed to go on for hours. In dreams he lost his shoes, his scapular, his Disability check. In an online forum he appealed to St. Anthony, the patron saint of lost objects. From the saint's profile pic, Anthony learned that he was in fact Pat Morita, the old Japanese coot who'd mentored the Karate Kid.

I have lost important objects, his dream self wrote. **Need your intercession asap.**

The saint responded with a string of emojis Anthony could not decode.

In the worst of the dreams, he was locked out of his house. Snow was flying, a monster nor'easter. The snow rose to his ankles, his knees, his hips. He was being buried alive in snow.

In desperation he messaged St. Anthony and received an autoreply:

On vacay in Florida with Dymphna ♥
Your call will be answered in the order received.

When the milk turned, he contemplated walking to Tedeschi's. Boots over his slippers, a parka over his robe. He was halfway out the door when a thought occurred to him: If he *were* locked out of the house, what exactly would he do? Call a locksmith? Maybe his father had a key, or maybe he didn't. It was a coin toss. Either way, Anthony would have to spend agonizing minutes in his father's company as they searched his sad apartment above Grandma Blanchard's garage. In his delicate state, the prospect was exhausting. It seemed a soul-crushing amount of effort just to get back to where he was at that very minute, inside the house.

He sat in a dark room holding his head.

Supplies dwindled. When the cereal was gone, he applied cream cheese to oyster crackers, which was difficult to do since each cracker was the size of a nickel. When the cream cheese was gone, he ate the crackers dry. When the oyster crackers were gone, he ordered more from Amazon.

He wished that Amazon delivered weed.

20

The conference room was packed with women—the entire full-time staff, plus thirty or forty of the volunteers. At the front of the room a projector screen had been lowered from the ceiling. Florine stood beside it, staring at a laptop. The room smelled faintly of her jasmine perfume.

She scanned the room, her lips moving slightly as she took a head count. She was dressed for battle, in a sleek dark suit and fine stilettos that could take your eye out. The rest of the staff were dressed in scrubs or blue jeans. Florine, as always, was the adult in the room.

"Thanks for being here, everyone," she said. As though they'd had a choice: an all-staff memo had informed them that the clinic would be closed to patients, the morning appointments rescheduled. This had happened before, but not recently. Even during a monster nor'easter, Mercy Street opened on time.

"As some of you may have heard, we have an ongoing security situation at the clinic." Florine spoke deliberately, choosing her words. "I know how rumors get started—I've heard some pretty outlandish ones already—so I wanted you to hear it straight from me.

"It has come to our attention that someone has been taking photos of our patients outside the clinic. We don't know who this person is, but we know it's happening because we've got him on video. The quality isn't great, so I'm going to turn down the lights to help you see."

The lights dimmed. Florine bent over her laptop and tapped briefly at the keyboard until an image appeared on the screen. It was the same footage Claudia had watched with Luis, the wide-angle view of the clinic entrance.

She'd watched it so many times that she could anticipate each frame: the protestors shifting and shuffling, Shannon F.'s jerky marionette steps as she made her way to the door, the guy in the Sox cap approaching from the edge of the screen like a hunter moving in for the kill. She felt a terrible anticipation as he raised the cell phone to his chest.

Florine paused the recording.

"This guy, whoever he is, has been uploading photos of our patients to a website. We have no reason to believe anyone is in physical danger, but our patients' privacy is a serious matter. We've been in touch with law enforcement for guidance on how to proceed."

Whispers in the room, a low hum of conversation. Florine turned up the lights.

"I know you have questions," she said. "Hit me."

A half dozen hands shot into the air. Good girls they were, polite and mannerly. They raised their hands and waited to be recognized, to be granted the right to speak.

"What about the website?" said Mary Fahey. "Do we know who built it?"

"The police are working on that," Florine said.

Another show of hands.

"This can't be legal," said Heather Chen. "Posting people's photos without permission. What about HIPAA?"

"I knew someone was going to ask that." Florine looked very alert, her sole mode of expression. "Here's the situation. According to our attorney, HIPAA is no help to us here. Health-care workers are legally bound to protect patient confidentiality, but the rest of the world isn't required to do so. And in Massachusetts, anyway, there don't seem to be any state laws that apply."

"Well, what about the site that hosts it?" Mitch called from the back of the room. "Can't we make them take it down?"

"It isn't that simple. There are First Amendment issues. I *know*," Florine said, at the groan of protest in the room.

Immediately ten conversations started at once. Florine knocked on the tabletop to get the group's attention, her silver ring loud as a gavel.

"People, people! Stay with me. This is important: we aren't the only clinic that's been targeted. The photos on the website were taken in multiple locations, probably in several different states. So there may be other state laws to consider."

"What about FACE?" Naomi asked.

"Too narrow," said Florine. "Physical force, threat of physical force, or physical obstruction. Unless this guy lays hands on a patient, or physically bars her from entering the facility, he isn't committing a crime.

"The point is, it's complicated. I don't have a lot of answers for you—yet—but I want you all to know that we're taking this very seriously. The police are aware of the situation and will be stepping up their patrols."

This was true. That morning Claudia had spotted a

BPD cruiser idling on Mercy Street, maybe fifty yards from the clinic's front door.

"If you see anyone behaving unusually outside the clinic, and especially if you see someone taking photos, let Luis know about it. I'm dead serious, people," Florine said in a husky voice.

The room fell silent. The director's poise was legendary. This was the equivalent of a normal person bursting into tears.

She recovered quickly. "That's all I've got for you at the moment. The safety of our staff and patients," she added (smoothly, in her TV voice), "is, as always, our primary concern."

When Claudia arrived at the deli, Phil was waiting.

"She lives," he said, clasping her briefly. "Where the hell have you been?"

"Nowhere. I've been nowhere." It was factually true. In the weeks since her visit to Maine, she'd been a stationary object. Except for work, she had scarcely left her apartment. Each morning she woke exhausted, as though the winter had finally caught up to her. There was simply nowhere she wanted to go. Holed up at home, she read trashy novels and watched *Dateline*. Occasionally she texted Phil to cancel lunch dates. Returning his phone calls seemed too complicated.

"Work has been crazy," she said—her all-purpose excuse.

She explained, then, about the security video, the freak in the Sox cap taking photos with his cell phone. She talked and talked, aware of the hysterical edge in her voice. She sounded crazy. She *felt* crazy. *If I didn't know me*, she thought, *I would think I'd lost my mind.*

Phil gave her his scrutinizing look.

"A website," he repeated, frowning. "Claudia, you're not making any sense."

"Wait till you see it." She pulled up the Hall of Shame and handed Phil her phone.

He scrolled and swiped, literally openmouthed. It was unsettling to see him at a loss for words.

"Wow. This is pretty elaborate," he said at last. "One guy did all this?"

"I don't see how. I mean, it's pretty clear they were taken at different clinics. I counted six different locations, and there could be more. He keeps adding more photos."

There was more she could have said. The dreams that woke her in the night, the hours—*hours*—she'd spent staring at the website. The hundreds of times she had refreshed that particular page.

"We know about one guy for sure, because we have

him on video. He came back the other day, but the security guard scared him off."

Phil said, "Have you talked to the police?"

"The police are aware. They've seen the video, they know what he looks like. Right now we're just waiting for him to come back."

"And then what?"

Claudia had been asking herself the same question.

"Well, that's kind of the problem. As far as we can tell, he isn't breaking any laws." She closed her eyes, suddenly exhausted. "But, you know, it's not harmless. There's a reason we're so careful about our patients' privacy. People are crazy on this subject."

The waitress arrived with a tray. Phil, as always, had ordered the special—today, a pastrami sandwich reeking of garlic. Claudia's omelet looked slightly congealed. The smell of egg was mildly disgusting. She pushed away the plate.

"You're not eating?" Again the scrutinizing look. "Claudia, are you all right?"

"I wish people would stop asking me that." Her head felt a little swimmy. The room was suddenly too loud, too hot. "I'm fine. A little tired."

"You need a break." Phil took a slice of toast from her plate and buttered it. "A change of scene. Weren't you supposed to go up to Maine?"

"I went. It was okay. I don't know what to say. It was—Clayburn," she said, as though that meant anything to him. In all the years they'd known each other, she had never once taken him there.

He handed her the toast and she took it, chewing obediently.

"Did Stuart go with you?"

"There is no more Stuart. Stuart is gonzo," she said. Whether he'd stopped calling, or she had simply stopped answering, wasn't clear and didn't matter. It was another argument in favor of the e-boyfriend—the most persuasive one, really. There was no need, ever, for a messy breakup. There was simply nothing to break.

Phil frowned. "I'm missing something here. What happened?"

I fucked my weed dealer, she did not say.

"Nothing," she said quickly. "No hard feelings. I wasn't that into him, honestly." Which was true, as far as it went.

She stole a glance at her phone.

"I have to run," she said, laying cash on the table. "I'm late for an appointment. My fucking mammogram. I'm *okay!*" she said, fake-exasperated. She had never been a crier. Now, for reasons she couldn't begin to articulate, she was near tears.

Despite the snow, the T was running on schedule. She took the Green Line to a busy neighborhood south of the Fenway, blocks and blocks of clinics and hospitals. It was a part of town she avoided studiously, except for this one day each year.

At the reception desk a nurse taped a paper bracelet around her wrist. In the waiting room she flipped through an issue of *Damsel*. She scanned the masthead for familiar names—her old colleagues, the assistant editors—but there were none she recognized. Twenty years later, everyone had moved on.

A young nurse appeared, dressed in pale blue scrubs. "Claudia B.?"

It was the standard HIPAA protocol they followed on Mercy Street. Claudia had used the same convention, first name plus initial, to sign the made-up letters addressed to "Ask *Damsel*." To protect the privacy of the imaginary reader, a woman living with secret agonies: cellulite, combination skin, weak, brittle nails.

She gathered her purse and coat and followed the nurse down the hall.

"Changing rooms are on your left." The nurse handed her a folded hospital gown and a locker key attached to a bracelet, a pink plastic Slinky to be worn around the wrist.

In the dressing cubicle, Claudia stripped off her sweater and stashed it in a locker. She put on the gown, a hip-length kimono wide as a Hefty bag, and wound the belt twice around her waist. As she shuffled down the hall to Gowned Waiting, she was aware of her purse, hanging ridiculously from her shoulder. The other women in Gowned Waiting looked ridiculous too, and intensely vulnerable—breasts hanging loose under the gaping kimonos, pink Slinky on one wrist, paper bracelet on the other. No one made eye contact. They all wanted to be invisible. They all wanted, simply, to disappear.

"Claudia B.?" the nurse called.

The other women in Gowned Waiting looked up expectantly. Claudia hugged her kimono around her and proceeded down the hall.

Entering the X-ray room was like stepping into a refrigerator. From a college photography class she recognized the smell, the distinctive odor of darkroom chemicals. The technician was an Indian woman in heavy black-framed eyeglasses, too large for her narrow face.

"May I see your bracelet, please?"

Claudia held out her wrist, confirmed her name and date of birth. The tech matched the digits to the numbers on the bracelet. Her eyeglasses—Claudia would remember this later—looked fake, unconvincing. They looked like they should be attached to a plastic nose.

"Given your family history, your doctor has ordered a 3D mammogram," the tech said. "I have a few questions before we get started. What was the first day of your last menstrual period?"

The eternal question.

"It's been a while," Claudia said. "A couple months, maybe? My cycles are kind of messed up."

"Perimenopause?"

"Probably." She'd had no symptoms yet, nothing resembling a hot flash, but at age forty-three, menopause couldn't be far away.

"Any chance you might be pregnant?"

Incredibly, she'd needed someone to ask the question. Until she was asked the question, the possibility didn't cross her mind.

That night, sleep was impossible. Claudia lay in bed with her hand on her belly—still flat, but not for much longer. On her way home she'd stopped at CVS and, though she'd already flunked one at the hospital, bought a pregnancy test. The second test was wishful thinking—a Hail Mary pass, just in case.

Hail Mary, full of grace. There was more to the prayer, but Claudia had never learned it. She understood the words only in football terms, the doomed audacity of the long-distance pass.

She lay awake and thought of her mother, gone forever. There was no one else she wanted to tell.

The numberless ways Claudia had hurt her. When she married Phil, she didn't invite Deb to the wedding. She knew it was an unforgivable breach. Her mother loved weddings. In Clayburn, they were raucous affairs, all-day bacchanals at the AmVets or the Rod and Gun Club. Deb, a perennial bridesmaid, had an entire closet full of hideous dresses in a vast range of sizes, each bought on layaway and paid for in installments and worn only once.

Deb loved weddings, even though—or maybe because—she'd never had one herself.

She wouldn't come anyway, Claudia told Phil, which may have been true. Her reasoning went like this: a city hall ceremony wasn't a real wedding. It was a statutory requirement, like taking a driver's test. And nothing short of a real wedding would get Deb to visit New York City.

With a city hall ceremony, she would be spared the necessity of introducing her mother to Phil's parents. She could have a normal wedding, like people on television.

Fat people look poor.

In the final year of Deb's life, Claudia was prickly, inattentive. If she ever logged into Facebook, she might have seen Nicolette's posts, requesting prayers for her sick mother. After the funeral, she went back and studied them. The language was vague. Nicolette's mother might have had a stomach flu or a bad head cold. The casual reader would never have guessed that after eighteen years of remission, Deb's cancer had reoccurred.

At the time no one knew this, not even Deb herself. She had no use for doctors—a common sentiment among medical support staff, the minnows at the bottom of a food chain in which MDs were the sharks. In all the years of Claudia's growing up, her mother never saw a doctor of any kind, never mind a gynecologist. Deb rarely spoke of what she called (on the phone to her sister, in a low voice) *female problems.* An annual exam—spreading her legs for a stranger—was a humiliation she could not bear.

Princess.

If the doctor had been a woman, someone might have talked her into it. But a male gynecologist—the only kind available in Clayburn, then or now—was out of the question. Deb's wariness stemmed from questions about the doctor's character. What kind of guy wanted to poke around *down there* for a living? A pervert was what kind.

When, several years after menopause, she started bleeding, she told no one. She simply took a maxi pad from the box under the sink.

If you happen to be a woman, all problems are female problems.

Failure to perform scheduled maintenance may void the warranty.

For a year, maybe longer, the cancer was confined to her uterus. At that point, a hysterectomy would have saved her. If her daughter—a licensed social worker, a women's health professional—had taken her to a gynecologist, she would still be alive. Instead the cancer spread to her liver.

Deb was a prude, and stubborn, and it was not inaccurate to say that she died of shame.

Her final weeks were spent on the old plaid couch, coffee-stained and embedded with cat hair, the DNA of several feline generations—the kittens and grandkittens of Mr. Whiskers, a stray cat that little Claudia (the budding sexpert, the future reproductive health professional) had mistakenly identified as male.

Her mother died as she had lived, with the TV playing. It was the only way she could fall asleep. When Nicolette found her, the *Today* show had just started.

Claudia could hear the theme song playing in the background when she answered the call.

The funeral lasted fifteen minutes. The young minister, a mild bald-headed man who'd never laid eyes on the deceased, seemed at a loss. Deb had been baptized at First Congregational, where her parents attended services at Christmas and Easter, but they'd been dead for years and the minister hadn't known them either. The crowd was small—Nicolette and her daughter, a handful of neighbors. Aunt Darlene came with her new husband and his portable oxygen tank, which he pulled behind him on a dolly as though walking a dog. There were a few other mourners Claudia didn't recognize: high school classmates of Nicolette's, her mother's coworkers from the County Home.

I didn't know Deb had another daughter, she was told more than once. Nicolette was the daughter they knew.

Claudia got out of bed and undressed in front of the mirror. Her body looked normal except for her nipples, which were bright red, like the mouth of a child after eating a cherry Popsicle. The same thing had happened twenty years ago, the last time she was pregnant.

She slipped on a bathrobe and turned on the television—tuned, as luck would have it, to a rerun of *Dateline*.

In preventing pregnancy—as in a murder investigation—the first forty-eight hours were crucial. The morning she crept out of Timmy's bed, Claudia had gone straight to work. She'd answered the hotline and counseled patients, spent hours looking at security footage with Luis. The following day she'd driven to Maine, thinking, all the while, of the unknown man who'd been watching the clinic, snapping photos of unsuspecting women and posting them to the internet.

In Clayburn, she'd stopped at Walmart to make a copy of Nicolette's key. On her way back to the trailer, she paid a brief visit to her aunt Darlene. As she performed these errands, she didn't even consider driving to a pharmacy for the morning-after pill—believing, not unreasonably, that she was safe.

Her confidence was reasonable. Women her age didn't get pregnant every day. Heather Chen, the nurse practitioner—a year younger than Claudia—had tried for two solid years. It took multiple rounds of Clomid injections, and three unsuccessful artificial inseminations, before she finally conceived in vitro with donor sperm.

For a perimenopausal forty-three-year-old woman with an erratic menstrual history, the odds of conception from a single act of intercourse were vanishingly slim.

She was a women's health professional, an authority in such matters. For years she had taken no chances. She blasted her system with hormones—the Pill, and later the Depo shot—and endured the side effects. Meeting Stuart—vasectomized, blessedly infertile—had freed her. A one-night stand with her weed dealer hadn't been part of the plan.

Truly, it wasn't that difficult to avoid getting pregnant. Her reasons, in the end, were the same as everybody's.

It just happened.

It was all my fault.

When *Dateline* ended, she dressed and set out driving. She didn't call or text; she just wanted to see him. What exactly she would say, she had no clue.

In the end it didn't matter. For the first time in the two years she'd known him, Timmy's windows were dark.

21

As a boy Timmy had been fascinated by astronauts, by space generally: the numberless planets spinning in their orbits, the unknowable muchness of the world beyond. Earth was just a speck, one tiny pebble on one undistinguished beach among many millions of beaches. He had not dreamed of becoming an astronaut, however. It was not an aspiration you had growing up in Grantham, where aspiration of any kind made you a target. Even as a child, he'd been a realist. Thinking about that now, decades later, made him sad, how a kid could learn, without ever being told, that some things could never be.

At that time, the early 1980s, movies and TV were rife with extraterrestrials and intergalactic adventures. To Timmy they seemed like entertainments for children. Fantasy did not interest him. Only the real thing would do.

It was just after his twelfth birthday when the teacher was sent into space—a regular person from Concord, New Hampshire, a straight shot up the highway from Boston. Timmy had seen her on television talking about the mission. She looked like his mother, his friends' mothers, a lady you'd see in the grocery store. When she opened her mouth, he heard his parents, his teachers. She sounded like every person he knew.

The morning of the mission, Timmy ditched school. He had done this before, met Andy Stasko at the seawall to smoke cigarettes and pass a flask of Jameson; but this time he didn't want company. At school the seventh graders would watch the launch together, Stasko and Dennis Link trash-talking the astronauts and especially Christa McAuliffe, the teacher being sent into space. This was expected behavior at any school-sanctioned activity, and normally Timmy would have joined right in. But the shuttle launch was different. He wanted to watch it alone, silently, reverently; to imagine himself into the capsule, in top condition from months of intensive training, strapped in and waiting for the count.

The launch started nine minutes late. In his parents' basement, Timmy sat in front of the television, waiting.

We have liftoff!

Sixty-five seconds into the launch, Commander Scobee went to full power. Timmy didn't understand, at first, exactly what he was seeing, the white smoke billowing in a serpentine chain.

The TV journalist went silent, endless seconds of dead air. When he finally spoke, his voice was shaky. *Flight controllers here are looking very carefully at the situation. Obviously a major malfunction.*

Something was very, very wrong.

Timmy sat there a long time, staring at the television. He wished that he were in school, where he would be unable to cry and wouldn't need to, because there would be girls on hand for that purpose. The girls would do the crying for you while you slagged on them and silently blessed them for the distraction, for sparing you the humiliation and pain. But Timmy was alone in his parents' basement. His mom and dad were at work, his brother and sister at school, and there was nobody, nobody he could call.

He left Pasco County at five in the morning, while the sky was still dark. He liked driving at that hour, no one on the road but the professionals. He set his cruise control at a prudent sixty-eight and settled in for the ride, I-4 to I-95, which would take him all the way to Boston. As he blew past his old exit, he felt a pang of guilt. He'd meant to stop and see the Tuna on the way down to Florida, but at the last minute had changed his mind. *Next time*, he thought. The mission demanded his full attention. He'd be more relaxed once he'd worked the bugs out. Next time he'd come early and spend a day fishing with his son.

No question, there were bugs. Last night, as he was loading the car, the trap had malfunctioned. The compartment simply would not open. He went through the steps again—driver's seat, defroster, front and rear windows, key card—and still nothing. Finally he called Alex Voinovich.

"What's the problem?" the kid asked. Techno music in the background, the cawing laugh of a drunken girl.

"The trap won't open."

Alex walked him through the steps in order. Still, the trap wouldn't budge.

"Are you sure?" Alex sounded skeptical.

Timmy said, "I am absolutely fuckin sure."

"Shit. All right. Bring it over in the morning and I'll have a look," the kid said—magnanimously, as though he were doing Timmy a huge fucking favor.

"I'm two thousand miles away. I can't bring it over in the morning."

"When you get back, then. It's probably a short. Simple fix."

If it's so simple, why did you screw it up in the first place? Timmy would have said, if there were any fucking point.

He packed the car in the usual way, as he'd done for years driving back and forth from Marcel's. He fit what he could around the spare tire. The rest he packed into two Igloo coolers. The weed was tightly bound in layers and layers of Saran Wrap, then crammed into large Tupperwares. With all that packaging it took up a lot of space.

Timmy thought, That is a fuckload of weed.

On top of the Tupperwares he arranged the beer cans, like that was going to fool anybody. If a cop got as far as opening the coolers, the beer cans wouldn't save him. If a cop opened the coolers, Timmy was already toast.

In the end he left half the product behind, in Wolfman's barn. *I'll get it next time,* he promised. He had enough to supply his regular customers for two months, three at the outside. He smoked a bowl to calm his nerves and, at last, got on the road.

He was getting too old for this.

Long ago he'd enjoyed the intrigue, the feeling of danger. To his teenage self, sneaking a joint in someone's basement had seemed radically adventurous. The fear of getting caught only enhanced the high. If weed had been legal, would he still be smoking all these years later? It seemed unlikely. Probably he'd have lost interest, the way he lost interest in drinking once a fake ID was unnecessary. It was the opposite of thrilling, it was somehow demoralizing, to bring home a sixer from the package store like a younger, slightly less defeated version of his dad.

That morning, watching the sun rise over a Shell station outside Deltona, he saw the truth clearly: for a middle-aged man, selling weed was a ludicrous way to make a living. He thought of his old buddy Dennis Link, the Massachusetts statie, now staking out speed traps in his stormtrooper boots. Was his own career path any less ridiculous? Dennis, at least, would have a state pension, a house to remortgage so he could send his kids to college. After twenty years of playing cops and robbers, Timmy had jack shit.

Like any displaced worker, he'd been resistant to the changes ahead. When weed became legal he would lose his profession, the only one he'd ever practiced. On the other hand, retiring from weed would open up his life. No longer would he spend his days waiting for the phone to ring. He would see the Grand Canyon, Hoover Dam maybe. Timmy knew these places only from television. In point of fact, he had never been anywhere.

While filling his gas tank, he made a decision: in a

year or two, when the Laundromat was up and running, he would quit smoking weed altogether. The idea was revolutionary. Until that moment, the possibility had never crossed his mind.

He got back into the car, wondering if Claudia had ever seen the Grand Canyon. One day they could drive there together, hours and hours on the open road, never saying a word.

Weeks had passed since their night together. At first he'd waited patiently. Sooner or later she would text him, or simply show up at his door.

Claudia Something. He had tried to recall everything he knew about her. She had a job, which was stressful. She'd grown up in Maine and liked cars and weed.

The point being that he had no fucking idea how to find her. Short of walking the streets of Cambridge and Somerville, questioning strangers—*Hey, do you know Claudia?*—he had no strategy at all.

He carried her with him. When their night together was still fresh in his memory, he had sketched her to give Connor something to work with. Connor got the body right: the small hands and slender legs, the naked torso compact and guitar-shaped. At Timmy's request, he gave her long hair. (Maybe Claudia could be convinced to grow hers.) After some discussion, Connor left the face blank.

Next time you see her, he told Timmy, *take a picture.*

But there had been no next time. The faceless woman on his back remained an outline, a void to be filled with something. The outline showed what was missing, an empty space shaped exactly like her.

By the time he reached the Georgia border it was late morning, the sun high overhead. He had forgotten his sunglasses. When he flicked on the air-conditioning, nothing happened. Whatever short had disabled the trap had also killed the AC.

Jesus fucking Christ.

He got off at the next exit, a curving ramp that peeled off into nowhere—a brand-new stretch of four-lane highway with empty fields on either side. He drove until he found a place to pull over, an abandoned gas station that looked ready for demolition, a crumbling patch of asphalt. What he needed, truly needed, was to smoke a bowl and collect his thoughts. Under the floor mat he kept, for just such emergencies, a small-bore pipe packed with a single hit of weed.

He parked and walked a discreet distance from the empty building before lighting the pipe. Immediately his brain cooled. He saw clearly the task ahead: daunting, yes, but not complicated. He'd driven I-95 more times than he could count. The fuckload of weed in the trunk was not important; it did not change the basic nature of the task. All he had to do was drive.

The little pipe was quickly exhausted. As Timmy shook the dregs onto the ground, he heard a noise behind him, a rustle of grass. He turned and saw a guy pissing into the bushes, a little meatball of a guy with a shaved head. The man shook himself and zipped and for no reason turned his head. Timmy saw, then, that he was wearing a uniform.

He hurried back to the Civic, faster than was prudent. He should have taken his time. He peeled out of the parking lot. Idling nearby was another car, a late-model Dodge Charger—solid black, with an elaborate antenna. He had smoked his bowl next to a pissing Georgia statie.

The Civic was sweltering, reeking of weed. As Timmy pulled onto 95, he discovered that its windows would no longer open. Except for the rear passenger-side window, which opened maybe three inches, they were now sealed shut.

As he drove, the car got hotter and hotter. He tried to think cold thoughts. Junior high hockey with frostbitten feet. Passing a flask at the boatyard with Dennis Link and Andy Stasko, freezing his nuts off. Claudia's cold hands on his back, his face, his shoulders and chest.

He'd driven maybe ten miles when he saw the blue lights in his rearview. He pulled over to the shoulder and waited in a pool of his own sweat.

The cop stepped out of his Tahoe. It was the same bald guy he'd seen pissing behind the gas station. He motioned for Timmy to roll down his window.

"I can't," Timmy said.

The cop seemed not to hear him.

"I can't," he said, louder this time. How did you pantomime, *My windows won't open?*

In a gesture of helplessness, he raised his hands.

He understood later that raising his hands had saved him. Reflexively, the cop reached for his weapon.

Timmy sat very still, his hands in plain sight, until the cop opened the driver's-side door.

"Sir, please step out of the car."

22

The world is full of signs.

This happened many years ago, in the early 1990s, somewhere in northern Nevada. Victor Prine was moving a load from Indy to Sacramento, a half day ahead of schedule, when he spotted a billboard along the highway.

ANNUAL EXPO GUNS AND AMMO
WEAPONS OF ALL KINDS

The hall, when he found it, was a low-slung bunker the size of an airline hangar. Who'd built it there, beside a barren stretch of road between Reno and Winnemucca, and for what purpose, were questions he didn't ponder.

The cavernous structure seemed randomly placed in the desert, as though it had fallen from the sky.

Inside, he walked the perimeter. The first person he met was a tall hatchet-faced kid in desert fatigues. He stood behind a card table piled with pamphlets and bumper stickers. Victor was then in his early forties. The kid was maybe twenty-five years old.

He handed Victor a business card.

"Is this you?" Victor asked, studying it. "Lon . . . Haruchi?"

The kid studied him intently, as though trying to determine whether the old guy was messing with him. "Do I look like my name is Horiuchi?"

When Victor laughed, the kid didn't even smile. His gaze was level, unflinching. "Seriously, man. That name means nothing to you?"

"Should it?" Victor said.

"Lon Horiuchi is an agent of your government, paid with your tax dollars. On August twenty-second, he gunned down an American citizen on private property while she was holding her child in her arms. Hor-i-uchi," he repeated, enunciating very clearly. "Remember that name."

His crew cut was fresh, mown short as velvet. Victor said, "Where'd you serve, son?"

"The Persian Gulf, sir." He spoke with a soldier's uninflected precision, a studied blankness.

Victor offered his hand. "Thank you for your service. I bet you did all right over there."

"I did my job." The kid had a grip like a tourniquet. His hand seemed to be made of solid bone.

Victor studied the printed card. "Why'd you give me this?"

"I give it to everyone. Every citizen needs to know what this government is capable of. I figure somebody sooner or later is going to be moved to do something about it."

It took Victor a moment to catch his meaning.

"That's the guy's home address?"

"Affirmative," the kid said.

There was a pointed silence, in which Victor studied the pamphlets on the card table. "What else have you got here?"

The kid handed him a bumper sticker: WHEN GUNS ARE OUTLAWED, I WILL BECOME AN OUTLAW.

Immediately Victor handed it back. "I'm with you, man. I heartily agree with that sentiment. But I'm a convicted felon, and I'll tell you right now, I'm not going to put this on my truck."

He never saw the kid again, though he believed, at the time, that he'd met plenty like him: young men just out of the service, trying to remember how the civilian world worked, if they'd ever known in the first place. It was the parallax of middle age—part laziness, part blindness. You assumed, always, that you'd seen it all before.

There was something in the air.

Months or years later, when the bombs exploded in Oklahoma City, Victor was driving. At a 76 truck stop outside Spokane, he saw the mug shot on television. He understood, then, how wrong he'd been. The kid at the gun show was like no one he'd ever known.

Tim McVeigh was long gone now, dead by lethal injection. At the federal prison in Terre Haute, Indiana, they'd put him down like a rabid dog. Victor thought of him at odd moments. Alone in his basement, organizing his preps and waiting for the shit to hit, he sometimes felt that he was being watched.

On a Monday night in early April, as he fired off another message to Anthony, he felt a familiar presence behind and above him, the unseen observer. It was a moment of reckoning. In that moment he saw clearly how he would look to a man like McVeigh, who, whatever his faults, had died with his boots on. Tim McVeigh had remained, to the end, a soldier. Victor Prine was an old man squinting at a computer screen.

He got up from his chair and went down to the

basement, took his bug-out bag from its hook on the wall. The bag was packed with unnecessary items, useless in an urban setting. Victor ditched the filtration tabs and bear spray, the waterproof poncho. That left enough room for a street map of Boston, his EDC and side holster, a box of ammo, and a handful of zip ties. Whether he would need any of these items was impossible to say.

At first light he set out driving, the bug-out bag on the seat beside him. Stashed beneath the passenger seat was the Mosin-Nagant. As he watched the log house disappear in his rearview, he wondered if he would ever return.

Victor Prine was on the road.

It was his natural habitat, the life he was made for. He could not remember choosing it. Driving, he wondered: Was this what people meant by happiness? He didn't feel happy, exactly. But he felt perfectly at ease.

Thirty years behind the wheel. On the road his loneliness had seemed normal. Only now—stripped of his rig, exiled for the rest of his days to ordinary life—did he feel hopeless, angry, and lost. The world excluded him. A female pushing a shopping cart down the aisles of Walmart, a young child strapped inside it. High school football games for which the entire town turned out, parents and grandparents rooting in the stands. At such moments he felt unfairly punished, by the someone or something that had decided, long ago, that every ordinary human pleasure was off-limits to him.

Kids in costumes, trick-or-treating. A car decorated with streamers—JUST MARRIED—dragging a pair of shoes behind.

On the road, such scenes were nonexistent. The highways were busy with truck traffic, solitary men hauling ass across the country. For thirty years Victor had encountered them at diners and highway rest stops, at roadhouses, at weigh stations. Wherever he went, he saw other versions of himself. He didn't speak to these men, didn't need to. It was enough to know they were out there, that he was not alone.

It seemed best to avoid the interstate, which was not a problem. Victor didn't mind the back roads. In his old rig the route would have been impossible, but in the F-150 he felt light and agile, the pickup nimble as a sports car. At a service station he bought coffee and a packet of peanuts and a scratch-off ticket.

The road dipped and weaved, winding through mountains. He scanned the dial for Doug Straight, but heard nothing but static.

The scratch-off ticket wasn't a winner, but it never hurt to try.

He'd traveled no more than fifty miles when his tooth began to ache. For weeks it had been mostly quiet, thanks to his soft diet, soup and oatmeal and Jell-O pudding, all of Randy's cooking pounded into mush. Now, without warning, the ache was back. He blamed the peanuts.

A shot of whiskey was the most effective solution, but sobriety left him with few options.

Pull it, already.

He thought or heard or possibly spoke the words aloud, in a strained voice that was not his own.

Things were breaking down.

He was at the stage of life when a man looked backward. There was so much life behind him and—no point in denying it—so little ahead.

He didn't regret his wild youth—the two tours of duty, the girls he'd balled, the hell he'd raised. *Regret* was not the right word. Though if he'd known then what he knew now, he would do everything differently. He would choose a sensible female and marry early, plant as much seed as she'd let him put there. He had learned, too late, that this was the only wealth that mattered: the saplings that would outlive him.

If he had it all to do over again, he would attend to his line.

Years ago, on the eve of his fiftieth birthday, Victor Prine took stock of his life. In the Army Buddies Usenet group, he made contact with a guy he'd known in boot camp, a Kentuckian named Larry Sweet. After Vietnam, Sweet had returned to his homeplace, a little mountain town called Mineral. With the aid of a magnifying glass, Victor located it on a map.

That summer, after dropping off a load in Louisville, he made a trip there. Sweet lived in a ramshackle farmhouse at the end of a rutted lane, flanked by an immense vegetable garden. As Victor rolled up in his rig, a woman in a straw hat knelt there weeding. When he explained who he was, Sweet's wife seemed happy to see him. Larry had gone to town but would be back shortly. Victor was welcome to wait.

Inside, she poured him lemonade. He drank it in a dim old-style parlor, studying the framed photographs that hung on every wall. His buddy was in every picture, the long horsey face and jug ears, the distinctive underbite. In certain photos he seemed to appear twice, as a teenager and as a very old man, Sweet's father or grandfather, maybe. To Victor it was a thing of wonder, the same face replicating itself over generations, unchanged and unchanging, without end.

They ate dinner on the screened porch, three generations gathered around the table: Sweet and his wife, their young sons and teenage daughter, and Sweet's elderly mother, who lived up the hill. When they joined hands to say grace, Victor held the wife's hand in his left, the daughter's in his right. The prayer was interminable, a long-winded dose of praising and blessing, but Victor didn't mind it. He would have sat there for hours. It was the first time he'd touched a female in many years.

He spent that night on a foldout couch, in the airless upstairs room Sweet's wife used for sewing. Lying awake, Victor could smell her in the room. She had impressed him powerfully, a brisk, practical woman who worked as a midwife, who grew vegetables and baked bread and made all the children's clothes. He saw that Sweet had chosen wisely. Acquiring such a female was like investing in a generator, an essential power source.

That evening, as they passed the dishes around the table, he'd come to certain realizations. The choice of a helpmeet wasn't as difficult as he'd made it. Females, in most cases, were just what they appeared to be. Victor had picked one who served liquor to strange men, who cursed like a sailor and dressed like a whore. A blind man could have seen that it would end badly. And yet, when she killed his baby, he'd been genuinely surprised.

He lay awake and thought of Sweet's daughter, sleeping on the other side of the wall. When he'd taken her hand for the blessing it had felt exactly like her mother's, a fact he found significant. Both were warm and strong and delicate, as though they were attached to the same woman. Their hands were exactly the same.

He rose early and left in darkness, while the family was still sleeping. He never saw Larry Sweet again. For the rest of his life he would remember that hot summer night, the teenage girl sleeping on the other side of the wall.

I should have taken her, he thought.

In retrospect it seemed the obvious solution. Sweet's daughter was small and slender. She weighed no more than a midsize dog.

By the time he crossed the New York border, his tooth was throbbing. In the rearview mirror he studied his swollen face. He wished that he had packed aspirin, though he was probably too far gone for that. At home in his medicine chest was the one remedy that sometimes worked, Orajel Plus, made for infants who were teething.

"Pull it already."

He spoke the words aloud, in a voice he recognized. It wasn't God's voice, or Doug Straight's or Tim McVeigh's, for that matter. He was speaking in his father's voice.

Things were breaking down.

What would happen on Mercy Street remained unclear.

In the first scenario, he would penetrate the clinic without resistance, his BCS. It seemed too much to hope for. How likely or unlikely this was, Victor could not say.

In the second scenario, he would be met with armed resistance—theoretically, at least, his WCS. But Victor Prine had never shrunk from danger. In his heart he was still a soldier, mentally and physically prepared to do what had to be done.

His jaw pulsed rhythmically.

Scenario three was the most complicated. In scenario three, he would be forced to pivot. If Columbia could not be located, the clinic offered other high-value targets—including, but not limited to, the abortionist himself.

Scenario three, it must be said, was vague to him. How he would find the abortionist, or recognize the guy when he saw him, was not clear. Better intel would have helped, a trusted lieutenant to make inquiries. What he needed, more than anything, was boots on the ground.

Of course, boots on the ground would have rendered the entire mission unnecessary. This was not a helpful thought.

In scenario four—his BCS—he would locate Columbia and contain her in an enclosed space.

He thought of the deer he'd lost in the woods north of Garman Lake, and of Larry Sweet's daughter. He would not make the same mistake again.

Pull it already.

In a gas station men's room in upstate New York, he reached into his mouth and pulled out the tooth.

Victor got back on the road.

His mouth was now on fire. Pulling the tooth hadn't solved the problem. Pulling the tooth had plunged him into new depths of pain.

Pull it already. His father's voice, predictably, had led him astray. It was a lesson he'd learned many times and ought to have remembered. Only a fool took advice from Lovell Prine.

He thought, helplessly, of Orajel Plus. In his fragile state, the very thought made his eyes tear. He imagined himself a baby crying out in pain, a beautiful young mother soothing him. Gentle fingers in his mouth as she rubbed the cream into his gums.

He got off at the next exit and spotted, in the distance, a CVS drugstore. He parked and went inside. The store was mostly empty. He walked up and down the aisles until he spotted what he needed. *Orajel Extra Strength. For relief of teething pain.* The package featured a photo of a round-faced infant, grinning broadly to reveal a single tooth.

At the cash register, a lady clerk was flipping through a magazine—a big round-faced gal, well past her prime, with meaty shoulders and a firm shelf of breast jutting forward like the prow of a ship. An ordinary female, nothing special. She would never have qualified for the Hall of Shame.

"You find everything all right?" she asked, barely looking up from her magazine. The hand turning the page looked plump and soft, the nails painted a pearly pink.

"Yes, ma'am." *Look at me*, he thought. *Please look at me*. Why this mattered so much, he could not possibly have said.

"Have a good one," the clerk said as she handed back his change.

Back in the truck, he studied his gums in the rearview mirror, the monstrous crater where his tooth had been. The crater was painful to look at, never mind touch.

He thought of the clerk's plump, white hands. He could go back into the store and ask her to apply it for him. Common sense stopped him. He was still sane enough to understand that it would end badly, that she would probably call the cops.

Driving soothed him. As he crossed the border into Massachusetts, the road climbed higher and higher, which surprised him. The northeast quadrant of the country was unfamiliar territory. For thirty years he'd avoided the eastern runs, the unending traffic this side of the Mississippi, a trucker's prejudice. He had pictured a different landscape entirely—flat and congested, an endless expanse of strip malls and big-box stores, the bleak, unending American sprawl.

Western Massachusetts looked nothing like that. Western Massachusetts, to his astonishment, was beautiful country. On a weekday afternoon there was no traffic to speak of. He passed a slow truck in the right lane, a snowplow with its yellow lights flashing.

Good Christ, it's April, Victor thought.

At that very moment, the snow started. Grit on the windshield, fine as sugar. The sky and the horizon were the same color, grainy and particulated. The road itself looked whitewashed, coated with a scrim of salt.

The road climbed and climbed. MT. GREYLOCK, HIGHEST POINT IN MASS. A stiff gust of wind took a swipe at his truck.

He passed signs for ski areas, for scenic overlooks. Snow swirled along the icy pavement, hovered mysteriously like steam or spirits. He thought wistfully of the tire chains he hadn't thought to bring, still hanging from sturdy hooks in Randy's barn.

The pain was making him perspire. A lick of sweat ran down his back. He wished he'd gotten himself an ice pack, something cold to hold to his jaw.

A skinny deer raced across the highway. Victor hit the brakes and regretted it immediately. His tires skidded crazily.

The road was glazed with invisible ice.

The truck slipped and slid; it could not get purchase. On April first, he'd swapped out his snow tires, as any sane person would do.

Pumping the brakes, he righted himself. The ache had spread to his left ear. Its fingers tightened around his throat. *Mercy,* he thought. When he reached the destination, Columbia would help him. The thought was nearly too much for him: her hands on his face, her fingers in his mouth.

His jaw pulsed like a second heart.

He thought again of the Orajel package. The baby's smile was sweet and trusting, as though all his pain had been relieved.

He wished the collapse would come already. He was tired of waiting. If shit was going to hit the fan, he wished it would hit soon. For fifteen years he'd planned and plotted. He hadn't counted on being old when it happened. An old man alone in the world—wifeless, childless, toothless, and possibly blind.

Mercy.

He gunned the engine up a steep grade that went on forever. As he crested the hill he saw—too late and too close—red taillights in front of him.

The world went white.

SPRING

SPRING

23

Long past the point when such a thing seemed inevitable, the thaw came.

In the last week of April, the final storm of the season gathered moisture over the Caribbean. *Here we go again,* said the NECN weatherman, looking tired. But this time the predictions were wrong. A high-pressure system pushed the frigid air northward—regifted, like an unwanted Christmas present, from New England to Canada, the land of moose and Tim Hortons and mild good manners. The final monster nor'easter of that godforsaken winter hit Greater Boston as driving rain.

A furious rain, fine as needles. The snow towers cringed and shrank; they softened into hillocks. The hillocks were pounded into oblivion, death by a thousand punctures. The accumulated grit of a wretched season washed into storm drains: road salt, motor oil, antifreeze, the tears of a hundred MBTA drivers. In Kenmore Square the roar was audible, a rushing underground river. Which direction it flowed, where or whether it emptied, no one cared to know.

On the North Shore, the South Shore, the storm surge was epic. Fish-smelling streets ran with salt water. A leveling wind whittled the dunes.

For three days and three nights, the rain kept coming. MBTA trains arrived on time. Parking spaces reappeared as if by magic. Boston returned to its regularly scheduled programming: fierce traffic and workaday surliness. The chip on the shoulder, F-bombs exploding. The crooked grimace, the harangue and complaint.

A hundred and ten inches of snowfall. After plowing 295,000 miles of city streets—twelve times the circumference of the earth—Boston road crews called it a wrap.

The thaw was good news for everyone. Good news for the new governor, sworn into office just before the first nor'easter; good news for mayors and city councilors and selectmen, who'd spent their entire snow removal budgets, and part of next year's, before the second one hit. Good news for bus drivers, for all drivers. For harried parents who'd burned an entire year's worth of vacation sitting home with restless kids, who had, in some half-forgotten past life, spent their days in school.

In late May, on the same weekend, the *Globe* and the *Herald* ran a photo of the very same snow pile, located at the back corner of a Dunkin' Donuts parking lot in Billerica—a pile so encrusted with soot and garbage, so many times melted and refrozen, that it had been rendered indestructible.

It's probably still there.

At the Wellways quarterly board meeting in Chicago, security measures were debated, a substantial investment in the Boston operation. At the clinic on Mercy Street, a new system was installed.

The new system was cumbersome. The exam rooms and surgical suite were reinforced with steel doors, each controlled by a thumbprint reader. The readers were highly sensitive. Hand lotion confused them. After Florine circulated a memo to this effect, the staff came to work unmoisturized.

Extra cameras were placed in the waiting room, the call center. An additional guard was hired to watch the monitors, while Luis manned the metal detector and looked inside backpacks and wanded the patients before waving them through.

Despite these measures, certain questions went unanswered. For months, Claudia and Mary monitored the Hall of Shame, but no new photos were posted.

The guy in the Sox cap (*my photographer friend*, Luis called him) was not seen again. As far as anyone could tell, he had never returned to Mercy Street.

As far as anyone could tell.

In the meantime, other things happened. The city turned its attention to politics, the upcoming presidential campaign. In New York, a B-list TV star descended an escalator, mugging for paparazzi. The world continued to turn.

That summer, without warning, the Hall of Shame went dark.

Questions remained. Who built the site, and why? Who owned the domain name? Wellways LLC mounted an investigation. Its legal counsel made inquiries. All requests for information went unanswered.

Luis's photographer friend never returned, or maybe he did. Maybe he's there right now, loitering on the sidewalk, wearing a different hat.

Life happens in increments. Early humans understood this, and so they invented time, a way of parsing the eternal.

A schedule was a critical component of right living, one of the necessary conditions for healing to occur.

Anthony worked the morning shift, seven thirty to two, with a ten-minute break in the morning and a half hour for lunch. Increments of time, filled with productive action.

He had not gone looking for the job. The job had come to him by way of his cousin Sal, who after his meteoric rise at Star Market had cut a deal with the competition and now ran frozen foods at Food Star, where he'd used his influence in invisible ways. This was the way of the world; Anthony understood this. His cousin had interceded in a saintly way, persuading the higher powers. Accordingly, blessings rained down. Anthony's application was fast-tracked. In no time flat, he was brought aboard as a part-time deli counter attendant. After completing the ninety-day probationary period, he would be eligible for more hours. The possibility of full-time was dangled. No promises were made, but Anthony could read the writing on the wall.

The job was satisfying. The pay was unimpressive—at the end of the month, he had less in his bank account than he'd collected on Disability—but there were other compensations. Free uniforms, an employee discount. No health insurance—not yet—but this fact did not trouble him. The doctors hadn't helped him anyway.

Other compensations. In the grand scheme of things, the paper-thin slicing of deli ham was of no great importance. Anthony knew this, yet he rose each morning with a sense of purpose. Instead of walking to St. Dymphna's, he walked to Food Star, where his presence was expected and needed. At the deli counter he uncovered the slicer, checked the Use by dates, shifted the inventory. At seven thirty the first customers arrived—old people, mainly. A few of the regulars greeted him by name.

The conversations were not taxing. He never had to grope for something to say. A friendly hello, a word about the weather, *Anything else for you?* When he handed over their cold cuts, the customers thanked him. His smile brightened their day.

It was nothing at all like working on the internet, fixing broken links and correcting typos for the faceless Father Renaldo, who issued curt commands and was never pleased. Anthony had given his notice via email, the only means of contacting Father Renaldo, and so was denied the gratification of quitting in person, due to having a better offer. Two days later he received a cursory reply: **OK, pls make those correx before you go. Yours in Christ, RC.**

At one time he'd spent entire days staring at his computer screen. Now he checked email maybe once a week. His online friends quickly forgot him. People came and went all the time, changing screen names and profile pics, ages, genders, identities. It was all made-up, really. Nobody was anybody, and neither was he.

Excelsior11, his second-best friend in the world, had disappeared completely—why exactly, Anthony would never know. He knew only that he'd stuck his neck out, spent untold hours lurking outside the clinic on Mercy Street. In retrospect it seemed pointless, a waste of effort. He'd sent the man dozens, maybe hundreds of photos. What Excelsior had done with them was anybody's guess.

At Food Star, Anthony saw people from the neighborhood—old classmates, friends of his parents. Several times a week he saw someone from church: Mrs. McGann and her senile husband, Mrs. Paone leaning on a shopping cart instead of a walker. Mrs. Morrison updated him on the barren daughter in Arizona. It was like old times.

Now that he had Food Star, he no longer needed St. Dymphna's. According to Mrs. McGann, Quentin the Quick had been reassigned to a parish in Leominster. Anthony didn't miss him at all.

He spotted her first, standing in line at the fish counter, no more than ten feet away. They hadn't seen each other in fifteen years. Naturally she had changed in that time, gained mass and solidity. Her hair was lighter than he remembered, the corners of her mouth sagging in some chronic disappointment. He thought she must have spent a lot of time frowning for her face to look like that. In a perverse way, this pleased him. The years spent with another man had not satisfied her. If she'd chosen Anthony Blanchard, her face might have frozen in an expression of joy.

Distractedly he apologized to a customer, who'd asked for a half pound of smoked turkey, thick-sliced. Anthony had given him thin.

Out the corner of his eye he watched the fish guy wrap up her order, an even pound of cod. How many people was she cooking for? Two pounds was a family-sized order, but a pound could go either way.

He put aside the pile of smoked turkey and tried again. With luck he could palm it off on another customer—smoked turkey was on special this week, and popular. If not, the mistake would come out of his paycheck.

A pound of cod could be dinner for two. Then again, she was a good-sized woman. She looked like she could easily demolish a pound of cod.

No wedding ring, he noted as she reached for the package of fish.

A year ago he'd have let the moment pass, and kicked himself later. A year ago he would have choked. But the new and improved Anthony Blanchard did not shrink from opportunity.

"Maureen!" he called, louder than necessary. Heads turned in his direction. He was aware of music playing, a jazzy version of "Do You Know the Way to San Jose?"

She turned, looking slightly startled.

"Maureen, hi," he said, his face flushed with heat. "It's been a long time."

"Oh, hi"—she glanced quickly at his name tag— "Anthony. Do I know you?"

It was a question you didn't want to hear from anybody, never mind the woman who'd initiated you into manhood. But Anthony was not deterred.

"Anthony Blanchard," he said. "I live on Lisbon Ave."

"Oh, *Anthony*," she said. Was he imagining it, or did her cheeks flush? "How are you?"

"Good," he said. "I'm good."

Maureen frowned as though trying to place him.

"Didn't you have an accident? Working on the Dig. Or maybe I'm thinking of someone else. Some guy got hit in the head."

"That was me." It wasn't exactly a claim to fame, it was not a thing you wanted to be known for, but it was better than nothing. "I work here now. In the deli."

"I see that," Maureen said.

Anthony pressed on. "It must have been your brother who told you. About my accident."

"You know Pat?"

He'd forgotten there was another brother.

"No, Tim. Me and him are best friends." Anthony remembered to breathe. "You still live in New Hampshire?"

"I'm staying at my mom's for now."

And this time he wasn't imagining it; this time she blushed for real. Miraculously, he thought of something to say.

"Hey, did Tim get a new phone? I texted him a couple times, but I never heard back."

Maureen moved in closer. She was now maybe three paces away—close enough that he could smell her hairspray, the minty gum she chewed.

"Timmy's in jail," she said in a low voice.

"Jail," he repeated stupidly. Bad news for Tim, no question, but Anthony found it comforting. At least his buddy wasn't ignoring him. There was a reason he hadn't answered those texts.

"I guess it had to happen sooner or later," Maureen said. "With what he was into."

"Where is he?" said Anthony. "Can I go see him?"

"Not unless you want to drive to Georgia. That's where they busted him. They say he was running drugs. *They say.*" Maureen shrugged elaborately. "I haven't talked to him. This is all secondhand from my uncle. Anyway, I should get going." She studied the package of cod in her hand, as if she wasn't sure how it had gotten there. "It was nice seeing you, Anthony."

"Wait." After all these years, he wasn't about to let her go. "Can you tell him Anthony asked about him? You know, if you talk to him."

"I probably won't. But yeah, sure."

"And keep me posted, okay? Like I said, he's my best friend. I can give you my number."

"That's all right," she said quickly. "I can just stop by the store. You're here every day?"

"Tuesday through Saturday," Anthony said. "Till two p.m."

"Okay, then. I'll see you around."

It wasn't exactly a date. But he would see her again, and next time she'd remember him. Gratitude filled him. He was sad for Tim, but mainly he was grateful. Tim, his best friend, had given them something to talk about.

Once again, Victor Prine was on the road.

On Saturday afternoons, his stepbrother drove him to Luther's house—thanks to its sturdy wooden ramp, the one place in Saxon County he could navigate on his own. In Luther's driveway he hoisted himself out of the passenger seat, waited patiently as Randy took the walker from the trunk. He clomped up the wooden ramp, knocked and waited. After some while, Luther rolled to the door.

They sat in the kitchen listening to the ball game on the radio, each nursing a single beer. On Saturday afternoons only, Victor allowed himself this small pleasure. He never drank more than one, for the simple fact that beer made him piss like a racehorse. In old age, at long last, he had learned to drink moderately. He could imagine no stronger deterrent than the fear of wetting his pants.

On Saturday afternoons he drank and listened to Luther. For the moment anyway, the Ebola virus had been contained. Luther, naturally, had theories. He talked about the mutability of the virus, the shadowy malfeasance of international corporations, the inscrutable motives of the Deep State. Victor did not agree or disagree. He was happy to defer to Luther, who had made a lifelong study of these matters.

At five o'clock, Randy came to get him. Slowly, painfully, he made his way down the ramp. He lowered himself gingerly into Randy's souped-up PT Cruiser. After a lifetime of driving big rigs, it was disconcerting to ride in a passenger car. The road raced beneath them like a conveyor belt, so fast, so close. Victor looked out at the world and read the signs.

TOUGH TIMES NEVER LAST. TOUGH PEOPLE DO.

Back at the log house he sank into the living room couch, as exhausted as if he had run many miles, and turned on the TV.

The details of the accident were vague to him, they lived in the realm of rumor and conjecture. The car he rear-ended in Massachusetts—a Toyota Prius—was totaled, though the driver was not hurt. He'd been distressed to learn, later, that she was pregnant. Though he had to wonder: What sort of female would put herself in such a situation, driving alone across the Berkshires in her condition? A pregnant female ought to take better care of herself.

The first time he came to, the EMTs were pulling him from the wreckage of the pickup. The second time, he was lying on a gurney behind a plastic curtain printed with tiny seashells. Victor verified his name and birth date and religious preference, and gave them a phone number to call.

My stepbrother, he said. *We're not blood-related.*

Eventually he was moved to a different room, surrounded by a different plastic curtain—putty-colored, printed with moons and stars. On either side of the curtain, male voices made phone calls. The voice to his left was possibly Mexican. Victor recognized a few words of Spanish: *mucho, hombre, gracias, nada.* The voice to his right spoke a singsong language that seemed wordless, an undifferentiated torrent of sound.

When he woke from the surgery he heard a female voice. The sound was achingly beautiful, recognizable American English. Gratitude filled him. After what seemed like months of solitary confinement, he was not alone.

He heard the voice several times before he saw its source, a heavyset Black female with a round smiling face. Ernestine was his age exactly, he learned later, though at the time he wouldn't have guessed it. The age of Black people was a mystery to him.

In the hospital he experienced a smorgasbord of humiliations, the daily trial of toileting. He could not wash or dress or shave himself. For these services and others, he was entirely dependent on Ernestine.

The services she performed were unspeakable. If she had been a White woman, he would not have survived it. The mortification might literally have killed him.

She placed the pan beneath him and removed it when he was done.

She worked in silence, which seemed preferable. On her left hand was a gold ring set with multicolored stones. Eventually his curiosity overcame him. One

day as she was changing his sheets, Victor asked about
the ring. His voice was phlegmy, nearly unintelligible.
Except for the Indian doctor who came and went, he
hadn't spoken to another person in days.

He cleared his throat and tried again.

"It's a mother's ring," said Ernestine. "My kids
gave it to me for my birthday." The gems were the
birthstones of her four grown children, three boys
and a girl.

Victor thought immediately of Doug Straight. A
Black female born in 1950 produced, on average, four
offspring. Again and always, Doug had been right.

Ernestine stripped the bed briskly, without fanfare.
She maneuvered him expertly, as though rolling a log.
"You never had any kids, Victor? Lift."

He lifted. The question had taken him off guard.

"No, ma'am," he said, blinking furiously.

There was a silence. Horrifyingly, he was near tears.

"That's sad," she said finally.

Victor said, "I think so too."

Another silence.

"I guess I never met the right girl," he added gruffly.
"Met a few wrong ones, though."

At this Ernestine laughed. Her laugh was remarkable, rich and melodic, a laugh that was larger than
them both. She laughed at what he'd said and what he

never could, at the dizzying variety of pratfalls and misfires and bitter regrets—absurd, brutal, irreversible, and irredeemable—a person, any person, could rack up in sixty-five years of living.

The moment passed, but Victor never forgot it. It was a pleasure he hadn't experienced in many years, or maybe ever: the simple joy of making a woman laugh.

Hospital days were like prison days, long and empty. Victor ate and shat and ate again, like a factory-farmed chicken. Mealtimes were the only events worth noting, the highlight of his day.

Each morning a slip of paper was delivered with his breakfast tray.

The slip of paper was vitally important. The patient was to note his preferences for breakfast, lunch, and dinner. Grilled cheese or tuna sandwich, meat loaf or spaghetti, oatmeal or scrambled eggs.

Victor filled out the form slowly, with great difficulty, the tiny type swimming before his eyes. Straight lines looked wavy. At the center of his vision was a blank spot, as though he were staring into a searchlight. He held the paper over his left shoulder and studied it out the corner of his eye.

Once Ernestine came into the room as he was filling out the form. "You need your glasses, Victor?"

"I can't find them," he grumbled—shamefaced, as though she'd caught him in some misdeed.

"Try these." She took off her glasses, bright red plastic, and handed them over. He was so flabbergasted he couldn't speak. There was nothing to do but put them on, the plastic warm from where it had sat on a Black lady's nose.

Victor stared at the slip of paper. At the edges of his vision the type looked clearer, but only a little.

"They're probably too strong for you. I'm blind as a bat." Unperturbed, she took the glasses off his face.

"It's not the glasses," he said, his heart racing. "I just can't see."

He had never said it aloud before. The next day an orderly came with a wheelchair and took him down to the second floor, where an Oriental woman put drops in his eyes. He stared at the chart on the wall and made his best guess.

Glasses wouldn't help him. That was the long and short of it. In accented English she explained that the hole in his vision was irreversible. Over time it would only get bigger. There was nothing to be done.

From the hospital he was sent to a rehab center. Medicare paid for thirty days. At rehab he did stretching exercises and watched television. He was issued special low-vision glasses that didn't help in the slightest. The occupational therapist taught him to navigate the world with his walker, to shower and dress himself.

In the end he went home to Saxon County. His brother Randy came to get him. The trip was seven hours long, the most time Victor had ever spent as passenger. His pickup truck had been totaled in the accident, his expired license surrendered. His driving days were done.

In the log house he mainly watched television. His computer sat idle in his office—the keyboard untouched, the screen dark. Since coming home from the hospital, he had turned it on only once. When he typed in the address for the Hall of Shame, he was greeted with a plain yellow screen.

This URL is now available from GoDaddy!

It took him a moment to absorb it: his domain name had expired. The Hall of Shame had disappeared from the world.

Curiously, he did not miss it. The young whores in their puffy jackets, the slide show set to music. The pain pills had killed his libido. He felt dead from the waist down and didn't care. His mad hunger for Columbia had faded like a dream.

He had failed in his mission. Victor understood, now,

that the defeat of the White race was inevitable, its decline irreversible. The Hall of Shame had been an inspired idea, but in the end it was too little, too late. His fortified basement—the shelves stocked with provisions, the arsenal of weapons—was likewise useless. He hadn't visited his preps in many months. The steep, narrow staircase was too dangerous to navigate, and anyway, it didn't matter. The End Times had already come.

Shit, meet fan.

He thought back on his time in the hospital, the weeks in rehab: the attending physicians, the Indian surgeon who'd pinned together his fractured pelvis, the Oriental optometrist who gave him the bad news. The anesthesiologist who'd sedated him, the physical therapist who'd tortured him for a solid month. Not one of these people was White. Victor's tribe had lost the game long ago; holed up in the mountains, he simply hadn't noticed. In Saxon County there were no Blacks or Orientals or Indians, no foreigners speaking in tongues. Quietly, without him noticing, they had carved up America and divided it between them, in whatever way suited them.

The collapse had come and gone.

Victor still mourned the White race, the once-great tribe now disgraced and diminished. But the urgency he'd once felt had dissipated, drained away like blood from a wound.

He lay on the couch and watched television. With his new satellite dish he found a station that aired westerns twenty-four seven, and watched hungrily. The hole in his vision didn't bother him. The stories were as familiar as the sky above. It was easy enough to fill in what wasn't there.

He'd seen them all before, or maybe he hadn't. In truth, it was hard to tell. The same characters appeared again and again: the solitary hero, the devious Indians, the saloon girls and kindly madams, the gruff sheriffs. *I'm the law in these parts.* From the corner of his eye Victor drank in the landscape, the wide-open spaces he recalled from his years on the road.

The cattle rustlers and ranchers, the brawling cow-pokes, the glory days of the White man. That America was gone now, lost forever, but Victor still had its embers—available to him day and night through the magic of satellites, beamed down from heaven to the disc on his roof.

"Please, Mother. Please don't kill your baby."

On Mercy Street, protestors came and went. This one was young, maybe thirty, with a Jesus beard and long dark hair in a ponytail. He reassured Claudia that God had a plan for her, that his ways were mysterious.

Claudia thought, *You have no idea.*

"I'm not your mother," she told him. "If I were, I'd tell you to stop harassing women in the street and do something useful with your life."

She plowed past him to the door and keyed in her new access code.

A higher power with a vivid imagination, a highly developed sense of irony. These weren't qualities she had ever associated with the protestors. It seemed unlikely that any god they believed in would operate in such a way.

Inside, Luis was waiting. "Claudia, this is stupid. You're going to get hurt. I'm putting my foot down. From now on, you need to use the garage."

Her usual argument was ready on her lips. His face stopped her, his genuine concern.

"All right, fine. I'll use the garage."

The protestors kept coming. For nearly ten years Claudia had stepped around them—feeling, always, that they couldn't touch her, that she'd developed a protective carapace. Falling pregnant changed that, as it changed everything. She had never felt so unguarded and unguardable, so utterly exposed.

Strangers found the pregnant body emboldening. Those who'd never been pregnant knew someone who had, and generously shared their expertise. Her landlady, the FedEx delivery guy, the homeless denizens of the Methadone Mile. She was advised daily about proper nutrition, the importance of sleep, the benefits of transcendental meditation or tai chi or alternate-nostril breathing. Who knew there were so many home remedies for heartburn, for water retention, for stretch marks and hemorrhoids and constipation and varicose veins? No bodily function was off-limits, because the pregnant body was everyone's. It belonged to the entire world.

Of course, she was not the first woman to make this discovery. Her peers had made it twenty years earlier. At age forty-three, almost forty-four, she was very nearly the last.

There is a fine line between concern and intrusiveness. Even her coworkers, who knew better, crossed it from time to time. Though they all wanted to, no one asked about the baby's father, *the man involved with this pregnancy.* Claudia volunteered nothing. It was a story she didn't know how to tell.

She kept her promise to Luis. Each morning she drove to work instead of taking the T. She parked in the underground garage, in the reserved space next to Florine's, and entered the building through a basement door, acutely aware that this was a luxury the patients didn't have.

Pregnancy changed everything. To the Access patients she said the same things she'd always said, but her words landed differently. To a woman unhappily pregnant, the counselor's swollen belly was a Rorschach test. The patient's reaction said more about her than it did about Claudia.

With the latecomers, especially, her pregnancy elicited strong emotions. On the worst fucking day of their lives, the last thing they needed was advice from one of the lucky ones, a middle-aged woman carrying—as far as she knew—a healthy baby. Once she'd begun to show, she handed off the latecomers to Mary Fahey. Claudia had trained her personally and trusted her completely. Her patients would be safe in Mary's large, freckled hands.

With the minors the situation was different. Claudia was older than most of their mothers, so unimaginably old that they assumed—correctly—that her circumstances were completely unlike their own. Her pregnancy interested them keenly. They asked whether she knew the baby's sex, or wanted to. Often this spun off into a conversation about their own future pregnancies, whether or not they would want to know. The minors spoke of future motherhood with warmth and enthusiasm, an experience they looked forward to. The minors weren't saying *no* to motherhood. They were saying, *Not now.*

For Claudia that answer was no longer possible. At her age, saying *not now* was the same as saying *not ever.*

Finding herself accidentally pregnant in middle age was the second-greatest surprise of her life.

The greater surprise was that she could do it. Unlike many of the patients she counseled, she was a functioning adult—healthy, employed, financially stable. She worked fifty feet away from an excellent gynecologist. Importantly, she was not in crisis. She felt ready to raise a child—clearheaded, unambivalent, sure.

In pregnancy she was always hungry. At first she found this alarming, the body taking over. For a person who loved to drive, there was something unutterably terrifying about a self-driving car. At the grocery store she filled her shopping cart. After a lifelong diet of processed garbage, she wanted fruit, fish, bread, vegetables. For the first time in many years, or possibly ever, she was hungry for actual food.

It was possible—likely, even—that these cravings were a form of atonement. Her future child, a girl, already had certain strikes against her. Half her genetic material had come from a man with an epic weed habit. (*All day, every day.*) The implications of this, its consequences for the next generation, were not clear.

Shortly after Claudia fell pregnant, she got in touch with a geneticist she'd once dated, a former e-boyfriend.

He assumed she was asking on behalf of a patient, a misconception she didn't correct. His response was distinctly unhelpful.

Anything's possible, he said. *No one knows anything.*

In the spirit of atonement she ate salads, drank smoothies. She did not smoke weed. Like the pregnancy itself, quitting had been an accident. Claudia had exercised no special discipline; she'd quit out of cowardice. After spending the night with Timmy, she'd been too embarrassed to call him and buy more.

When she told Phil about her pregnancy, he was dumbfounded. It was the first time she'd seen him at a loss for words.

"How did this happen?" he asked finally.

"In the usual way."

"Stuart?"

"God, no."

If it were anyone else, she would have dodged the question. At work, especially, she avoided the subject. She was a reproductive health professional. There was no easy excuse for her lapse in judgment, her failure to contracept.

"It was someone else," she said finally. "We're not in touch now. I knew him for a couple years." It wasn't much of an explanation, but it was all she was prepared to offer. "He was a friend."

According to her mother, Claudia had been a late talker. Until the age of three she never said a word. When she finally spoke, her first word wasn't *Mama*, and it certainly wasn't *Daddy*. Her first word was *No*.

Naturally enough, she said it to Deb.

For most of her adult life, she'd said *no* to everything. *No* to marriage and *no* to daughterhood, *no* to food and *no* to love. She'd said *yes* to sex, it was true, but only to a certain kind: curated sex, electronically screened and vetted sex. When an e-relationship ran its course, she started over with a new e-boyfriend who would be, in the end, not so different from the last one. This was in no way surprising, since she had selected him using the same filters: education, profession, political views, zip code.

If she were to remove all the filters, she might've gotten someone like Timmy.

One Christmas Eve she went to see him. Her mother had been dead for just three months. Claudia planned to spend her first orphan Christmas alone in her apartment, asleep if possible. To execute this plan, she needed a supply of weed.

Timmy's porch light was on, his giant TV tuned to the Travel Channel. A celebrity chef in a leather jacket was eating blowfish in Osaka.

"No way would I eat that," he said, as if Claudia had accused him of doing so. "No fuckin way."

After smoking a bowl they were both ravenous. Timmy tried to order Chinese food, but at midnight on Christmas Eve, even Jade Garden was closed.

Claudia followed him into the kitchen, a room she had never entered: scabby linoleum and ancient appliances, an electric stove that looked grimy and possibly dangerous, its burners wrapped in yellowed tinfoil. Lined up on the counter were cereal boxes, a twenty-pack of Top Ramen, a toolbox, and a sack of rock salt.

They stood shoulder to shoulder, staring into the refrigerator.

"This is bleak," Timmy said.

"Hang on." Claudia rummaged through the drawers and came up with a half stick of butter, speckled with toast crumbs, and a few plastic-wrapped slices of American cheese.

She hadn't made Cheesy Ramen in twenty-five years, but she made it that night for her weed dealer on her first orphan Christmas. They dined side by side in front of the television, the way she'd eaten every meal for the first seventeen years of her life.

"If I'm ever on death row, I want this to be my last meal," Timmy said with his mouth full. "I want you to come make me these fuckin noodles."

He said, "This is the most incredible thing I have ever eaten in my life."

Don't you want to find him?

She tried one last time to see him—midway through her second trimester, when she was just beginning to show. She was counting on her belly to speak for her, to articulate what couldn't be said.

Timmy's apartment was empty. The tapestry had been taken down from the front window, and she could see clearly into the empty living room. His furniture was gone, the capacious couch and magisterial recliner and massive wide-screen TV. Claudia stood on the porch a long time, looking into the apartment, trying to memorize it. She knew that she would never return.

"Can I help you?"

She turned to see a pink-cheeked man in a Bruins jersey, holding a laminated sign. APARTMENT FOR RENT.

"I was just about to hang this." He was maybe sixty, with longish hair and a gold chain at his throat. "The place is available first of the month. You wanna see it?"

"Yes," said Claudia, her heart beating loudly. *Yes, that is exactly what I want.*

She followed him inside.

"I just listed it this morning," said the landlord. "Already I'm getting calls out the wazoo."

The apartment was clean and empty, filled with sunlight. Without Timmy's outsized furniture, his imposing physical presence, the place felt smaller, not larger. It still smelled faintly of weed.

"Sorry about the smell. I'm having the floors redone next week. That should take care of it."

She followed him into the kitchen. The cruddy linoleum had been replaced with wood-grain laminate, the moribund stove with a ceramic cooktop.

"That's a brand-new refrigerator," said the landlord. "Energy Star–rated."

"Terrific," Claudia said.

"You know the neighborhood? It's a great location, walking distance to the Orange Line. At this price, the place will go fast. I'd put in an application today, if you're interested." His eyes dipped briefly to her waist, or maybe they didn't. She was at the stage in her pregnancy when she was prone to imagining such things.

"Any questions for me?" he asked.

Claudia hesitated only a moment.

"The old tenant," she said. "Where did he go?"

It was a bizarre question, but if the landlord thought so, he gave no sign. He looked a little sleepy, his eyes red-rimmed and bleary. It occurred to her that he was probably high.

"Moved away," he said. "Out of state, I think."

"Do you know where?"

"Couldn't tell ya. He didn't leave a forwarding address."

A mobile phone rang in his pocket, the first few bars of "Danny Boy."

"Excuse me, I gotta take this." He handed her a business card from his pocket. BARRY PROPERTY MGMT. "You want to fill out an application, just give me a call."

He stepped back into the apartment, closing the door behind him.

Claudia lingered a moment in the vestibule, staring at the closed door. She imagined it opening again, Timmy appearing out of nowhere in his stocking cap and layered T-shirts. What exactly would she say?

At that moment she heard footsteps on the landing. A small round woman was struggling with a package, an immense fruit basket wrapped in clear yellow plastic.

"Do you need help with that?" Claudia called.

"It's arright, I got it. Can you grab those bags, maybe?" The woman nodded toward two large shopping bags sitting on the landing.

Claudia picked up the bags and followed her upstairs. The door of the second-floor apartment was ajar, a radio playing. Cooking smells wafted into the hallway, cumin and maybe garlic. Claudia's stomach squeezed violently. She'd eaten just an hour ago. Now she was salivating like a hungry dog.

"Let me put this inside," said the neighbor—Latina maybe, her speech accented. "Hang on, I'll be right back."

Claudia waited in the hallway—why, she wasn't sure—until the woman reappeared. She took the bags from Claudia's hands and set them inside the door.

"Thanks. Timmy used to do that. He was always carrying things for me. I heard you asking about him." Her eyes lingered at Claudia's midsection. "I've seen you here before."

Claudia felt her face heat.

"He didn't move away," said the neighbor. "He went to jail."

Claudia's stomach groaned audibly.

"Jail," she repeated. "Are you sure?"

"That's what people are saying." The neighbor raised her hands, palms up: What could you do? "I knew what he was into. But he wasn't a bad guy, you know? I liked him."

Claudia said, "I liked him too."

She could find him if she wanted to. It would take some effort, but she could do it. She didn't know his last name or his age or where he was now or how long he'd be there, but those questions had answers, and answers could always be found.

When she thought of him at all, which wasn't often, she remembered the way they'd talked to each other, their conversations mediated by television. She could place him easily in her childhood, on the sagging couch between Deb and the fosters. Claudia gave Timmy his own TV tray, his paper plate, his plastic cup of cola. In this way it seemed that he'd been with her for her entire life.

He was her kind.

They weren't in love and never could be, but for a time he'd felt like home to her. In the terrible year after her mother died, his apartment was the place she went to.

His porch light was always on.

Timmy was gone now. There was power in knowing this. The knowledge made all things possible. She couldn't imagine having a child with him. She could only imagine doing it alone, as her own mother had done.

When she fell pregnant, she had a choice to make. That the choice wasn't automatic or obvious is a truth no one wants to hear. Falling makes for a better story: falling pregnant, falling in love. If she fell in love with Timmy, or with her future child, if she fell in love with the idea of motherhood, she would be a more sympathetic character. This hasn't changed, and likely won't: We prefer our heroines helpless. Helpless means blameless.

It wasn't her fault. She simply fell.

Some weeks later, her pregnancy clearly showing, Claudia drove to Clayburn. "I'll stop by Saturday afternoon," she told Nicolette's voice mail. But she didn't say why.

They sat at the kitchen table. Nicolette moved aside a pile of junk mail, catalogs, and unopened bills, a child's coloring book. From her handbag Claudia took a piece of paper.

"What's this?" Nicolette said.

Claudia took a deep breath—cigarettes and air freshener, the smell of her entire childhood. "The title to the trailer. It's yours now. Mom"—she said experimentally—"would want you to have it."

The decision, once she'd made it, seemed entirely obvious. Not for a minute of her life had she wished to own a single-wide trailer—a place she'd never live in and couldn't bring herself to sell, if such a thing were even possible. A tin can, fifty feet long and eighteen feet across; the home her mother had made for them. Its resale value was approximately zero. The trailer's worth couldn't be expressed in dollars. Another metric was required, a currency Claudia would have to invent herself.

"This is just for the trailer," she explained. The land beneath—her grandfather's—now belonged to his one surviving child, her aunt Darlene. "I don't think she has any plans for it, but that's between you and Darlene."

Nicolette studied the paper in her hand.

"Keep it in a safe place, okay? You don't want to lose it." Claudia looked around at the chaos of the trailer. *Get a safe deposit box*, she thought but didn't say.

"I have something for you too." Nicolette got up from her chair and brought a plastic laundry basket from the living room. "Darlene said you were having a girl."

She set the basket on the table. Inside were pools of silky nylon fabric, hot pink and turquoise and buttercup yellow. "I used to wear these on Skylar." Nicolette touched the cheap fabric tenderly, almost reverently. "She can't fit into them anymore."

Claudia knew this. Judging by recent Facebook

photos, Skylar—now six years old—was a little butterball. Claudia wondered, fleetingly, if she had plumped up on purpose, to avoid wearing these godawful outfits.

Nicolette held up a dress for Claudia's inspection. The shiny purple bodice was studded with rhinestones, the green satin skirt cut to resemble a tail.

"The Little Mermaid. Mom loved this one," Nicolette said, her eyes glittering with tears.

And Claudia—who would never in a million years inflict such a costume on a child—felt her own eyes tearing.

"Thank you," she whispered. Then she did a thing she had never done, not even at their mother's funeral. She took Nicolette into her arms.

In pregnancy she was always tired. Making a person, it turned out, was exhausting work. For the first time in many years, she slept deeply and dreamed vividly. According to *What to Expect When You're Expecting*, this was common. The dreams of pregnant women were full of magical creatures. In dreams they gave birth to dragons, to snakes and monsters.

Claudia dreamed none of these things.

For all of her childhood, and most of her adulthood, she had fallen asleep thinking of her mother. As she drifted off to sleep, she pictured where Deb was at that very moment: in her waterbed in the back corner of the trailer, or snoring on the old plaid couch. Either way, a TV would be playing. Only after she'd located her mother could she fall soundly asleep.

As long as her mother was alive, she didn't consider making another person. She didn't feel the need. Deb's death changed that, as it changed everything. Suddenly, brutally, she was no longer a daughter. Nothing in her life had prepared her for this loss.

In pregnancy she dreamed of her mother. A different type of person might have taken this as evidence—proof that Deb was still out there, some piece of her alive in the universe, what believers refer to as a soul.

The first time it happened, Claudia woke up laughing. In the dream she carried her mother inside her, the baby version of Deb, mother and daughter nested inside each other like a set of Russian dolls. Soon, soon, she would give birth to her mother. In the dream she had found this ridiculous, but also correct and delightful.

It was the best possible thing.

Acknowledgments

I am grateful to the John Simon Guggenheim Foundation and the American Academy of Arts and Letters, for their generous support during the writing of this novel; the Shanghai Writers' Association, for enlarging my world; and the Banff Centre for Arts and Creativity, the Ucross Foundation, Mac-Dowell, and PLAYA, where portions of the book were written.

Over the course of three New England winters, Mary Cerulli and Karen Wulf opened their homes to me. Sara G., Ashley S., Rachel P., and Lia R. entrusted me with secrets. When the music stopped, Josh Barkan gave me hope.

Bill Clegg, Dan Pope, Malachy Tallack, and Joshua

Ferris read early drafts and offered advice and encouragement. Karen O'Brien generously shared her medical expertise.

In one way or another, every page of this novel is a gift from Rob Arnold. His contributions can't be quantified.

Finally, I would like to thank my publishing family at Ecco—Dan Halpern, Helen Atsma, Miriam Parker, and Jonathan Burnham—for giving my work a home. Again and always, I am grateful.

HARPER LARGE PRINT

We hope you enjoyed reading
our new, comfortable print size and found it
an experience you would like to repeat.

Well – you're in luck!

Harper Large Print offers the finest in
fiction and nonfiction books in this same larger
print size and paperback format. Light and easy to read,
Harper Large Print paperbacks are for the book lovers
who want to see what they are reading without strain.

For a full listing of titles and
new releases to come, please visit our website:
www.hc.com

HARPER LARGE PRINT